RIDERS IN DISGUISE

To Mom and Dad.
Thanks for raising me in this insane city.

And to Collene. Miss you.

PATRICK ANDERSON JR.

Jitney Books

"Let us reflect in another way, and we shall see that there is great reason to hope that death is a good, for one of two things:—either death is a state of nothingness and utter unconsciousness, or, as men say, there is a change and migration of the soul from this world to another. Now if you suppose that there is no consciousness, but a sleep like the sleep of him who is undisturbed even by the sight of dreams, death will be an unspeakable gain...for eternity is then only a single night. But if death is the journey to another place, and there, as men say, all the dead abide, what good, O my friends and judges, can be greater than this?"

Plato, *Apology of Socrates*

"...Perhaps the whole root of our trouble, the human trouble, is that we will sacrifice all the beauty of our lives, will imprison ourselves in totems, taboos, crosses, blood sacrifices, steeples, mosques, races, armies, flags, nations, in order to deny the fact of death, which is the only fact we have. It seems to me that one ought to rejoice in the fact of death—ought to decide, indeed, to earn one's death by confronting with passion the conundrum of life. One is responsible to life: It is the small beacon in that terrifying darkness from which we come and to which we shall return..."

James Baldwin, *The Fire Next Time*

Tribe: noun /trib/

A social division in a traditional society consisting of families or communities linked by social, economic, religious, or blood ties, with a common culture and dialect.

Tribalism: noun /ˈtraɪ.bəl.ɪ.zəm/

The state of existing as a tribe, or a very strong feeling of loyalty to your tribe.

MEETING HELD JULY 28TH, 1896

FOR INCORPORATION OF THE CITY OF MIAMI, FLORIDA

The County Supervisor of Registration certified that
there were 424 registered voters in the territory to
be incorporated.

This number consisted of: 243   WHITE
                           181   BLACK
                           424   TOTAL

Of those registered voters, 368 were present at
the meeting.

This number consisted of: 206   WHITE
                           162   BLACK
                           368   TOTAL

Record Negro Vote in Miami Cast Under Heavy Police Guard, *May 3, 1939*

City Rejects War Homes for Negroes, *August 18, 1944*

KKK 'Needed' In Nation Declares Florida Leader, *July 19, 1949*

End to Anti-Negro Sentiment Could Be Soon, *September 29, 1955*

Student Riot in Cuba Quelled, *December 1, 1955*

Fidel Castro Is Set Free in Mexico, *July 26, 1956*

Castro's Miracle Becomes Dust in a Year, *January 1, 1960*

Cubans Take Our Jobs, Negroes Claim, *October 18, 1961*

Children Fly High in Secret Escape Routes from Cuba, *March 9, 1962*

Cuban Children Find 'Asylum of Love', *March 12, 1962*

Tempers Flare, Mayor's Blamed for Liberty City Riot, *August 10, 1968*

Miami 'Negro Removal' Stirs Dispute, *June 5, 1969*

Cubans, Negroes Could Control Politics in Dade, *September 25, 1969*

Sebastian Burgos Named Mayor by City Commission, *April 20, 1973*

Burgos is Right—Re-Think Miami Metro, *July 16, 1978*

Part One: Drive
Wednesday, July 11, 1979

"Good times, these are the good times,
Leave your cares behind, these are the good times,
Good times, these are the good times,
Our new state of mind, these are the good times."

Chic, "Good Times"

"You've got to know when to hold 'em,
Know when to fold 'em,
Know when to walk away,
And know when to run."

Kenny Rogers, "The Gambler"

1.

Tommy stubbed his cigarette out in the ash tray on Greg's enormous wooden desk as Greg mm-hmm'd into the phone. A panoramic window behind Greg's head looked out on the employee lot. Tommy's Trans Am sat alone in the back.

"Sell it," Greg said into the phone, sucking on a Benson & Hedges. The voice on the other end clucked something and Greg pulled the cigarette from his lips. "No, I said *sell* it. Now."

The voice clucked some more and Greg grunted, dropping the phone back in its cradle. He smashed his spent cigarette next to Tommy's and leaned back.

"Tommy, it's been a while," he said. "Feel like I never see you anymore."

Tommy forced a smile. "I'm out there," he said. "Every day…"

"I hear ya," Greg said. "How's the missus?"

"She's good. Getting big."

"She'll get bigger yet. You're lucky if she ever gets back to form. Lord knows mine didn't. How far along is she?"

Tommy cleared his throat. "Six months."

"And this is your second, right?"

"Yeah.

"Gonna be some smart ones," Greg said. "Like their dad. Number crunchers. Hit the slots early, home by five-thirty. Clean as a whistle."

Tommy's face hurt from smiling. "Yeah, uh…Sara at reception said you needed me for something?"

Greg scratched his chin. "You watch Carson last night?"

Tommy blinked rapidly. "Johnny Carson?"

"One and only."

"Uh…no," Tommy said. "Little late for me. I'm usually asleep by then."

"Tom, sometimes I forget how much of a square you are," Greg said, rolling his eyes. "No offense."

Tommy did something he didn't think was possible and smiled even wider. "None taken."

"It's a good characteristic," Greg said. "Career like this. Means you're reliable. Any company will be lucky to have you. Should be easy."

Tommy's smile disappeared. "Should be—"

"So, Carson's got Don Rickles on last night, right?" Greg said, chuckling. "And the guy—I don't know if you've seen his stuff. The guy's a certified asshole but if he ain't goddamn hilarious. Started just *berating* Carson *and* the audience and they're all just eating out of the palm of—"

Greg noticed Tommy's blank stare and his laughter faded.

"Anyways, Carson's a genius in my book," he said. "It's a great show. Nice way to end the evening." Greg opened one of his desk drawers as he spoke, pulling out a brown folder and flipping it open to a stack of clipped papers. Tommy's name stood in bold print on the top sheet.

"I'll keep that in mind," Tommy said.

"You definitely should." Greg's eyebrows shot up. "Hold the phone, says here your name's—" He squinted at the paper. "Toe-mass Moon-owes?"

"Tomás," Tommy said. "Muñoz."

Greg glanced at him. "Sounds Latin."

"Cuban," Tommy said.

"You don't say?" Greg plopped back in the chair. "Cuban, huh? Whole time I'm thinking you're just a regular white guy." He frowned. "You don't have an accent though."

"I was raised here," Tommy said. "Came over when I was a kid."

"Wait," Greg said. "Were you one of those—what're they called, the—" He snapped his fingers. "The Peter Pan kids?"

"Pedro Pan," Tommy said. "But yeah."

Greg looked at him with awe. "Wow, I remember reading about y'all in the paper back in like middle school. Look at you now, huh?"

"What's going on, Greg?" Tommy asked. "Did I do something wrong?"

"*Wrong?*" Greg said, scoffing. "Tom, why would you—of course you haven't done anything *wrong*."

Tommy said nothing. Greg pulled at his collar, glanced at the folder then looked back at Tommy with a deadness in his eyes.

"You haven't done anything wrong, Tom," he said. "If anything, you're—I don't know. Maybe you're too right."

"Too right," Tommy echoed.

"Too good," Greg said. "At your job, I mean."

Tommy's right thumb rubbed feverishly against his middle finger. "Too good at my job."

"Yes," Greg said, raising his fingers in air quotes. "'Over-qualified' is the word they keep throwing around. Every fax, every letter, every other paragraph. Over-qualified, over-qualified like, what the hell does that even *mean*?"

Tommy's fingers burned.

"I'm gonna be straight with you, Tom," Greg said. "If it was up to me, you wouldn't even be in here right now. Unfortunately, it isn't. Economy's in the tank, company's looking to cut costs so—"

"I'm a cost cut," Tommy said flatly. "Is this because I asked for a raise?"

"This has nothing to do with that," Greg said. "There's just been a concerted effort to bring on younger, more, um...*afford*able—"

"Greg, I'm twenty-five," Tommy said. "How young are you talking here?"

"Tom—"

"High school students?" Tommy said. "College interns?"

"Tom, I can't—"

"Free labor masquerading as opportunity," Tommy muttered.

"Excuse me?"

"I'll save you the speech." Tommy stood and straightened his tie, a striped black and blue one Clara got him last Christmas. "How long do I have?"

Greg twirled a pen between his fingers, staring at the open folder.

"Brass wants y'all cleared out by the end of the week," Greg said.

"Y'all?"

"Meeting with Brandon and Luke too." He glanced at Tommy. "Please keep that to yourself."

"Brandon," Tommy said. "The man just bought a house."

Greg cleared his throat. "There is a severance package," he said. "Couple of month's pay and a solid rec—"

"All due respect, Greg," Tommy said. "Screw your recommendation."

At his desk, Tommy grabbed his jacket and messenger bag and was packing up whatever he could when his desk phone rang. He let it trill twice before picking it up. Clara's voice floated above the living room TV in the background.

"I miss you," she said. "Come home."

Tommy flashed a genuine smile. "It's barely past eleven," he said. "I've been gone like two hours, max."

"Sounds like a good enough workday to me," she said.

"Actually," he said, glancing over at Greg's office. "Luck would have it, I'm leaving early."

"Really?" Clara said.

"Should be home soon," he said. "Gonna stop for smokes."

"Ooh can you pick up eggs? And milk? I'm trying the recipe my uncle's girlfriend gave me at the party Saturday. That vanilla crème cake you liked?"

"So that's the reason you called," Tommy said.

"Of *course* not," Clara said. "I just miss my husband."

"Right."

"And an onion. I'm making meatballs for dinner."

"Yum," Tommy said.

Clara breathed into the receiver. "Everything okay?"

"Great," he said. "Amazing. I'll get the stuff. Love you, see you soon."

Tommy put the phone down, grabbed his bag and headed for the door. He passed a tax attorney's office and three For Lease signs on the way downstairs, pushing out into the early afternoon sun. He walked to his car, tossed his things in the backseat and climbed in, starting the engine. Letting it rumble for a moment, he grabbed the vibrating steering wheel then pressed the gas, once, twice. A rising tide filled his chest and he slammed on the pedal, the engine roaring as Mick Jagger's voice burst through the speakers:

SCARRED OLD SLAVER KNOWS HE'S DOIN' ALL RIGHT!

Tommy yanked the tape out of the 8-track player and the music cut off. Gripping it with a shaking fist, he eased off the pedal, panting in time with the idling engine. A black man wearing old corduroys and a tattered vest with no shirt walked by on the sidewalk, trailing a beat up, overflowing shopping cart. Tommy watched him until he passed, then opened the glove compartment and tossed the tape inside. He pulled out another and pushed it in the player, grabbing the gear shift and kicking the clutch as Robert Plant shouted:

AND YOU KNOW HOW IT IS!

Tommy pushed in the cigarette lighter.

I REALLY DON'T KNOW WHAT TIME IT WAS!

Pulled his pack of Marlboros from his pocket, shaking the last cigarette into his palm.

SO I ASKED THEM IF I COULD STAY A WHILE!

The lighter popped out and Tommy lit up. He rolled his window down, smoke billowing into the afternoon air. Throwing the car in reverse, Tommy squealed out of the parking lot, flicking ash onto the asphalt outside his old job.

2.

Exit 8 on I-95 and take MLK Blvd west past the rows of vacant parking lots and darkened storefronts; past the men in wheelchairs holding signs (*a penny for my pain, thank you*); past the balding palm trees on 9th and 10th and 11th ave to NW 12th Parkway smack in the middle of The Beans.

AKA Liberty City.

Rows of squat apartments stretch north, three story buildings to the south connected by clotheslines heavy with laundry, like cobwebs. Bordering one of the city's main through-streets, The Beans resembles much of Miami from the outside. Talk to somebody in the know though, and they'll point out that only one in five spots around here have a working AC.

AC was one of the few things Rig missed about school.

Lying on a twin mattress tucked in the corner of the living room, he fanned himself with a copy of *The Slave Dancer*. The bedroom door at the end of the narrow hallway opened and his dad emerged, stumbling over Rig's lanky legs on the way to the kitchen. He turned to his son.

"Que haces?" he said.

Rig let the book fall open on his chest. "Reading."

"Ain't he supposed to be in summer school?" his dad hollered at his mom.

"Not this year," Rig's mom called back. She came out of the bedroom in a housedress, hand over her protruding belly. Nudging Rig's dad aside, she rounded the kitchen counter and grabbed a glass from the cupboard, filling it with tap water. Rig's dad touched the small gold crucifix swinging around his neck, his brown skin gleaming with lotion.

"You should be out there then," he said, pointing at the front door.

"Eddie, let the boy read," his mother said. "You're supposed to be gettin' to work anyways."

"Got another half hour," he said.

"The bus comes in fifteen."

"I'm trying to have a conversation with my son."

"And I'm having a conversation about this empty goddamn fridge!" Rig's mom yelled. "Katzen told you if you're late again he's docking your pay and you keep acting like this baby isn't—"

"Gail," Rig's dad said. "Mi amor. Cállate. I'm leaving in a second."

Rig's mom scowled and sipped her water. His dad pointed at Rig's book. "Who gave you this?"

"Mrs. Tyson," Rig said.

"Esa mujer," his dad said. "Sounds like you're her favorite."

"The boy's smart," his mom said.

"She said I'm reading two years ahead of the other kids," Rig said.

"You'll learn more out there than you will in here," his dad said.

Rig sat up, his butt touching the ground through the warped mattress springs. A smirk crossed his dad's face and he bent over, shoving his fingers into Rig's head of curls. His hand was warm, rough, pleasant until his dad twisted Rig's head around and grunted.

"What happened here?" he asked, rubbing a bald spot above Rig's temple.

"Nothing," Rig said, pulling his head away.

"Boy, don't act stupid," Rig's mom snapped. "Tell Papi what happened."

Rig looked up at the ceiling. "I was at the park and this kid took my book."

"And?" his dad said.

"So I hit him." Rig lowered his voice. "I wasn't even bothering nobody."

"Bothering *any*body," his mother said. "You reading those books or just skimming them?"

"They took your book so you hit them?" his dad said. He pointed at the bald spot. "So how'd that happen?"

"They hit me back," Rig said.

"Don't sit there acting like an angel," Rig's mom said. "The boy's mom came over while you were at work, Eddie. Rig broke his nose and knocked out one of his teeth. Lucky she know Tanya, know we're good people so she let it go. But you cannot always *solve* things with *violence*, Rig."

Rig's dad squatted in front of him. Rig focused on the hazel flecks in his dad's brown eyes, identical to the ones he saw in the mirror every day.

His dad lowered his voice. "But did you win?"

"Eddie do not encourage him!" his mom yelled.

Rig glanced at his mom then back at his dad. He nodded. His dad winked, pushing Rig's head playfully and walking over to his wife.

"I'll be back later," he said, kissing her cheek and tapping her butt.

"You better," she said.

Rig's dad kissed her again on the lips. "Te amo."

"Gross," Rig said.

"Only reason you exist," his dad said, grabbing his keys off the counter. The apartment door closed behind him and the room was silent. Rig's mom stared after her husband.

"Papi don't like reading?" Rig asked.

"Doesn't," his mom corrected. "And he does, he just reads different things than you and I."

"Like the newspaper?"

"Like the newspaper," she said. "Don't pay him any mind. Keep reading."

"I already finished this one."

"Read it again," she said. "Sometimes they're better the second time."

Rig nodded. His mother turned to the small kitchen window looking out on the gray concrete next door, her dark skin shiny in the outside light. Rig picked up the book, slipped it under his mattress and grabbed some faded black shorts off the carpet, checking the pocket for the crumpled five-dollar bill he'd snuck out of his dad's wallet earlier that morning. He got dressed and slipped on his sneakers, duct tape holding the bursting seams together.

"Can I go out?" he asked.

Rig's mother looked at him, the corners of her eyes wet.

"Back by dinner," she said. "And stay out of trouble."

Rig kissed his mother on her cheek, sniffing the vanilla scent of her skin.

Outside, Rig passed an old picnic table and a couple of cement-filled truck tires in the Crystal Palaces courtyard, some teenagers sitting cracking jokes and smoking cigarettes. An empty chip bag and some scraps of newspaper floated by. The heat stuck to Rig as he held a hand up for the few neighbors sitting in the shade, his forehead prickling with sweat. Music carried from an unseen window, James Brown screeching over funky drums. Small children ran after a ball, a burly woman strolling behind them. Mrs. Anselbury—Rig's mom's friend—walked towards her apartment. Rig let out a whistle and she waved.

Ducking through clotheslines, Rig passed windows with large and small statues of Jesus in various poses of torture: carrying his cross, nailed to his cross, taken down from the cross. A strong breeze blew and wind chimes rang. He stepped onto 62nd street, strolling past King Square Park, a landmark in

The Beans where one could find any combination of neighborhood youths hanging out at any given moment, most innocently, some not so much. Rig crumpled and uncrumpled the five-dollar bill in his pocket, watching the teenagers play ball on the rundown court. His worn shoes scuffed the chipped sidewalk. A car drove past in the opposite direction, a white couple in the front seat laughing while a kid Rig's age peered at him out the back window. Rig stared back until the car disappeared on the horizon.

That's when he noticed the white van.

It sat a block away from the park at the stop sign on 11th ave, the sun gleaming off the windows. Rig pulled his hands out of his pockets and balled them up. The van crept closer then pulled to the side of the road, idling across the street from Rig. The driver's door opened and an old man with the darkest skin Rig had ever seen stepped out, cigarette hanging from his lips with a cloud of smoke around his head. He wore faded overalls and a t-shirt, patches of gray in his beard and temples. Leaning against the fender, he nodded at Rig.

"What up, Young Blood."

Rig stayed quiet.

"You Eddie's boy, right?" the man said. "Eduardo? And Gail?"

Rig hesitated then nodded.

"I knew yo' Mama from." He made a shooing motion over his head. "Way back when. Went to school together, 'fore yo' daddy moved y'all out to Goulds. Glad y'all back home."

Rig stayed quiet.

"What they call you?" the old man asked.

"Rig."

"Rig, huh?" The man flicked his spent cigarette. "How old you is, Rig?"

"Eleven," he said.

"I'll be damned," the man said, whistling. "You a big'un for just eleven. The hell they feeding you?"

"I don't know you, man," Rig said.

The man revealed a gap-toothed grin. "That's right, you don't know me from Adam," he said. "I hear that but see—I see a young brother like you walking 'round the neighborhood, middle of summer, nice day like this, and I ask myself—" The old man held his hands out. "—what's he looking for?"

"Ain't lookin' for nothin'."

"See boy, you might *think* you ain't looking for nothing," the man said. "But I'm guessing you *is*. You just don't *know* you is."

Rig turned to walk away. A muffled yell from the van turned him back around. The old man rolled his eyes.

"Alright fine," he said, walking over and sliding the side door open to reveal two sweaty boys Rig's age sitting on stacks of old cardboard boxes filled with newspapers. One of the boys was long and gangly, Rig's height but skinnier. The other kid was short with clumps of muscle running up his arms and legs.

"Come on, Left," the short one said. "Goin' make him think we hustlers."

The old man nodded. "Alright, you sell him on it then."

"We slangin' newspapers," the kid said to Rig, pointing at the old man. "Lefty get the boxes and we go 'round sellin' 'em on the street."

"Saw you walking and Otis here thought you might be up for it," Lefty said.

Rig studied the old man and the two boys then shook his head. "I'm good."

"You good?" Otis said. "But you ain't even doin' nothin'."

"I'm good," Rig repeated.

"Just an offer, Young Blood," Lefty said, holding his hands up. "Guess you good on making some money too, ain't nothing wrong with that."

"How much money?" Rig said quickly.

"Depends how hard you work," Lefty said.

"It's fifteen cents a paper," Otis said. "Most people toss a quarter. We keep the dime." He pointed at the other kid. "DJ made five bucks last week."

Rig checked the street for cars and crossed, climbing in the van. Lefty slammed the side door shut and got back behind the wheel. The van shuddered as it pulled off from the curb.

Sitting on the wheel well, Rig ran a hand across the metal interior. Patches of mold festered in the corners and the entire cabin smelled like old dirty socks. It was hotter inside than out, sweat dripping off Rig's chin. Rig looked at the other boys. Otis's shoes had even more duct tape holding them together than his own. DJ's shoes looked new by comparison, though the seams were swollen. Otis twisted one of the little knots of hair poking out all over his head, like raisins. DJ's hair was cut close, almost bald. Rig pulled at his curls, the stacks of newspapers catching his attention.

"*Miami Rise*," he read aloud.

"Lefty's homeboy makes it," Otis yelled over the rumbling truck. "The news they don't give you in the other paper. Black folk news."

Rig grabbed a copy and scanned a couple headlines. They stopped at a red light and Lefty turned to them.

"We're heading south a ways," he said. "Catch the lunch crowd in Kendall. You need me to pass by your ma's or anything, let her know you gone?"

Rig shook his head.

Lefty winked. "Let's get up outta here then."

The light turned green and they drove west until the projects gave way to I-95, shifting into US-1. Otis tapped Rig on the shoulder.

"You that nigga whooped Marquise ass at the park," he said.

Rig said nothing.

Otis nudged DJ with his shoulder. "Told you it was that nigga."

"You messed his nose up bad," DJ said. "Knocked out his tooth."

"He started it," Rig said.

"I believe it," Otis said. "Him and his cousins always starting something."

"I hear y'all back there," Lefty yelled. "Y'all need to stop quarreling with black folk. Reason we can't never come up, constantly fighting each other."

Otis rolled his eyes towards Rig, lowering his voice to just above the van's rumble. "*Everybody* talking 'bout that shit, bruh." He patted the back of his hand against Rig's chest. "Respect. Can't stand them niggas. Fuck 'em."

"Told y'all to stop with that language," Lefty yelled.

Otis sucked his teeth. "My bad, Left."

"I heard why y'all had to move back, Rig," Lefty said, looking at Rig in the rearview mirror. "Messed up how they did your old man."

Rig shrugged.

"How long was he up for?" Lefty asked.

Rig hesitated. "Two years," he said.

"He got out not too long ago, right?" Lefty said.

Rig's left eye twitched a little. "Last Thanksgiving."

"Bet you glad to have him back."

Rig nodded and looked out the window at the transient landscape. Lefty let him be and focused on the road as they passed Grand Ave, coasting through the Gables and South Miami before pulling onto a grassy plain off Kendall Drive. The southern stretch of US-1 lay ahead of them, Dadeland Mall looming to the right. In the parking lot, the aqua-colored Dadeland Tower stretched up fifty feet, a giant "D" bolted to the top.

Lefty shut off the van and stepped out, walking around to open the side door. He grabbed a small folding chair strapped with Velcro to the back of the passenger seat and motioned for the boys to get out.

"Grab some boxes and let's get up under that shade," he said, pointing to a tree a few yards away.

The boys each grabbed a box just as flashing red and blue lights reflected off the van's peeling tints. A single whoop from a police siren made them all turn to the street. In the furthest right lane of US-1, two cops stepped out of a patrol car and sauntered up to the group. Both men wore sunglasses, their skin bright red.

"Afternoon, boys," one of them said. "What we got going on here?"

"Just selling some newspapers, officer," Lefty said, staring up at the blue sky. "Figured we could get a little business done on a fine afternoon like this."

"Did you now?" The officer smirked at his partner. "We'll gladly let you boys get on with it then. Soon as you show us a permit."

Lefty's eyes faltered, though his grin didn't budge. He nodded and placed his folding chair on the ground, reaching into his pocket.

"Easy," the cop said, hand flicking to the gun at his waist. "Slow."

Lefty kept his eyes on the officer, carefully pulling out a slip of paper. The cop took it from Lefty's outstretched hand. On the street, a short line of traffic had built up behind their stopped patrol car, horns punctuating revving engines. The cop kept his hand on his gun, studying the permit. When he finished, he looked up at Lefty, then at the three boys. He pointed at the intersection.

"Make sure you stick to that corner," he said, then pointed at the boxes of newspapers. "And take it with you when you're done. Don't need the litter."

"Yes sir, officer," Lefty said.

The cop handed Lefty back his paper and followed his partner back to their vehicle. Seconds later they were gone. Lefty planted a smile back on his face.

"Grab some boxes," he said, picking up his chair. "We got papers to sell."

Lefty ambled away, DJ following. Otis stared after the cops.

"Only 'cause they got that badge and gun," he said. "Nothin' but some scared ass crackers without 'em." He turned to Rig. "Let them muhfuckas ride through the Beans without they shit."

Otis put an imaginary gun to his head and pulled the trigger. He smiled at Rig and Rig smiled back, the boys joining Lefty and DJ under the tree.

3.

Dropping her pen, Tina leaned back in her desk chair and studied her notes for a moment before looking up at the wall above her bed. A picture over her nightstand was creased where it had been folded and stashed in one of her mother's albums, a water-stain blurring the bottom left corner. In it, her grandfather's lying on a hammock strung between two palm trees. His eyes are closed, a smile beneath his bushy mustache, one hand cupping a straw hat against his large belly. The family house in San Juan sits blurry in the background. In a smaller frame next to that photo, Tina and her brother Fernando stand in the living room at their old house in Orlando. Fern's arm hangs over her shoulder, familiar faces frozen in the background. A picture of Tina's mother and father hugging outside a church sits to the right, her mother wearing a flower-print dress, her father handsomely garbed in a loose suit and tie. Too much exposure had faded the image so their outfits looked gray.

The bedroom door opened and Tina's mother, Luisa, poked her head in, bringing the smell of coffee with her. Faint lines creased her mother's forehead and the corners of her eyes, a few streaks of gray in her otherwise silky black hair. An unlit cigarette hung from her fingers.

"Dame el cepillo," she said.

Tina handed her the hairbrush. Her mother stared at her dress.

"Adónde vas?"

"The mall," Tina said. "Gonna write and take some pictures."

"Tú siempre escribiendo," Luisa said. "No wonder you can't keep a man, estás enamorada de tu pluma."

"Yep," Tina said. "That's the reason."

"You should look for a job while you're there," she said. Tina gave her a look and her mother stared back at her. "Qué?"

"I work at Ernesto's, Mami," Tina said.

"Ay, mija. That is no job. They do not even pay you."

"Mami, I get paid."

"So *that* is what you're going to do the rest of your life?"

"There's nowhere in the mall I'm going to work for the rest of my life either," Tina said. "And Ernesto doesn't have to pay me. I work for tips."

With one look, Tina's mother assessed her outfit, her hair and the ribbon holding it up.

"Eres guapa," she said, matter-of-factly, then bellowed into the hallway. "Maria! Ven acá!"

Luisa glanced at her daughter once more then closed the door. Tina unclenched her jaw and tightened the ribbon in her hair. Grabbing her journal, she slipped it into her camera bag and stepped into the hallway just as her twelve-year-old cousin Maria came out of the bathroom. Tina bumped into her, throwing an arm over Maria's thin shoulders.

"Your Tia summons you," she said, laying her cheek on the girl's head and whispering menacingly. "She's got *the brush*."

"I can't wait 'til I'm your age," Maria said.

"Ay," Tina said, fluffing her cousin's curly hair. "My head hurts for you."

"I couldn't put my eyebrows down last time," she grumbled.

"We all go through it," Tina said. "Be glad it's not Ita. She yanks whole handfuls out by the roots." Tina twisted her fingers into claws and stuck them in Maria's face. "She's got *man* hands."

Maria groaned.

In the living room, Maria's mother Lupé sat on the couch drinking coffee and watching the news on their small black TV. Sipping from her mug, the lenses on Tina's aunt's thick glasses fogged from the steam. A table separated her from a second matching couch in the center of the living room, a plate of butter cake sitting next to another coffee mug and a folded copy of the *Miami Tribune*. Tina's hairbrush lay on the edge of the table near a heavy wooden chair with a plastic cover. Sitting by the open living room window, Tina's mother puffed her L&M.

"Mami," Tina said, guiding Maria over to the wooden chair. "You're letting the air out."

"The air I am paying for," her mother muttered.

Tina plopped her cousin on the ground in front of the chair. A commercial on the TV ended and the news returned with an image of an older man with a kind face waving to a crowded room. The caption: *Burgos Under Fire Again*.

"They are so mean to him," Lupé said. "Like he is the city's problems."

"If it was up to them he would not have that job," Tina's mom said. "I know from when they say boricua mayor, it is too good to be true."

"Technically he's not our mayor," Tina said.

Her mother brushed her off. "Miami is so confusing."

"It's really not," Tina said. "There's City of Miami and there's Miami-Dade. We live in Miami-Dade." She pointed at the TV. "He's City of Miami's mayor."

"City of Miami, Miami-Dade," Her mother curled her lip. "It is all Miami. Makes no sense."

"What *really* makes no sense is why we have two city councils," Tina said. "Which is the point I think the news people are trying to make."

"And the point *I* am trying to make," Tina's mother said, stubbing out her cigarette. "Is they would not say that si él fuera un gringo. He is Puerto Rican so of course he is unnecessary."

"I really don't think that's what's happening, Mami."

"I like him as the mayor," Lupé said. "He is handsome."

"Yes, *that* is what makes him a good mayor," Tina's mother said, closing the window. Moving to the wooden chair, she sat on the plastic with a noisy plop and looked up at Tina, jutting her chin towards the lone coffee mug.

"Pa ti."

"Gracias, Mami," Tina said, sitting across from her aunt.

Tina's mother shoved her hands into the bounty of hair on her niece's head. "Mi sobrina," she said. "When is the last time you washed?"

"Sunday," Maria said.

"Con coco?"

Maria shook her head.

"Lupé," Tina's mother said, looking at her sister.

Lupé didn't look over, taking another sip of her coffee. "They are still talking about Jonestown."

Tina glanced at the TV. "All those people."

"Pobrecitos," Lupé said.

Tina's mother pulled her niece's head back. "You must use coco," she said. "It keeps your hair strong and shiny. You want your hair to look good, right?"

"Yes, Tia."

"You won't get a husband with a head full of snakes," she said. "Not one who can take care of you." Without looking up, she motioned towards Tina. "End up like your prima."

"Thanks, Mami," Tina said, glaring at her mother. "Really appreciate that."

Her mother picked up the brush from the coffee table, pushing it into Maria's hair. It coughed through some knots and a whimper escaped Maria's lips. Tina's mother rapped a knuckle on her head. "Paraté."

"Ay, Luisa," Lupé said, whipping around. "Solo es una nena. Be gentle."

"Oh, *now* you hear me," Luisa said, waving a dismissive hand at her sister. She nodded at Tina. "That man sniffing around. Cómo se llama?"

Tina furrowed her eyebrows. "What man?"

"The man you were with the other night," her mother said. "Por cine."

Tina sighed. "Derek."

"Derek," her mother said, brushing Maria's hair with a calmer touch.

"We went on one date," Tina said. "Like a month ago. That was it."

"Por qué?"

"Why are we talking about this now?"

"He seemed nice," her mother said.

Lupé smirked. Tina shot her aunt a glare. A headline on TV announced NASA's Skylab returning from a six-year stint in orbit.

"What happened to this Derek?" Luisa asked.

"Nothing, Mami. It was one date."

Tina's mother shrugged, separating her cousin's hair into two strands and plaiting them together with jerking motions that made Maria's cheeks twitch.

"You are not getting any younger," Luisa muttered.

"I'm twenty-one, Mom," Tina said. "You act like I'm Rose Carter's age."

"You all live differently—"

"Than you did in San Juan," Tina finished. "I know. I've heard."

Luisa clenched her jaw. Tina looked back at the TV. The four of them sat in blissful silence for all of thirty seconds.

"I guess it is better, the way they do it here," Luisa said to Maria.

"Here we go," Tina said, sighing.

"When I was a girl," Luisa said. "The girl find a man and they love each other to the ends of the earth. The men crawl on hands and knees, begging the girl to be his. And she would be his and give herself to him. And these men give back and take care of her for the rest of her life. Una buena vida."

"Yes, mother," Tina said, rolling her eyes. "That's exactly how it goes."

Luisa stopped braiding, pulling Maria's head back again. "But some men— los degenerados—sometimes these men leave that girl holding dead flowers at the altar. And the man disappears, rides his horse to the next town to do it again to another, and another. Can you imagine?" She shook her head. "Los *hombres*, con three, four familias all on the island?"

"Mami," Tina said.

"Men possessed," Luisa continued. "With the lust of the devil. God is not in their hearts. Pueblo a pueblo, deshonrando. How could you catch him? How could you know what type of man he is?"

"Pobrecitos," Lupé said.

"Did you know anybody like that, Tia?" Maria asked.

"Sí, sit still." Tina's mother pushed Maria's chin down and kept braiding. "We call her Paola la Pobre. Un hombre—un *macho*—seduced her y la daño. Ever since, she says nothing, nada. She doesn't even leave the house she's lived in desde que era una *niña*."

"Mom," Tina said. "I really don't think she needs to hear this."

"Por que?" she said. "If your father were alive, he would tell you. His family lives two houses from her."

A knock at the front door brought Lupé to her feet. A small elderly woman entered, waving hello to the room before disappearing down the hallway. Lupé grabbed a sewing kit off the dining table and followed the woman to the back.

"Your Tio called," Tina's mom said.

Tina froze, her eyes on an image of Jimmy Carter at a podium. She looked over at her mom. "Which one?"

"Raul," her mother said.

Tina flinched.

Her mother squinted at her. "What is that? That face?"

Tina knocked back the rest of her coffee and grabbed her bag, slipping on the black flats she kept near the front door. She walked over to her mother and cousin, kissing them each on the cheek.

"Me voy," she said.

"Párate," her mother said. "What is this? Why are you leaving like that?"

"I'm not leaving like anything, Mami," Tina said, glancing at Maria.

Luisa stared back at her daughter. "Adónde vas?"

"To the mall," Tina said. "Like I told you literally five minutes ago."

"I'm almost done," she said. "Te manejo."

"It's right there," Tina said. "Quiero caminar."

"Por cuanto tiempo te vas?"

"I didn't realize this was an interrogation," Tina snapped.

Tina's mother gave her a look. Tina squeezed her eyes shut.

"I don't know how long," she said. "I'm gonna take some pictures and write for a bit, grab something to eat maybe. I'll be home later."

Luisa said nothing, her fingers working furiously. She finished Maria's hair and pulled a pink ribbon from the front pocket of her housedress, tying it around the braid. "Ahí. Perfecto."

Tina sighed. "You working at the hotel or bowling alley tonight?"

"Hotel," her mother said.

Tina nudged her, smiling. "Can you get some shampoo?"

Her mother tried not to smile back and failed, giving her a nod.

Maria looked up at Tina with forcibly raised eyebrows. "You want to watch a movie tonight?" she asked.

"We'll see," Tina said, rubbing Maria's cheek. "I'll try to get back in time."

"She won't," her mother said.

Tina pinched her cousin's nose, glared at her mother then walked out.

4.

It's always the same day: April 30th.

Ralph knows because Sanders is always sitting to his left in the helicopter and he always tells Ralph—yelling into his headset over the steady *whap-whap-whap* of the rotors—

"My boy turns three today."

Sanders stares at a crumpled photo of his wife and son, holding the picture in his lap like a newborn baby next to his M-16.

"Wife says kids born end of April got a good outlook," he says. "End up smart, successful."

"That so?" Ralph says.

"And funny," Sanders adds. "Kid's gonna be the next Lenny Bruce, God rest his soul."

"How's she know that?" Ralph asks.

"That horoscope bullshit," Sanders says.

"You into that crap?" Ralph asks, the helicopter jerking them side to side.

"Hell no," Sanders says, making a face. "Bunch a female mumbo jumbo. But it's a nice thought."

Sanders holds out the picture and Ralph takes it. The smiling boy sits on his mother's lap on a park bench, both distinctly Vietnamese, the kid sharing Sanders' elongated nose and puffy lips. His wife is thin and beautiful with a sadness in her eyes that looks permanent, and it's always then Ralph thinks:

Didn't Sanders hop a bird stateside a month ago?

He looks up and both Sanders and the pilot are gone. He looks down at his hands and the photo is gone too. Ralph's alone in the helicopter that's not in the air but parked on the roof of the U.S. embassy in Saigon, and there's a ton of commotion on the ground. He untangles himself from his harness and climbs out, walking to the edge of the roof. Throngs of people storm the embassy's exterior, waves of bodies smashing against the gates like a tsunami.

The second Ralph looks over the edge of the roof—as if on cue—the pamphlets start falling. Raining down from the sky with no preamble like dead birds, littering the area around the helicopter. At the same moment, sirens sound off in the distance. Ralph stoops to pick a pamphlet up, even though he knows what it says inside. The cover's stamped with the acronym S.A.F.E. Ralph flips to the first page: a map of Saigon. He flips the page again and there's a short insert:

> *Note evacuational signal.*
> *Do not disclose to other personnel.*
> *When the evacuation is ordered,*
> *the code will be read out on Armed Forces Radio.*
> *The code is: The temperature in Saigon is 105 degrees and rising.*
> *This will be followed by I'm Dreaming of a White Christmas.*

Ralph reads that last line and ten feet away the helicopter's radio crackles to life, a man yelling through the distorted signal:

"*The temperature in Saigon is 105 degrees and rising!*" The man sucks in a rattling breath then wails. "*I repeat, the temperature in Saigon is 105 degrees and rising!*"

The voice disappears, replaced by a cheerful musical intro, Bing Crosby sliding into the speakers:

I'mmmmm dreaming of a whiiiiiiite Christmas.

Somewhere, in some Saigon radio station, a record skips.

I'mmmmm dreaming of a whiiiiiiite Christmas.

The record skips again. Ralph looks down as the throng of people jump the gate, some running spikes through their feet and falling to the floor, mouths open in silent, anguished screams.

I'mmmmm dreaming

There's a sudden crash as the gate collapses, bodies flowing towards the embassy building.

of a Whiiiiiiite Christmas

The building shakes beneath Ralph as the mob knocks the heavy doors down like they're made of cardboard.

I'mmmmm dreaming

People flow back out the front doors with couches thrown over their shoulders, chairs, tables, desks, running with contraband against the crowd.

of a Whiiiiiiite Christmas

The crowd grows louder, their shouts traveling up the building towards him, echoes muffled behind the main stairwell door, a dozen feet from the helicopter. Too late, Ralph rushes for his M-16 just as the stairwell door bursts open and dozens of women—*hundreds* of them it seems—swarm onto the roof, surrounding Ralph with their hands held out, their faces dirty and tear-streaked, grabbing at him, screaming

"Take us, please!"

I'mmmmm dreaming

"We will give you money! Gold!"

of a Whiiiiiiite Christmas

"We will give you sex! Good sex!"

I'mmmmm dreaming

The stairwell door flies open again and scores of men in military uniforms with machetes storm the roof and start hacking the women to pieces,

of a Whiiiiiiite Christmas

blood and limbs and shards of bone flying everywhere, splattering Ralph's face, Ralph unable to move or breathe, eyes fixed on the men's facial features

I'mmmmm dreaming

or *lack* of facial features, each of them raising their machetes and bringing them down on the women's shoulders and arms and heads with nothing but pale skin where their eyes and noses and mouths should be and as Ralph stands frozen, one of the faceless men runs at him with his machete raised, bringing it down just as Ralph lets out a—

Ralph shot up in bed, feeling a hand on his back and turning with his arm raised to punch his attacker. Amanda flinched away, wide eyed. Ralph shook himself, put his arm down and leaned back on the headboard. Squeezing his eyes shut, he sucked in a deep breath.

Amanda faced him, tense. "Same dream?"

Ralph glanced at her as the phone trilled on the nightstand. He snatched it up, Sergeant Daniel Murphy's gruff voice on the other end.

"Code thirty, Grove," he said. "Swing by the office, we'll ride together."

"Roger," Ralph said, dropping the phone back in its cradle. He stood and stretched, feeling Amanda's eyes on his back. He glanced at his wife and she smiled, the corners of her eyes crinkling in a way that was new to Ralph. Ralph forced a smile back, heading to the closet and pulling out a blue suit.

"Was that Danny?" Amanda asked.

Ralph grunted, pulling on his pants and standing in front of the mirror.

Amanda sighed. "What is it now?"

"Shooting in the Grove," Ralph said, pushing the lapels of his shirt into his pants and buckling his belt.

"They've had you on doubles for weeks now," she said.

"Thin as the department's getting," Ralph said. "No choice."

"You know exactly what's happening here, Ralphie."

Ralph turned to her. "What?"

"Same as I've been telling you," she said, sitting up. "It's the immigrants. They've been a problem for years and nobody's addressed it and *now* look."

"I'm going to the Grove," Ralph said, facing the mirror again. "This isn't an immigration issue."

"You heard they bought out the radio station," she said. "WNMS. Turned it on yesterday, nothing but Spanish."

"What's your point, Amanda?"

"My point is it's criminal what Carter's letting happen," she said. "How do we know these people are who they say they are?"

Ralph looked over. "How do we know anybody is who they say they are?"

Amanda opened her mouth then closed it again, considering.

"The city's just getting crowded," Ralph said. "More people's bound to bring hostility, hostility breeds agitation, agitation breeds crime. This isn't some abnormal occurrence. Just sucks it's happening on our watch."

Amanda pulled the covers to the side, lying at an angle in the mirror that made her look like a funhouse version of herself, blonde hair and gray eyes and thin nose and lips all disproportionate.

"I just don't know how any of you guys do it," she said, scooting off the bed and walking to the bathroom. "And the absolutely *insane* women who think they can do your job?" She scoffed, shook her head. "Even when you were overseas, I kept thinking…he's gotta just run at some point, right? Come back to me, I mean. Like, he can't just *stay* over there, can he?"

"Run, right," Ralph said, smirking. "Would've gone well with my C.O."

"You know what I mean."

"Court martial looks great on the résumé, actually."

"How come you never talk about it?" she asked.

Ralph glanced at her in the bathroom doorway. "About what?"

"The war," she said. "You *never* talk about it."

"Nothing to talk about," Ralph said, grabbing his badge. "Heard one story, you've heard 'em all."

"But don't you want to—I don't know, get yours out?" she asked. "I read this psychologist in Cosmo, said it's really not good to keep all that in."

"Did he, now?" Ralph said.

"Says it's not good to have all this pent-up negative energy."

"I don't spend time dwelling on stuff, Mandy," Ralph said. "There's nothing *to* get out. No 'negative energy.' Nothing."

"I just—"

"I have to go," Ralph said. "Murphy's waiting."

"How is he?"

"What's with all the questions, Mandy?" Ralph barked. "You practicing for some marathon or something?"

Amanda shrank into the bathroom.

"Feel like I'm on the other side of an interrogation table," he said.

Amanda said nothing.

Ralph squeezed his eyes shut, forcing a thin smile.

"Danny's fine," he said.

"Okay," she said, closing the bathroom door.

Ralph grabbed his keys off the dresser. "I'll ring if I can't make it for dinner," he called out. "Love you, bye."

Passing Mikey's bedroom at the end of the hallway, Ralph peeked in on his sleeping son, taking in his tiny facial features, almost identical to his own. Mikey stirred and opened his eyes, smiling at Ralph before turning over and passing back out again. Closing the bedroom door, Ralph headed through the living room out to the front.

Outside, Ralph picked up the newspaper off the grass and followed the path to his Plymouth, climbing in and shaking the paper open onto the front seat. Scanning the headlines, he sucked his teeth and shook his head, turning the engine and blasting the AC. The car smelled faintly of puke, a department-issued radio and siren attached to the dashboard. The radio crackled some staggered call signals as Ralph took off his jacket and draped it over the back of his chair, adjusting his .38 in its side holster. He plucked a pack of Kools from his shirt pocket and lit one up, smoking as he pulled out of his driveway and headed south through Miami Shores towards the downtown precinct.

Twenty minutes later Ralph pulled up outside the building on 14th street, cruising to a stop on the sidewalk as Sergeant Daniel Murphy stepped out.

Ralph threw the newspaper in the back, Murphy climbing in the passenger seat. Pulling back into traffic, Ralph tugged at his shirt collar, sweat on his forehead.

"Lady at the store told me this suit was summer weight," he said, grabbing another Kool from his pack. "All I feel's the weight of summer."

"Gonna get hotter yet," Murphy said, pulling a Rocky Patel cigar and Zippo from his jacket pocket.

"Always does in this damn city," Ralph said, lighting up with one hand, the other on the steering wheel. "What's this thirty about?"

They puffed their smokes while Murphy gave Ralph the rundown: young black male shot and in critical condition on the way to the hospital, patrol at the house waiting for them. Murphy finished as they rode south on Biscayne towards Coconut Grove, smoke billowing out both open windows. Weaving in between the slower cars, Ralph felt Murphy's eyes on him and glanced over.

"What?"

Murphy pulled his cigar from his mouth. "You look like shit."

"Thanks."

"Still ain't sleeping?"

"That obvious?"

"Could use those bags under your eyes for storage," Murphy said.

"Been trying to help Amanda more with Mikey."

"Three-year-olds," Murphy said, shaking his head. "Ain't gotta tell me."

"'Bout to be four next month."

"Good age," Murphy said. "They start to calm down a little."

"Thank God."

"Just a little."

"I'll take it."

"How much overtime did you put in last month?" Murphy asked.

Ralph shrugged.

Murphy shook his head. "Told you to pace yourself, Williams."

"I have a feeling I'd be tired no matter what," Ralph said.

"Gonna get more tiring longer you do this, believe me" Murphy said. "By the way, department's got a vehicle for me next week. You and Weis can go back to jacking each other off or whatever it is you two do in your free time."

"Weis's doing just fine without me," Ralph said.

"Good," Murphy said. "Gonna have to split you up anyways. People we've lost, can't afford my best running together. We're getting some new blood, you two gotta bring them up to speed."

"Whatever you say, boss."

Murphy glanced over at him. "You sound less than enthused."

Ralph gave Murphy a look of surprise, pulling the car to a stop at a red light. "Sorry," he said, sighing. "Woke up with Mandy in my ear."

"They do that," Murphy said. "There's a reason I'm twice divorced. It ain't the job."

"Then I go and open the *Tribune*," Ralph continued, pointing over his shoulder. "And they're still spouting their bullshit."

Murphy snuffed a laugh. "They've got a lot to talk about when it comes to us these days."

"It's just like—" Ralph shook his head. "—Some days I wonder if there's any real point to what we're doing."

Murphy scratched the stubble on his chin. "How do you mean?"

Ralph flicked his cigarette out the window as the light turned green. "It's like the entire—I don't know, defense system of this society is fucked. Like every day the world gives a little less of a shit about its own safety."

"Bleak."

"It's only when I'm wearing this I think like that though," Ralph said, fingering the badge on his right hip. "Then I get home, and I look at Mikey—"

Ralph's voice petered out. Murphy stared out at the passing businesses on US-1 as they turned into the Grove, headed towards a street blocked off by patrol cars and flashing lights. Ralph held his badge up to the window and one of the patrols waved them through, pointing at a faded-green shotgun house near the middle of the block. Ralph nodded at the man and drove forward.

"My pops, the son of a bitch," Murphy said as Ralph pulled the car to a stop outside the rundown house "Before he passed, he always used to tell me it ain't good to get complacent about nothing. Gotta keep it fresh." He tapped a finger against his temple. "Boredom breeds mistakes. Mistakes get you killed."

"Solid advice," Ralph said, cutting the engine.

"It was," Murphy said, climbing out of the car. "Old man wasn't an asshole all of the time."

The living room inside the house was sparsely decorated, half a dozen milk crates stacked in the corner next to a couch. A dark-skinned, lanky kid with broad lips and an afro stood in the kitchen, a patrol officer leaning against the wall on the opposite side of the room staring at the kid with obvious disdain. The kid wore an oversized Miami Dolphins t-shirt with holes in the pits. He flailed his arms as he talked, his shirt billowing around him. Ralph and Murphy stepped through the front door, glanced at the patrol, eyed each other then pulled out their notebooks. Ralph trailed Murphy as they approached the kid in the kitchen.

"He just ran in from the street," the kid was saying, pointing at a burglar-bar-covered window. "He was by the bus stop and they rode up and shot—"

"Alright hold on," Murphy said, holding up a hand and glancing at the patrol again. "No sense yelling at the man."

"I ain't yelling at him, he just ain't list—"

"Slow down," Murphy interrupted, pointing at himself. "I'm Sergeant Daniel Murphy." He nodded at Ralph. "This is Detective Ralph Williams."

"'Sup," the kid said nervously.

"Now, who'd you say ran in from the street?"

"Richie," the kid said. "My brother."

"And Richie's the one on the way to the hospital right now?"

"Yeah, with Mama. And Marcus went—"

"Who's Marcus?" Ralph chimed in.

"My cousin."

"And how old are Richie and Marcus?" Murphy asked.

"Richie sixteen," the kid said. "Marcus seventeen."

"And you?" Murphy asked. "Name and age?"

"Claude, man," the kid said. "I'm fif—what this got to do with Richie?"

"I need you to start over, Claude," Murphy said, placing his leatherbound journal open on the kitchen counter. "Tell us what happened. Slowly."

Claude sucked his teeth. "Richie over at the bus stop talking with Marlene. Said he was just standing there then they drove up and shot—"

"Marlene," Murphy said. "Who is Marlene?"

"Richie's girl," Claude said.

"And where is she?"

"With Marcus and 'em ridin' to the hospital."

"So who shot Richie?" Ralph asked.

"Said he don't know," Claude said.

"He doesn't know who shot him?" Murphy asked.

The kid shook his head. Ralph and Murphy glanced at each other.

"So he got shot," Murphy said. "Comes back in the apartment and—?"

"Marcus come running in the living room," he said. "See Richie got shot. Mama come in from hanging clothes and start screaming then she call 911."

Murphy turned to Ralph. "Take a look."

Ralph tucked his notepad in his back pocket and headed to the door.

Stepping down the concrete steps, Ralph noticed a group of teenagers sitting outside an apartment across the street, their conversation stopping the moment he walked out. Ralph ignored them, turning to the patrolman.

"You the first officer on scene?" he asked.

"No," the patrol said. "My partner, Jackson."

"Where's he at?"

"With the vic at the hospital."

Ralph gave him a look. The man was golden tanned, thin nose with a blonde buzzcut. Bushy mustache, shades reflecting the blazing sun.

"He's supposed to stay here," Ralph said. "Secure the scene."

"That's what I told him," the patrol said.

Ralph was about to head down the path towards the street when the patrol cleared his throat. Ralph glanced over at him.

"Sorry," he said, nodding at the door. "Just—the doorknob. Sir." He raised one of his feet, as if checking for dog shit. "And the steps."

Ralph looked at the faded brown doorknob. He looked down at the steps beneath his feet, the porch shrouded in shadows with the sun directly overhead.

"Lemme get your Maglite?" Ralph asked, holding his hand out.

The cop pulled his flashlight from his belt and handed it over. Ralph turned it on, shining the beam on the front steps and the doorknob. He grunted and walked down the concrete path to the street, looked around then returned and handed the flashlight back to the patrol.

"What's your name, officer?" Ralph asked.

"Terrence," he said. "Terry. Pullman."

Ralph nodded and stepped back inside. Pulling out his notebook, Ralph cut Murphy off in the middle of his questioning.

"When your brother came in the house," he said to the kid. "After he got shot. Where did he sit? While your mom called 911?"

The kid looked confused, then pointed at a couch against the wall.

"Right there?" Ralph said.

The kid nodded.

Ralph walked over to the couch. "Where's the blood?"

The kid's eyes fell to his shoes and he said nothing.

"Detective Williams asked you a question," Murphy said.

"We cleaned it up," the kid mumbled.

"Cleaned it up?" Ralph asked. "With what?"

The kid pushed off the counter and walked to the hallway closet, opening the door and grabbing a laundry basket filled with bloody towels. Ralph and Murphy walked over and looked at the contents. Ralph picked one of the towels up between his thumb and index finger, holding it away from his body.

"You used this to clean up the couch?" Ralph asked, dropping it back in the basket. "This is a lot of blood."

The kid put the basket back in the closet, speaking quietly. "We turned over the cushions."

Ralph walked over and flipped the middle couch cushion to reveal a large, damp stain the shape of Texas. Ralph turned to Murphy, nodding at the door.

"No blood on the knob," he said. "Or the path headed in."

"Okay," Murphy said, sliding his notebook back in his pocket. "I think I know what happened here."

"I told y'all what happened," the kid said.

"You all were in here playing with a gun and your brother got shot," Murphy said. "By either one of you or himself."

Murphy paused. The kid avoided his eyes, said nothing.

"Now if you quit the bullshit and come out with the truth," Murphy continued. "Then I won't have to take you in. Where'd you hide the gun?"

"Ain't no gun," the kid said.

"Jesus H. Christ," Ralph said. "Where's the goddamn gun, kid? We don't have time for this shit."

"What gun?" the kid said, bringing his shoulders up near his ears. "Don't know nothin' 'bout no gun."

"Your brother or your cousin or one of you has the goddamn gun," Ralph said. "Sooner we get it, the sooner we can be on our way."

"They ain't shoot Richie in here," the kid said. "They shot him out—"

"You're lying," Ralph yelled. "Y'all were in here fuckin' around, probably don't even know how to use the goddamn thing and you up and got your brother shot. Accident or not, it's gonna happen again if you keep playing fuckin' stupid. Where's the gun?"

"Ain't no gun, man," the kid said.

Murphy walked towards the door, motioning for Ralph and Terry to follow.

"You think about how you want this to go," he called back to the kid. "If your brother dies in that hospital, we're coming back here with a warrant, finding that gun and arresting you for manslaughter."

Murphy paused by the front door, looking back at the kid. The kid said nothing. The three men exited the apartment.

Outside, Murphy turned to Officer Terry.

"What's your partner's name?"

"Jackson," Terry said.

"First officer on scene—"

"Already went over that," Ralph said. "Terry here pointed out the lack of blood outside."

Murphy looked Terry up and down then patted the patrol on the shoulder. "Good eye. We could use more of that in homicide."

"Thank you, sir," Terry said, the corners of his mouth twitching.

"Gonna need you to stick around for a bit," Murphy said. "Least 'til we swing by the hospital."

Terry nodded. Murphy and Ralph headed back to Ralph's dull-blue Plymouth Satellite, climbing back in.

"Me and this Jackson gonna have a talk," Murphy grumbled.

"Bet he's not even at the hospital," Ralph said.

"Nothing worse than a lazy cop," Murphy said, looking over at Ralph. "Got a little heated in there, huh?"

Ralph shook his head. "It's just already been a long fucking day."

"There's a 7-Eleven next to the hospital," Murphy said. "Sounds like you could use a cup."

Ralph smiled. "Donut too if they're fresh."

"Fresh or not," Murphy said. "Better than nothing."

5.

Tommy parked at the Publix on Le Jeune and killed the engine. Strolling inside, he headed for the produce section and had a carton of eggs and a single bagged onion in hand when he heard his name. He turned to find a brown-skinned man with a curly afro and a bushy mustache walking past the meat freezers towards him.

"Luchi," Tommy said, surprised.

"Parcero," the man said, hand outstretched. Wearing an off-white guayabera and brown slacks, Luchi held a bag of charcoal under his arm, his face lit up with a smile. A year since meeting Clara's uncle and Tommy still marveled at how the man seemed so much larger than his five-three frame, his ostrich-skin shoes almost child-size.

Tommy took Luchi's hand and Luchi slapped a palm down on his shoulder, shaking his arm. Tommy noticed Luchi's fingers then, the blackened, wrinkled tips, like charred hot dogs.

"Que bueno verte," the man said.

"Funny running into you here," Tommy said. "Clara was just talking about that cake your girlfriend made for the party last weekend." Tommy snapped his fingers. "Forgive me, her name totally slipped my mind."

Luchi's eyes flashed with something that made Tommy's stomach sink a little before he smiled again.

"It is no matter," he said. "La fiesta. Is good, eh?"

"Very good," Tommy said. "Had a lot of fun. Probably drank too much, to be honest."

"Too much drinks," Luchi said, waving him off. "Dis not a thing."

"Tell that to the hangover I had the next day."

"Dis happen if you *stop* drinking," Luchi said.

"True," Tommy said. "Feels good to let loose every once in a while."

Luchi cocked his head to the side, nodding. "Let loose," he echoed.

Tommy held up the items in his hands, leaning towards Luchi and lowering his voice. "Gotta get this home. Can't leave a pregnant woman waiting too long, she'll rip your head off."

"*Dis* is a thing," Luchi said.

"Definitely a thing," Tommy said. "But maybe you can—"

"Ju still looking for work?"

Tommy froze, his eyes narrowing. He waited for Luchi to elaborate but the man just stared at him.

"Work?" Tommy said.

"Sí."

"No," Tommy said. "I mean—I have a job."

"But ju no like this job," Luchi said, mimicking the act of typing in midair. "Numbers all day, Clara say to me. All you do, numbers numbers numbers."

Tommy forced a smile. "Clara said that?"

"Sí," Luchi said. "She say ju hate it. Ju say you, eh." He snapped his fingers. "Human adding machine."

"Wow," Tommy said, chuckling. "Can't believe she told you all that."

"If ju are okay, ju are okay," Luchi said. "Pero five hundred dollars, un poco de trabajo, no numbers."

Tommy squinted at the man. "Did you say five hundred dollars?"

"Sí."

"Five hundred American dollars?"

Luchi nodded.

"Five hundred dollars to do *what* exactly?" Tommy asked.

"Manejar," Luchi said. "Drive."

"Drive," Tommy repeated. "Drive what? Who? Where?"

Luchi scratched his stomach. "Ju know what it is I do for work, Tommy?"

Tommy shrugged. "Clara said something about imports and exports."

"Sí, imports," Luchi said, smiling. "It is good business. But you will help."

"Driving?"

"Ju know Me-ah-me, no?" Luchi raised an arm, sweeping it around.

"I mean…yeah," Tommy said. "Lived here my whole life."

Luchi switched the bag of charcoal to his other arm. "So I tell ju a place, ju can go to dis place easy?"

"If it's in the city, yeah," Tommy said. "Sure."

"And ju will take dis job?" Luchi asked.

"Whoa," Tommy said, holding a hand up. "I didn't say that."

"No?" Luchi asked.

Tommy dropped his hand. A woman with a shopping cart strolled past them, a boy sitting in the front pretending to drive it like a race car.

"You *just* want me to drive?" Tommy asked.

"Sí," Luchi said.

"That's it?"

Luchi nodded.

Tommy swiped the corners of his mouth. The grocery store's intercom crackled to life and a man mumbled something unintelligible.

"This isn't for like—a bank robbery or anything like that?" he asked, smiling and loosening his tie. "I'm no good for jail. Bad for my health. Plus leaving Clara and Adam alone and all that."

Luchi laughed. "No robbery," he said. "Y no jail. Ju will go me campadre's house, get di car, take me my house."

"And you'll give me five hundred dollars for that?"

"Sí."

Tommy paused. "Why?"

Luchi put a palm to his chest. "Mi sobrina," he said. "Clara, ella te ama. She love ju Tommy. Dis mean ju are good man. So I give ju work."

An image of Greg's enormous wooden desk appeared in Tommy's mind.

"What the hell," he said, shaking Luchi's hand. "I'm in."

Luchi pulled a silver ball-point pen and a small spiral-bound notebook from his shirt pocket and ripped off a sheet, using the back of the notebook to scribble. He placed the pen and notepad back in his pocket and passed the sheet to Tommy. Two addresses were listed, one above the other.

"Ahí," Luchi said, pointing at the top address. He pointed at the second address. "Drive di car aquí." He held up two fingers. "Dos y media."

"Two-thirty," Tommy said.

"Two-thirty," Luchi said, backing away.

"See you then," Tommy said.

He watched Clara's uncle drift down the bread aisle and disappear as suddenly as he had arrived. Glancing at the sheet of paper in his hand, Tommy checked his watch: half past eleven. "Two-thirty," he repeated.

Walking to the registers, Tommy floated through the checkout motions, adding a pack of Reds to his purchases. Back in his Trans Am, he lit up a cigarette, switching the tape in the 8-track to the b-side. "Black Dog" started and he put the car in gear, squealing out of the parking lot and headed back north on Coral Way.

Tommy was halfway home when he realized he forgot the milk.

6.

The Jeep had no doors.

Rig had never seen a car with no doors before. Not one that worked.

The white man behind the steering wheel flipped him a quarter and Rig handed him a newspaper. The man tossed the paper on the passenger seat and turned up his radio.

Dropping the quarter in his pocket, Rig crumpled the five-dollar bill in there then smoothed it out again with his palm, watching DJ work the opposite sidewalk. Otis stood four cars away next to a red Cadillac with dark tints, the driver's window halfway down. Squatting, Otis pulled a lumpy plastic bag the size of a golf ball from his sock and dropped it in a folded newspaper. He handed the newspaper through the window to the driver, who exchanged it for a bill. The window rolled up, the light turned green and the red Cadillac pulled off with a short honk. Rig watched the car until it disappeared then turned back to Otis, finding the boy standing a couple of feet away, an unwavering intensity in his eyes.

"What you starin' at?" Otis asked, hands clenched at his side.

Rig noticed then just how much taller he was than Otis. Wider too, his midday shadow like a blanket.

Rig smirked. "Yo' mama."

Otis tossed Rig a side-eye and laughed. He glanced at Lefty sitting on a lawn chair smoking under a tree. The old man stubbed out the cigarette and lay his head back, draping a towel over his face.

Otis turned back to Rig. "You down to hit the mall?"

Rig glanced over at Dadeland, the mall sparkling like the Land of Oz.

He looked back at Otis, shrugged.

Otis called out to DJ. "You comin'?"

"I ain't tryin' to hear mama's mouth again," DJ called back.

"Always actin' like a bitch," Otis muttered, and without warning the boy bolted across the street.

Rig hesitated for a second then ran after him. Hopping a line of bushes into the parking lot, they bee-lined towards the Tribute Tower, crouching behind the pillar. Rig waited for a shout or approaching footsteps or anything. When nothing came, he poked his head around the corner. Lefty dozed away under the tree, DJ standing at the intersection staring after them.

"He ain't goin' tell Lefty?" Rig asked.

"DJ ain't no snitch," Otis said, brushing his hands on his shorts.

The mall loomed ahead as the boys crossed the parking lot, pushing through the glass entrance past a cafe to the right, rays of sunshine streaming in from the overhead skylight, dust particles lit up in the air. A giant statue of a horse stood in the middle of the promenade, surrounded by a circular pool of water. Rig leaned over the marble edge, peering at piles of pennies and nickels settled at the bottom. A toddler stumbled over from his parents' side, steadying himself on the edge of the pool with a quarter held up in one hand. His father followed behind, lifting the kid and waiting for him to drop the coin in the water. It made a tiny plop as it hit and the boy giggled. The dad smiled too, his expression fading when he noticed Otis and Rig. He put the toddler down and grabbed his hand, looking back at the boys with a sneer.

"Why they throwing money in there?" Rig asked.

"S'posed to make a wish," Otis said. "Or some shit."

"Then what?"

"S'posed to come true."

Rig pulled the single quarter from his pocket and studied it.

"I ain't throwing money in water for no wish," he said.

"Lefty'd lynch yo' ass anyways," Otis said. "Most of that's his."

Delving deeper into the mall, the boys passed clothing stores, a luggage store, a shoe repair and a slew of kiosks advertising everything from cigar boxes to ceramic ballet figurines. Rig ignored them all until he spotted a purple banner with *Magic City Books* printed on it in medieval-style lettering. Heading for the neon-lit sign like a moth, Rig paused just inside the entrance to inhale the pungent scent of old books. A couple of tables in the center of the small space displayed dozens of hardcover novels. Stacks of boxes sat against every wall in every corner, filled with paperbacks. Shelves of books hung on the walls around the room, a couple of small overflowing plastic barrels set up next to the tables. Walking up to one barrel labeled *Discount Bin$*, Rig picked up a book and studied the cover art: a white man sitting on a desk holding a gun, a white woman in a red dress with only her legs visible sprawled across the floor.

Otis came up behind him.

"Fuck you doing?" he said. "Lefty goin' figure out we gone, ain't got time for this."

"Check this out," Rig said, holding the book up.

Otis took it and looked it over. "What is it?"

"Rage," Rig said, reading the cover. "A novel by Richard Batch-man." Rig read the caption to himself, then out loud: "His twisted mind turned a quiet classroom into a dangerous world of terror."

Otis smirked. "You like reading and shit," he said, handing the book back.

Rig shrugged, opening to the first page. Otis nudged him, nodding past Rig's head at a rack of comic books set up on the back wall.

"Now that's *my* shit," Otis said, hopping over to the display.

Rig joined him as Otis grabbed one of the comics. The cover showed a room half in disarray, half neatly kept. Batman approached a couch with a menacing look on the visible portion of his face. A man sat on the couch wearing a suit split purple and orange plaid, half of his face grotesquely disfigured on the orange side. A silver dollar sat on his palm.

"This my nigga right here," he said. "Batman stay whoopin' on fools."

"He ain't really got superpowers though," Rig said.

"That's why he's the shit," Otis said. "He just like you and me, 'cept he got enough money to buy all this shit make himself super just like these other fools. *Cash* that nigga's power."

Rig picked up another comic: Spider-Man clinging to the side of a wall as a masked woman wearing a full black outfit pounced from above, a mane of white hair waving above her head. Rig flipped to the first page.

"Y'all need to buy those if you want to read 'em," someone yelled. Rig turned to find a short round man glaring at them from behind the cash register.

Rig glanced at the cover price: forty cents.

"I got it," he said, taking the Batman comic from Otis and heading to the register. The cashier watched them, his glare fading and his chin tilting back as Rig got closer.

Rig dropped the comics on the counter. "How much?"

The cashier glanced down at the items as if they'd materialized out of thin air. He tapped each of them. "A dollar," he said. "Even."

Rig reached in his pocket and pulled out the crumpled five-dollar bill.

Otis stared at it as Rig handed it over. "You made that today?"

"No," Rig said. "Got it from my mom's."

"And you spending it on *this*?" Otis said, letting out a sharp laugh.

"Why not?" Rig asked.

"Nothing, nigga," Otis said. "Just like—ain't you *hungry*?"

At that exact moment Rig's stomach growled. "Yeah, actually."

The cashier's drawer dinged open and the man with the ponytail handed Rig four singles, bagging the comics.

"They got a place out back," Otis said, shaking his head. "You a funny cat."

Rig frowned. "Why?"

"You gotta be the only nigga in The Beans spendin' cash at a bookstore."

"It's like you said," Rig said. "I like reading."

"Guess so," Otis said, as if it were an inexplicable phenomenon. "You a wild nigga for real though."

"No loitering," the cashier spit. "Take your purchases and leave."

Rig and Otis looked over at the man in unison: pale and balding with large wide-framed glasses and a frayed ponytail, a ring of acne around his lips. The man looked Rig in the eyes and saw something that made him lean away. Otis tapped Rig on the chest and headed for the exit. Rig kept his eyes on the cashier, taking his time walking out with the *Magic City* bag clenched in his fist.

"Fucking cracka," Otis grumbled as they headed for the exit.

"Whatever," Rig muttered, pushing the door open. "Just angry 'bout life."

As the boys spoke, a white van circled towards the lot from the north. At first glance Rig noticed something odd. Bulky, was the word that popped into his head, though he wasn't sure he was using the term right. The van looked like a regular van—like Lefty's but newer—and at the same time seemed bigger than one, as if somebody had taken a regular van and stretched it at the edges.

"Check this out," Rig said, tapping Otis's arm.

The van entered the lot and pulled into an open space next to a Mercedes Benz facing two store entrances: *Royal Liquors* and *Maraschino's Deli*. The van's brakes hissed, the engine idling. Something clattered inside and the van shifted. A moment later the front doors opened and two men hopped out wearing jeans and leather jackets. They stood shorter than Rig, the passenger walking with a confident gait, the driver bouncing on the balls of his feet. The summer heat shimmered off the concrete around them. The men glanced in their direction and Rig looked away, staring at a wrinkled movie poster for *Mother, Jugs & Speed* with Bill Cosby, Raquel Welch and Harvey Keitel. The tag line: "*They don't call them that for nothing!*"

Otis stared right back at the men. "Fuck is up with these chicos?" he said. "Hot as hell, they dressed like it's New York."

Rig peeked over as the men pushed through the *Royal Liquor* entrance.

As soon as they disappeared Otis walked towards the van.

Tensing, Rig clenched the *Magic City* bag in his fist and hurried after the other boy. They stopped in the shade of the van, looking up at the words stenciled just below the tinted windows: *Happy Time Complete Supply Party*. The stencil was fresh, a few dark streaks where the paint had been applied heavily. A small hole with metal covering it stood below the painted words.

Rig left Otis to walk around the van's rear bumper, running his hand on the warm metal. On the other side he found the same set of stenciled letters, streaked with globs of paint:

Happy Time Complete Party Supply

Rig walked back to Otis, reading the stencil on that side out loud:

"Happy Time Complete Supply Party."

"Yeah," Otis said.

Rig motioned for Otis to follow him back to the other side of the van, pointing at the stencil there.

"Happy Time Complete Party Supply," he said. "They got the last two words switched around."

Otis stared at the mismatched stencil then burst out laughing, a high-pitched and unhinged sound that infected Rig. Hands dropping to his stomach, *Magic City* bag slipping down his wrist, Rig laughed and Otis laughed louder and the boys both laughed until they cried, sucking in breaths around the guffaws.

Rig couldn't remember the last time he laughed like that.

They were still laughing when Rig looked through the liquor store window at the men from the van. They faced two other men standing behind a cash register, the one on the left wearing a fedora with a white button-down, the other a Miami Dolphins t-shirt with a cigar in his mouth and a bottle of dark liquor in hand. The men from the van talked animatedly at the two men behind the register, the sun glaring off the window and making it hard to see the details. Rig squinted as Otis's laughter subsided behind him.

Rig's smile faded. "They got guns," he said.

"What?" Otis said.

Rig pointed at the store and opened his mouth to repeat himself as the men raised their guns and pulled the triggers and all hell broke loose.

7.

Ralph pushed out of the convenience store with Murphy behind him, both detectives holding steaming cups of coffee.

"Goddamn bathroom smells like the Orange Bowl after a game," Murphy grumbled, tucking a bag of donuts under his arm.

"You were expecting something else?" Ralph said.

"Some professional courtesy maybe."

The sun broke cover from a couple of clouds and beamed down on them. Ralph's skin prickled, sweat popping up on the back of his neck. He slapped at the itching sensation as faint gunshots rat-a-tatted in the distance.

Ralph froze, cocking his head to the side. Murphy took a bite of glazed donut and opened the passenger door of Ralph's Plymouth.

"You hear that?" Ralph asked.

Pausing with one leg in the car, Murphy followed Ralph's gaze east on Kendall Drive.

The gunshots sounded off again.

The sweat on Ralph's neck went cold.

"Dadeland," Murphy said.

Ralph turned the car on, twisting the volume on the police radio. A frantic dispatcher screamed through the speakers.

—fired at Dadeland Mall, all available units respond!

"Let's go!" Ralph yelled, dropping his coffee in the cup holder and slamming the door. Murphy hopped in and Ralph flipped on the siren, throwing the car in reverse. The Plymouth's back tires spun before catching traction, shooting the car towards the exit. Ralph whipped it onto Kendall Drive with horn blasts trailing after them. Murphy dropped his bag of donuts and braced against the dashboard.

"Don't fucking kill us!" Murphy yelled.

"I'm not!" Ralph snapped as they fishtailed around a Camry turning at the Galloway/Kendall intersection.

Skidding to a halt in an empty lot across from the mall, Ralph threw the door open, stepping out into chaos. Crowds of people near the main building of the mall ran screaming, ducking for cover while on the opposite end of the lot, bullet flashes lit up the tinted windows of a white van with its fender crushed against the Dadeland Tribute Tower.

Ralph pulled his .38 special and took off running as the van reversed, switched gears and sped off. The steady blast of bullets conjured phantom jungle smells in his nose.

"That's fucking military grade!" he yelled.

Murphy's footsteps pounded after him. "Cut them off through the alley!"

The van careened around the parking lot towards the rear exit as half a dozen patrol cars turned onto Kendall from US-1, squealing into the mall. Dozens of officers hopped out with guns drawn. The van rounded a Jordan Marsh and disappeared, taking the gunshots along with it. Ralph hopped a hedge, knocking over an abandoned shopping cart rolling into his path as they approached the department store. Twenty feet away, the sound of squealing tires and a dull thud brought Ralph to a skidding halt. He turned to find Murphy airborne, legs splayed and his jacket billowing around him.

Murphy hit the sidewalk and rolled to a stop in a patch of grass near a parked Impala. Ralph cursed, running over. Murphy pushed himself up slowly.

"Shit, Sarge," Ralph said, breathlessly. "You—"

"Go!" Murphy yelled, hopping on one leg. "I'm fine dammit, go!"

Ralph glared at the car that hit Murphy, a Corolla stopped in the middle of the lot. A woman sat behind the wheel, hand held to her mouth, eyes filled with tears. A little boy sat crying in the passenger seat. Ralph jabbed a finger in the woman's direction then took off running again.

Bursting onto 84th street near 72nd ave, Ralph spotted the white van stopped at the intersection behind the mall. He approached with his .38 raised, sucking in deep breaths. Ducking below the rear windows, Ralph blinked sweat from his eyes. He poked his head around the back of the van and quickly returned to his position, taking a second to register what he saw.

No clear view of the driver's side.

Ralph ticked off three seconds then rounded the corner, crouching below the driver's line of sight and passing a porthole in the side of the van, the hole ragged from bullet flashes. Aiming his gun at the side mirror, finger twitching against the trigger guard, he sucked in another breath and backed away from the van in an arc, gun raised.

Empty.

Ralph scurried back up against the van. He let out a huff then risked a quick peek through the driver's window.

Nobody.

Ralph's aim wavered. He looked out at the streaming Snapper Creek canal, glistening in the afternoon sunlight. Looking back at the van, he studied the stencil: *Happy Time Complete Party Supply* with a phone number listed beneath.

Moving to the back of the van, Ralph raised his gun again and pulled one of the rear doors open. It barely let out a whistle.

Ralph lowered his gun, taking his finger off the trigger guard.

"You get those sons of bitches?" Murphy called out, limping up behind him with his.38 drawn, the right sleeve of his jacket torn at the shoulder. He stopped just short of Ralph, staring inside the van.

"Shit," he exhaled.

"Yeah," Ralph said.

The van had been fitted with extra layers of metal siding, the mirror-tinted windows on the rear doors blocking the view from the outside world. The floor was upholstered with red shag carpet, two fuel cans shoved against the right wheel well. Eight Kevlar vests hung from hooks attached to the van's reinforced roof, surrounded by a dozen other hooks holding a couple submachines and automatics. Below—strapped to a tripod in front of dual ports drilled into the side of the van—was a mounted .50 caliber M2 Browning. Hundreds of rounds of ammunition sat in crates on the ground. Spent bullet casings littered the carpet.

Ralph picked up one of the used shells, rolled it in his palm, sniffed it.

"They left all this behind," Murphy said.

Ralph dropped the casing back on the floor of the van.

"Like nothing," he said, nodding at the tripod. "That's a BMG. Haven't seen one since 'Nam."

A line of patrol vehicles screeched to a stop at the intersection, blocking off the road.

"Wait'll they get a load of this shit," Murphy muttered.

Ralph stared inside the van with haunted eyes, a sense of dread settling deep in the base of his spine, like cancer.

8.

Sitting at the coffee shop near Dadeland's entrance, Tina snapped pictures of the horse statue glistening beneath the skylight. Two black boys wearing oversized clothes stood by the wishing well. Tina took shots of their small faces as they walked away then put her camera down, sipping her coffee and jotting a quick description of the horse statue in her journal (the phrase *accentuating dynamics* floated to the surface of her mind). She was picking her camera back up when gunshots sounded off from the back of the mall. Scattered cries drifted over, spreading through the crowd like an electrical current. A few shoppers started jogging towards the mall entrance.

Tina turned her ear to the sound. More gunshots rang out.

Grabbing her bag and journal, Tina left her coffee and weaved through the fleeing patrons towards the back of the mall, pushing through the double doors just as the rattling gunshots stopped. She skimmed past a group of wild-eyed women, her eyes adjusting to the scene. Bringing her camera up, she snapped the liquor store's destroyed entrance, scanning the area through the lens. Bullet casings and shattered car windows cut a trail through the parking lot back to Jordan Marsh. The crowd outside the liquor store grew. Tina moved close enough to glimpse the dead bodies lying inside. She was about to snap a picture when a group of people stepped in the way. Lowering the camera, she noticed the two black boys she'd photographed earlier staring at the liquor store entrance, their dark skin stark against the mob of white faces.

A hand clamped down on Tina's shoulder. She looked up at a police officer wearing a brown uniform and a grim expression.

"Gonna need you to head inside, ma'am," he said.

Another officer came over and pulled the two black boys off to the side. Two dozen other cops milled about, trying to gain control of the crowd.

Tina held up her camera. "I'm just taking some—"

"Miss," the cop said. "We have to secure the area. You need to go inside."

Tina bristled. "But they're already gone."

"Lady, I'm not going to ask—"

"She's with me, Officer Pendleton."

Tina and the officer both looked over at a woman with very large sunglasses and teased blonde hair, holding up a lanyard around her neck with a press badge clipped to the end.

"She's our photographer," the woman said.

"Ms. Brathwaite," the officer said. "This isn't the—"

"We're on the job, Officer," she said. "Just like you."

The officer sighed. "Just don't get in the way."

"Same to you, officer," she muttered as the cop disappeared into the crowd.

Tina faced her savior. The woman took off her sunglasses and cleaned them with the hem of her puffy green blouse. Her eyes were sky blue.

"You should've just lied," she said, putting the sunglasses back on. "Told them you worked with us. Half the time they don't check badges, especially not at active scenes." She pointed at Tina's hands. "Any film in that thing?"

Tina looked down at her camera, then back up at the woman with a nod.

"Come on," the woman said. "See what's left to catch."

"Come on where?" Tina said.

The woman faced her again. "To find that van."

Tina said nothing. The woman placed her hands on her hips.

"This is a one-time offer," she said, nodding at Tina's camera. "I find somebody else with one of those and you're shit out of luck."

"Yes," Tina said, looking down at her camera again. "Yeah. Sure."

"Good," she said. "The name's Emilia by the way. Stay close and keep that thing snapping."

Tina followed Emilia through the bustling crowd of onlookers down a side road next to Jordan Marsh, pausing every few seconds to photograph the destruction. Coming out at the Snapper Creek canal, they saw a white van with a crushed front fender parked at the intersection half a block away. Emilia ran to the guardrail lining the canal and crouched, Tina right behind her. Parked facing north, the van gleamed in the sun like a pot of gold. A man in a suit holding a gun approached it from the back, another man in a suit limping up behind him. Emilia sucked her teeth.

"Detectives got here already," she whispered. "Only two though, we can work with that."

Tina opened her mouth to ask what she meant but Emilia was already gone, shuffling towards the detectives. Tina cursed and followed. The detective near the van opened the van's rear doors, looked inside and lowered his gun, taking a step back. The second detective hobbled up behind him and soon both of them stood staring into the van, trancelike. Both men wore close-cropped hair, one younger than the other. Tina snapped some pictures of them.

Following Emilia to the bridge that ran over the canal, Tina arced around the front of the van, crossing the street towards the dented front bumper. The transfixed detectives barely moved. Using the van to stay out of their line of sight, Tina stood in the street a couple feet away while Emilia peered inside.

A slew of patrol cars appeared, blocking off the intersection. The older detective jogged over to the scrambling officers. Tina got in a dozen shots before the younger detective popped his head around the corner of the van.

"Hey!" he barked. "What the hell do—stop that!"

Emilia stepped away from the van, looking at the detective. "There's only 108 miles on the odometer."

"Emilia, this is an active crime scene," the detective said. "You can't just touch things."

"I'm not touching anything," she said. "And hello, Detective Williams. How's your day going?"

"Like shit and you know it," the detective growled, pointing across the street. "I need you two to step back."

"There's only 108 miles on the odometer," Emilia repeated, staying put.

"Ms. Brathwaite, I'm not going to ask you again," the detective said through gritted teeth. "I need you to get across—"

"It's brand new. Is what I'm trying to say."

"Hi, Emilia," the older detective said, trotting over from a patrol car.

"Hi, Danny."

The older detective glanced at his incensed partner and smirked. "Williams, it's fine." He placed a hand on Emilia's shoulder. "What do you got?"

"There's only 108 miles on the odometer."

"Really?" Detective Danny said, raising an eyebrow.

Emilia pointed at the van's dashboard. Detective Williams glared at them. Tina raised her camera and started snapping again, the film running out after a couple of clicks. She deftly removed the used roll and placed it in an empty film canister, dropping it in her bag and laying a new one.

"You from the paper too?" Detective Williams asked.

Tina startled at the question. The detective's eyes were an intense shade of green that made her want to look away. She resisted the urge and was about to answer the question when Emilia cut her off, swooping over from the van.

"Yes, she is," Emilia said, turning to Tina and hissing. "What's your name?"

"Valent—," Tina shook her head. "Just Tina."

"This is Justina, our new photographer," Emilia said to Detective Williams, glancing at Danny. "What's in the cabin has you both so captivated?"

Detective Danny glanced at his partner then motioned for Emilia to follow him. Emilia rounded the van's rear bumper and looked in the back, her mouth dropping open as she waved Tina over. Tina walked the few steps, turned the corner and gasped. She raised her camera and started snapping. The sound of the shutter drew Danny's attention, his face growing dark.

"You mind if I borrow that for a moment?" he asked.

"Borrow her camera, Danny?" Emilia said.

"Forensics isn't here yet," Danny said. "Wanna get this while it's fresh."

"I'm sure they'll be here soon," Emilia said, nodding at Tina's camera. "That's the *Tribune's*. You wanna be held liable something happens to it?"

The detective frowned at the camera, raising his hands and backing away. "Worth a shot."

"No pun intended," Emilia muttered, winking at Tina.

Behind them, the uniformed officers created a barricade at the intersection, onlookers flocking over. Emilia walked the van's perimeter, scribbling on a notepad. The Detectives stood close by, seeming indecisive until another white van with *Dade County Medical Examiner* stamped on the side pulled up, parking across the canal bridge. Two men in plain gray outfits walked over holding boxes of equipment. Detective Danny perked up, barking orders.

Closing her notepad, Emilia glanced at Tina and motioned towards the mall. She waved to Detective Williams and whistled at Danny as she jogged across the street, Tina on her tail.

"We gotta get back," she yelled, holding up the notepad.

"You need a statement?" Danny said.

"I'll get one from your desk later," Emilia said, nodding at the growing mob. "You guys have your work cut out for you."

"Understatement of the year, that one," he said.

"This whole damn city's an understatement," Tina muttered under her breath, putting her camera back in its bag.

Emilia let out a quick bark of laughter that startled Tina. "That's a good one," she said, pulling Tina towards the mall lot. "Gonna use that one. Come on, we need to call this in."

9.

Miguel remembers things that happened before he was born.

Men with rifles emerging from the dirt like zombies, setting fire to acres of land at a time. People crying out for loved ones, jerked from their beds, lined up and gunned down, their blood splatters dark against pitted concrete walls. Women running with screaming children clutched to their chests. The smell of death and decay, towns filled with more dead bodies than live ones.

Whenever Miguel tells Jose about these things he remembers, Jose tells him it's Papi's fault. Says the stories their father told their mother infected their home, blocking out any real chance at happiness. Miguel was still in the womb—Jose no more than four—when their mother got the news that her husband was dead. Killed after an unsuccessful attempt to take the Palanquero Air Force base during *La Violencia*. The years that followed were hard on Mama, turning her into a hard woman. Prior to the war, their father had been a successful Anthropology professor who owned a bit of land—generational land, passed down from his great-grandfather to his grandfather and so forth. Land that was taken away when local conservative farmers decided they'd had enough of PLC supporters. As an open and proud PLC member, Papi was one of their first victims.

"Es por esto que luchamos," Jose would always say.

This is why we fight.

Jose looking Miguel in the eyes, hand gripping the back of his neck. "Está en nuestra sangre. Luchar por lo que es nuestro."

It's in our blood. To fight for what's ours.

These were the words Jose had repeated to Miguel when the short man with the bushy mustache and afro handed them two brand new passports, their faces pictured next to names Miguel didn't recognize. A week later Miguel took his first flight ever—an engineering miracle—into Miami International Airport where the same short man with the bushy mustache and afro picked them up and brought them to Giselle Benitez's house in West Kendall.

La Madrina. The Godmother.

Lounging in the living room of a house five times bigger than any Miguel had ever seen, wearing more jewelry than Miguel thought humanly possible, La Madrina had assessed them with a skeptical eye before turning to Luchi.

"Bueno," she said, parting her lips to reveal the prominent gap between her two front teeth. "Más como ellos."

More like them.

Now, sitting on the wheel well in the back of the white van, Miguel held a Mac-10 and thought about his brother's motto. *Esta en nuestra sangre.* Jose sat in the driver's seat holding a pistol. Luchi sat in the passenger's, stroking his mustache. A giant machine gun mounted on a tripod in front of Miguel sat aimed at two holes drilled into the side of the van and covered with movable aluminum caps.

The Mac-10 slipped through Miguel's sweaty fingers and hit the shag carpet with a dull, metallic thud. Miguel snatched the gun back up, holding it against his stomach. Jose and Luchi twisted around to look at him, the van creaking. Miguel took a deep breath, forcing himself to look Luchi in the eyes. A violent lightning storm crackled in the man's pupils.

"Todo bien?" Luchi asked.

Miguel nodded.

"Seguro?"

"Está bien, Luchi," Jose said. "Vamonos."

Luchi kept an eye on Miguel for a second longer then looked back at Jose.

"Recuerda," he said. "Giselle quiere enviar un mensaje."

Giselle wants to send a message.

Pulling a vial from his pocket, Luchi opened it and dumped white powder into the patch of skin between his thumb and index finger. He handed the vial to Jose and snorted the powder in one quick sniff. Jose did a line as well, leaving a ring of white around his nostril. He held the vial out to Miguel. Miguel shook his head. Jose shrugged, handing the vial back to Luchi.

Opening their doors, Jose and Luchi stepped out of the car, barely hiding the gun barrels beneath their black jackets. They slammed the doors with heavy thunks and headed inside the liquor store.

The moment they were gone Miguel snatched up the water bottle next to his foot, twisting the cap off and taking a swig. He sighed with pleasure, splashing some on his head and swiping water off his face just as a flash of movement outside caught his attention. Miguel grabbed the gun, pointing it at two black boys approaching the back of the van. They both wore dusty, faded shirts and shorts with black high-top sneakers covered in duct-tape. The tall one carried a blue bag. Miguel aimed the gun and the boys kept walking towards the van without hesitation. Realizing they couldn't see him, Miguel lowered his gun and watched.

The kids walked out of view. Miguel held his breath. Their footsteps stopped close by. Silence, then some muffled talking. Miguel cocked his head to the side, glancing at Jose and Luchi in the liquor store. They both faced the men behind the counter, arms pressed against their sides.

The boys suddenly burst out laughing.

Miguel jumped, banging his head against the ceiling. Cursing, he glared in the direction of the kids' laughter. It died down a few seconds later, giving way to yelling coming from inside the store.

Miguel turned back towards his brother and Luchi.

Standing across from the register, Luchi shook a fist at the two men on the other side of the counter. The men stood frozen, stark fear in their eyes. The man in a Miami Dolphins t-shirt with a cigar in his mouth said something and Luchi swung his gun up. The muzzle flashed and the man fell backwards, the cigar disappearing along with the rest of his face. The man's t-shirt filled with holes, his chest deflating like a crushed piñata as he pirouetted to the floor. Thick bloody chunks of flesh painted the wall and shelves behind him, an accompanying red mist floating into the air like pepper spray. The man on the left in the fedora and black vest tried to duck out of the line of fire, the bullets catching him simultaneously. Bright red dots appeared all over his shirt, opening like blooming roses as he flew back into the wall. The man crumpled to the floor, his fedora falling off.

Jose raised his pistol seconds after Luchi, his arms jumping as the thunder of expended bullets intensified, like two planes crashing into each other. The interior of the liquor store disappeared in a cloud of dust.

Emptying their clips, Jose and Luchi dropped their guns and walked out the front door, trailing smoke. On the sidewalk, Luchi pulled a pistol from the back of his jeans and blasted out the liquor store's front window. He shot half the clip into the store then emptied the rest into the Benz parked next to the van. The car's windows caved in, the tires blowing out one by one until the whole body fell on its suspension. Luchi's gun clicked empty and he threw it to the ground, he and Jose climbing back in the van. Inside the deli next to the liquor store, screaming patrons lay on the floor with their hands over their heads. A woman with a huge purse clutched to her chest tripped and slammed into the deli entrance, tears and mascara smearing the glass.

Jose bounced up and down behind the steering wheel, grinning so wide it seemed to cut his face in half.

"Puta *madre!*" he yelled.

"Maneja!" Luchi barked, reaching for one of the Uzis hanging from the ceiling. He fell back into the passenger seat and scowled at Miguel, pointing at the mounted machine gun. "Que haces hijo de puta?"

"Eh, sí." Miguel gave the machine gun a forlorn look.

Luchi snapped his fingers in Jose's face, slapping him on the leg and pointing at the steering wheel. Jose revved the engine a couple of times then sped backwards, throwing the van in gear and slamming on the gas. Miguel braced himself as the van shot off.

Luchi spun on Miguel again. "Dispara!" he shouted, pointing at the machine gun again. "Dispara la pistola, parce!"

Miguel grabbed the gun's double grip, squatting for balance. Luchi rolled his window down and aimed the Uzi outside. Weaving through a patch of parked cars, the van sped past the entrance towards the back of the mall. Miguel centered the gun barrel on the left porthole, reached over and twisted the aluminum cap open. He settled back to a crouch, took a deep breath, and squeezed the trigger.

A pounding roar hit the side of the van, the reports so loud Miguel's eardrums registered exactly five blasts before all sense of hearing cut out with a faint pop. Left behind was only the physicality of each shot hitting him in the chest like heavyweight punches. The gun bucked in his grip. Two seconds after pulling the trigger his shoulders felt about to shake out of their sockets; in ten seconds his arms were numb. Bullet cartridges flew out the side of the gun like quarters from a slot machine jackpot.

The van bounced off a divot in the concrete and careened to the right. Jose overcorrected, veering hard left and sending the van into a slide. They nearly skirted past a parked pickup truck, clipping the back bumper just enough to send them spinning into the Dadeland tribute tower. The van's right headlight crunched against the concrete pillar and Miguel went flying, soaring above the red shag carpet and slamming into the back of Jose's seat.

The engine cut out.

Luchi slapped Miguel on the shoulder.

"¡Dispara!" he yelled again, pointing at the machine gun.

Miguel got back to the gun slowly. Luchi dropped his spent Uzi and frog-walked past Miguel to grab another one. Miguel placed his palms against the handles of the machine gun again, but his fingers wouldn't curl around the grips. Luchi screamed for Jose to get the car started. Jose smashed his foot down on the gas pedal, twisting the key in the ignition. The engine sputtered.

Squinting out the porthole—which was now the size of a small plate, ragged with bullet holes around the edge—Miguel noticed some movement near the wreckage of the liquor store. The two black boys from earlier came into view, standing outside the store, staring after the van. Blue bag crumpled in the tall one's hand. Behind them, swarms of people streamed out of the deli.

Hicimos esto, Miguel thought.

The kid holding the bag squatted and grabbed something off the ground. Holding up the gun Luchi tossed, he tapped the short kid on the arm and said something. The short kid nodded and the taller kid opened his blue bag, dropping the gun inside.

Miguel mouthed the word *no*.

Está en nuestra sangre.

The engine roared to life and the injured van shot off, Jose taking them towards the back of the mall. Luchi stuck his Uzi out the window and rattled off some more shots. They flew around the last fifty feet of parking lot past Jordan Marsh onto 82nd street.

"¡Aquí!" Luchi yelled, pointing at the approaching intersection. "¡Detente!"

Jose slammed on the brakes and the van skidded to a halt in a patch of grass on the NE corner of 72nd ave. Across the street, a brand-new Toyota Corolla sat idling. Luchi hopped out of the van and walked to the other car, opening the passenger door and climbing in.

Miguel sat in front of the machine gun, staring out the porthole. Jose snapped his fingers in his brother's face but Miguel didn't respond. Jose pushed him. Miguel fell to his side, facing his brother. Jose yelled something that sounded like he was speaking through a thick plaster wall. He smacked Miguel's cheeks, said something else then bounded out of the van after Luchi.

Pushing himself up, Miguel crawled across the carpet. An angle of sunlight streamed in through the open front door, catching on something as he passed, one of the many shell casings littering the area. A faint, swirly fingerprint stood out on the side. He picked up the bullet casing as if it were a talisman, studying it in the sunlight for a second before slipping it in his pocket.

Climbing out of the van, Miguel stumbled over to the Corolla, about to follow his brother into the backseat when a spasm hit his abdomen. He lurched away from the car, grabbing the concrete railing and leaning out over the canal. Belching, a stream of bile poured from his mouth into the murky water. He puked until his intestines seemed about to turn inside out, then wiped his mouth with the back of his hand and staggered back over to the Corolla, opening the door and falling inside. The car took off seconds later, leaving the damaged van and its contents sitting at the corner of the intersection like a discarded trophy.

10.

The light ahead turned red and Clara downshifted, the Trans Am coming to a shuddering stop. Glancing at Tommy, she plucked the unlit cigarette from his mouth and tossed it out the window.

"What the hell?" Tommy said, lighter raised. "Why'd you do that?"

"How many times do I—" Clara took a deep breath and put a hand on her swollen belly. "For the *zillionth* time, honey. The doctor said not to smoke around the baby."

"He said smoke *outside*," Tommy said, sticking his arm out the window. "We're *outside*."

"Can it wait?" she snapped. "For me, honey? Is that too much to ask?"

Grumbling, Tommy put the lighter away. The light turned green, Clara fiddled with the gear shift and the car lurched forward.

"So you just ran into him at the supermarket?" she asked. "And he just offered you the gig, right there?"

"Right here," Tommy said, pointing at the approaching intersection. "And yes, Babe. For the *zillionth* time."

"Smart ass."

"Takes one," he said, tossing her a side-eye glare. "I still can't believe you told him all that shit about me hating my job."

"He asked," she said. "He's my uncle. What am I supposed to do?"

"You met him like six months ago," Tommy said.

"He's the only one on my mom's side who's ever reached out," she said. "I didn't even think there was anyone left. I have to get to know him."

"I guess," Tommy muttered.

"It's just so *odd* though," she said. "Five hundred dollars to drive. It's such a weird thing to ask somebody you barely know."

"That it is," he said.

"The money will come in handy though."

"That it will."

They turned right at the next intersection onto a shady, pock-marked street that ended in a cul-de-sac. Clara pulled the car around to a run-down house, the car trembling to a stop. She fiddled with the gear shift and sighed.

"What?" Tommy said.

"We've gotta do something about this car," she said.

"The car's fine. You just don't know how to drive stick."

"It's fine for *you*," she said. "How're we all gonna fit? And the car seat?"

"You wanna talk about this now?"

"Doesn't matter when I bring it up," she said. "It's always an issue with you. Same with the crib."

"I told you I'm putting the crib up this weekend."

"You said that last weekend."

"Last weekend I was busy," Tommy said. "Hanging out with *your* uncle and *your* friends."

"So they're just *my* friends?"

"I guess we're talking about this now," Tommy muttered, slumping down.

"Daddy, look!"

Tommy turned to his son lying across the backseat with a pile of green military figurines in his lap. Adam raised two of them and smashed them together, making an explosion sound. Tommy smiled and glanced at Clara. She stared past him at the house, the front lawn a mixture of dirt, patchy brown grass and weeds. Two cars sat next to each other near the front door, one old, one new.

"You sure this is the right address?" Clara asked.

Tommy glanced at the slip of paper in his lap, then up at the numbers on the rusted black mailbox a few feet away. "Looks right."

Clara stayed quiet. Tommy looked over and she sat squinting at him.

"I'm starting to have a bad feeling about this," she said.

"You have a bad feeling about everything," Tommy said. He leaned over and planted a kiss on Clara's forehead, sniffing her hair, a mixture of coconut and sweat. He waggled a hand across Adam's head then climbed out.

"Call me when you can," Clara said, giving the house a weary stare.

"Will do," Tommy said. "Drive safely, please. The brake's not a typewriter."

Clara stuck her tongue out and pulled off, the car vibrating down the street. Tommy headed up the concrete path to the entrance. Knocking twice, he stood to the side as footsteps approached and the front door opened on a man who resembled Luchi in size, afro and mustache. He wore khaki pants and a black tank top, his mouth twitching as he chewed on something.

"Que?" he said, his voice raspy.

"Hey," Tommy said. "Luchi sent me."

The man slammed the door, his footsteps fading away into the house.

Tommy frowned and faced the street just as a thick cloud passed over the sun. The shadows of tree branches crept towards him like fingers and he felt a sudden spark of inexplicable fear. The footsteps in the house returned. The door opened and the squat man held out his left hand. A ring with two keys sat nestled in his palm.

"Aquí," he said, pointing at the brand-new Corolla in the yard. "Ahí."

He slammed the door again and the lock clicked.

Tucking the keys into his palm, Tommy pulled out his cigarettes and lit one up, sucking it down to the filter as he strolled over to the Corolla. He climbed in, savoring the new car smell, running his hand across the beige interior and admiring the spotless back seat. He slipped the key in and the car started with a purr. Flipping on the radio, he twisted the dial through some Cheap Trick, Donna Summer, Sister Sledge and some static before settling on a Chic track.

Pulling out of the driveway, Tommy headed south through residential neighborhoods out to Sunset Drive. Ten minutes later he approached the back end of Dadeland Mall and slowed to a crawl. He glanced at his watch: two-thirty, on the dot. Hitting a U-turn at the intersection, he parked on the bridge over Snapper Creek, facing north with the intersection behind him. He checked the area. Nothing.

Tommy flipped on the air conditioner and turned the radio up loud, pulling out another cigarette.

"*Mama don't want you,*" he sang, the car filling with smoke.

Tommy looked out at the flowing canal reflecting the sun's high arc. The song ended and a Tide commercial began. Tommy finished the Red and rolled the window up, sitting through more commercials and a Kenny Rogers track before a white van sped around the corner behind him, squealing to a stop at the intersection. The van's doors flew open and Luchi hopped out, crossing the street at a brisk pace. A man Tommy didn't recognize came out after, followed seconds later by a third man stumbling across the street to puke over the canal railing. Tommy turned off the radio and rolled the window down as Luchi opened the passenger door. The sudden influx of sounds caught him off-guard: slamming footsteps, distant screams, wailing police sirens.

Tommy looked over at Luchi. "What the hell's going on out there?"

"Drive," Luchi said, settling into the passenger seat.

The back door opened and one of the men fell inside, babbling in Spanish incoherently. The other man finished puking, wiped his mouth with the back of his hand and staggered over to the car.

"What the hell is hap—"

"Drive!" Luchi barked.

"*Where?*" Tommy yelled back. "I need a dest—"

"Puta madre, *drive!*" Luchi pointed straight ahead. "Fucking *drive!*"

The puking man fell into the backseat and Tommy slammed on the gas, the Corolla hopping off the curb into the street. The white van became a small dot in the rearview mirror. Luchi scowled at the men in the back.

"Maricones," he muttered.

The puking man said nothing, his eyes haunted, his breathing ragged. He sat behind Luchi, slouched with his arms pressed against his sides. The one sitting behind Tommy continued rambling, clapping his hands together with a manic grin on his face. They looked about Tommy's age. Both men had the same crooked nose, brown eyes and shaggy hair.

Luchi pointed at the turning lane near the Sunset intersection and Tommy made a left, the mall disappearing from view. Removing his jacket, Luchi ran a hand over his afro.

"Ju say ju from Miami, Tommy, no?" he asked.

Tommy frowned. "Well—no, actually," he said. "I was born in Cuba. Came when I was a kid."

"Eres Cubano?" Luchi said, surprised.

"Barely," Tommy said.

Now Luchi frowned. "No hablas Español."

"I grew up in a Catholic orphanage," Tommy said. "Nuns kind of beat the Cuban out of me. I get a little here and there, but I'm pretty much a gringo."

"Ah," Luchi said, opening the glove compartment and rummaging around. "Un huérfano. Vida triste. Tienes hermanos?" He glanced over. "Ju have brothers? Sisters?"

"No," Tommy said.

"Tengo dos hermanos," Luchi said, holding up first two fingers, then a third. "Y Clara's mamá."

"Really?" Tommy said, raising his eyebrows. "Clara told me you were her mom's only brother." He glanced at the men in the backseat. "This them?"

"No," Luchi said, pulling a gray revolver out of the glove compartment. "Dey are dead."

Turning, Luchi pointed the gun at the man sitting behind Tommy and pulled the trigger twice. The shots went off like bricks smashing right next to Tommy's ear. The man's voice cut off abruptly as his chest deflated and his head snapped back, a bullet smashing through his eye and painting the rear windshield with bloody chunks. His chin fell to his chest, a ragged, meaty hole in the back of his skull.

Tommy's whole body seized up and he jerked the steering wheel to the left, swerving into oncoming traffic as Luchi quickly blasted two shots at the man sitting behind him. A black Impala skirted around them, horn blaring. Tommy swerved back into the right lane, hands gripping the steering wheel so tight his knuckles popped. The man behind Luchi slumped in his seat, holding his midsection with blood dribbling between his fingers. Another hole in his shoulder blossomed red. His mouth opened and closed with no sound.

Luchi glared at Tommy.

"Maneja recto, parce!" he yelled, motioning towards the whimpering man. "Mira. Mira esto."

"Sorry," Tommy coughed out, pressing his shaking body against the door.

Luchi faced the gut-shot man again.

The man's eyes filled with tears, a line of blood slipping from the corner of his lips down his cheek.

Luchi leaned over and pushed the gun under the man's chin.

"Se acabó," he said.

An explosion of gore painted the other side of the windshield. Both bodies sank down. The sharp scent of cordite and copper filled the car, overpowering the lingering cigarette smoke.

Luchi settled back in his seat, placing the gun on his lap.

They cruised west on Sunset, the bodies slumping further down with every bump in the road until Tommy thankfully couldn't see them anymore. The gunshots echoed in his head. His wrists shook against the steering wheel. Luchi pulled a stained yellow towel from the glove compartment and picked the gun up, cracking the barrel and emptying the bullet casings into his lap. Closing the barrel, he wiped the gun with the towel, as if polishing a piece of woodwork. They approached 107th ave and Luchi grunted, pointing at a dusty patch of sidewalk near the canal. Tommy pulled the car over, a cloud of dirt billowing around them. Luchi dropped the empty gun on the seat and hopped out with the bullet casings in hand, strolling over and dropping them in the canal. Getting back in the car, he pointed at the intersection ahead.

Tommy cut across traffic and took a left on 107th, keeping the car at the speed limit. The cordite had dissipated once Luchi opened the car door, leaving the coppery smell of blood and what was now very clearly human feces. They rode over a bump and the body behind Tommy bounced against the door, the ragged hole in his head appearing then disappearing from view. Tommy squeezed his eyes shut for a moment then opened them again, concentrating on the road.

Luchi finished wiping the gun and placed it back in the glove compartment. At the intersection on Kendall Drive, he pointed right and Tommy turned. Two blocks down, he pointed again and Tommy pulled into an apartment complex, parking the car on a stretch of mulch near a giant Oak tree behind the complex's welcome sign. Luchi climbed out and opened the back door, raising his foot to hold up the dead man as he fell. He straightened the body out and grabbed the man's limp arms, tossing them across his chest. Heaving him up onto his shoulder, Luchi paused to look in the car at Tommy.

"Vas a ayudar?" he said.

Tommy's stomach lurched. He forced a swallow. "You want me to help?"

"Tommy," Luchi said, exasperated. "Why do I pay you for?"

Tommy squeezed his eyes shut again, nodded and opened his door. Stepping out into the bright Miami afternoon, he looked up at the Oak tree. Ten feet away, cars flew by on Kendall Drive.

"Venga," Luchi hissed, dragging the body towards the tree. "Apúrate!"

Tommy counted to three and opened the back door. The dead man's arm slipped out. The hole in his head where his eye used to be winked up at Tommy. Tommy sucked in a breath, grabbed the guy's still-warm hands and pulled. The body slid out of the car and hit the ground with a thud. Tommy dropped the arms, his mouth filling with saliva. Turning to the sign at the entrance, he puked up chunks of tuna salad and bile. Luchi stood by the tree watching with amusement. Swiping his mouth with the back of his hand,

Tommy lurched back over to the body lying in the dirt. Grabbing the arms, he heaved the dead man across dead leaves and mulch over to where Luchi had dropped the other body, hidden behind the tree.

Luchi brushed his hands on his pants and climbed back in the car, slamming the door.

Tommy forced himself to look at the man he'd just dragged over. A fly landed next to the bullet hole where his eye used to be, hopping inside. Tommy looked away, waiting for the nausea to dissipate. He spit on the ground then climbed back behind the wheel.

Pulling out of the complex, Tommy couldn't keep his eyes off the blood-soaked rear windshield. They approached another section over the Snapper Creek canal and Luchi motioned for Tommy to pull over. Rolling his window down, he opened the glove compartment and pulled out the revolver and towel, tossing them both in the water. He rolled the window back up and Tommy pulled off. They were driving a full minute before Luchi spoke.

"Dis is—" he said, motioning towards the back seat. "Dis no personal."

Tommy said nothing.

"No trust," Luchi said, looking out the passenger window. "Ju must trust."

Tommy spoke in a gravelly tone. "Where are we going?"

"Mi casa," Luchi said, pointing ahead. "I show you."

Tommy nodded and drove.

11.

Leaving the van with the techs, Ralph and Murphy headed back towards the murder scene, Ralph glancing at Murphy as they walked through the mall's rear parking lot.

"You know the *Tribune's* the reason the department's in the mess it's in right now," Ralph said. "And we're just letting them photograph active crime scenes? Promising quotes?"

"*Are* they the reason?" Murphy asked. "Seems to me the *department* is the reason the department's in the mess it's in."

"Doesn't mean what they're doing is right," Ralph said. "That last article Emilia wrote was just a smear campaign."

"Have you read it?"

"Yes, and yes, those guys were idiots," Ralph said. "Any squad worth its salt knows you gotta check the address before a raid. She's making it seem like we're *all* that fucking stupid."

"There's that," Murphy said, pausing at the side alley they'd used to chase the white van not twenty minutes ago. "And then there's the one she wrote about how the biggest assholes among us are always getting assigned to areas like Liberty City. *That's* a department problem."

"Every city's got issues," Ralph said. "Job's hard enough without a microscope over our heads."

"It's not the paper's job to care about our feelings," Murphy said. "The fourth estate's a necessity in a functioning democracy. They're here to report the truth. Regardless whether we like it or not."

"Whose truth?" Ralph said.

"Trust me, Williams, I'm with you," Murphy said, heading into the alley. "Dealing with Emilia and her kind is like sticking your fingers in an electrical socket. Woman's a fucking hawk, never met someone asks more questions in ten seconds. My point is, she's good at her job and gets what she wants whether we play ball or not. So why not play? Tell it the way *you* want?"

"And what happens when she takes what we say out of context?" Ralph said. "Now my word's being used against me?"

"Can't say the same for all of them but Emilia plays it pretty straight," he said. "Like to think she's as fair as they come."

Rounding the corner, they came up on the bombed-out entrance to the liquor store, surrounded by a frenzied crowd with patrols trying and failing to control the situation.

"Goddammit," Ralph said, running with Murphy towards the growing throng of gawkers. Grabbing the badge at his hip, Ralph raised it high in the air. "Public Safety Department, need you to create a path, people."

Nobody moved.

"People!" Ralph barked. "Back! Up!"

The crowd parted and Ralph and Murphy weaved their way to the front. They broke through and Ralph clipped his badge back at his waist. Stepping over mounds of shattered glass in the mangled doorway, Ralph froze, his eyes going wide as his gaze fell on the bodies.

The man on the left was missing the vast majority of his face, his lower jaw hanging against his shoulder by a tendon, a gaping, meaty hole where his eyes and nose should have been. The other man was missing his entire forehead, his t-shirt soaked through with blood and filled with more bullet holes than Ralph could count with a naked eye. He held a bottle of Chivas Regal that somehow remained intact.

Ralph looked away, noticing two black boys who stood out in the mostly white crowd. Their eyes were fixated on the bodies. One of them held a blue shopping bag. Three uniformed officers pushed through the mob and Ralph unclipped his badge, raising it again. The patrolman up front nodded.

"Gomez," he said, pointing first at himself then the other two officers. "McKenzie and Madison. What do you—" The man saw the bodies and his voice cut short, his face turning a sickly gray. "Holy shit."

"Need you to block all this off," Ralph said, noticing an Uzi lying on the ground in front of the register, another on the sidewalk. "And secure the guns, make sure nothing disappears before CSI gets here."

As he spoke, a pair of white vans appeared in the parking lot. The doors flew open and a dozen techs jumped out, pushing towards the scene. One of them approached Ralph's position holding up a camera and Ralph stepped aside, convening with Murphy outside the deli next door.

"Emilia kept saying the van had 108 miles on the odometer," he said.

"Almost new," Murphy said. "You saw the words don't match?"

"What?" Ralph said.

"The words," he repeated. "On the side of the van. Says Happy Time Complete Supply Party one side. Party Supply on the other."

Ralph shook his head, looking again at the mangled bodies in the liquor store. "None of this adds up."

"Guessing the number they listed is disconnected," Murphy said. "Or never existed to begin with."

"This drug dealer war that city council keeps yammering about," Ralph said. "Last week it's the main item on the docket. Now this."

"Makes sense," Murphy said. "Like that turnpike mess a couple months ago. Same brazenness. Left all their shit behind then too."

"The *balls*," Ralph said. "To do this in broad fucking daylight. Starting to feel like Chicago. Dodge City, Capone's days."

"Back then it was booze," Murphy muttered. "Always something."

"You make anything illegal there's gonna be a market for it," Ralph said. He hocked a wad of spit onto the sidewalk, then turned and slapped his palm against the deli's metal window frame. He faced Murphy again with his hands on his hips. "What if we had caught up with them earlier? There's a fucking BMG in the back of that van. I haven't seen anything like that since I was wading through the fucking jungle." Ralph touched his sidearm. "And I was carrying a lot more than this."

Murphy studied Ralph for a moment. "You know you were recruited because of your service record, right?"

"Sure," Ralph said. "Half the department's served."

"And it's that half keeping us afloat," Murphy said. "My guess is that half's gonna have to figure out how to deal with this shit and help get everybody else up to speed. A lot of these men have never seen anything like this before."

Ralph took a deep breath. "When I got back. After I got—you know, *used* to being back. When I first got my badge, the guys I met on the drug beat. You know what they used to bitch about?"

Murphy scratched his reddened cheeks. "Paperwork?"

"No," Ralph said, chuckling. "I mean, yes. But no." He shook his head. "Chasing down potheads with bags of grass shoved down their pants. Biggest complaint was fucking ball sweat."

Murphy smiled, poking the tear in his jacket sleeve. "Did I ever tell you my stepdad was a bookie?"

Ralph frowned. "What's that got to do with anything?"

"Moved me and Mom down from New York after my brother died," he said. "When the Army was done with him he ran numbers from our apartment up in Tampa, same when we moved down here." Murphy gave the sky a melancholy look. "Real piece of work. Bolo, everybody called him. Never knew his real name. He held books for some of the guys in the department actually. Might have helped me land my first post in '65, unconfirmed rumors and such."

Ralph stood quiet. A couple of patrol officers approached on the left.

"Sir," one of them said to Murphy.

"I know," Murphy said, holding a hand up. "One second."

The patrols headed back inside the liquor store.

Murphy cracked his neck. "One day I come home from school or work or something. Bolo's in the living room watching TV, all excited. Cheering like the Braves just won the goddamn pennant. But it's January, spring training hasn't even started."

As he spoke, a van squealed to a stop in the parking lot, *WTVJ Miami* stenciled across the side. A man jumped out of the passenger seat holding a microphone, two other men carrying a video camera out the back.

"What was he cheering about?" Ralph asked.

"Politics," Murphy said, eyes on the news van. "Some report on the state legislative session. They were going back and forth on gambling, same old song and dance. Put it to another vote, and the legislature knocked it down. Again." Murphy paused. "Bolo the Bookie was jumping for joy."

A couple of patrolmen intercepted the approaching reporters and Murphy moved in that direction. Ralph grabbed his arm, stopping him in his tracks. "Wait, what's all that supposed to mean?"

Murphy nudged Ralph's arm away. "You asking me to elaborate?"

"Yeah," Ralph said.

Murphy nodded at the reporters. "I'm not in the habit of going into too many details around the press, Detective. You should show the same restraint."

Ralph's shoulders dropped. Murphy chuckled.

"I'll give you something," he said. "Bureau Commander wants to announce it himself though, so you've gotta act surprised."

Ralph said nothing.

"You're right," Murphy said. "About us needing a specialized response to these—" He glanced over at the crowd outside the liquor store as an officer unrolled some yellow tape. "—new developments. Everybody's on board, from the Mayor to the Director on down." Murphy patted Ralph on the chest. "They're booting me up to Homicide Captain next week, complete with a special unit. Eighteen-man squad, backed by considerable resources."

Ralph's eyes went wide. "Captain?"

Murphy nodded. "Stated goal is to sniff out and eradicate this new threat."

"How 'bout that?" Ralph said, offering a lazy salute. "Congrats, Cap."

"Save it," Murphy said. "You start next week too. And before you ask, yes, it comes with overtime."

Ralph froze.

Murphy nodded. "Thought you'd like that."

Ralph squinted. "A brand-new squad?"

"Gave it a name and everything," Murphy said, nodding towards the bodies. "You want to find some meaning in all this bullshit, some purpose, then here it is. Help me catch these fuckers. And all their kind. And start finding me some people to fill out the department. We're gonna need it."

"That uni from the Grove today," Ralph said. "He's MPD, but I wouldn't have noticed the doorknob detail if it wasn't for him."

"I'll put in a request," Murphy said. "Need his badge number."

"Assuming it'll be on the report when he files," Ralph said, wincing. "Shit, we just left him there."

"More pressing matters," Murphy said, moving again towards the reporters.

"They give it a name?" Ralph called out. "The unit?"

Murphy brushed the comment off. "Something generic, Special Investigations Team or the like."

Ralph chuckled. "Put a lot of thought into it, didn't they?"

"Department's known for a lot of things Williams," Murphy said. "Their poetic sensibilities is not one of them."

"Guess it doesn't really matter," Ralph said.

"They could call it the Shit Squad for all I care," Murphy said, nodding towards the liquor store, now surrounded by reporters. "Long as it works."

12.

Emilia slammed the payphone down, wiping her ear with her blouse and walking back to her '75 Caprice idling at the curb.

"I swear it's like talking to a five-year-old," she muttered, climbing behind the wheel. "Have to repeat everything twenty times and oh my *God* those phones are fucking disgusting."

Tina looked up from her notebook. "Your boss?"

"Front desk," Emilia said, holding up a leather journal. "Always call the story in when you get it, in case you lose your notes." She pointed at Tina's camera bag, sitting at her feet. "Don't ever let a cop use that by the way. Probably never get it back."

"Noted," Tina said, closing her journal and sticking her pen behind her ear.

Pulling out of the gas station, Emilia sped north on US-1 with the wind whipping through the open windows. The shadows of palm trees in the median brushed over them. Passing 17th avenue, US-1 forks into I-95 and Biscayne and Emilia veered right, stopping the car at a red light on Rickenbacker.

Tina looked around.

"Where are we going?" she asked.

"The Trib—" Emilia paused, smiling. "You have no idea who I am."

"I mean…Emilia, right?"

Emilia laughed. "Of course, my narcissism rearing its head. Here I was thinking you were looking for a job."

Tina leaned away from her. "A job?"

"Okay let's do a proper introduction then," Emilia said, holding her hand out. "Emilia Brathwaite. Miami Tribune, Metro department."

"Brathwaite," Tina said as the light turned green. "Yeah…I think I've read some of your stuff actually."

"I can tell it was memorable."

Tina flushed. "I'm sorry, I just—"

"I'm kidding," Emilia said. "I'm not out here writing Pulitzer material. It's metro, in Miami." She turned her head to the side. "Though this story's sure to draw some national attention."

"I'd be surprised if it didn't," Tina said.

Emilia squinted at her. "How old are you, Justina?"

"Tina," she said. "Just. Tina."

Emilia laughed again. "Just, Tina," she said. "More evidence that context always matters. How old are you just Tina, if you don't mind me asking?"

"Twenty-one."

"You handle the camera well," she said. "You taking classes?"

"No," Tina said, looking down at the camera. "My dad bought it for me in high school. Sort of taught myself."

"Best way to learn," she said. "What do you do for money?"

"Serve tables a couple nights a week at this restaurant near our house."

"'Our,'" Emilia said. "Who's 'our'?"

"My family," Tina said. "Mom, me, my aunt and cousin. And my brother, but he lives in Orlando now."

"So you're sharing rent." Emilia nodded. "Side gig doesn't hurt either. I did a little waitressing when I first moved here. Seems like forever ago now."

"You're not from Miami?"

"Jersey."

"No way, me too," Tina said. "We're originally from San Juan though."

"Puerto Rico," Emilia said. "Such a beautiful place. I stopped there once on a cruise."

"We moved to Jersey when I was six," Tina said. "I've always kinda felt like I'm from both."

"You, mom, aunt, cousin," Emilia said. "And dad?" Tina hesitated and Emilia put her hand up. "Sorry if this sounds like an interrogation. Part of the trade. I like to get to know the people I work with."

"My dad died," Tina said. "Couple of years ago. Heart attack."

"Oh," Emilia said. "My condolences."

"He would have flipped if he knew I was anywhere near what just happened," Tina said, looking out at the passing high-rises. "My mom's definitely going to."

"Moms tend to do that."

"Where in Jersey are you from?" Tina asked.

"Hoboken," Emilia said. "You?"

"Across the bridge in Newark," Tina said.

"I hated Newark," Emilia said, smiling. "No offense."

"None taken," Tina said. "I was happy when we moved. I hated the winters up there."

"How old were you?"

"Fourteen," Tina said.

"Big transition."

"It was...weird," Tina said. "For a little while at least."

A large building appeared ahead, rising until it covered the skyline. Large letters bolted to the concrete foundation high above the plexiglass entrance spelled out the company's branding in bright lights: *Miami Tribune*, set above a smaller *El Tribune Español* sign. A giant barge moored to a dock partially blocked the Biscayne Bay waterfront, waves rippling towards the islands dotting the horizon. Emilia pulled around to the back and parked, cutting the engine and hopping out of the car. Tina grabbed her camera bag and followed.

"What you're seeing now is not the norm," Emilia said. "Most everybody goes through the front. Perks of being here this long."

Emilia held the back door open for Tina then headed down the hallway to a reception area near a bank of gray elevators. She jabbed the buttons until one of the doors dinged open, pressing the fifth-floor button inside and leaning against the wall. Tina stood next to her, clutching her camera bag, shifting from one foot to the other as the floor numbers changed. Emilia nudged her.

"Don't worry," she said, winking. "They're mostly harmless."

The elevator doors opened on organized chaos.

The sheer enormity of the open-plan, football-field-sized newsroom left Tina awestruck as she stepped off the elevator, dodging a man speed-walking past her with his nose buried in a thick book. Streams of people darted around the room, rifling through notepads and stacks of loose papers. Others sat at their desks flipping through Rolodexes with telephones jammed to their ears. Emilia pulled her own journal from her purse and flipped through it as she navigated the crowded area. Floor-to-ceiling windows fitted the north-side of the room, looking out at Miami Beach and the vast ocean beyond. To the west, lines of skyscrapers stood against the backdrop of Overtown and—a couple miles out—the Orange Bowl Stadium. Rows of desks lined the smoke-filled room, each one covered in disarray: overflowing ashtrays, grimy typewriters, stuffed organizers and folders bursting at the seams.

"Sorry," Emilia said, stopping midstride to make a sweeping gesture around the room. "Welcome to the Jungle." She pointed at various clusters of desks.

"Sports is there, politics there, obits on the other side. Business and entertainment over there, editors in the outer offices."

Eyes shifted in their direction. Emilia stopped at a cluster of desks in the back, where a line of women speaking loudly into headsets banged away on black typewriters.

"And here we have Metro," Emilia said.

Tina looked around. "Pretty busy, huh?"

"This?" Emilia said, waving a hand. "Nothing. You should see it during election cycles." Emilia snapped a finger at one of the women at a typewriter. "Shirley, I need that transcript."

Without pausing her phone conversation, the woman grabbed some papers and held them out to Emilia. Emilia reached for them and Shirley held on, placing a hand over her headset.

"Couple of messages too, E," she said.

Emilia took the stack of yellow slips Shirley handed over, shuffling through them as she walked over to a desk with *E. Brathwaite* tacked to the front panel. The desk was covered in items vying for space: directories, photographs, reams of paper with scribble on them. Tina sat in an adjacent chair, placing her camera bag on the ground and crossing her legs. Something caught the corner of her eye out the wall of windows to her right; a white seaplane with blue stripes swooping towards the *Tribune* building. Tina waited for it to turn, but the plane barreled towards them, getting closer and closer until Tina grabbed the corner of Emilia's desk, bracing for impact as the plane veered upwards at the last second, disappearing out of view.

Tina relaxed, looking around to see if anybody else had noticed the stunt. The room pulsed with activity, undeterred. A man at the desk behind Emilia's banged away on his typewriter, sporting a wrinkled Grateful Dead t-shirt tucked into equally wrinkled brown corduroys with no belt. His nameplate read *J. Malone*. He glanced up at Tina, did a double take, then resumed writing.

Emilia pulled a pack of Virginia Slims from her purse, holding it out. Tina waved them off. Shrugging, Emilia lit one up, grabbing a black ashtray from one of her desk drawers.

"Did you notice anything interesting about the van?" she said.

Tina raised an eyebrow. "Besides the arsenal of guns?"

"The exterior," Emilia said. "Under the driver's side mirror."

Tina closed her eyes and pictured the van, then shook her head. "What?"

"A dealership emblem," Emilia said. "Coleman Ford. Econoline."

"So we call them," Tina said.

Emilia opened her desk drawer and pulled out a phonebook, flipping through the pages. She stopped on one and ran her finger down, pausing on an entry. Grabbing her desk phone, she dialed the number and opened her notebook. The phone rang a couple of times before someone answered.

"Hi, yes, this is Emilia Brathwaite, with the *Miami Tribune*. May I speak with your supervisor please?"

Emilia waited on hold until another tinny voice came on the line.

"Emilia Brathwaite here," she said. "*Miami Tribune*, Metro department. I'm calling in regards to the van purchased from your dealership that was used in the shooting that took place at Dadeland Mall earlier today."

The typing at the desks nearby stopped, and Tina felt eyes turn in their direction. The squeaky male voice on the other end of the line rambled for ten seconds before putting her on hold again. Emilia put the phone to her shoulder.

"You should get some new clothes," she said. "This whole thing doesn't really work in dresses."

"What are—" Tina paused, looking down at her spring dress. "I like th—"

"Not what I mean," Emilia said. She put the phone to her ear and listened for a second then lowered it to her shoulder again. "When I first got this gig I dressed nice too. High heels, silk scarves, the nines. You step in enough swamps and witness enough crime scenes though, you'll see. Flats and slacks, breezy blouses and the like. And jumpsuits, gotta get you some of those. I've got two, purple and beige. Always handy."

"Emilia, I have no idea what—"

"And waterproof boots," she said. "If you can get your hands on some. Might not seem like it but trust me, they're worth it."

"Emilia—"

Emilia held up a finger. "Yes, I'm here," she said into the phone. She scribbled down some numbers in her journal, thanked the man and hung up. She turned the notepad to Tina. "Got it."

Tina stared at Emilia's scribble, making out an address. "What'd he say?"

"That his dealership isn't in the armament business," Emilia said. "They must have customized the van after they bought it. He remembers them though. Couple of Latin guys came in and bought it last week. Cash." She tapped the notebook. "This is the address they left on the paperwork."

An older, balding man stepped out of one of the periphery offices marked *Managing Editor* and walked over to them, giving Tina a perfunctory glance before planting both fists on the edge of Emilia's desk.

"You were at Dadeland," he said.

"Just got a lead on the van's owner," Emilia said.

"Channel 7's calling it the War Wagon."

"War Wagon," Emilia said, nodding. "I like that. I'm gonna use that."

"This is serious shit, Emilia."

"I was there, Fred," Emilia said. "You don't have to tell me."

"Whoever did this," he said. "These people aren't playing around."

"If the scene they left behind today is anything to go by," Emilia said. "Then I feel justified in saying these men have no idea *how* to play around."

"Which is why I'm not sure I want you poking around in this." He glanced at Tina again. "Not the way you normally do at least."

Emilia rolled her eyes, glancing at Tina. "The ever-valiant Fred, worried for my safety."

"Someone has to be," he said, crossing his arms.

"I'll be fine, Fred."

"Emilia—"

Emilia cleared her throat loudly. "When have you ever seen me shy away from a story for absolutely *any* reason?"

"Which is great," Fred hissed. "Exemplary behavior for a reporter under normal circumstances. That was *before* Stewart got his head blown off."

"My *God*, man," Emilia groaned. "This is the United States, not Nicaragua."

"We are not in the United *States*," Fred said. "We are in *Miami*. There is a very real difference."

Emilia rolled her eyes over to Tina, nodding at Fred. "Meet Frederico Russo, managing editor." She side-eyed him. "And by managing I mean always managing to be a pain in my ass."

"Bring one of the interns with you at least," he said. "For the lead. To ease my mind, please?"

"Unnecessary," Emilia said, nodding at Tina. "I've got her."

"And who is she again?" Fred looked at Tina. "Who are you?"

"Our new photographer," Emilia said.

"Tina," Tina said, holding out a hand. "Tina Rivera."

"Rivera," Fred said, shaking her hand. "Never seen you before."

"Hence the word 'new,'" Emilia said. "She just started today actually."

Fred's face went through a multitude of emotions in the span of seconds, confusion to recognition to anger and finally disdain.

"Emilia," he said.

"Fred."

"We *have* photographers," he said.

"And not one of them got the shots of Dadeland she did," Emilia said, tapping Tina's shoulder. "Give it to him."

Tina rummaged in her bag, pulling out a single film canister.

"Moments after the shit hit the fan," Emilia said, pointing at the rolls. "Outside the liquor store where it happened. The van. *Inside* the van."

Fred rubbed his forehead, staring at the canister like it was a bar of stolen gold. "I have to see the shots," he said.

Tina handed the film to Fred.

"We've gotta go," Emilia said, grabbing Tina and pulling her back towards the elevators. "The shots are good though. I'll let you know if the lead has legs."

"I've gotta run this downstairs," he called after them. "And she has to fill out paperwork. She needs her credentials!"

"Later!" Emilia yelled back over her shoulder, pulling Tina onto an elevator as the doors closed.

They descended in silence, the doors opening again on the lobby. Emilia stepped out and Tina stayed in the elevator, holding the door open.

"Emilia," she said. "Wait."

"What?" Emilia said, turning to her. "Come on, you gotta hop on these leads before they dry up."

"Why did you just tell Fred I'm your new photographer?" Tina asked.

Emilia gave her a skeptical look. "Because…you are?"

Tina shook her head in disbelief. "What the hell is happening?"

Emilia smiled. "You just got a job." She stood at attention, offering Tina a mock-salute. "Welcome aboard. Now let's go."

13.

Rig remembered the day Papi got arrested. He was four, sitting in the living room when two burly men in uniform kicked in the front door. Tore the house apart searching before they emerged from his parents' room holding a plastic bag of grass.

"Niggers and their reefer," one of the cops said, laughing.

Rig remembered them handcuffing Papi in front of the whole neighborhood, dragging him across the patched concrete to a paddywagon parked at the curb.

This was back in Goulds, at the edge of where Homestead and Miami meet. Rig didn't like thinking about that place. He still had vivid dreams with his mother's screams as the soundtrack. She didn't talk for a week after the arrest, and even when she came back to him things were different, her voice filled with a sadness that made Rig want to click his heels and snap his fingers and whisk them away to a foreign land like those fairy tales at school.

Sitting on a curb with a cop standing over them, barking questions, Rig thought about that day. Otis sat next to him, responding to the cop with a series of grunts and shrugs. A commotion nearby interrupted the back and forth as Lefty pushed through the crowd.

"Those boys are with me officer," Lefty said, glaring at Otis. "What the hell y'all doing over here?!"

"Gonna need you to calm down, sir," the cop said, standing between Lefty and the boys.

"I'm calm, officer," Lefty said, backing away. "No trouble. I'm just in charge of these boys. Gotta get 'em back to they mamas."

The cop glanced back at Otis and Rig. "You with this man?" he asked.

Otis nodded. The officer looked at him skeptically.

"Alright," the cop said. "See that they get right home. Boys've been through a lot today."

Lefty planted a hand on Rig and Otis's shoulders and followed them through the chaotic parking lot, guiding them away from the mob floating around the demolished liquor store like vultures. The crowd parted and men wearing white coats pushed two gurneys with black body bags out onto the sidewalk, headed to the Medical Examiner van parked nearby. The sheets beneath the bags were soaked with blood. Lefty pushed Rig and Otis in the other direction.

Back at US-1, DJ jumped up from Lefty's lawn chair as they approached the van. Lefty marched Rig and Otis over, opening the van's side door. Otis glanced back at DJ.

"Snitchin' ass," he said under his breath.

"Ain't nobody snitch on nobody," Lefty snapped, wheeling around and pointing at the slew of flashing police lights in the mall lot. "Y'all could've gotten hurt in all that, and then what?"

Rig, Otis and DJ said nothing. Lefty walked to the driver's side. The boys climbed in and Lefty started the engine, gripping the steering wheel, wrists shuddering, knuckles pale. Eventually he looked back at them, offering the boys a tight-lipped smile. He nodded at the bag gripped in Rig's fist, hidden between his knees.

"What you got there?"

Rig glanced at Otis.

"Comic books," Otis said.

Lefty squinted at him, holding his hand out. "Lemme see."

Rig carefully pulled the two comics out of the bag and handed them to Lefty, sliding the bag itself under his leg.

Lefty took the comics, studying the covers.

"You like reading," he said, glancing at Rig. "You should read some real books sometimes."

"I read real books," Rig said.

Lefty held the comics up. "You pay for these?"

"Yeah," Rig said.

"You sure?" Lefty said, more to Otis.

"He had cash on him," Otis said.

"Where you get that from?"

"My mama," Rig said.

"And you used it to buy this?" Lefty said, handing the comics back to Rig.

"Yeah," Rig said, handing the Batman comic to Otis. "You can ask the man at the store."

Lefty nodded. "Good thing, reading," he said, pointing at Otis and DJ. "Maybe you can get these knuckleheads to try it."

"I read," DJ said, staring at the comic in Otis's hands. "Sometimes."

"Sure you do," Lefty said, facing forward again. "Let's get y'all back home."

Lefty pulled the rattling van back onto US-1 and pushed north. The afternoon traffic was light, the interior of the van cooler than when they'd driven over. Rig and Otis stayed quiet, staring out the window with haunted looks on their faces. DJ looked back and forth from one boy to the other then tapped Otis on the shoulder.

"Bust a rhyme," he said, putting his hands to his mouth.

Otis smiled and DJ started blowing into the cups of his palms. Otis nodded to the beat. Rig glanced over and watched the two, fascinated. Otis opened his mouth and his voice came out raspier than usual.

Yo it's O-dawg, yeah you know just how I be
Always rockin' the scene, that's why they call me Rocky
Stay so fresh and clean, for the ladies I mean
Hand the mic to Rig, can he spit? We'll see

Otis pointed at Rig. Rig said nothing, squinting at the other two boys, curiosity gleaming in his eyes.

"Nigga, spit a rhyme," Otis said, nudging him. "Fucking up the flow."

"I don't—" Rig paused.

DJ kept blowing into his fists.

The van rumbled.

Rig closed his eyes and nodded to the beat, letting it fill his mind.

Considering his words, he ran some lines through his head and opened his mouth, lyrics seeming to flow not out of him but through him:

Yo it's Rig, a simple name that rhymes with big
Description of my size and every second I live
Searchin' for paradise in a city filled with pigs
Lookin' at us and ain't got two shits to give
Ya dig?

DJ dropped his hands, him and Otis staring at Rig with their mouths open.

Otis held his hand out. "Respect, my nigga." He glanced at DJ with his eyebrows raised. "Goddamn. I guess ya boy can spit."

"Dropping you off first, Rig," Lefty called out. "Then DJ. And Otis—me and yo' mama goin' have a talk."

"Come on, Left," Otis whined.

"It's happening. Get used to it."

Otis crossed his arms, pouting.

"Can you drop me off where you picked me up please?" Rig asked.

Lefty switched his stare to Rig, nodding. "No problem, Young Blood."

They approached an intersection and Otis hopped forward, pushing his face against the window. "There they go right there!"

DJ and Rig looked out at two boys walking in the opposite direction down 7th avenue. One of them had a metal clip bandaged over his bruised nose.

"Marquise," Otis said. "That's the nigga Rig fucked up at the park."

"Who's the other guy?" Rig asked.

"Day Day," DJ said. "Marquise's cousin."

"He was there too," Rig said. "Didn't do nothing, just stood there."

"'Cause he a bitch," Otis said. "Him and Marquise the same type a asshole. Can't stand none of them Indigo City ass niggas."

"What's wrong with Indigo City?" Rig asked.

Otis sucked his teeth. "Bunch a snitchin' ass muhfuckas."

"Day Day's pops the one got O's pops locked up way back," DJ said.

"Fuck all a them," Otis said.

"My tia stay in Indigo City," Rig said.

"Yo' what?" Otis said, raising an eyebrow.

"My auntie," Rig said. "Tia mean auntie in Spanish."

"Shit," Otis said, leaning away from Rig. "This nigga a chico."

"You know Spanish?" DJ asked.

"A little," Rig said.

"Whatever, yo *tee-ah* need to move," Otis said. "Fuck Indigo City."

"Place look just like where we stay," Rig said.

"'Cept it ain't," Otis said.

Lefty pulled the van over to a curb and put it in park, climbing out and walking around to open the side door. Rig stood and DJ leaned forward, holding out his hand.

"Nice meeting you, brother," he said, slapping Rig's palm.

Otis gave Rig a nod. "We 'round the block."

Rig hopped out and Lefty closed the door, patting Rig on the back and shimmying back to the driver's side. Rig stared at the busted taillights as the van rattled through the stop sign. It turned left on the next block, disappearing.

Cutting back through the Crystal Palaces courtyard, Rig passed a party in progress. A cloud of smoke hung over the back porch as a dozen adults swayed and laughed, plastic cups in hand. The familiar scent of marijuana filled Rig's nose. Some of them waved towards him as he passed. Rig waved back, shyly.

Stopping outside his front door, Rig looked at the purple *Magic City* bag in his hand. Taking out the Spiderman comic, he walked around to the side of the building and crouched next to a three-foot square patch of dirt surrounded by cinder blocks, heaving one of the blocks aside to reveal a hole about half a foot deep and a foot wide. Dirt spilled onto the items buried in plastic: a wallet with nothing but a driver's license for some lady named Bertha Williams; a smooth, round rock Rig had found in an abandoned lot that gleamed with gemstones in the sunlight; a sheathed, rusted hunting knife he'd found strolling behind the supermarket on 62nd street a few weeks back. A backfiring car engine startled him and he shoved the *Magic City* bag into the hole, replacing the cinderblock.

Rounding the corner back to his apartment, Rig was about to knock on the front door when it opened, his mother standing in the doorway with the right half of her hair set in a tight black bun on her head like an anemone, the other half bleached blonde and resting on her shoulder in wet, curly strands. Her swollen belly stretched the waist of her sweatpants, the house phone jammed between her shoulder and cheek with the cord stretching across the kitchen.

Rig hid the comic behind his back. His mother studied his face for a second then told the person on the other end of the phone line to hold on.

"I thought I heard you out here," she said. "Where you been all day?"

Rig shrugged.

His mother turned her head to the side, studying him. "What's wrong? You look like you saw a ghost."

"Nothing," Rig said. "I'm fine."

Rig's mom waved him inside, shuffling back to the kitchen. A parade of chemical smells wafted in a cloud of steam above the sink, a cosmetology textbook open on the counter.

Rig walked over to his mattress and plopped down, sliding the Spiderman comic underneath. His mother told the person on the other end of the line to hold again and put the phone to her chest.

"Papi said five dollars was missing from his wallet this morning."

Rig said nothing.

His mom widened her eyes. "Rig?"

"I don't know," Rig said, shrugging.

Rig's mother opened her mouth just as someone banged on the front door. Rig tensed.

They both flinched when the banging came again.

"Alright damn," she said, putting the phone down on the counter.

As his mother approached the peephole, an intense wave of fear washed over Rig, his skin getting cold, his mouth dry. It was a foreboding fear; a fear that his mother opening that door would let in something evil.

Inescapable. Damnable.

A muffled voice from the other side yelled, "*Gail, they got him!*"

"Mama," Rig said, hopping up. "Mama, wait."

Rig's mother's eyes widened around the peep hole.

"No," she said. "No no no not again."

"Mama, wait!"

Rig's mom threw the front door open and started screaming.

14.

Holding her notebook up to block the sunlight, Emilia squinted at the numbers on the sides of the conjoined apartment buildings, comparing them to her scribble.

Standing next to her, Tina stared out at the strawberry fields that started half a block away, stretching towards the Everglades. "I didn't even know they built anything this far west."

"Not gonna stop either," Emilia murmured. "They'd build straight into the swamp if the city let them." She pointed at one of the buildings. "That one."

"You sure we should be doing this?" Tina asked, following Emilia towards the stairwell. "Maybe Fred was right."

"Fred's never right," Emilia said. "The editors are never right, always remember that."

"What if the guys from Dadeland are in there?" Tina whispered.

"Then we'll try and get a quote," Emilia whispered back.

"But isn't—"

"If I avoided every story that seemed dangerous," Emilia said. "I'd never get anything printed."

Tina said nothing. Emilia paused at the stairs, one foot up on the first step.

"You know—I hated being a woman when I first got this job," she said. "Hated it, wished I had a penis for all of six months until I realized it's all these assholes think with." Tina stifled a laugh. Emilia smiled. "All of the editors were men, and any time one of us female reporters made an error, no matter how—insignificant, you'd never hear the end of it. Carping on about the newsroom becoming a henhouse. Terrifying, that I might get that label. Then I got a few features, got them in by deadline, made the front page. All of a sudden there's a lot less griping. You know?"

"I—think so?" Tina said.

"The point is if you want to do this, you can," Emilia said. "But you've got to really *want* it."

"Emilia, I met you what—four hours ago?" Tina said, looking up at the ceiling. "I don't even know what's *happening* right—"

"You want to be in the paper," Emilia said. "You want your name on those pages. I know the look. I've had the look so I know the look and listen—" Emilia faced Tina, folding her arms. "I don't know yet why I like you Tina, but I do. And I've only gotten this far by trusting my instincts. After today, if those pictures pan out, you've got a foot in the door so—" She patted Tina's shoulder. "Let me get you the rest of the way in."

Tina nodded and Emilia nodded back.

Headed upstairs to the third floor, they approached Apartment 19 cautiously. At the yellow door, Emilia raised her hand to knock and paused, glancing back at Tina. Tina nodded and Emilia gave the door three solid raps. Soft footsteps approached from inside. The lock clicked and the door creaked open on a pretty blonde about Tina's age. She wore a small black bikini, a blue towel draped over her shoulder. Her skin was tanned, her eyes blue as the sky.

"Hi," she said. Midwestern accent. "Can I help you?"

"Yes," Emilia said, looking up at the gold-plated number 19 next to the door. She looked down at her notebook. "You live here?"

"Um, yeah," the girl said. Her voice was bubbly, her smile plastered. "Just moved in."

"Just moved in," Emilia echoed.

"Mm hmm." The girl touched the towel on her shoulder. "About to head to the pool. First time. Are you all here about the air conditioner?"

"No, we work for The Tribune," Emilia said, flipping through her notebook. "Do you know the person who lived here before you?"

"No," the girl said. "I was just looking and saw an ad in—yeah, in your paper actually. The Tribune."

"And you didn't have any problems getting the place?"

"No," the girl said. "I'm sorry, what was your name?"

"Emilia," she said. "This is Tina. We need to speak with the person who lived here before you."

"Oh, I mean… I don't know what to say." The girl scratched her neck. "I replied to the ad, paid my first and last and the landlord gave me the key. The apartment was empty when I came to see it."

Emilia tapped a pen against her notebook then slapped it closed. "Thanks, sorry to bother you."

"No problem," the girl said as Emilia pulled Tina down the hall.

Back in the car, Emilia flipped through her notebook while Tina stared out at the fading afternoon.

"Maybe try the landlord," Tina said. "He might know where they went."

"I can tell you exactly where they went," Emilia muttered, putting the car in gear. "Colombia. Or Mexico. Or the bottom of the ocean for all we know. This is a dead end. Probably literally."

Emilia pulled out of the complex, heading east back towards US-1.

"What now?" Tina said.

"Now I put what I've got together into something coherent by deadline," Emilia said. "As for you, I've stolen enough of your time today."

Tina sat back in her seat. Emilia reached over and touched her arm.

"Don't worry," she said. "I'll make sure you get your credit, and payment. Matter of fact—" Emilia tossed her notebook into Tina's lap. "Write down your info. First and last name, telephone, address."

Tina scribbled down the information and handed the notebook back. They stopped at a red light and Emilia glanced at Tina's writing.

"No wonder," she said. "You live right next to the mall."

"I had just walked over when everything started."

"Walked?" Emilia said. "No car?"

Tina shook her head.

"I'll give you a ride in the morning," Emilia said, pulling through the intersection. "Don't make a habit of it though. Either get a car or figure out which bus you've gotta take."

"I'm saving up for one actually," Tina said.

"I'm kidding," Emilia said, reaching over Tina's lap to open the glove compartment. She pulled out a card and handed it to Tina. "If you ever need a ride, call me."

Tina studied the card:

Emilia Brathwaite
Staff Reporter, Metro Department
Miami Tribune
305-555-4631

"And when I say anytime," Emilia said. "I mean anytime. That's my desk number but my house is on the back. There's a police scanner next to my bed so I'm up anyways."

"Thanks, Emilia," Tina said. "Really."

"Thanks for bringing your camera today," Emilia said.

They passed Dadeland, half a dozen patrol cars and a bunch of news vans parked near the destroyed liquor store, the entire area cordoned off with yellow tape. The mall disappeared behind them and Emilia turned left on 77th. Tina pointed at her house and Emilia pulled into the driveway.

"You can help me with my rounds in the morning," Emilia said. "Stopping at the precincts to check arrest reports. Pick you up here at seven thirty?"

Tina nodded and climbed out of the car. Emilia rolled down the window.

"You've got some paperwork to fill out," she said. "Bring some pens. And your camera. I'll bring the morning edition."

Emilia tapped the horn as she drove off, Tina waving after her.

Unlocking the front door, Tina stepped inside the dimly lit living room. Tia Lupé sat on the couch, Maria on the floor next to her, the TV bathing them in a blue glow. The moment Tina appeared they both jumped up, Maria running over and throwing her arms around Tina's waist. Lupé clasped her hands together, tears in her eyes. Tina stared at them both, confused.

"Happy to see you guys too," she said.

"On the news," Lupé said, sitting back down and nodding at the TV. "The shooting at the mall."

"We thought something happened to you," Maria said, her voice muffled against Tina's stomach.

"I'm fine," Tina said, stroking her cousin's hair.

"Tu mama dijo que la llames," Lupé said.

Tina clenched her jaw. "I'll call her now."

Extracting herself from Maria's grip, she walked into the kitchen and poured herself a cup of water. She picked up the phone hanging on the wall next to the sink and dialed the hotel her mother worked at, navigating through three line switches before Luisa appeared on the other end.

"Mija!" her mother said in a winded voice. "Where—you're gone all day? You don't call, nada, and then—they are *shooting* at the *mall* and you—"

"I'm okay, Mami," Tina said.

"But you were at the—"

"Yes, I was there," Tina said. "But I wasn't near the—"

"You were *there?*" her mother gasped.

"Mami, I'm fine," Tina said. "I wasn't near the shooting and I actually, um—" Tina cleared her throat. "I got a job."

"A job?" her mother said. "Where?"

"At The Tribune."

"Las noticias?" Luisa said.

"Sí, Mami."

"What can you do at the newspaper?"

Tina frowned. "Pictures," she said. "Maybe even write for them someday. I took some photos of what happened today and—"

"And they are going to pay you?" her mother said. "For pictures and writing? Enough to live?"

"I mean, we haven't—" Tina's voice cracked and she coughed. "Yeah. Yes. They are."

"Ay, Valentina," her mother said. "Mira, I don't know why you are so difficult. I have told you, I will talk to Beatrice and you can have the job at the hotel, no problem."

"I'm not going to work at the hotel, Mami," Tina barked. She pulled the phone away from her ear, cursing under her breath.

"What is wrong with the hotel?" Her mother's voice sounded distant, tinny.

"Nothing," Tina said, putting the phone back to her ear. "There's nothing wrong with the hotel. I'm just saying I have a job already." Tina held up two fingers. "*Two* of them now."

"I do not understand your gener—"

"What is there to understand, Mami?" Tina said.

"Why are you raising your voice?" her mother asked.

Tina pulled the phone down again, her jaw shaking with the force of her gritted teeth. She put the phone back to her ear, catching her mother in the middle of talking.

"—attitude this morning, what is wrong with you?"

"What do you mean, Mami?" Tina asked.

"The way you left this morning," she said.

"I don't know what you're talking—"

"I bring up Tio Raul," her mother said. "Every time I say something about Raul you get upset."

Tina froze. Her eyes watered. Twisting the phone cord around a finger, she pulled it tighter until the tip of her finger turned bright red. "You keep acting like he's some sort of saint," she whispered.

"He is your tio," she said. "Mi hermano."

"Is there anything else, Mami?" Tina said, a tear slipping down her cheek.

"These children—"

"Mami, I've gotta go," Tina yelled. "Love you bye!"

Tina slammed the phone down. Swiping tears from her face, she walked back into the living room.

"Todo bien?" Lupé called out.

"Fine," Tina said, disappearing down the hallway to her room.

15.

Turning into the strip mall, Ralph parked outside the Guns and Ammo store, the radio playing "Folsom Prison Blues" at low volume. He raised his right arm, willing his hand to stop shaking. Placing two fingers against his neck, he felt his pounding pulse, squeezed his hand into a fist and opened the car door, climbing out.

A bell rang over his head as he entered the shop, the door slamming behind him. He took off his sunglasses and slipped them in his jacket pocket, scanning the glass display cases lining the walls to his left and right. Across the room, behind the cash register, a man stood with his arms crossed, flexing his flaccid biceps. He wore a blue tank top and a gray cap over his mullet, the hat sporting a stitched imprint of a cartoon woman with disproportionately large breasts wearing a cowboy hat and a tiny rebel flag bikini.

"How can I help you?" the man drawled, chewing something in the corner of his mouth.

"Looking to upgrade," Ralph said. He let his suit jacket open as he approached the register, revealing his holster. He unclipped his badge and placed it on the counter.

"No problem, Officer," the man said, his demeanor shifting. He nodded at Ralph's holster. "What's that you got there, a .38?"

"Good eye," Ralph said. "Smith and Wesson, nineteen blue steel."

"Nice piece."

"Nice enough," Ralph said. "Need one can handle more shots. Not too much bigger. Still gotta holster it."

"Reckon the Browning's what you're looking for," he said, walking around to one of the display cases. He pulled a ring of keys from his pocket and opened it, sliding out a sleek black pistol. He pulled back the slide, cocked the hammer and pulled the trigger with a click. "Nine-millimeter. Fourteen shots. Reliable."

Ralph took the gun, sighted it, popped the clip and checked the chamber. Pulling his .38 out of its holster, he tested the nine in its place.

"How much?" he asked.

"That one'll run you one-fifty," he said. "Includes registration and all that."

"I'll take it," he said. "And a box of rounds."

"Sure thing," Mullet said, heading back behind the counter. "Five percent discount, on account of you being law enforcement and all."

"'Preciate that," Ralph said.

"No, sir," Mullet said, his expression going serious. "Thank *you*. Thank all of y'all for what y'all do."

Ralph nodded.

"The way the newspapers rail against y'all," Mullet said, disgusted. "Acting like *they* could do *your* job. Makes me sick. Gotta turn everything into a race issue. Like the blacks ain't always complaining about something. I tell you—I almost joined the force myself, back in '69. Couldn't, on account of my knee problems. But I wanted it. Wearing that badge." He nodded. "Nothing but honor in that."

Ralph said nothing, offering a smile.

"Let me get ya squared away," Mullet said, tapping the register.

Ralph studied the other display cases while Mullet got the paperwork in order, his eyes falling on a pump-action shotgun, three feet long with a thick black barrel. Closing his eyes, Ralph pictured the Uzis hanging from the ceiling in the War Wagon, the tripod mounted M2 machine gun. He opened his eyes and tapped the glass display.

"This too," he said. "And some shells."

Back in his car, Ralph shoved his .38 in the glove compartment and slipped his new 9mm in the holster, moving his arms around to test the feel. He tossed the shotgun in the passenger seat and caught a glimpse of his reflection in the rearview mirror: day-old scruff on his cheeks, bloodshot eyes. Blinking hard, he started the car and pulled back onto Miller Drive, headed north.

Downtown, Ralph parked on 2nd ave and walked into the five-story PSD building through the back entrance. He checked in at reception then headed upstairs to the third floor, past the coffee shop down the hallway to the door marked "Homicide." He entered a room with a dozen or so stark, government-issued metal desks lined up in rows, most of the seats empty with detectives milling about. One of the sergeants standing by the coffee room spotted Ralph and held up a hand. Ralph raised his in response, dropping his jacket on his chair. Stacks of folders and a dozen or so yellow slips of paper littered his desk's surface. Ralph pulled out his notebook and slapped it down just as Detective Richie Weis rolled his chair over.

"You were at Dadeland with Murphy?"

"Getting started on the paperwork now," Ralph said.

"Goddamn shit-show," Weis said, glancing around. "Where's Murphy?"

"Stayed behind," Ralph sighed. "Wanted to double check the scene."

"So you saw the vics?" Weis whispered.

"What's left of them," Ralph said, rummaging through the scattered notes on his desk.

"Glad I wasn't there," Weis said. "Got four shootings last week alone. One guy in the head in a bathroom. Brains all over the tiles."

"Heard about that," Ralph said.

"Never seen a mess like it," Weis muttered.

"We weren't even supposed to be there," Ralph said. "Only in the area 'cause some kid got shot in the Grove. Gonna be here all goddamn night now."

"Speaking of," Weis said, nodding at Ralph's desk phone. "Amanda called a couple times."

Ralph picked the phone up, nodding at the other detective. Amanda answered on the second ring.

"Hey babe," Ralph said.

"Your son is driving me insane," she said.

Ralph rubbed his forehead. "So he's just my son now?"

"He got that annoying streak from you, not me," she said.

"That why you called?" Ralph asked. "To tell me our son is just as annoying as I am?"

"I saw you on the news," Amanda said.

Ralph paused. "You did?"

"In the background, next to Danny." She lowered her voice. "You were there? At Dadeland?"

"We were nearby when the call went out, yeah." He leaned back in his seat. "What're they saying?"

"Who?"

"The news, Mandy," Ralph said. "What's the news saying?"

"Oh, it's horrible," she said. "All of it. Two men killed, bunch of people injured. They said it might be related to that Turnpike thing last month?" She gave a little gasp. "And they showed the van, that—that war wagon, they're calling it?" She lowered her voice. "Jesus, Ralph. Who are these people, to be doing things like this?"

"That's what we're trying to figure out," Ralph said.

"They're keeping you on the case?"

"Funny you should ask that," Ralph said. "Danny told us right after—"

"He looked thin," she interrupted. "You sure he's okay?"

Ralph frowned. "He's fine. He just got pro—"

"He say anything about Crystal?" she asked, lowering her voice.

"Why are you whispering?" Ralph asked.

"I read this article in Cosmo today about what divorce does to a person," she said. "It really can make you go a bit crazy."

"Danny's fine, Amanda," Ralph said, rolling his eyes at Detective Weiss. "The divorce was like two years ago."

Amanda breathed softly on the other end. "Sorry. Just asking."

Ralph squeezed the bridge of his nose. "Was there anything else, hon?"

Amanda sniffled. "I think I'm getting sick."

"You've been saying that for like two weeks," Ralph said.

"I know," she said. "I think maybe it's allergies."

Ralph placed the phone against his chest, counted to three, then put it back to his ear.

"I'm sorry to hear that, hon," he said. "I'm gonna be here late, got a lot of paperwork. You want me to bring you anything on my way home?" He forced his voice to stay steady. "Or do you think you'll be fine for the evening?"

"No, I'm okay," Amanda said. "I just wanted to make sure you're safe."

Ralph's shoulders slouched.

"I'm sorry you don't feel well," he said. "Really. Put Mikey to bed early, tell him I said so. Try and get some rest. I'll join you when I get back."

"Okay," she said. "I love you."

Ralph paused for just a half-second. "I love you too," he said.

They hung up and Ralph planted his elbows on his desk, cradling his forehead in his palms.

"All good on the home front?" Weis asked.

"As good as can be," Ralph said. "All things considered."

"See how long that lasts," Weis said, grabbing his coat and badge. He winked at Ralph. "Amount of overtime we got coming our way."

Weis disappeared, leaving Ralph focusing on the new weight in his holster.

A wave of commotion floated over from the bulletin board near the lieutenant's office, a group of detectives talking excitedly as the lieutenant added a couple of new entries to the list of open cases. Ralph sauntered over, grabbing the closest man and giving him an inquisitive look.

"Two John Does," the detective said. "Just got the call, found them at the entrance to those new apartments off Kendall and 107th."

Ralph's ears tingled. "How'd they go?"

"Gunshots," he said. "One to the chest and face. Other guy in the stomach and shoulder then kill blow under the chin. Dumped behind a tree."

"You're with me on this one, Williams," Murphy said from behind Ralph.

Ralph turned, Murphy staring at him grimly from the doorway. The hairs on the back of Ralph's neck stood up.

"I haven't started the paperwork on Dadeland," Ralph said.

"Get some unis on it," Murphy said, nodding at the chalkboard. "Techs found an empty casing in one of the Doe's pockets. Matches the M2 Browning." He glanced at the other detectives eavesdropping on their conversation. "Can't be sure 'til we get lab results but my guess is these are our shooters. Somebody cleaned up after themselves."

Ralph glanced at the bulletin board again—at the two instances of *John Doe* listed in red at the bottom of the extensive list—then followed Murphy out.

16.

Bending his knees, Eddy Lopez stretched his long arms out at his side. The cop leered at him, crouched in a wrestler's stance. Eddy kept his arms moving in a circle, searching for an opening. Twenty yards behind him, a second cop stalked over from the courtyard benches. The Crystal Palaces project apartment complex came alive, doors opening, wide eyed residents creeping out to gossip on the small patches of concrete at their back doors. The party Rig had passed on the way home stopped in its tracks, all the guests wandering across the courtyard to get a better view.

"Eddy!" Rig's mom yelled from their apartment. "Behind you, the cop is *behind* you."

"Mama, the baby!" Rig said, holding fast to his mother's waist, struggling to pull her back inside as she clawed at his arms, pushing towards the door.

The cop in front of Rig's dad swiped at him then retreated. Eddy balled his hands up and growled.

"Come on then, fucking pig," he spit. "Tired of y'all harassing me, man, come on. Straight up, face to face."

"Been looking forward to this, Eddy," the cop said. "I'ma enjoy whoopin' yo' monkey ass."

Behind Eddy, the second patrolman came around a tree and bolted towards him. Rig's mom yelled again and her husband finally heard her, turning just as the cop launched into the air. His shoulder hit Rig's dad square in the stomach and the two men fell to the ground, wrestling and trading blows with heaving grunts. The other cop ran over just as his partner threw a right hook into Eddy's ribcage. Rig's dad screamed and fell, hard. Both cops hopped on his back, twisting his arms behind him.

Rig's mother grabbed hold of the door frame, pulling so hard the veins in her neck bulged. Her belly bounced beneath her maternity pants.

"Mama!" Rig shouted. "You gotta stop, that's the pol—"

"That is yo' *Daddy!*" she snapped, spinning on him and back-handing him in the face.

The blow rocked Rig, dots swimming in the corners of his eyes. Pushing him away, his mother bolted across the courtyard, holding her belly with one arm. The crowd outside grew louder, a couple of rocks and sticks flying in the cops' direction. Rig put a hand to his stinging cheek and ran after his mom. He was ten feet away when she collided with one of the cops, almost knocking the man on his ass. Catching his balance, the cop turned and shoved Rig's mom. She screamed out as she fell, landing on her back with a loud *oof*.

Rig was reminded then of the fight he'd gotten into at the park, with Marquise and his cousin. The feeling that had risen in him when they snatched his book, how that disrespect had felt like a color, a red so deep it had tinted the entire world around him. He saw that same red again now.

His mother hit the ground and Rig shifted trajectory, baring his teeth and lunging at the cop.

The cop's eyes widened at the sight of an oversized eleven-year-old flying at him. Rig reached for the man's neck and was inches away when the cop sidestepped, sticking out his foot and catching Rig's ankle. Rig flew face-first to the ground and hit the grass with a thud, air bursting from his lungs. He scrambled to push himself up but the cop was on him, shoving a knee in his back and twisting his arms.

"Get the fuck off me!" Rig yelled. "Don't touch my Mom!"

"Your mom pushed *me*, kid!" the cop screamed in his ear.

"Officer, please," Rig's mom cried.

Rig twisted around to see his mother standing a few feet away, holding her belly with tears streaming down her cheeks.

"He didn't do nothing," she said. "He was just trying to help. I'm—I'm sorry I pushed you. That's just—it's—that's my husband and I—" Rig's mother floundered, falling to her knees and holding her hands out. "Please."

The officer sitting on Rig's back twisted his arm more and Rig screamed. The pain seemed to last an eternity before the cop released him, pulling Rig to his feet and pushing him towards his mother. Rig grabbed her, clinging to her.

Eyeing the mother and son, the cop helped his partner handcuff a defeated Eddy Lopez. They pulled Rig's dad to his feet, Eddy's face stained with dirt, sweat and tears, his gold chain and crucifix lying in the grass at his feet. Shirt torn, pants covered in grass stains, a knot forming above his right eyebrow. The crowd jeered around them.

"Niggers getting riled up," one of the cops said.

The other cop looked around. "Get him in the car before this shit starts getting ugly."

"Check him first."

The cop holding the handcuffs patted Rig's dad's pockets then reached down the back of Eddy's pants. Rig's dad gave a half-assed show of protest as the cop pulled out a freezer bag filled with greenish-brown buds.

"Bingo," he said.

The other cop scowled at Rig and his mom. "You want we book 'em too?"

The cop holding the bag of weed glanced around the courtyard, seeing nothing but angry faces in return.

"Leave 'em," the cop said, shaking a finger at Rig. "But don't pull no shit like that again, boy. Ain't gonna end well for you next time."

Rig glared at the men. The two cops dragged Rig's dad to a patrol car parked on the street, opened the back door and shoved him inside.

"Can't remember last time I had to run five blocks *and* fight a nigger," one of them said, his voice carrying over with the wind. "Fucker's too big to be that goddamn fast, should play for the Dolphins."

"Told you to hit the gym," the other cop said. "Fat fuck."

The cops laughed and climbed in, the patrol car squealing off.

Rig's mother raised her face from his chest, her cheeks and nose a mess of tears. Her mouth moved silently. Rig tilted his ear towards her.

"Not again," she whispered. "Not again."

The gleam of his dad's gold chain and crucifix caught Rig's eye. He let his mother go, walked over and picked it up. Dangling the cross in front of his face, he turned back to his mother who was standing with a hand over her belly. There was something on her maternity dress, down below her waistline; a dark stain spreading across her crotch.

"Mama," Rig said, pointing.

Rig's mother looked down. When she looked back up, her eyes were empty. Rig grabbed her before she fell, holding her up.

Rig glanced around at the dissipating crowd, most of the people going back in their homes. The music at the party resumed. Rig tilted his head up to the sky, turning a deep, dark purple. Rig's mother leaned against him as they walked back to their apartment. Rig helped her inside, turned and looked out at the courtyard then closed the door.

17.

Luchi plopped down on a lawn chair across from Tommy, a plastic table separating them. The living room was otherwise bare aside from a small chest of drawers against the opposite wall and the couch Tommy sat on. Luchi picked up the pack of Reds sitting on the table and held it out to Tommy. Tommy raised a quivering hand and grabbed one, nodding thanks without looking Luchi in the eyes. Raising his lighter, Tommy studied the jittering flame, willing the cigarette to stop shaking between his fingers.

Dumping the rest of his pack out, Luchi proceeded to squeeze the tobacco out of each cigarette into a small mound of brown flakes in the middle of the table. He pulled a plastic bag of grayish-white powder out of his pocket and dumped some onto the pile of tobacco, mixing it with a rusty spoon then using the spoon to feed the concoction back into each empty cigarette wrapper. Twisting the ends of the repackaged cigarettes, he held a flame under them until the white papers turned a yellowish brown.

Placing one on his bottom lip, Luchi lit up, his eyes glazing over.

He pointed the butt of the laced cigarette at Tommy. "Quinientos. Sí?"

Tommy glanced at Luchi then immediately looked away.

"Five hundred," Luchi said. "American dollars, no?"

Tommy ran the words through his mind. "Yeah," he croaked.

Luchi stood and walked over to the chest of drawers, pulling out a wad of cash. He tossed it and the roll hit Tommy's leg. Tommy twitched away. Luchi laughed, a startlingly high-pitched sound.

"Ju are, eh—" Luchi held his arms up, scarecrow-like. "Asustado."

Tommy picked up the cash, fanning through the crumpled stack of twenties and tens. "So," he said, his voice cracking. "What now?"

"Now?" Luchi said through smoke as he stubbed out the foul-smelling cigarette. "Ahora limpiamos, parce."

Shoving the wad of bills in his pocket, Tommy followed Luchi outside to the Corolla, parked in the driveway beneath the afternoon shade of a large oak tree rooted at the curb. They walked around the side of the house to a small wooden shed, covered in peeling white paint. The door creaked as Luchi pulled out a dirty yellow bucket and a black hose, handing one end of the hose to Tommy and attaching the other to a faucet sticking out the side of the house. Luchi turned on the faucet and Tommy filled the bucket then heaved it over to the Corolla. Luchi came up behind him with the running hose.

"Limpia," Luchi said, handing Tommy the hose and pointing at the car. "Di window, di seat, todo."

Tommy stared dumbfounded at the car as Luchi headed back towards the house. The moment he was gone, Tommy let out a breath he hadn't realized he was holding. A chill ran up his spine, causing a shudder as he approached the car. He opened the back door and gagged, holding his arm over his face as he surveyed the gory scene. The thickest amounts of blood and brain matter were confined to the headrests and the rear windshield, though some had also seeped into the seats. The smell was horrific, smacking him in the face before he could block it out.

Tommy's stomach lurched and he turned away, hacking into the grass.

Luchi returned with gloves, some sponges and two stiff-bristled brushes.

"Ay, Tommy," Luchi said, placing the cleaning supplies on the car trunk. "Ju stomach es weak, parcero." Luchi made a fist and rapped it against his paunchy midsection. "Cómo el acero. Ju need más bandeja paisa."

Tommy wiped his mouth with the back of his hand, avoiding Luchi's eyes as he turned the hose on the backseat. A steady flow of red-tinted water etched a veiny course down the driveway.

"Que desastre," Luchi said, staring in the car from the other side. "Ju know es di bullets, eh? Cómo se dice doommies?"

Tommy stopped spraying, squeezing his eyes shut. "Dumdums," he said.

"Sí dumdums," Luchi said. "Hace un lío, no?"

Tommy shook his head. "They make a mess, he says."

"Sí," Luchi said. "Un mess"

Tommy took a deep breath, glanced up at the sky then forced himself to face Luchi. "You sure you don't want to just get rid of this thing?"

"Rid?" Luchi said.

"Of the car," Tommy said. "Just scrap it."

Luchi sucked his teeth, patting the roof. "Dis car es good, parcero. De Japan, no American. Es better."

"That's debatable," Tommy said.

Luchi narrowed his eyes. "Que coche tienes, Gringo?"

"Pontiac," Tommy said. "Firebird."

"Firebird," Luchi said, his eyes widening. "La película, Smokey and di Band-it, eh? Burt Reynolds?"

"You got it," Tommy said, surprised when the corner of his lips twitched towards a smile before settling back into a thin grim line. "He's actually the reason I bought it."

"Very good car," Luchi said, patting the Corolla again. "Japones es mejor."

"I'm just saying," Tommy said, pointing at the mess inside. "This might be a lost cause."

"I change dis," he said, waving Tommy off. "Di car, it will be like brand new, no problem."

Tommy squinted at Luchi. "Then—all due respect—why the fuck are we doing this?"

"Porque, Tommy," Luchi said, as if talking to a child. "We cannot go to ju casa like dis, eh?"

Tommy froze, his entire midsection clenching up the same way it had earlier in the car when the gun went off in his ears. Like two bricks smacked together. He started shaking, clenching his jaw in an effort to make it stop.

"My casa," Tommy said. "You—you're coming to my place?"

Luchi turned to the house. "No me puedo quedar aquí," he said. "So I stay with ju y Clara."

"You're going to stay with us," Tommy echoed.

"Pocos días," Luchi said. "Den ju go New York, y I go Colombia por que esta—" He waved his fingers at the sky. "—Dis is over."

"New York," Tommy said.

"Clara tambien, y Adam," Luchi said. "Tommy, todo bien. All es good."

Tommy looked in the car again. "I just—" Tommy shook himself, glanced over at Luchi. "I have to talk to Clara."

Luchi sucked his teeth. "Por que? Ju are di man, no? Ju must ask ju wife? Como un niño?"

Tommy said nothing. Luchi seemed confused. Then he smiled and nodded.

"Clara esta embarazada," Luchi said, rolling his eyes and putting his hands in front of his belly as if he were pregnant. "I forget. Children are good. I have two, en Colombia. Cuatro y seis."

Tommy forced a smile, raising the hose and blasting the inside of the car some more. When the water running down the driveway turned clear, Tommy dropped the hose and grabbed a pair of gloves and a sponge. He and Luchi alternated sponging and hosing until they could see out the rear windshield again, then they used the brushes to scrub the seats and carpet, dyed from their original beige to a deep, dark brown.

"Que mierda," Luchi said. "Ju are no fun, Gringo."

Hopping over to the driver's side, Luchi started the car and switched on the radio. A news broadcaster's voice wailed into the car speakers:

"—SUSPECTS IN TODAY'S GRISLY SHOOTING AT DADELAND MALL WHICH LEFT TWO DEAD AND AT LEAST SIX IN—"

Luchi twisted the dial. A second later he let out a whoop.

"Di man en black!" he yelled, pointing at the radio. "Johnny Cash es di man, eh? Te gusta?"

"Yeah," Tommy said.

"I like dis song very much," he said. Then, to Tommy's surprise, Luchi threw his head back and started singing loudly. "*Yippie I ohhh, yippie I yayyy…dose riders innn disguise.*"

The corners of Tommy's lips twitched again, a wonder. He kept scrubbing and the offensive smell faded, replaced with a lemon soapy scent. The radio switched to some Dolly Parton and the tension was just beginning to seep out of Tommy's shoulders when he ran the brush between the seats and found something glistening. He held it in his gloved palm. Gray and fleshy, like a rotting section of ground beef. Tommy tossed it at the grass, bracing against the nausea that came and went without incident. Tommy wondered for a moment if he was already getting used to this, then went back to scrubbing.

An hour later, Tommy climbed in the driver's seat, his hands raw, every muscle in his body tight. Luchi locked up the house and bounded over to the passenger's side. Checking through the smeared rear windshield, Tommy reversed out of the driveway and headed towards his apartment. The streets were empty on a work night, the lights blocking out the stars so it seemed like Tommy was driving through a ghost town floating in nothingness.

Pulling into his apartment complex, Tommy headed to the rear lot and parked. He reached for the key in the ignition and Luchi grabbed his forearm, pressing his own against it, slapping his other hand around the back of Tommy's neck. He pulled Tommy in close until their eyes were level. His hands were rough, hot. His breath stank of the laced-cigarette smoke. Tommy swallowed repeatedly until the urge to vomit went away. Luchi pointed at Tommy's temple, then his.

"We are parceros now, Tommy," he said. "Ju okay, I okay. Ju no okay, I no okay. Sí?"

Tommy willed himself to stop shaking. His arm steadied and he nodded. Luchi let him go, leaning against the door.

"Go now," he said. "Talk to Clara. Make it okay."

Tommy climbed out of the car and slammed the door, stumbling against the side of the car and bracing there for a second. He waited until his stomach settled and his head stopped spinning before heading upstairs and almost walking past his apartment. He paused at the front door with his keys raised. Lowering his arm, he looked over the railing at the Corolla idling in the lot. Luchi stared up at him. Tommy faced the door again, closed his eyes and heard the bricks slamming in his ear, saw the man's right eye disappear, smelled the lemon soapy scent mixed with the fumes of death.

Twisting the key in the lock, Tommy opened the door just as Clara came racing down the hallway holding her belly.

"Damn, babe. I thought you guys said it would only take a couple—" Clara froze, her eyes widening in horror. "What the hell happened to you?!"

Tommy looked down at his red-stained shirt. When he looked back up, his eyes were filled with tears, his jaw trembling.

"I got laid off," he said, then collapsed on the floor.

Assassins Open Fire in Dadeland Mall Liquor Store, *July 12, 1979*

Realtor Murdered At Open-House; Drug-Related, *August 12, 1979*

Dolphins Down Bills; Fins 20-0 Against Buffalo in '70s, *October 15, 1979*

Five Policemen Suspended in Death of Motorcyclist, *December 28, 1979*

Emilia Brathwaite, Miami Tribune, Metro

Five Public Safety Department Officers were arrested today in connection with the death of thirty-three-year-old motorcyclist Arthur McDuffie. Four of the officers—Isaac Davis, Milton Wyatt, Wilford Hanley and Arturo Menendez—are being charged with manslaughter. A fifth officer—Sergeant Horace Ewing II—is charged with being an accessory after the fact.

Authorities investigating the incident charge that the officers stopped Arthur McDuffie on the night of December 17th following a high-speed chase. The officers are accused of savagely beating McDuffie during the stop using heavy-duty flashlights and nightsticks. Investigators say the officers then turned their weapons on McDuffie's motorcycle, destroying the vehicle and reporting the incident as a traffic accident.

"This was no accident," said Homicide Captain Daniel Murphy, part of the PSD team investigating the matter. "The accident report was filed as a cover for what really went on that night."

According to Captain Murphy, the chase for McDuffie began after the insurance agent ran a red light. The initial report stated that McDuffie lost control of his motorcycle and crashed, losing his helmet and striking his head on the concrete pavement. McDuffie was rushed to the hospital where he slipped into a coma. Five days later, he was dead.

"His skull was cracked like an egg," said Dr. Lewis Adams, Dade County's Chief Deputy Medical Examiner. "Whoever did it used a long, heavy blunt object and hit him repeatedly. This was a hell of a beating."

All five officers involved have been suspended without pay. Four of the officers were booked downtown at the Dade County Jail and released on $12,000 bonds. The fifth officer—Hanley—is reportedly out of town.

Virginia Klein Goodman, the McDuffie family attorney, has filed a multi-million-dollar wrongful death suit against both Dade County officials and the Public Safety Department.

Hundreds Weep at Funeral for Arthur McDuffie, *Dec 29, 1979*

McDuffie Trial Moved from Dade County, *March 1, 1980*

Black Leaders Fear McDuffie Trial in Tampa, *March 13, 1980*

Carter Agrees to Accept 3,500 Cuban Refugees, *April 14, 1980*

Protestors: Send Cubans Elsewhere: 'They'll Take Our Jobs', *May 3, 1980*

Controlled Chaos: Day 17 of 23,000-Person Cuban Exodus, *May 8, 1980*

Retarded People and Criminals Included in Cuban Exodus, *May 11, 1980*

Officials Estimate 50,000 Cuban Refugees and Counting, *May 12, 1980*

McDuffie Beating Called 'Justifiable Force', *May 16, 1980*

Magic Johnson Drops 42; Lakers Down 76ers for NBA Title, *May 16, 1980*

Part Two: The Riot
Saturday, May 17, 1980

"Early one morning while making the rounds
I took a shot of cocaine and I shot my woman down
I went right home and I went to bed
I stuck that loving .44 beneath my head."

Johnny Cash, "Cocaine Blues"

"Ain't No Stoppin Us Now!
We're on the move!
Ain't No Stoppin Us Now!
We've got the groove!"

**McFadden & Whitehead,
"Ain't No Stoppin Us Now"**

1.

Ramon had nothing but a sandwich and the clothes on his back when he got to the boat. Raising his nose, he sniffed the ocean, a scent he hadn't been allowed to enjoy in the three years since his article on El Jefe was published. Three long years that inexplicably ended this morning when guards grabbed him from his cell, drove him to the Mariel port and pushed him towards the 36-foot *Olo Mundo*. The boat rocked side to side as dozens of passengers boarded. Ramon stood at the stern, listening to the *Olo Mundo*'s protesting captain. The boat was only meant for his seven family members, he said. Not the other forty-something people Cuban soldiers had shoved onboard. The soldiers laughed as if the captain had told a great joke and gave the man two choices: leave with everybody or leave with nobody. The captain reluctantly climbed back on his boat and started the engines.

Waves crashed against the ship's starboard as the soldiers guided the *Olo Mundo* out into the straits for the eight-hour ride back to Florida. Patrols assured everybody through shrill bullhorns that the seas would calm once they got underway. Huddling with the crowd on the deck, Ramon looked out at the eight-foot chop and thought otherwise. Eventually he and some others headed below-deck to the cabin.

The sun had just cracked the horizon when one of the *Olo Mundo*'s twin engines died.

Ramon felt them slowing to a crawl, several adults and children crouched around him in the belly of the boat. He glanced out a porthole just as a wave slammed into the ship hard enough to make his stomach lurch.

Another wave hit right after, then another.

The *Olo Mundo* dragged ten feet south before capsizing, tossing everybody in the cabin upside down.

Screams echoed in the small space, rattling Ramon's ear drums as he tried to balance on footing that felt as unstable as the ocean itself. Water burst through the door, filling the cabin. A mother held her baby above the water, two children next to her flailing to stay afloat.

Ramon turned back to the porthole, grabbed onto a metal railing and dug his heels in beneath the rising water. Using his weight as momentum, he kicked the glass, then kicked it again. On the third kick a crack formed. Gathering all his strength, Ramon launched himself at the porthole and the glass shattered, water pouring into the cabin. He'd barely lowered his leg when one of the other adults bolted past him, jumping feet first into the rushing water and jamming his entire body into the hole. Ramon cursed and pushed the guy's shoulders. The man screamed. Ramon pushed harder and the man slid through, leaving behind bloody shards of glass in the porthole.

Ramon motioned the parents and children over, helping a mustachioed man and his daughter. A couple pushed through with a baby, another man with a young boy and girl. Ramon urged them all to hold their breaths and swim straight for the surface. The room continued to fill as he helped the last person out, his head barely above water.

Taking a lingering look around the almost submerged cabin, Ramon held his breath and swam out the porthole.

Breaking the surface, Ramon grabbed onto a piece of plastic floating nearby, catching his breath and taking in the scene. The upturned blue hull of the *Olo Mundo* sank, surrounded by flailing bodies trying to find purchase. Two of the ship's fifty-gallon gas drums had spilled out into the sea, the sickening stench filling Ramon's nostrils. A gas slick surrounded the boat in psychedelic colors, the acidic combination of salt water and fuel burning his eyes. A man nearby clung to an upturned table. Another splashed towards an errant life jacket, grabbed it and put it on a screaming little girl. Securing the straps, he kissed the little girl on the forehead then seemed to deflate, sinking below the water's surface. The girl screamed for him. He did not appear again until minutes later, floating on his stomach thirty feet away. He bobbed for a bit then disappeared again for good.

Ramon wondered then about sharks.

A young woman swam towards him with a toddler held above her head. Ramon kept one hand on the plastic holding him afloat, reaching the other out for her. Instead of taking it, she handed him the baby, then sank below the surface, staring at her child until the water consumed her.

Ramon put the baby on the plastic. The baby screamed. Seconds later, helicopter rotors approached in the distance. Search lights appeared, beaming off the *Olo Mundo*'s sinking prow. Ramon held the baby in place, the skin on his arms ablaze. A few feet away, a sobbing man gripped one of the empty butane tanks bobbing in the waves.

Hovering above the wreckage, the helicopter lowered its winch, pulling survivors up one by one. The helicopter came to Ramon and the winch descended. He grabbed it and cried out as the skin on his hands sheared off on the metal wire. Gritting through the pain, Ramon tied the winch around the toddler's waist and yanked it, watching as they pulled her up.

He waited for the winch to come back down.

He waited, and he waited some more.

He looked up through blurry eyes and saw the rescuer in the helicopter looking down at him. Saw the sadness in the man's face as he held up the winch wire, broken and frayed at the end. The last bit of the boat sank below the sea and the helicopter flew away, leaving Ramon and a couple dozen others splashing around.

Eventually Ramon's arms and legs gave out and he sank into the ocean, watching the sunrise through a cloud of saltwater.

He had thought about this moment for a very long time and was surprised when all he felt was relief.

That it was all over.

2.

Rig poured the steaming water from the pot into the bathtub, testing it with his pinky. Satisfied, he put the pot back in the kitchen and returned to the bathroom, closing the door and stripping down. Sliding his long frame into the tub, he grabbed a chalky bar of soap and lathered up, studying the blackened grout between the gray wall tiles. A knock at the bathroom door startled him out of his reverie.

Rig's mother poked her head in with a towel draped across her shoulders.

"Hurry up," she said.

"I just got in," he said.

"Rig, I gotta get to work," she said. "Hurry up."

She closed the door and Rig muttered to himself, washing soap off his arms and legs. He opened the drain and the grayish water swirled down. Climbing out, he dried himself in front of the dusty mirror, staring at his awkward reflection, hair wet and hanging in curls to his shoulders.

"Rig, hurry up!"

Rig opened the door to his mother standing with one hand on her hip. She nudged him aside, leaving him standing in the hallway damp and perturbed.

Dressing in his typical black shorts and t-shirt, Rig donned his gold crucifix and tucked it under his collar, turning on the 13-inch black and white TV his Tia Magda gave them after his dad went away. He sat on a stack of milk crates, twisting the dial to CBS and slapping the side of the TV until the image cleared. A rerun of *Fat Albert* started, the one where Shawn walks around with his dad's gun, Albert snitches on him and Shawn almost blows his hand off. Halfway through the episode Rig's mom stepped out of the bathroom and retreated to her room. Seconds later, Otis Redding crooned from the radio, drowning out the TV.

Rig scowled at his mom as she danced her way back to the living room wearing a blue blouse and gray slacks. She grabbed a pair of sneakers by the front door, humming as she slipped them on.

"I can't hear the TV," Rig said.

"What?" she said.

"I can't hear!" Rig yelled, pointing at the TV.

His mom glanced at the cartoon and waved him off, opening the fridge and pulling out some bread, lunch meat and a jar of spread. She sang and swayed as she made her sandwich, her thick hair hanging in knotty strands around her face. Rig watched her and relaxed against the wall, his scowl fading. Wrapping her sandwich in aluminum foil, his mom returned everything to the fridge, glancing at Rig and catching him staring.

"What?" she said.

Rig shook his head and looked back at the TV. The song on the radio ended and a commercial for a car dealership started. Rig's mom walked into the room and the radio shut off. She came back out and stood in front of him with her hands on her hips.

"You visiting Papi with me tomorrow?"

Rig said nothing, touching the crucifix under his shirt.

"Rig."

"Do I gotta?" he asked.

"Do you *have to*," she corrected. "And yes, you do but—"

"Then why you even asking," Rig muttered.

"Rigoberto Lopez-Campbell," she said. "He is your father."

Rig stared at the TV.

"Keep acting like he did something to you," she grumbled. "He ain't do anything *to* you."

"*Didn't* do anything," Rig grumbled.

"Boy don't get smart with me!"

Rig slouched his shoulders.

"How many times does he have to apologize?" she said.

Rig pulled at a strand of his hair. His mother sighed and went muttering down the hallway, reemerging with an elastic band stretched across her fingers.

"I'm gonna be at the shop 'til close," she said, putting her hair up. "Your tia's picking me up in a bit and she's staying for dinner. Maybe she can talk some sense into you."

Rig rolled his eyes. His mom stomped over to the TV and switched it off, cutting his protests short with a steady brown finger.

"You need to watch that attitude," she barked. "You think I forgot that shit you pulled last week?"

"I was watching that," Rig said.

"Boy don't play with me!"

"Mommy," Rig whined.

"Save it," she said. "I'm tired of these constant calls about you fight—"

"They started it!"

"So you *had* to finish it?!"

"Idiot just kept poking me," Rig said, crossing his arms.

"I don't care! You walk away!"

"I told him to stop and he didn't," Rig said. "I hate bullies."

"So you hit him?"

"What am I supposed to do?" Rig yelled.

His mother's finger shot back in the air, her voice falling to a growl. "Watch your tone. Don't make me smack you."

"You always sayin' listen to Papi," Rig said, lowering his voice. "And he always sayin' stick up for myself. I just did what Papi said."

Rig's mother stood with her fists balled at her side, a mixture of anger and sadness in her eyes. Someone knocked at the door and she waved him off.

"I can't," she said. "Gonna be late for work messing around with you."

Grabbing her purse and sandwich from the counter, she opened the front door and Tia Magda poked her head in, her dyed-red hair pulled up in a tight bun that looked like a doorknob.

"Por qué los gritos?" she said. "I can hear you guys from the courtyard."

"Your nephew is—" his mother started, cutting herself off with a wave. "I don't have time for this right now. I gotta get to work."

Magda looked at Rig "This about your dad?"

Rig shrugged.

Magda looked at Rig's mother and rubbed her shoulder. His mother fiddled with her keys, looking at Rig with something like longing in her eyes.

"Don't cause any trouble," she said.

"I don't," Rig said.

His mother nodded and walked out. Tia Magda smiled at him and Rig smiled back. She glanced behind her then whispered at him.

"We'll talk later," she said. "But I get it. Believe me, I get it."

"Tell *her* then," Rig said.

"She's your mom," she said. "I get her too."

Rig rolled his eyes and his aunt smiled at him, closing the door and leaving him alone. He walked over to the TV and turned it back on. A minute later he sighed and turned it off again, studying the living room and his bed. Rays of sunshine streamed through the slits between the window blinds, falling on a roach scurrying up the wall behind the couch. Rig threw his sneaker and hit it dead center, leaving a brown smear on the wall. Wiping the residue on the carpet, he slipped his shoe back on and pulled up his mattress, grabbing the wad of bills that lay there next to a paperback Hardy Boys novel. He checked himself in the bathroom mirror then walked out of the apartment, locking the door with a single loose key.

Strolling through the courtyard out to 62nd street, Rig headed for the gas station on 65th. An abandoned lot appeared on his right, a caterpillar on the sidewalk crawling towards a patch of grass on the property. Rig crouched to get a closer look. His shadow fell across the caterpillar and it stopped moving, raising the front half of its body in the air. Its legs moved rhythmically, the wave-like motion hypnotizing.

Dropping back down to the concrete, it resumed crawling.

Footsteps drew Rig's attention away from the caterpillar and he looked up as a man wearing jeans and a tank top approached at a brisk pace. Rig opened his mouth to stop him but nothing came out, and he watched in horror as the back of the man's shoe came right down on the caterpillar with a slight crunch. The man looked down at Rig without breaking stride. The green smear on the sidewalk stood a couple of inches from the grass.

Rig glared after the man as the man turned the corner at the end of the block and disappeared.

Continuing towards the gas station, Rig looked back every couple of seconds until the green smear was indistinguishable from everything around it.

3.

Ralph was sipping coffee in the kitchen—Mikey sitting across the living room watching cartoons and eating a box of animal crackers—when the large rotary phone bolted to the wall above the stove rang. Ralph picked it up, the voice on the other end speaking before the receiver got to his ear.

"—the paper?"

"Hey Danny," Ralph said.

"Did you see the paper?"

"Not yet," Ralph said. "Was just about to grab it."

"Read the cover story," Murphy said. "Did Pullman contact you about the vics in Spring Garden?"

"Not directly, dispatch called. I'm meeting him now." Ralph paused. "What's got you so worked up?"

"Brathwaite wrote another goddamn article." Murphy said, papers shuffling in the background. "I don't know who keeps talking to her but I thought I made it clear she is no longer a friend of the department."

Ralph glanced at his son. "What's it saying?"

"Between her making us all look like assholes and the fucking FBI gutting the goddamn division," Murphy said. "I don't know how this city expects us to do our jobs. It's down to you, Weis, Fry. The most senior detectives I've got on staff now."

"We're building though," Ralph said. "Your words."

"Gonna be hard to build anything with the fucking Emilias of the world yanking the rug out every morning edition."

Ralph smiled. "I remember you telling me once to be nice to her."

Murphy grunted. "I also told you she's a fucking hawk. Secure the scene with Pullman then report in."

"Got it," Ralph said.

Ralph placed the phone down and called a goodbye out to Amanda. She yelled something back that Ralph couldn't make out. He hesitated, almost went down the hall towards her then walked over to Mikey instead, ruffling his son's hair. He walked out the front door, locking up behind him and pulling a pack of

Kools from his jacket. Lighting one up, he grabbed the gray bundle lying on the walkway, shaking the newspaper open on the half-wall surrounding the front patio. A headline caught his eye, tucked in the bottom corner beneath another article about the McDuffie trial:

Murders Up 61 Percent, Arrests Off
By Emilia Brathwaite

Ralph finished his smoke and folded the paper under his arm, flicking the cigarette on the sidewalk.

Climbing into his Plymouth, Ralph tossed the newspaper in the passenger seat and rolled the windows down, reversing out of the driveway. He lit up another Kool as he weaved through traffic with the windows open, wind ruffling his hair, the palm trees in the median casting flashing shadows across the windshield. Merging onto I-95, he drove ten more minutes then exited, pulling up outside a modest home in Spring Garden. He parked across from the half dozen cruisers and vans crowding the street corner, placing his police placard on the dashboard. Climbing out, he ducked under some yellow tape, passing a medical examiner's van with two wheels up on the curb, a couple of patrols smoking cigarettes against the side. Ralph threw them a salute and hopped the steps to the front porch as Detective Terry Pullman stepped outside, pulling off a pair of plastic gloves with a grim expression set on his reddened face. He saw Ralph and raised his eyebrows. Two years behind Ralph, Terry looked even younger, his skin unmarred by either wrinkles or scars. His forehead glistened with sweat, beads running down his thin nose. Terry pulled out a handkerchief and swiped his face.

"Might wanna take a sec, Sarge," he said to Ralph. "Before you head in."

"And why would I want to do that?" Ralph asked.

"Pretty grisly," he said. "Never seen anything like it."

Ralph looked out at the street, the bright sky overhead, heat shimmering off the concrete. The neighborhood was nice, well-landscaped trees and bushes lining the sidewalks. Ralph pulled out his cigarettes and shook out two, handing one to Terry. Terry produced a lighter, sparked his up then held the flame out for Ralph. Ralph coughed lightly on his first puff, then took another.

"What am I walking into?" he asked.

"Adult male and female in the main bedroom," Terry said. "Can't tell the exact cause of death yet 'cause…well, you'll see."

"Need to get used to detailed descriptions, detective," Ralph said.

Terry shot him a side-eye. "Mail on the dining table says Alvin and Paola Montes," he said. "Got an address book too."

"You logged them?"

Terry nodded. "Adolescent male, same condition in the second bedroom, assuming he's—"

"They did a kid?" Ralph said, his eyes flashing with disgust.

"Yeah," he said. "Thought dispatch told you."

"I'd remember if they did," Ralph said, finishing his cigarette and tossing the butt in the bushes. "Jesus Christ, they're doing kids now."

Ralph pulled a small bottle of Old Spice from his jacket and shook some onto his fingertips, swiping it under his nose. He held the bottle out for Terry who did the same. They each pulled pairs of latex gloves from their pockets, snapped them on and walked inside. Steady nervous chatter filled the living room almost as completely as the stench of death. Pausing in the foyer, Ralph took slow deep breaths until the nausea subsided then followed Terry past the milling officers to a narrow hallway with three doors.

The first door led to a bedroom with techs buzzing around. Ralph entered and froze, his stomach turning. A tech in a white coat to his left dusted an area on the floor near a disheveled closet. Two other coats took pictures of the bare queen-size bed in the center of the room. The bed itself was wood frame, lion's feet knobs at either end of the large headboard. A woman lay naked on top of the mattress, cotton sheets tied to the knobs securing her ankles and wrists. Her eyes and mouth were open, a trickle of brown running from her lips to her left ear. A ragged slash stretched beneath her chin from one side of her neck to the other, the mattress beneath her soaked a brownish red.

Directly across from the woman, a man sat in a chair facing the bed, his arms and legs also tied to the bed with sheets. His head lay back, his mouth wide open. Two gaping bloody holes yawned where his eyes should have been. On his lap lay two severed eyeballs, glistening in the sunlight streaming through the cracks between the blinds. His throat was also slit, the front of his formerly white tank top drenched brown.

The smell—a mixture of blood and excrement—watered Ralph's eyes. He blinked away tears. A pinkish-gray blob lay on the woman's left breast. Ralph looked back at Terry, pointing at the blob.

"Is that—"

"Her tongue," Terry said.

Ralph blinked. "Where's the kid?"

Terry backed out of the room and the two headed past the bathroom to another bedroom at the end of the hall. A stone-faced officer stood outside, the door ajar. A tech moved around inside. Terry pushed the door open, motioning for the coat to give them the room. The man stepped out and Terry entered, leaning against a small blue nightstand and crossing his arms over his expansive chest. Ralph stood just inside the doorway, surveying the single twin bed and the little boy lying on top. He couldn't have been more than eight or nine, his scrawny frame sprawled across the mattress, legs hanging off the edge. Thin brown hair and a small nose. Ralph stared at the boy's face until he looked like Mikey, his son.

Shaking himself, Ralph focused on the boy's injuries. The slash across his neck, his Flintstones sheets soaked through with blood. Lying on top of his t-shirt on the smiling cartoon face of Mighty Mouse were two ragged pieces of flesh. Bloody holes gleamed in the overhead light where the boy's ears should have been. His eyes were open and glassy.

Ralph looked back down the hall, towards the other bedroom.

"Tongue," he said. "Eyes, ears."

"Couldn't just kill 'em," Terry said. "Had to mutilate 'em."

"The three monkeys," Ralph said. "See no evil, hear no evil, speak no evil."

Terry raised an eyebrow. Ralph headed back to the other bedroom, Terry following behind. A black nightstand stood next to the dead woman on the bed, a thin layer of white dust coating the surface beneath a scattering of pills. Ralph swiped a trail through the dust with a latex-covered finger then picked one of the pills up, turning to the techs.

"We know what these are?" he asked.

"Looks like 'ludes," one of the men said. "Can't be sure 'til we test."

"No signs of resistance," Terry said. "Makes sense whoever did this drugged them up."

"We'll know more when we run the blood samples," the tech said.

"You get this too?" Ralph asked, pointing at the powder.

The tech nodded and Ralph squatted next to the nightstand, opening the single drawer to find a bible and a six-shooter revolver. He pulled a pen out of his pocket and used it to pick up the gun by the trigger guard, turning and holding it up. The tech held out a plastic evidence bag and Ralph dropped it in, looking back in the drawer. In the spot where the gun was, an edge of the drawer's bottom looked frayed. Ralph reached in and pulled at it. The bottom shifted a little so Ralph took out the bible, dropping it on the bed next to the dead woman. Getting a good grip, he pulled the drawer's false bottom up and out. Ralph placed the thin piece of wood next to the bible and pulled a large plastic bag of white powder out of the drawer, followed by four thick stacks of cash and another smaller bag filled with pills.

Terry walked over as Ralph laid the items out. His eyes went wide and he stared at the dead couple with renewed purpose.

"Guess we got motive," he said.

"Maybe," Ralph said, motioning to the tech. "Let's get this bagged up too."

The coat went to work. Ralph peered closer at the woman. She was young, early-twenties maybe, Hispanic and beautiful, thick brown hair splayed around her head. She lay with her ankles about a foot apart. One of the techs had bagged her tongue while Ralph was in the kid's room, leaving a slashed red stain across her left nipple.

"Can we get—" Ralph said, turning to nobody in particular. "We need anything else, or can we cover her up? Get a little bit of dignity in here?"

One of the techs produced a gray blanket and Ralph covered the woman, tucking the blanket below the cavernous wound in her neck. He turned to find Terry staring at the contents of the nightstand as the coat bagged them—the powder, the pills, the cash—with an unmistakable glint in his eye.

"What is it?" Ralph asked.

Terry looked at him and shoved his hands in his pockets. "Nothing," he said. "This is just batshit crazy."

Ralph motioned Terry out into the hallway.

"You find anything else?" Ralph asked. "Before I arrived?"

"Didn't really get to look around much," he said. "Everybody got caught up with the bodies the moment we got here."

Ralph nodded, taking in the sickly expression on Terry's face. "Remember your first case?" he said, giving his partner a small grin. "Thought they were all gonna be that easy, huh?"

Terry snorted a laugh. "Fucker shoots a guy in the head and can't keep his mouth shut to save his *life*." Terry put up air quotes. "'I'm tired of the black man fucking up the white man's world.' Guy was out of a movie."

"Nut jobs are easy," Ralph said, looking around the room. "Whoever did this was calculated. No weapon, I'm assuming."

"Nothing," he said. "Told the patrols to keep an eye out."

"No signs of struggle, no break-in." Ralph walked back to the living room. "They had to have known whoever did this."

"So we canvas the neighborhood," Terry said. "Check that address book, look for known associates."

"My guess is these two weren't very social," Ralph said. "We know who made the call?"

"Anonymous."

"Of course," Ralph muttered, pointing at one of the techs as he walked out of the room with an evidence bag. "Get everything to the M.E. soon as you guys are done." He pulled Terry towards the front door. "We gotta get to the precinct. Murphy wants to meet."

"No problem," Terry said. "Maybe you can help me get started with all this paperwork when we're done."

"Seniority," Ralph said over his shoulder. "Means I can tell you to go fuck yourself on that one, Detective."

4.

Sticking her purse under her seat, Tina climbed out of Emilia's car, shading her eyes as they walked the couple of blocks towards the Orange Bowl lot.

"Are we even allowed in there?" Tina asked, glancing at Emilia.

Emilia looked up at the stadium, the giant structure looming larger with each step. She held out her press badge.

"Powerful thing right here."

The sun beamed, both women sweating seconds after exiting the car.

"How long are these people gonna have to stay here?" Tina asked.

"The honorable Mayor Burgos would be a good person to ask about that," Emilia muttered, sticking a pen in her hair. "If he were actually concerned with being mayor."

Tina chuckled. "Not a fan?"

Emilia smiled. "I'm not a fan of his priorities."

"My mom and aunt adore him," Tina said. "Think that's got more to do with him being from San Juan."

Emilia nodded. "How about you?"

"I don't care either way," Tina said. "Politics give me a headache."

"I don't hate him," Emilia said. "I just don't trust people whose entire motivation in life is money."

"We passed by his place near the Omni the other day," Tina said. "It's honestly ridiculous."

"Please, enlighten me," Emilia said. "What does one need with thirteen bathrooms? Does he have thirteen penises? Thirteen anuses?"

Tina laughed. "Thirteen anuses. Imagine."

Emilia wrinkled her nose. "I'd rather not."

They crossed the street headed towards the crowd of bodies surrounding the gated lot just outside the storied stadium. Home to the Miami Dolphins, the Orange Bowl had enough parking and bathrooms to house the hundreds of people a day arriving from Cuba. Concession stands now served as service stations. Thousands of refugees slept on canvas cots, if lucky; blankets spread on dirt floors if not. Stamped on the stadium walls above them, the Dolphins and University of Miami insignias were a stark contrast to the drab tents populating the lots outside. A layer of police and National Guardsmen stood outside the fence regulating the crowd. Inside, people stood in various lines, waiting for everything from pillows to food.

"I've been meaning to ask," Tina said. "Do you know who the Tribune sent down to cover Mariel?"

Emilia shook her head. "Editors on that beat are keeping them anonymous, just in case. Apparently Castro's got spies everywhere." Emilia lowered her voice. "Between you and me though, I haven't seen Julie around in like a month." She shrugged. "Just saying."

"You couldn't pay me enough to go over there right now," Tina said. "Cuban spies. Sounds like some James Bond story."

Emilia paused, looking up at the sky. "I ever tell you my first husband worked for the CIA?"

Tina stopped midstride, facing Emilia. "Excuse me, what?"

"One day I'm picking up some groceries, using his car," Emilia said. "Go to put the bag in the trunk except when I open it, the thing is filled with guns."

"Guns?"

"Dozens of them," she said. "Rifles, shotguns, handguns."

"Holy shit," Tina said, shaking her head. "That's—what'd you do?"

"Confronted him, obviously," she said. "And he tells me yeah, his job as a manager at Publix is real. But he's *also* got this CIA gig. The guns were for some anti-Castro activists. Checked his trunk a couple days later and they were gone, had no choice but to believe him."

"That is an insane story, Emilia," Tina said. "Truly. Like, holy shit insane."

"Probably one of the reasons it didn't work out," Emilia said, continuing towards the stadium. "Though I like to think it was the drinking and cheating."

"Every time you tell me about your past I get tired," Tina said. "I haven't been through half of what you've been through."

"Stick around," she said. "You'll get there. Life has a way of…piling up."

Approaching a table with a platoon of servicemen, they cut their conversation short just as a commotion started at the fence, a man bolting for the compound and scurrying to get over and in. A few Guardsmen dragged him down, slapped zip-ties on his wrist and hauled him off. The soldiers in front of Emilia and Tina laughed.

"Craziest shit I ever seen," one of them said.

"That been happening a lot?" Emilia asked, handing her press badge over to the soldier.

"Couple times a day, at least," he said, studying the placard. "You two work for the paper?"

"Yes," Emilia said, nodding at Tina. "She's one of our photographers. Tell me, why are they trying to get in?"

"Bunch of reasons," the man said. "Some got family in there. A lot of them are just trying to help. Crazy, ain't it? Talk about taking care of your own." The man finished jotting down their info and handed Emilia back her press badge, pointing to a row of tents on the south side of the lot. "You ladies stay in the designated area. You'll see the signs."

They thanked him and walked towards the fences. Tina felt eyes and looked over at two patrol officers glaring at her and Emilia. Emilia looked over too, stopping in her tracks. The cops shook their heads and turned their backs to the women, leaning into each other conspiratorially.

"Take it they recognized me," Emilia said.

Tina frowned. "What's their problem?"

"Write enough bad things about police and you're bound to get the high school treatment," she said. "Even if everything you say is true."

Entering the compound, Emilia pulled Tina towards the first row of tents. They paused outside one and Tina peered through her camera lens at a brown-skinned woman sitting on a plastic chair. Emilia tapped her pen against her cheek and studied her journal, each page filled margin to margin on both sides. Tina snapped a photo of a black number eight stitched above one of the open tent flaps. The woman in the tent looked at her and Tina seized the opportunity to take her picture. She lowered her camera and held up her hand. The woman remained expressionless, leaning back on the plastic chair with a faint squeak.

"They're going to have to clear this place before football season," Emilia said, looking around as if she were the one in charge of that particular task.

"I think the city's got a lot more to worry about than football," Tina said.

"You'd think so," Emilia said. "Until the sports junkies lose their bets."

Tina snapped a pic of the stadium, lowering the camera. "You're right, this city's priorities really are messed up."

Emilia touched Tina's arm. "I confess another reason I brought you along. You up for translating?"

Tina shrugged. "Sure."

"Just gotta find the right subject," Emilia muttered, tapping her pen against her lip. She spotted a man speaking to a group of thirty or so people and drifted over, Tina on her tail. The orator was brown skinned with slicked back hair. His hands did not stop moving as he spoke. He wore tan slacks and a brown belt that looked new. The sleeves on his buttoned t-shirt were rolled up.

"What's he saying?" Emilia asked.

"He's talking about the differences between Cuba and Miami," Tina said. She listened for a couple of seconds. "Telling them how to find a job and get a room. You want him?"

"No," Emilia said, searching again. "I need a family."

Emilia grabbed Tina's arm and pulled her down another row of tents. Tina snapped pictures as they passed, Emilia peering at the many faces. The rows stood twenty to thirty tents long, with more rows than Tina could see without climbing above the lot. The air seemed clogged with dust, each tent covered in a layer of grayish-brown soot. An old man lay on a cot with his eyes open, staring at nothing. A couple of barefoot kids ran by chasing a half-deflated soccer ball rolling unevenly through the dirt.

Emilia stopped in front of a tent where a man and woman sat with two small kids, a girl and a boy. The kids' shirts were stained, their skin ashy. The mother laid between them on a cot, the man standing sentry just outside the tent. He made eye contact with first Emilia then Tina, flashing a smile that revealed a couple of missing teeth.

"Them," Emilia said.

Tina let her camera hang around her neck, waving at the man as she approached. He shoved his hands in his pockets and nodded.

"Buenos días," Tina said, motioning towards Emilia. "Mi amiga aquí es una reportera de las noticias de Miami Tribune."

The man glanced at Emilia and raised his hand in greeting.

"Le gustaría hacerle algunas preguntas." Tina swept her arms around the parking lot. "Ella está escribiendo un artículo sobre este lugar."

"Sí," the man said, nodding. "No problem."

"Bueno," Tina said. "Como se llama?"

"Jose," he said, turning to his wife and kids. "Mi esposa, Lucia. Mis hijos, Javier y Pilar."

"Qué hermoso," Tina said, smiling. "Si no es demasiado problema, nos gustaría oír de su viaje aquí."

The man's expression went dark and he said nothing at first, just stared off into the distance as if sifting through his thoughts.

Emilia leaned towards Tina, keeping her voice low. "What'd you say?"

"I asked him to tell us about his trip here," Tina whispered.

Jose started speaking slowly, deliberately, gaining momentum as the details spilled forth. A minute later Emilia and Tina couldn't shut him up if they wanted. Tina translated as fast as she could, holding the man's eyes as he told them about the fishing village forty minutes outside of Havana where the only distinct landmark was the Cuban Naval Academy, a colonial relic sitting in the local hills. This was Mariel harbor, they'd been told by the soldiers ushering them onto a boat. And that endless expanse of sea out there was the Florida Straits, a straight line from Cuba to Key West. He talked about the fishing charter named Big Baby, how they boarded it ahead of another 150 people, the last of which were clearly not right in the head. He talked about the other boats waiting for families, the people on them sunburned and dehydrated. Dozens of boats arrived each hour, while barely any left. Patrols floated around the area, soldiers with machine guns and Soviet flags on their armbands. Cuban citizens in tourism skiffs went around charging high prices for ham sandwiches, bags of shrimp, boxes of chicken and rice and quarts of watered-down rum.

Jose would not talk about the actual boat ride, not in front of his kids. But, he told Tina, the trip took an entire day, sunrise to sunset, and it was the longest day of his entire life.

It was then his daughter piped up, excited about a prized detail.

"Sabíamos que estábamos en los Estados Unidos," she said, grinning. "Cuando vimos la máquina de Coca Cola en Key West."

"What's she saying?" Emilia hissed.

Tina smiled. "She says she knew they were here when they saw the Coca-Cola machine in Key West."

Emilia jotted it in her notes.

Tina faced Jose. "Cuanto tiempo llevas aquí?"

"Una semana," Jose said. He nodded at the children's mother, sitting next to them. "Estamos esperando al tío de mi esposa que él pueda patrocinarnos y podamos irnos."

"They've been here a week," Tina said. "They're waiting for his wife's uncle to sponsor them so they can go." She looked at Emilia. "Anything else?"

"No, that's good," Emilia said.

Tina turned back to the family. "Gracias," she said, clasping her hands together. "Has sido de gran ayuda."

"No," Jose said, touching his wife's shoulder. "Es agradable hablar con alguien que no está tan de caído como nosotros."

His wife nodded, the hint of a smile touching the corner of her mouth.

Tina and Emilia thanked the family again and returned to perusing the rows of tents. They stopped twice more to interview a couple with no children and a single mom with two before heading out the front gates.

Outside, they passed a payphone and Emilia tapped Tina's shoulder.

"Get it started," she said, holding out her car keys. "Gonna call this in."

Tina took the keys and Emilia walked away. Looking up at the looming stadium, Tina raised her camera and took a few wide shots before heading back to Emilia's car. She climbed in the passenger seat and turned the car on, packing up her camera and pulling out her notebook. She was jotting some notes when Emilia walked up and climbed behind the wheel, opening her own notebook to scribble some more. Their pen scratches filled the silence between them.

Emilia finished and closed her notebook. "You remember your first day?"

Tina looked over. "What about it?"

"That dress you were wearing," Emilia said, smiling. "And those shoes. I can't believe you ran around in those."

"Like I knew what was gonna happen," Tina said.

"Oh, you looked gorgeous," Emilia said.

"I just wanted to have a relaxing afternoon," Tina said. "I didn't expect a goddamn shootout."

Emilia looked her up and down. "A year later, now look at you."

Tina looked down at her outfit: faded jeans, plain black t-shirt, black boots laced tight.

"So you're saying I look like shit," Tina said.

Emilia rolled her eyes, looking out the window at the stadium. Her smile faded. "There's this thick air of sadness around this place," she said.

"I know what you mean," Tina said. "It's stifling."

"I just hope these people end up getting somewhere. Anywhere but here."

"Me too."

Emilia put her notebook away and grabbed the pack of Virginia Slims off the dashboard, shaking two out. She handed one to Tina and they both lit up. Emilia switched on the radio and they settled back, smoking to Reba McEntire.

"Gotta make a stop," Emilia said. "Drop something off at a friends, if you care to join. Head to the office after."

Tina looked at her watch. "I've gotta get some work done before class."

"When's that?"

"Seven thirty."

"Plenty of time," Emilia said. "How you liking it? School?"

Tina shrugged. "Kind of boring actually. The professor drones. And there's too much homework."

Emilia laughed, putting the car in gear. "Sounds like college to me."

Tina gave the Orange Bowl one last glance as it faded into the distance.

5.

Clara grabbed the back of Tommy's neck and mashed her lips against his, moving in rhythm with him, faster and harder until Tommy arched his back and grunted. Clara wiggled her hips against him and Tommy's face turned red, his eyes rolling back, veins standing out in his neck. Wheezing out a breath, he fell on her, gripping the sheets in his fists. Clara squirmed beneath him, grabbing his butt with both hands and pulling him in. Soon they grew quiet, their naked torsos tangled in the sheets of their California king-size. Sunlight streamed through Venetian blinds, birds chirping outside their window. A Curtis Mathes wooden TV took up the wall opposite the bed, pictures of Tommy and Clara, Adam and baby Lorena in frames on top.

Tommy grabbed a black Walkman and headphones from his nightstand.

"What're you listening to?" Clara asked.

Tommy pressed play and slipped the headphones over her head.

Clara grimaced.

"That's AC/DC," Tommy said with mock offense. "You don't make that face for AC/DC."

"It's so loud," Clara said, reaching for her own yellow Walkman on the opposite nightstand. "Here."

She put the headphones over Tommy's head and pressed play, a crooning doo-wop rhythm starting.

Re-mem-mem

Re-mem-mem-mem-ber

Re-mem-mem

Re-mem-mem-mem-ber

Tommy took off the headphones and climbed out of bed with a blank expression on his face.

"What's wrong?" Clara asked, the delight in her eyes fading. She glanced down at the Walkman as if it were defective. "I thought you liked The Earls."

"No," Tommy said. "I mean yeah, I do, it's not that. It's just—" Tommy slipped into his bathrobe, forcing a smile. "Just reminded me of this song my mom used to play when I was a kid."

"What was it called?" she asked.

"I don't remember," Tommy said, nodding at her Walkman. "It sounded kinda like that though."

"Sing it," Clara said, wrapping her arms around a pillow.

Tommy gave her a look. "You know damn well I can't sing."

"Try, please?" she said. "You never talk about back then."

"'Cause I barely remember back then."

She stuck out her bottom lip. Tommy sighed, closing his eyes. Opening his mouth, a song sprang forth in a scratchy whisper.

"*Era una noche de luna,*" he sang. "*Cuando yo la conocí.*" He paused, shaking his head. "That's all I got."

"I like it," she said. "What does it mean?"

"You are the worst Colombian ever."

"*Half*-Colombian," she said. "Not my fault mom wasn't around."

Lorena's wail filled the hallway outside their room.

"Great timing," Tommy said, heading for the door.

"I got her," Clara said, hopping up and grabbing her own robe.

Down the hall, Clara headed for Lorena's room while Tommy poked his head into Adam's. Toy figurines and racecars littered the floor, the room otherwise empty. Heading to the living room, he found Adam in front of their brand new 35-inch Panasonic, watching cartoons and eating peanut butter from the jar.

"Hey, Bud," Tommy said, ruffling his son's hair. "That's not breakfast."

"I'm not hungry," Adam said.

Tommy took the peanut butter and spoon out of his son's hands. "Then I guess you don't need anymore of this, do you?"

Adam opened his mouth and Tommy cut him off with a stiff finger.

Depositing the peanut butter back in the fridge, Tommy put his headphones on and pressed play on the Walkman, headed out the front door. He grabbed the newspaper off the front step and shook it open, the music blasting so loud he barely heard the voice.

"Que es eso?"

Under the open newspaper, Tommy saw leather shoes on oddly small feet, standing on the walkway that led from their front gate to the porch. He lowered the newspaper. Luchi beamed at him. Tucking the newspaper under his arm, Tommy pulled his headphones off.

"Luchi," he said, reflexively searching the area. He found two cars—a Mercury Cougar and a BMW—sitting a quarter mile down the street, the front seats occupied by shadowy figures. "Wasn't expecting you 'til ten."

"I come early," Luchi said.

Tommy nodded at the cars. "They don't have to park all the way down there you know."

"Dey are fine," Luchi said, nodding at the headphones. "What is dis?"

"This?" Tommy said, pulling the device out of his robe. It was rectangular, the size of a paperback novel on the racks at supermarket checkout lanes. He took the headphones from around his neck and held them out to Luchi. "It's a Sony Walkman. Just got it."

Luchi put the headphones on and Tommy pressed play.

Looking up at the sky, Luchi nodded to the shrill music. "Who is dis?"

"AC/DC," Tommy said.

"It is loud, eh?" he said. The song ended and Luchi took the headphones off, handing them back to Tommy. "I like."

The front door opened behind Tommy, Clara stepping out with Lorena resting on her shoulder.

"Tío," she said, surprised. "I didn't know you were joining us. I'd have made some breakfast."

"It is fine," Luchi said. "I will eat later. I come for Tommy."

"I've gotta get dressed," Tommy said. "Come in, hang for a minute."

"Yes," he said, swiping his sweaty forehead and glaring at the sun. "Que maldito calor."

Inside, Luchi waved to Adam in front of the TV and Adam waved back shyly. Clara put Lorena in her highchair and resumed stirring a bubbling pot of porridge on the stove.

Luchi nodded at Lorena, leaning on the kitchen counter opposite Tommy. "She grows fast."

"Way she eats, no wonder," Tommy said.

"She's definitely got your appetite," Clara said.

"Lorena," Luchi said, beaming. "El nombre de tu madre."

"Her middle name," Clara said.

"Middle name," Luchi repeated, nodding.

"What've you guys got planned today?" Clara said.

Tommy glanced at Luchi. "Up to your uncle."

Luchi smiled, a gesture that took ten years off the man. Clapping a hand down on Tommy's shoulder, he shook him a little, looking at Clara. "Tu esposo es de gran ayuda." He glanced at Tommy. "He helps very much. Un regalo de la nada. A gift from nowhere."

"I'm glad to hear," Clara said. Tommy noticed her smile was painted on. "He seems…he's enjoying the work."

"He is a good driver and good with numbers," Luchi said, raising his hands to the sky. "Dis is a blessing in our business, a man who is good with the numbers. Most of di men I work, dey cannot count to ten."

"While I do enjoy the praise," Tommy said, pushing off the counter and heading for the hallway. "I gotta get dressed."

In the room, Tommy closed the door and leaned his back against it, taking in the panoramic view: giant bed against the rear wall with two wooden nightstands on either side; state-of-the-art TV with pictures of his family on top; double sliding glass door overlooking a nearly Olympic-size swimming pool surrounded by enough land to play football on and a lake with a fountain beyond that.

Two loud blasts rang out in the hollow chamber of his memory, like bricks being smashed together.

Tommy closed his eyes, waiting for the echo to fade. A few minutes later he was dressed in jeans with no belt, a yellow polo tucked at the waist. He looked around the room again then headed back to the living room, kissing Clara and the kids goodbye and walking out with Luchi.

The BMW and Mercury Cougar down the street sprang to life as they reached the front gate, speeding towards them. The driver of the Cougar hopped out and threw Tommy the keys, walking back to the BMW. Tommy got behind the Cougar's wheel, Luchi in the passenger seat. Pulling out a vial from his breast pocket, Luchi dumped a bit of powder out and snorted it off his fingers. He held it out towards Tommy and Tommy hesitated.

"You want or no, parcero?" Luchi said, shaking the vial in his face.

Tommy took it and dumped some into his pinky nail, holding his finger up to his nose and snorting. It burned like fire for a second and his face went numb. He handed the vial back to Luchi.

"It is true, you know," Luchi said, grabbing a cigarette from the pack sitting on the dashboard.

Tommy pulled out his Marlboros, his left leg hopping. "What's true?"

Luchi pointed at Tommy's house. "You do good," he said. "Very good. Ayudas mucha gente importante. Dey will not forget. Dey *do* not forget."

"Appreciate that," Tommy said, putting the car in gear.

"You are happy here?" Luchi asked. "Dis house?"

"Very," Tommy said, pulling off with the BMW close behind. "Thanks for setting this up. I don't think we could've lasted another month in New York. Place was driving everybody crazy."

"Yes," Luchi said. "New York is different. Very busy."

"Extremely busy," Tommy said, dragging on his Marlboro. "Colombia on the other hand—" Tommy whistled. "That was something else. We should've gone there."

"Cali is beautiful, eh?" Luchi said. "We will go again. En tiempo."

"Looking forward to it," Tommy said, finishing his cigarette and tossing it out the window.

Cuban salsa played on the radio as they left Miami Shores, turning onto Biscayne headed south against the weekend traffic. They stopped at a red light on NE 79th street and Luchi patted his arm.

"Mucho dinero, Gringo," he said, with no pretext. "We will make more than Clara can spend. And—escuchame Tommy—Colombian women spend money like no other."

"Believe me, I know."

"Dis house you are living," Luchi said. "It is nothing. I will find you better."

"That's really not necessary," Tommy said. "This place is great and—"

"You will have more great," Luchi said, pulling a buzzing beeper from his waist and dropping it on the dashboard. "Necesito un telefono."

"We passed one in that plaza back—"

"Go," Luchi said, all joviality gone from his voice. "Now."

Tommy whipped the car around and headed back north, pulling into a shopping center with a Publix and a gym. He parked in front of a phone booth near the back of the lot and Luchi grabbed the beeper, slamming the door behind him.

Taking a deep breath, Tommy ran a hand through his hair, his leg still shaking. Luchi closed himself into the phone booth and pulled some quarters from his pocket, pushing a couple into the coin slot and jabbing at the keypad. He held the phone to his ear, speaking with his head down, shuffling his feet.

Tommy ran down the radio dial, pausing on a news broadcast.

"—expect Jurors in the McDuffie trial to take anywhere from a couple of days to weeks to deliver the verdict. McDuffie was beaten to death last December in what many in Miami's Black community are calling—"

The passenger door opened and Luchi poked his head in.

"You have quarters?" he said.

Tommy reached in his pocket and pulled out a couple of coins, dropping them in Luchi's palm: two quarters, a dime and a nickel. Luchi dropped the dime and nickel on the seat and slammed the door. Tommy focused back on the radio, running the dial some more and pausing on an angry voice.

"—about us, huh? What about the people already living here? I mean, don't get me wrong. What happened at that Peruvian embassy sounded horrible like—you heard about it, right? Reports say Castro wasn't even feeding them. They're eating cats and whatnot and—no disrespect to what these people are going through but they should be sending them to Alaska, not holing them up in—I mean, the Orange Bowl? Football season's in two months. And these 'spics, they're getting all sorts of benefits that other people, other U.S. citizens, aren't getting, believe me. I'm telling you, people, been saying it for months now. Castro's draining his swamp into our backyard. Mark my words, we're all gonna be picking up the tab for our esteemed Mayor Burgos and his—"

Movement from the corner of his eye drew Tommy's attention back to Luchi as he barked something into the payphone then banged it back into the receiver. Picking the phone right back up, he dropped another quarter into the slot and dialed another number. The phone seemed to ring forever before Luchi banged it back into its carriage, picked it up and banged it again and again until the phone fell apart in his fist.

Leaving the remains hanging, Luchi exited the phone booth.

Back in the passenger seat, Luchi breathed heavily. He glanced at Tommy, reached over and patted the back of his hand against Tommy's chest. The skin beneath Tommy's shirt tingled uncomfortably.

"Tengo hambre," he said. "You are hungry?"

"Not really," Tommy said. "Don't usually get hungry 'til—"

"Maybe dis is our last meal alive, Gringo," Luchi said, squeezing Tommy's leg and pointing at the steering wheel. "You will eat."

6.

Rig walked into the convenience store and grabbed a bag of jellybeans and a can of RC Cola, dropping two bills on the counter by the register. The cashier—a Hispanic man with brooding eyes—handed him back a couple of coins and Rig grunted thanks. Outside, Rig found Otis and DJ leaning against a concrete block near a gas pump, Otis with a bag of chips, DJ pouring a pack of roasted peanuts into his mouth. Rig popped the tab on his soda and took a swig, dapping his friends up.

"Fuck you been at?" Otis said, glancing over at DJ. "Ain't seen this nigga in like a week."

"Mom's been sick," Rig said, tearing open the bag of jellybeans with his teeth. "Just went back to work today."

Otis smirked. "You gotta babysit yo' Mama now?"

"She don't like me out when she home," Rig said.

"Sound like a hostage," DJ said. "This ain't Iran, bruh."

"She been trippin' since pops went up."

Otis let out a world-weary sigh. "Moms be trippin'."

"And Pops be goin' up," DJ added.

"Y'all seen Lefty 'round?" Rig asked.

"Not for a minute," Otis said, scrunching up his face. "Who the fuck was talking 'bout Lefty?"

"Just thought of him," Rig said.

"I ain't seen him neither," DJ said.

"Lefty ain't hittin' us up no time soon," Otis said.

"What?" DJ said. "Why?"

"He found out 'bout that weed, huh?" Rig asked.

Otis squinted, shaking his head. "You know Left and Black are boys from way back, right?"

"Black?" Rig said. "Like, your uncle, Black?"

"Black used to run with Left's little brother before he got locked up," Otis said. "Black the one set up that whole newspaper thing."

Rig and DJ glanced at each other.

"So where Lefty at then?" DJ asked.

"I don't know," Otis said. "Black say he ain't seen him much neither. Started hanging out with some niggas in Hialeah."

"Damn," DJ said.

"Almost fucked up the cash flow," Otis said. "That newspaper shit was legit. Black always say, you gotta have legit you wanna sell shit ain't legit."

"What you be selling that shit for anyways?" Rig asked, pouring some jellybeans into his palm and handing the bag to DJ.

"To make money, nigga," Otis said, scoffing. "Da fuck else for?"

"But they be locking people up for that shit," Rig said. "Papi ain't gettin' out for a minute."

Otis laughed. "That Papi shit be trippin' me out, bruh. I be forgettin' you a chico." He waved Rig off. "Yo' Pops ain't play the game right. Black done schooled me since I was a jit. I got this shit locked."

"Still wrong though," DJ said.

"Says who?" Otis said.

"The law."

"Laws made by a bunch a white people," Otis said. "Mad 'cause weed a nigga drug. Black man can't have a fuckin' *plant*, they go and make laws 'gainst it. This shit from the earth, nigga. Same place we all from. Can't be no laws 'gainst that."

Rig smiled. "Out here actin' like Weed Jesus."

"The Ganja Messiah, nigga," Otis said, dapping him up.

"Should call dem joints 'Christ Almighty,'" DJ said.

"Yo, that ain't a bad idea," Otis said. "One hit a dis Christ Almighty and I swear you'll be seein' *God*."

The boys laughed as a red candy-painted Corvette sitting on gleaming twenty-two-inch gold rims turned the corner on 62nd and pulled up next to a nearby pump. Otis held a hand up to his eyes, squinting in exaggerated fashion.

"Goddamn!" he said, letting out a shrill whistle. "Carl 'bout to *blind* me with them shits."

"Who's that?" Rig asked.

Otis sucked his teeth. "Come on, nigga. Who ain't heard of Chevy Carl?"

"Me," Rig said.

"You 'bout the only one," Otis said. "Nigga's fly as fuck."

"Buddy got five other ones just like that," DJ said, nodding at the Corvette. "All types of colors too. Blue, black, yellow."

"Cold as ice," Otis said. "Carl been in the game for a minute."

The Corvette's door opened and Curtis Mayfield poured from the speakers. A short, round man stepped out wearing a red zoot suit with butterfly collars and matching bell bottom pants, his hair done up in processed curls. A long gold-rope chain swung side to side around his neck, a diamond-encrusted Chevy medallion hanging from the end. He closed the door and sunlight gleamed off a diamond pinky ring on his right hand. Rig caught a glimpse of a beautiful girl with a caramel complexion and long black hair sitting in the passenger seat wearing a tiny skirt before the door closed, tinted windows hiding her away. A couple of younger kids ran up to Carl begging him to let them fill the Chevy up. Carl pulled a roll of bills out of his pocket and started handing out twenties, telling them to pump his gas and wash his windshield and make sure nobody touched the paint job. He set them all up then headed towards the convenience store, pausing next to the boys.

"You Black's fam, right?" he said, wagging a finger at Otis.

"He my uncle," Otis said, a nervous excitement in his voice.

"You tell Black I said what's up," Carl said, pulling his bank roll from his pocket again. He peeled off three twenties and handed them out to the boys, then disappeared inside the store. Rig stared at the bill as if it were a gold bar.

Otis shoved his twenty in his pocket and winked at Rig. "Told you. Nigga cold as ice."

Chevy Carl walked back out a moment later and the driver's side door of his Corvette opened, seemingly on its own. Rig got another glimpse of the girl in the passenger seat. She looked over at him with sparkling green eyes, her skin shiny in the afternoon heat. Rig noticed a sadness in her gaze just as Carl climbed in and slammed the door closed. The Corvette started with a roar and slipped back out on the street.

"Cold, bruh," Otis said, watching the red dot dwindling in the distance. "Trying to get on *that* nigga level."

"Need bread for that," Rig said.

"And you outchea askin' why I be sellin' this shit," Otis said, snatching the bag of jellybeans out of DJ's hand. Digging one out, he eyed Rig. "Why they call you Rig? That ain't yo' real name."

Rig snorted a chuckle. "How you goin' tell me what my name is?"

"Ain't goin' matter no ways," DJ said, rolling his eyes at Rig. "Nigga don't even know *my* real name. And we been boys since first grade."

"Fuck you mean?" Otis said, wrinkling his nose. "It's Darryl."

"*Darren*," DJ said.

"Darryl, Darren," Otis said waving him off. He nodded at Rig. "What's yo' real name?"

"Rig."

"Just Rig?"

"No," Rig said. "But I ain't tellin' y'all."

"Why not?"

"'Cause y'all dumb," Rig said.

"Nigga you dumb," Otis said. "For real bruh. How we yo' boys and we don't even know yo' real name?"

Rig glanced at DJ and DJ shrugged. Rig sighed, rolling his eyes.

"Whatever," he said. "It's Rigoberto."

"Rigguh-*who*?" Otis burst out laughing. "*Fuck* kinda name is that?"

Rig's cheeks got hot. "Exactly why I ain't wanna say nothin'."

"For real though," Otis said. "Where that from?"

"It's Nica," Rig said.

"It's nigga?" Otis said, confused. "What?"

"*Ni-ca*, nigga," Rig snapped. "Nicaragua. Where my pops from."

"If that ain't some chico ass shit right there," Otis said.

"You know chico just means boy, right?" Rig said.

"Don't matter, chico ass nigga," he said, laughing harder. "Yo' moms from Nigga-whatever too?"

"Naw, Jamaica."

"Oh, so you a yardie," Otis said. "My pops from down that way."

Rig tapped DJ's leg. "How 'bout you?"

"His pops dead," Otis said.

"I know, nigga," Rig said. "I mean why they call you DJ?"

"Long story," DJ said.

"No it ain't," Otis said. "Dis nigga's mom won some bread playing jai alai a while back, bought herself a stereo. Turntable, tape deck, speakers—"

"We ain't gotta tell this story again," DJ said.

"'Bout a week later," Otis said. "They having one of them block parties and this nigga *Darren* sat by the DJ the whole time, watching him spin. Next day, he took his mama's Marvin Gaye LP and tried to spin it like buddy at the party. Fucked up the whole record." Otis broke out laughing.

"Mama was *maaad*," DJ said, smiling. "Whooped my *ass*."

"Been DJ ever since," Otis said.

Across the street, two familiar figures approached from the north. Rig squinted through the summer haze, recognizing Marquise and his cousin Day Day. Otis noticed them too and scowled.

"These niggas," he muttered, tossing the empty jellybean bag in the trash and slapping Rig on the shoulder. "We 'bout to head to Black's spot, niggas playing bones. You down?"

Rig nodded, eyeing the two boys in the distance.

Leaving the gas station, the trio walked west on 62nd street past the entrance to King Square Park. Rig tensed when three PSD cars turned into the lot, a slew of cops hopping out and hurrying towards a small crowd of fifty or so people standing in front of a stage set up in the middle of the park. A woman in a suit and a couple of other cops congregated onstage near a microphone. One of the cops stepped up to the mic, his voice carrying out to the street where Rig and crew stood watching.

"Good afternoon," the man said. "My name is Captain Daniel Murphy of the Public Safety Department, and before I introduce the guest of honor, our state attorney, Ms. Janet Reno, I'd like to say a few words about what we're doing to make your neighborhood—"

"I ain't trying to listen to no fucking pigs right now, bruh," Otis said.

Rig stared at the growing crowd, a sinking feeling in his gut as he jogged after his friends.

7.

Housed in a brand new Downtown building, the Miami Police Department (MPD) employs roughly 660 officers who cover the dense, mostly urban heart of the city. Conversely, patrol of Miami's outskirts falls to the Public Safety Department (PSD), with over two thousand public servants operating out of six stations scattered across the city's various municipalities. Most of the time, jurisdictions keep PSD officers well away from their MPD brethren. However, through a classic combination of districting magic and bureaucratic gerrymandering, Liberty City is split between both departments, with MPD covering forty percent of the community and PSD overseeing the rest out of the Central District headquarters.

Entering that PSD Central Precinct on NW 14th street, there's a checkpoint at reception, the room filled with frenzied uniforms running ten calls behind since the year began. Hit the elevator up to the second floor and pass Cup O' Joe's on the left, serving coffee and donuts 7 AM to 7 PM. Turn right and push through the door to Homicide, where open-plan desks sit in rows and office doors line the back wall, each of them labeled Major, Shift Commander, and Captain respectively.

Ralph and Terry sat in two chairs under the Captain sign, Ralph holding a folder. Cocking his ear towards the door, Ralph listened to the voices inside: Murphy sitting behind his desk with the D.A. sitting across from him, and the PSD Commander Lippman pacing the room, his muffled words traveling back and forth through the walls.

"This can't continue, Murph," Commander Lippman said.

"We're doing what we can," Murphy said. "There's only so many options with the limited resources we—"

"*Limited resources?*" Lippman yelled. "I seem to remember giving you one *hell* of a clearance to increase manpower in, what, January? This Special Team of yours, what's the progress on that?"

"We've lost a lot of men since then with these invest—"

"Do *not* blame this on the Feds," The Commander snapped, slapping a hand down on Murphy's desk. "That doesn't explain these numbers. You know the national clearance average last year?" Lippman waited half a second. "Seventy-two percent. We're at fifty-one. Fifty-one percent. Do you know what that means?"

"Yes, I—"

"That means *half* the murders happening in this goddamn city are going unsolved. That is un-fucking-acceptable."

"There's also the Mariel business—"

"The Governor's sending reinforcements on that," Lippman said, lowering his voice. "But the mayor is focused on the city as it is *right now*. I brought you in to head the department because I believed you could get a handle on this shit. So far you are proving me wrong. Get it under control, now. Or I'll find somebody who can."

The door opened and Commander Lippman stormed past Ralph and Terry. Ralph peered in the office. Murphy leaned back in his chair, rubbing his forehead. Sitting in the corner like a sentry, Detective Richie Weis stared at a stack of papers on his lap. Next to him, the D.A. stood from his seat, brushing his tie down flat.

"I'll be back later with those warrants," he said, and headed out the door. He nodded at Ralph and Terry as he made for the exit.

Closing the door behind them, Ralph and Terry sat across from Murphy. Weis looked up at them and nodded, focusing back on the papers in his lap. Ralph handed Murphy the folder in his hands and Murphy dropped it next to a copy of today's *Tribune*, glancing at the newspaper with disgust. He opened the folder, flipped through the papers inside then slapped the folder closed, rubbing his forehead again.

"A goddamn kid too," he muttered.

"I'm thinking he might not be theirs," Terry said. "Woman's too young. Could be a brother. Nephew. Boarder, maybe? Part of whatever ring they're involved in."

"Any suspects?"

"Not yet," Ralph said.

"Find some," Murphy said, handing the folder back to Ralph. "Find somebody, get them booked, clear the case."

"We've got patrols canvassing the area," Terry said. "But my guess is this is the same M.O. as the others so it's gonna be hard—"

"Find out who the hell is doing this shit and bring them in," Murphy said. "Or find somebody who goddamn *knows* the person who's doing this shit and bring *them* in." He jabbed a finger at the folder. "Get. It. Cleared. You're detectives, right?"

Ralph and Terry looked at each other. Murphy stared at them.

"Uh…yeah?" Terry said.

"So *detect*," Murphy said, plopping back in his chair. "Jesus Christ, what is happening to this city?"

Ralph and Terry stayed quiet. Weis cleared his throat. Ralph glanced over and he and Weis made eye contact, something passing between the two men. Handing Terry the case folder, Ralph stood and opened the office door. Terry followed, stepping past Ralph into the main room and turning to find Ralph holding the door, still standing in Murphy's office. Ralph held his palm up.

"Five minutes," he said.

Terry frowned. Ralph closed the door on his partner and returned to his seat. Murphy opened his desk drawer and pulled out a bottle of Rolaids, popping one in his mouth and taking a swig from a water mug on his desk.

Ralph pointed over his shoulder. "Commander seems pretty riled up."

"Same ol' shit," Murphy muttered. "Too much crime, not enough clearance. Too many corrupt cops, not enough good ones. Goddamn imbalance." He glared at Ralph. "The whole lot of you can't spell for shit, by the way. Reading field reports is like deciphering a foreign goddamn language."

"Commander's acting like *we're* the reason we're short-staffed," Weis muttered. "Fucking Escander case shitted all over us."

"I'd be okay never having to hear that name again," Murphy said. He pointed at the door. "Outside of you two and Fry, average time on the job out there's not even two years." He slapped a hand down on the newspaper. "And now the mayor's out here calling cops racists."

Ralph turned his head to the side. "He said that?"

"What he actually said was the whole state of Florida is racist," Weis said. "But I get your point."

"Was just telling my daughter yesterday," Murphy said, rubbing both his eyes. "Things are starting to feel like that Lucy episode where she's working at that chocolate factory and the conveyor belt's moving too fast and chocolates end up everywhere. Only replace the chocolates with bodies. I'm meeting with Congress next week."

Ralph and Weis looked at each other. "Congress?" they said in unison.

"Federal, not state," Murphy said, picking up the newspaper. "Have to give testimony on the current state of crime in America. Meanwhile, the goddamn *Tribune's* out here making us look like a bunch of incompetent assholes."

"Can't really fault them for doing their job," Weis said.

"There's a difference between doing your job and taking everything out of context," Murphy said. "Every article it's like we're some evil—I don't know, Nazi empire. And this fucking McDuffie fiasco, their lawyer on TV every goddamn night screaming to high heaven. Doesn't matter what the facts are they just—" He pointed a finger at Ralph then Weis. "Nobody in this unit talks to the press 'less they run it by me first."

"After what me and Terry just saw," Ralph said. "I think the media and McDuffie are the least of our worries. These new vics, they—" Ralph shook his head. "There's no M.O. for this, Danny. It's like there's a war going on that we can't see. And we're the ones who are supposed to stop it."

"I don't think we should disregard McDuffie," Weis said. "Been out with patrols the past couple of days. People are really paying attention to this trial. Especially Liberty City. You can feel the heat out there."

"Guys are taking bets," Ralph said, nodding towards the bullpen. "Word got out the jury's released. Pool's leaning towards no conviction."

"Probably won't get a verdict 'til next week," Murphy said, waving the comment off. "Let 'em blow off some steam."

"If the guys who beat McDuffie get off they'll be reinstated," Weis said.

"And if the city deems them fit to wear a badge again then so be it," Murphy said. "Listen, you two know the situation. FBI's got a vendetta against us. Four guaranteed convictions and I'm down to a handful of day-shifters for a city that seems hell bent on murdering itself into oblivion." Murphy opened his hands. "We can only use what we've got."

"I hear you," Ralph said.

"Outside of Fry I don't trust anybody who isn't in this room right now anyways," Murphy said.

"What about Terry?" Ralph said.

"What about him?" Murphy said, an edge in his voice. "Something happening with your partner, Sergeant?"

Ralph sighed. "No, sir."

Murphy squeezed his eyes shut. "The reason I stuck him with you was to keep an eye on him until we can properly assess his potential."

"That's fine," Ralph said, adjusting his collar. "But I'll say it again, Danny, I'm not compromising for the guy. I got a weird feeling about this one."

"Weird feeling based on what?"

Ralph looked Murphy in the eye for a moment then shook his head. "Nothing specific," he said. "Just saying. If I ever see something suspect, I'm reporting it."

"Wouldn't expect anything less," Murphy said. "But to be clear: it is your job to get him where he needs to be."

Ralph nodded. Weis rolled up the stack of papers on his lap and stood, stretching. Murphy stood too, motioning for the door.

"You two get outta here," he said "Gotta get to this rally in King Square park. People swear we don't do anything, gotta go stand in this heat now and convince them we're good at our jobs."

"Who else is going?" Weis asked.

"Janet Reno's supposed to be there," Murphy said. "Captain Riley from MPD. The PIO who put it together went to high school with McDuffie."

"Maybe it'll help," Weis said.

"We'll see," Murphy said, ushering the men out of his office. "Get that report filed after the morgue. And make sure it reads good." He fluttered his fingers through the air. "Director likes 'em all *nice*-looking."

Back at Ralph and Terry's adjacent desks, Terry sat with the triple homicide report open in front of him. Nearby, a couple of patrols giggled at one of the detectives writhing in his seat, as if being shot by imaginary bullets.

Ralph stared at them. "The hell's wrong with Maxwell?"

"He was at that airport shooting last week," Terry said. "Says that's what the vic looked like when they got to her."

Ralph glanced at his partner. "And that's supposed to be funny?"

"What else you gonna do?" Terry said. He nodded at Murphy's office. "What was all that about?"

"Nothing," Ralph said, shrugging on his jacket. "Come on."

Terry grabbed his jacket and jumped up. "Where we going?"

"Morgue," Ralph said. "Lunch first though, I'm starving."

Taking the elevator down, they headed out to Ralph's Plymouth. Ralph had the door open when he paused to look back at the building, sucking his teeth.

"Forgot the goddamn radio," he said.

Terry pulled his jacket aside, revealing a walkie-talkie clipped to his belt.

"That works," Ralph said, and the two detectives headed out.

8.

By time cocaine gets to the states—at whichever nightclub or gala or backseat of a limo it lands—it's already been bounced around half the western hemisphere. Depending on who's heading the operation, the coveted white powder begins its journey as a plant in either Peru or Bolivia, out near the Eastern slopes of the central Andes where the climate is narco-perfect. The diversity of vegetation in this sub-tropical terrain—over two hundred species of orchids alone—is rivaled only by the disparities in altitude, the combination forming picturesque, mist-filled valleys where water vapor from the nearby rainforest allows the coca leaf to thrive. Depending on the location, the coca produced results in either a greenish-brown elliptical-shaped leaf (*Viva Bolivia!*) or a pale green oval-shaped leaf (*Viva Peru!*). The cocaleros running these farms grow the plants in two-acre plots called vocals, with fourteen-thousand coca plants per. After the initial growth phase, the coca's harvested four times a year, at which point the cocaleros literally reap the benefits of their labor, their livelihoods depending on those bountiful yields. The whole family's out there in the field, packing wet leaves into repurposed flour sacks cinched at their waists. After drying the harvested leaves in the sun, the farmers hike the loads uphill by llama, dropping them off at labs set up in the mountains where the leaves are dumped into vats and treated with a reacting alkaline solution (i.e. lime) which separates the unnecessary alkaloids from the prized cocaine alkaloid. Remove the dead coca leaves and soak the whole mess in giant casks of kerosene, toss in some sulfuric acid and mix until a variety of throwaway salts appear along with the main target: cocaine sulfate.

Or—as the cocaleros call the gray goo that's left at the bottom of the barrels after they dump the waste—pasta de coca.

From its homeland, Peruvian and Bolivian coca paste is shipped to Colombian traffickers (*Qué más, Pablo!*), where a few fiendish narcos skim off the top to mix it with tobacco, creating a potent cigarette known as bazuko (Luchi's roll-up of choice). The majority of the paste ends up in labs in the Colombian jungles, where the goo's soaked in more drums of kerosene and mixed with more chemicals that transform it into layers of soppy crystals which are dried and filtered over and over again until the cocaine base is achieved.

At its purest, cocaine base can be smoked, not sniffed. Another chemical bath is required, this one consisting of hydrochloric acid, acetone and ether—the main ingredient—before the familiar white powder makes an appearance.

At this point the final product is packaged and shipped via plane to various checkpoints in the Caribbean and Miami, a fact the Navy and Coast Guard became privy to in the late '70s leading to significant difficulties in smuggling. That was until a certain Cuban revolutionary-turned-dictator opened his borders and bombarded Miami's shores with bodies. With ninety percent of the Navy and Coast Guard consumed by the Mariel situation, massive opportunities opened for smugglers to move their weight, opportunities they gladly took advantage of. Washington will eventually estimate that an extra billion dollars' worth of coke slipped into Miami in the summer of 1980 alone.

Including a 200-kilo shipment that left from Cali yesterday morning.

The same 200-kilo shipment that was lost in the Everglades last night.

Tommy weaved through traffic as Luchi spoke, the ocean air whipping through the open car windows.

"Lost?" Tommy yelled over the wind, hitting the horn and swerving around a car stopped in the road with its left blinker on. "How's it lost?"

"Di pilots," Luchi said. "Dey drop di bags, dey land di plane, dey go get di bags. But di police are dere too, looking for di—cómo se dice cazadores?" He waved the question off. "Di police find di bags."

Tommy swallowed thickly. "Two hundred keys?"

"Yes," Luchi said. "And now we do not find Bilsner."

"Did you call him?" Luchi threw Tommy a heated glare and Tommy held a hand up, the other on the steering wheel. "I take it he didn't answer."

"No," Luchi said. "Di Morenos, dey will blame dis on him. And so dey will blame us."

Tommy looked back at the street as the light at 79th turned yellow, a large crowd gathered at the corner holding up signs that Tommy didn't get a chance to read before blowing through the intersection. He glanced in the rearview mirror past Luchi's men in the BMW at the throng of black fists.

"Where am I going?" Tommy asked.

"Di Barnacle."

A sour feeling rose in the pit of Tommy's stomach. "You *actually* wanna eat right now?"

"What else is dere to do?" Luchi said, looking at him funny. "Di bags are gone. Tengo hambre."

Crossing Rickenbacker to Key Biscayne, they pulled into The Barnacle lot and parked up front. Luchi's men parked a few spots over near the restaurant's back deck and the glistening bay beyond, a smattering of boats floating near the shore. They took a table inside, Luchi's men sitting close by as the waitress approached with glasses of water. Luchi ordered rum, neat, and a steak, medium rare. Tommy ordered a gin and tonic and a loaded baked potato. Luchi's men ordered sodas, eliciting a look of suspicion from the waitress as she retreated.

The waitress left and Luchi pushed his chair back, leaving without explanation. The waitress returned with their drinks, placing Tommy's in front of him. Tommy forced a smile, touching the sweaty glass.

"You can go ahead and get me another," he said.

The waitress left and Tommy knocked half the drink back in one gulp. Luchi returned, sitting and taking a sip of his rum.

"I try again to call Bilsner," he said.

"Maybe he's asleep," Tommy said. "Plane came in at four which means he was on the ground 'til sunrise. Could be passed out."

"Could be," Luchi said.

Tommy chugged the rest of his drink. The waitress brought his second round and he handed her the empty glass. Luchi waited for her to leave, then leaned across the table.

"Bilsner is dead," he said.

"Luchi, come on," Tommy said. "We don't even know—"

"If he is not at di meeting today," Luchi said. "He is dead."

Tommy's throat seized up. He forced a swallow. "The meeting?"

"Yes," Luchi said.

"What meeting?"

"With Pepito."

The waitress brought their food—Tommy's loaded potato and Luchi's mid-rare sirloin with a side of rice pilaf. Luchi grabbed a fork and knife. Tommy pushed his plate to the side and leaned over his drink.

"You're meeting with Pepito," he said.

"We are," Luchi said, cutting off a sliver of steak and scooping some rice onto the fork.

Tommy grabbed his drink, trying to keep his voice steady. "Don't you think that's something you should've told me?"

Luchi shoved steak in his mouth, chewing thoughtfully before pointing his fork at Tommy. "Por qué?"

"Why?" Tommy chuckled.

"Yes," Luchi said. "Why should I tell you we are meeting with Pepito?" He paused. "You will not go?"

"I didn't say that," Tommy said, leaning back.

"No," Luchi said. "Because you go. I tell you, I do not tell you, you go because I say you go." Luchi cut off another piece of the steak. "You work for me. I tell you what you need."

Tommy glanced at Luchi's men sitting nearby, looking out of place in the restaurant. One wore tan shorts and a plain black t-shirt, the other corduroys and a tank top, both their faces holding perpetual scowls.

Tommy knocked back the rest of his drink, dropping the glass on the table and sighing. "What are we going to say? At this meeting?"

"No sé," Luchi said. "But if Pepito does not like it, we are dead also."

The waitress walked by. Tommy touched her arm. She looked over at him and he pointed at his drink.

"Make it a double," he said.

9.

The brown house on NW 88th street had a sloping roof and a well-manicured patch of grass separating two slabs of concrete that served as the driveway. Emilia parked behind a caravan of vehicles, she and Tina climbing out. They approached the front door as a tall black man walked outside, a cigarette dangling from his lips and a halo of gray hair puffing out under his straw boater's hat. The man startled when he saw them, gathered himself then held the door open.

"Afternoon, ladies," he said with a bright smile that wrinkled the corners of his eyes.

Tina smiled back, entering the dimly lit house. Passing a kitchen counter covered in trays of food, they made their way to the living room where a dozen or so people sat with paper plates in hand, a couple of kids playing with toy soldiers in the hallway. Aside from Emilia and Tina, everybody in the house was black, a fact Tina found impossible to ignore.

A group of women crowded around a small TV. One of them turned to Tina and Emilia and startled. She walked over and embraced Emilia.

"You came," she said.

"I said I would," Emilia said. "I brought you something."

Emilia pulled a book from her purse and handed it over. The woman took it and read the title: *Our Bodies, Ourselves: A Book by and For Women.* The cover showed two women holding a sign that read *Women Unite.*

"I kept thinking about our talk," Emilia said. "Figured you'd appreciate it as much as I did."

"Thank you," she said, clutching the book to her chest. She eyed Tina. "And who's this?"

"One of our photographers." Emilia said, placing a hand on Tina's shoulder. "Tina Rivera, this is Claudette. She was friends with Arthur."

"We all were," she said, motioning around the room. "He was a good man, loved by many."

"I am so, so sorry for your loss," Tina said, taking the woman's hand.

"Not me so much I'm sorry for," Claudette said, looking around the room. "His sister was here earlier. Don't think she wanted the crowd though. Everybody talkin' 'bout the trial."

"I'm still surprised they let the jury out on a Saturday," Tina said.

"It is odd," Emilia said.

"Of course they'd rush it," Claudette said. "They just want to put it behind them, forget it ever happened. Problem is we ain't *never* goin' forget."

"Heard anything new?" Emilia asked.

"No," Claudette said. "Arthur's mama up there now with his wife and the babies. We saw her on TV yesterday. She looked so…angry."

"She's got every right to be," Emilia said, looking around the room. "Look how many people loved him. It's a tragedy."

"He was a good man, and talented," Claudette said, pointing at a couple of men sitting in front of the TV. "Those two used to work with him over at the insurance company. His team sold more than any other firm in the state. They were talking about promoting him beginning of the year."

Emilia rubbed her shoulder. "Hopefully this verdict will be some relief."

Claudette sighed. "Truth is, wouldn't nobody even know Arthur's name if you hadn't wrote those articles. Ain't usually this much noise 'bout a black man beaten by police. People mad on Arthur's behalf. You did that."

"I just did my job," Emilia said. "And not that well I might add. Editors gutted most of what I wrote, took all the teeth out. It took Ms. Goodman raising hell for people to start listening."

Claudette smiled. "That lawyer do got a whole lot of hell-raisin' in her."

"The best do," Emilia said.

Claudette's eyes went wide. "Where's my manners, Lord. Y'all hungry? Can I fix you a plate?"

"I'm fine, thanks," Tina said.

"Just ate," Emilia said, reaching for her hip. She pulled out her pager. "Sorry, it's the office. Can I use your phone for a second?"

"Sure," Claudette said, pointing at the kitchen.

Emilia walked away and Claudette saddled up next to Tina. "So you take pictures for the Tribune?" she asked.

"Yeah," Tina said. "I want to start writing more though. I'm taking some classes right now."

"I read the paper," Claudette said. "Way I see it, pictures just as important as the words. Helps make the point, you know?"

"It does, yeah," Tina said. "Always thought of photography as a hobby, didn't think I'd ever actually make a career out of it."

"Life got a way of bein' unexpected, don't it?"

Emilia reappeared from the kitchen, her face pale and gray, her eyes haunted. She pulled Tina aside.

"That was Fred," she said. "They just got an update on the Newswire. Verdict's in."

Tina frowned. "Already?"

"They're going to announce it soon," Emilia whispered. "We have to go."

"Now? Why?" Tina said, concerned. "You look like you saw a ghost."

Tina barely had the words out when a commotion started near the TV, Claudette's guests all speaking at once.

"They done!" one of the men yelled. "They got the verdict, they 'bout to announce it."

The room's collective attention turned to the TV. A camera zoomed in on a judge sitting next to a row of six jurors, one of the jurors standing with a piece of paper in hand.

"*We, the jury of Hillsborough County on this 17th day of May, 1980, find the defendant Wilford Hanley, as to count three of the information, manslaughter by unnecessary killing, not guilty. We, the jury, find the defendant, Isaac Davis, as to tampering with or fabricating physical evidence as charged in count five of the information, not guilty. We the jury find the defendant Milton Wyatt, as to count three of the information, tampering with or fabricating physical evidence, not guilty. We, the jury—*"

The rage in the living room grew like slow-moving lava. Claudette turned to Tina and Emilia, her eyes filled with pain and something new: a deadness, as if part of what made her human had just slipped out of her soul.

On the TV, one of the acquitted officers—Arturo Menendez, the caption said—grinned into the camera.

"*Thank God this country still has people who are honest and believe what's right.*"

Emilia grabbed Tina's hand and pulled her towards the front door, holding her own hand up towards Claudette. "We *really* have to get back to the office," she said. "But I'll be in contact. This isn't over."

At the door, the man with the gray afro and boater's hat walked in, glancing at them curiously as they breezed past. Climbing in Emilia's car, Tina stared outside at the bright blue sky. Emilia said something that sounded like it was traveling underwater and Tina turned to her.

"Huh?"

Emilia turned the car on. "This is bad. This is not going to end well."

"They let them *all* go?" Tina said.

"You don't get it," Emilia said. "None of them do. These people were hinging on that conviction. There's gonna be—"

Emilia cut herself off and put the car in gear, pulling away from the house and heading back to US-1. About a mile south of Claudette's, Tina saw the first picket signs on a corner. Emilia noticed them too and slowed, shaking her head.

"This is just the beginning," she said, speeding away.

10.

A rock flew across 12th avenue, slamming into the coupe's passenger door. The white man inside yelled behind rolled-up windows, squealing past an ice cream truck jingling its way in the opposite direction. Otis saw the food truck and took off running, leaving Rig and DJ staring at the couple dozen protesters at the intersection chanting with picket signs raised.

Justice for McDuffie!
Stop Killing Our People!
Right the Unrightable Wrong!

"You saw who threw that rock?" Rig asked.

"Probably one of them shorties right there," DJ said, nodding at a couple of kids their age screaming next to some trash cans. "All everybody been talking 'bout, them cops killed that McDuffie cat."

"Heard my mom's talking 'bout that shit last night," Rig said.

"Fuck them pigs," Otis said, walking up with a hot sausage in hand. "They better lock they asses up."

The boys continued to the next intersection, passing an apartment with a radio sitting on an open windowsill, "Rapper's Delite" blasting into the afternoon. Otis finished his hot sausage and tossed the wax paper, jumping in front of his friends and dancing like a robot. DJ ran up next to him and started convulsing, his movements growing more fluid until his limbs seemed made of spaghetti, flailing to the beat. Rig watched and laughed. Otis stopped to watch DJ too. DJ struck a finishing pose, arms crossed, feet spread wide.

Otis pointed at him. "Nigga think he a Jackson."

"That was solid," Rig said.

"I can teach you," DJ said, breathless.

"Hell yeah," Rig said.

"Y'all gay as fuck," Otis said.

"Fuck you nigga, *you* gay," DJ said.

"Fuck *you*," Otis said, pushing DJ. DJ pushed him back and Otis slapped Rig in the chest and the boys chased each other down the block whooping and hollering. They passed an abandoned tenement and Rig startled when two teenagers poked their heads out the only window that wasn't boarded up. One had his hair in braids running down to his shoulder. The other guy was bald.

"Got that fire," the bald one said. "Sweet Brown Sugar, get you lit."

"We good, bruh," Otis said, waving him off.

Rig studied the teenagers. The bald one returned an unwavering stare.

Turning onto 15th avenue, they headed for the cluster of green apartments where Otis lived, four men sitting outside one of them at a plastic table talking and slapping dominoes down. A red nose pitbull chained to a pipe a couple feet away drank from a metal water bowl. In the background, a radio blared the call signs for WEDR as a Sister Sledge track started.

One of the men at the table spotted the boys and stood up, bringing Otis in for a hug. He was well over six feet tall, dark as burnt toast with a short afro and a thick gold chain around his neck. Wearing black Dickies and a black t-shirt, he held a plastic cup half-filled with dark liquid. He dapped DJ up, glancing at Rig. The pitbull let out a soft growl near his feet.

"You a big muhfucka ain't you?" the man said, sizing Rig up.

"This my boy Rig," Otis said, turning to Rig. "This Black."

Black studied Rig for a second. "He the shorty broke Neville's kid nose last year, ain't he?" Black turned to the other men at the table, all of them sporting ropes of gold jewelry with plastic cups of liquor on the table in front of them. One man held a tattered book on his lap: *The Fountainhead* by Ayn Rand. "What's Neville's boy name again?" Black asked.

"Marquise," one of them said.

"Marquise," Black echoed. "Shorty's nose still crooked."

"He asked for that shit," Otis muttered. "All them Indigo City ass niggas asking for it."

"Done told you about that," Black said, spinning on Otis. "Ain't right. All this niggas 'gainst niggas shit. Y'all playing *right* into these cracka's hands."

Otis sucked his teeth. "Come on, unc. That ain't how shit work these days."

"Boy don't be telling me how shit work like I don't already know," Black said. He took a sip of his drink. "So this Rig, huh? Hell of a name. Ain't that what they call them shipping trucks? Big rigs?"

"Shorty built like one," the man holding the book said.

"You ain't lyin'," Black said, taking his seat at the dominoes table again. "You play ball, Rig?"

"Sometimes."

"Pop Warner?"

Rig looked at him blankly.

"Big as this nigga is, he don't need it," Black said. "Just goin' end up hurtin' them other shorties. Soon as he hit freshman year coaches goin' snap his ass up." Black pointed at the man with the book. "This here my partna Talvin." He pointed at the pitbull. "And this here Booze. Call him that 'cause he act like a crazy drunk." He waved at the other two guys at the table. "Don't matter who these niggas are."

One of the guys sneered, his white tank top stained with something reddish-brown at the bottom. "Way to make a nigga feel wanted."

"Nigga don't nobody want you 'round here," Black said.

The other men at the table laughed. Tank Top grumbled, slapping a domino down. The pitbull plopped down on the concrete, panting.

Black took another sip of his drink. "How old you is, Rig?"

"Twelve."

"Goddamn, *twelve*?" Tank Top yelled, kicking the man sitting across from him, a light-skinned brother wearing an MLK t-shirt, corduroys and brown boots. The man looked up from his dominos for the first time since the boys arrived, giving Rig a double take.

"Goddamn, da fuck dey feeding you?" He glanced at Black. "He play ball?"

"Nigga, I just asked him that," Black said.

"You hear Leanne's boy starting next year?" Tank Top said. "That shorty there fast, boy. Say he might play for FAM."

"Who said that?" Black asked.

"Whole 'hood," MLK-shirt broke in. "FAM recruiting him. Heard they looking at Frank's kid too."

"Which Frank?" Tank Top said.

"Robertson," MLK said. "What's his kid's name again, um—" He snapped his fingers a couple times. "—Darnell."

"Yeah that little nigga can ball," Black said.

"Saw him out at Northwestern last week," MLK said. "Burnin' *everybody*. Ain't even break a sweat."

The men slapped dominos down as they spoke. Otis took a seat on the grass against Black's apartment, Rig and DJ following suit. The song on the radio ended and the DJ swooped in smoothly.

"This is WEDR, James Roscoe here with an update on the trial for the killers of Arthur McDuffie. The jury in Tampa appears to have come to a verdict concerning the fate of the four charged police officers. We'll deliver that news once it's available. In the meantime, Michael's here to rock with you."

"Shit don't even matter," Tank Top said. "Even if they lock they asses up. Arthur still dead."

"Solid nigga too, man," MLK said. "I knew his Mama, used to baby-sit my sister back in the day."

"I know his sister," Black said. "Goddamn saint, that woman. Dis nigga Art just livin' his life, ridin' his hog. They go and bust his head open, for what? Swear to God, felt the same like King died when I heard that shit."

MLK and Tank Top grunted in agreement.

"Y'all trippin' if you think they goin' to jail," Talvin said, closing his book. "They moved the trial to Tampa for a reason. People up there ain't nothing but some cop-loving crackas, whole jury full of white folk. Pigs goin' be back in they blankets by Monday."

"Yuh-huh."

"Ain't no white folk goin' send a cop to jail for bussin' a nigga' head."

"You know you right."

"Damn sho ain't happenin.'"

"Otis!" a woman's voice yelled.

Otis, Rig and DJ looked over at an apartment across the courtyard. A woman wearing a headwrap, housedress and pink sandals stood hanging laundry up on a clothesline.

"Yeah!" Otis called back.

"Where yo' sister at?"

"Fuck'm I supposed to know," Otis said to Rig and DJ, his voice low.

"I heard that!"

"I ain't seen her!" he yelled back.

"O, go find yo' sister!"

"Mama!" Otis whined.

"Boy! Go find yo' goddamn sister!"

"I'm right here, Mama!"

A teenage girl who resembled Otis approached from the street with another pudgier girl, each of them carrying plastic crates.

"Where you been?" Otis's mom yelled.

"Can y'all quit hollering all over the place?" Tank Top said. "Black, yo' sister sound like a goddamn banshee."

"Shoulda heard her growin' up," Black muttered, slapping a domino down.

"Black folk ain't worth shit to none a them," Talvin said. "Not the police, not them judges, not the jury."

"That's why they took down Mr. Jones," Black said. "First nigga superintendent, knew damn well they wasn't goin' let his ass stay. Over some fucking bathroom pipes."

"Like these crackers don't be doin' worse shit," Tank Top said.

"Y'all heard how they did that cat in Overtown?" MLK said. "Chuck something. The teacher."

"Chuckie Anderson," Tank Top said. "Kicked the nigga's door down and fucked him up. Ain't find shit, still booked his ass for resisting."

"How you goin' resist in yo' own crib?" Talvin said.

"They always got resisting to fall back on," Black said.

"At least Chuck breathing," Tank Top said. "What's JJ's kid's name again?"

"Tyrell."

"Yup, Tyrell," Tank Top said. "Shot that nigga right in the head. One minute he taking his sister home from school. Next minute boom, he gone."

"That one right there pissed me the fuck off bruh," MLK said, gritting his teeth. "Like why the *fuck* you got a gun pointed at the shorty head when you already got cuffs on 'em? How's *that* an accident?"

"I just said it," Talvin said. "We ain't. Worth. Shit. Ain't nothin' but numbers to them."

"Hate us like we stole somethin'," Tank Top said, looking over at Otis, Rig and DJ. "Y'all too young to remember, but this whole hood used to be full of white people. Back when niggas stayed in Overtown."

"'Til they ran I-95 through that bitch," Talvin muttered.

"Shit was nice," Black said.

"Forced us out here," Talvin said. "Moment we showed up dem crackers ran they asses off. You know I was the first nigga at Holmes?"

"You only tell that story every time you come over!" Otis's mom yelled.

"Woman, mind yo' damn business!" Black yelled back. The men laughed. Otis's mom glared at her brother, grabbed an empty laundry basket and walked back inside her apartment.

"Mama walked me up in there first day like a trophy," Talvin said. "Only nigga in the whole class. End of the year, wasn't one white kid left."

"Ain't got to do nothing but look around," Tank Top said. "Broken sewer, holes all up in the street, can't get a coat a *paint* in this bitch. And now they got all these goddamn Cubans showing up like they—" He turned over his dominoes, forfeiting. "Talked to that nigga Melvin, work at the Orange Bowl. Every one of them Mariel niggas get clothes, a hundred-something dollar check, a place to stay *and* a doctor's visit."

"Meanwhile baby mama went for food stamps the other day," MLK said. "They told her they was out. How you goin' be out of food stamps? City glad to give shit to *anybody* 'cept niggas."

"Bottom rung of the totem pole," Talvin said. "Why I ain't got no hope they goin' lock up these pigs killed Arthur. Niggas is dispensable to them."

A gunshot rang out in the not-so-far distance, breaking through their reverie with a jolt as sharp as lightning. Booze jumped up and started barking insanely. The steady slap of running footsteps got Black out of his chair as a teenager in a black tee and loose jeans appeared from around the corner, bunching the waist of his pants in his fist. He skidded to a halt in front of Black. Booze barked louder, yanking on his chain. Otis scooted over and grabbed the dog, calming him.

"What up, Marcus?" Black said, looking past the kid. "Fuck you running from like that?"

Marcus glanced at Otis and pointed at the radio. "Turn it up."

Otis raised the volume. A woman's voice came over the speaker, distorted through her phone line.

"—*crying shame this jury, this all-white jury goin' just turn those officers loose after what they did? How long can we keep taking this nonsense? When are we going to rise up?*"

The line clicked. The DJ's voice returned, his typically smooth lilt strained.

"*Thanks for the call. Phone lines are full, and we here at WEDR want you to be heard. We understand that this is a time of hardship, and we feel for our community, but we also urge you, folks, please remain calm and keep the peace. I'm getting word that there will be a demonstration this afternoon outside of the Metro Justice Building—*"

Everybody looked back at Marcus again.

"They let them go," Marcus said. "Not guilty. All of 'em."

The pain in the men's faces right then was so raw it made Rig's stomach hurt. MLK and Talvin turned over their dominoes.

Black shook Marcus's shoulder. "How many we got at the house?"

"Just me and Poonk," Marcus said. "Belly went out for food an hour ago."

"Head back," Black said. "We'll meet y'all there."

Marcus nodded and ran back in the direction he came. Black flexed his hands over and over, the veins in his neck standing out. Suddenly, he grabbed the handle of Johnny Walker and hurled it at the nearby sidewalk, the glass shattering on impact.

"You can smell that shit," Talvin said. "They goin' riot tonight."

"Let's ride," he said, marching into his apartment. Talvin followed, Tank Top and MLK behind him. Otis jumped up but Black poked his head back outside, putting a hand on his nephew's thin chest.

"This grown folk business, Young Blood," he said.

"But I thought—"

"Hold it down here," Black said, slamming the door.

Otis plopped back down next to Rig. "This is fucked up," he said.

"I can't believe they let them go," DJ said.

"I can," Otis mumbled.

"What you wanna do?" Rig asked.

Otis glanced at him but said nothing.

Black's apartment door opened again and Talvin walked out carrying a duffel bag. Black followed, holding a pistol that seemed to disappear in his giant grip. Tank Top appeared holding a shotgun with MLK at the rear holding another black pistol. Black paused next to the boys as the rest of his men walked over to a red '75 Impala parked across the street.

"Watch Booze for me," he said, running a hand over Otis's head.

Otis nodded. Black walked over to the Impala and climbed in. A second later the car pulled off.

The moment they were gone Otis stood and walked back towards 62nd street. DJ and Rig hopped up and followed, catching him as he rounded the corner. The same two teenagers—braids and bald head—poked their heads out of the abandoned tenement window.

"Got that fire, Sweet—"

"We good, nigga!" Otis snapped.

Walking back towards King Square Park, they found the 12th avenue intersection even more crowded with protesters than when they'd passed earlier. Flames shot out of a trash can at the corner and someone kicked it, burning garbage spilling out onto the street. A car swerved around it and slowed, an older white man in the driver's seat staring bewildered into his rearview mirror. Someone from the crowd heaved a rock at the car and the vehicle's rear windshield exploded. The driver sped off, leaving a trail of burning rubber. Half a block down, residents in Crystal Palaces where Rig lived pulled out aluminum chairs and sat in front of their whitewashed bungalows to watch.

Rig felt a hand on his shoulder and turned to Otis holding a handful of small rocks. DJ stood behind him in an abandoned lot a couple of feet away, eyes wide with something on the border of fear and excitement.

Otis's stare was deadly serious. "What you thinkin'?" he said to Rig.

Walking over to the abandoned lot, Rig picked up a rock the size of his fist.

Rig turned back to Otis and tossed the rock in the air, catching it and holding it at his side. "Fuck we waiting for?"

11.

A giant sign on a beam rises from the roof of the green building at the corner of NW 7th avenue and 75th street: *Jumbo's*. The restaurant's logo—a cartoon shrimp wearing a top hat—is stamped on every door. Signs tacked to the outside walls and curtained windows make bold declarations:

Generous Portions

Prices are Right

Jumbo's Stands the Test of Time

Ralph pulled his Plymouth into the Jumbo's lot and parked. Across the street a small crowd stood at a corner, chanting and holding up cardboard signs.

"Everybody knows about Jumbo's," Terry said, climbing out of the car.

"Everybody around *here* knows about Jumbo's," Ralph said.

"Exactly."

Ralph froze mid-step. "Bullshit."

"What?"

"You're from 'round here?"

"Yup."

"Bullshit," Ralph repeated.

Terry paused at the restaurant's doors, shaking his head and chuckling. "Why would I lie about that?"

"You grew up in Liberty City?"

Terry pointed across the street. "Me and Mom lived four blocks that way."

Ralph watched the protesters. A couple of stragglers joined the crowd, swelling its dimensions. "Where's mom now?" he asked.

"Passed," Terry said.

"Sorry."

"Don't be," Terry said, opening the door. "World's better for it."

A few guests sat scattered throughout the restaurant, some at the booths by the windows, others on barstools at the lunch counter. Ball lights hung from the ceiling, potted plants on shelves, walls covered in posters and news clippings of prominent Hurricanes and Dolphins football players.

At the register, Terry glanced out the window at the protesters again. "Think that's gonna be a problem?"

Ralph looked outside, pursing his lips. "Not like we can do anything about it anyways. Director was clear, back off Central."

A young waitress with flawless dark skin came over holding a pot of coffee, beaming at Terry.

"How you doing today, Detective Pullman?" she asked, grabbing a mug.

"I keep telling you, Shirley," he said. "That's weird. Just call me Terry."

"And I keep telling you that wouldn't be respectful."

"Bah, respect," Terry said, accepting his coffee. "Who needs it?"

She winked at him. "The usual?"

"Yeah."

She flashed her smile at Ralph. "And what's your name, handsome?"

Ralph glanced at Terry. "Uh...Williams. Ralph Williams."

"Nice to meet you," she said. "What'll it be Detective Williams?"

"*Sergeant* Williams, actually," Terry said, winking.

"Well well," Shirley said. "What'll it be, Sergeant?"

"Um—the usual too, I guess?" Ralph said, looking dazed.

"To go," Terry said. "On the run, gotta get to the morgue."

"Lunch before the morgue?" she said, curling her upper lip.

"Better than after," Terry said, smiling. "Tell your sister I said hi. Me and her need to catch up."

"Oh, she'll like that," Shirley said. She grabbed the pot of coffee and headed to the open kitchen where a man with skin so dark it looked purple stood sweating over the grill.

Terry reached for the closest sugar container and prepared his mug, glancing at Ralph's bewildered expression.

"What?"

"Her sister?" he said, staring after Shirley.

"We went to high school together," Terry said.

Ralph let out a belly laugh. "You're yanking my chain, right?"

Terry smiled. "I really don't understand what is so hard to believe about—"

"You're white," Ralph said. "From what I can tell, you are very white."

Terry sipped his coffee. "I didn't know whites weren't allowed here."

"Oh, we're allowed," Ralph said. "It's just been my understanding over the thirty-odd years I've lived in this city that they have absolutely no interest in exercising that right."

Terry rolled his eyes. A couple minutes later Shirley returned from the kitchen, placing two plastic bags on the counter in front of them. Terry waved off Ralph's cash and handed Shirley a twenty, told her to keep the change then grabbed a glass ketchup bottle and poured a glob in his container. Ralph glanced at the spread: scrambled eggs and hash browns covered in cheese with a side of toast. Resealing his bag, he followed Terry back out to the car. They were settling inside when a pickup truck came honking through the intersection, swerving around a dark-skinned teenager standing in the middle of the street with his arms straight up in the air. Terry stared at the crowd of protesters, grown to a couple dozen.

"Wonder what the rest of the neighborhood's looking like," he said.

Ralph put the car in gear. "Murphy's over at that King Square rally."

"That's down the street."

"Gonna pass by and see how things look."

"What about the morgue?" Terry said.

"Bodies aren't going anywhere."

Turning left on 12th, Ralph headed down to 62nd street, pulling up to the park. He stopped at the curb and tossed his police placard on the dashboard. Terry scarfed down a couple forkfuls of egg and placed his tray on the seat, following Ralph. They approached a stage erected in the middle of the park, joining the crowd of eighty or so standing in front. The department PIO spoke into a microphone. Offstage, the MPD Captain stood next to Janet Reno, the State Attorney. Half a dozen officers stood sentry onstage. Captain Murphy was nowhere in sight.

"—the dilapidated exercise equipment," the PIO said. "The broken swings, the basketball courts in need of maintenance. This area has been neglected long enough. And with your help, we would like to change that, and end the cycle of crime and degradation that has plagued this community for years. We would like to bring back King Square."

A smattering of applause was cut off by a commotion stirring its way from the front of the crowd. The PIO put his hand over the microphone, turning to the group onstage behind him. Then, suddenly, Reno was gone, whisked away by three officers to a car waiting outside the park. The MPD Captain disappeared next. The officers guarding the stage gave each other confused glances. The PIO got back on the microphone.

"Folks, we're having some technical difficulties so we're going to take a momentary break. We will return shortly."

"Not guilty," a voice said from Ralph's left.

Ralph looked over as Murphy walked up to them.

"The whole lot of 'em," he added. "Not guilty."

Terry's eyes widened. "On all counts?"

Murphy nodded. "Reno just got the news, the director paged me a few minutes ago," Murphy looked around the area. "You two stick around the area, in case things get testy."

"Sure thing," Ralph said.

"Low profile though," he said. "City's telling patrols no sirens, no chases, no drug arrests, no domestics. Assume the Chief's gonna go the same route."

"Roger that," Terry said.

Murphy looked at his watch. "Roll call's in an hour so everybody'll be fresh. I'm heading to the office, see if they need anything."

Murphy patted Ralph's arm and walked away. Ralph glanced around at the dissipating crowd, most of whom seemed more confused than angry. Motioning for Terry to follow, he headed back to his car. In the driver's seat, he opened his lunch and started eating. Terry climbed in and did the same. Chewing a mouthful, Ralph looked around at the busy traffic on 62nd, the growing crowds of protesters at all four corners of the 12th avenue intersection. He put another forkful in his mouth and closed the tray, placing it in the backseat and putting the car in gear.

"This ain't gonna end well," he said.

Terry looked over at him with a piece of toast in hand. "Ya think?"

Ralph snuffed a laugh and pulled off.

12.

Emilia weaved in-between traffic south on I-95 while puffing on a cigarette, twisting the radio dial. Tina smoked her own, her notebook open in her lap, pen in hand, pulse pounding in her forehead. Emilia paused on a news broadcast and turned the volume up:

"—miles off the coast of Key West. Authorities believe the Olo Mundo's tragic malfunctions were a result of overloading, as many have accused Cuban soldiers at the Mariel harbor of placing too many passengers on boats, in addition to not providing—"

"The trial," Emilia hissed, twisting the dial to another news station.

"—reached in the trial of four police officers accused in the beating death of Arthur McDuffie last December. The six-juror panel submitted a full acquittal for all four men on charges ranging from conspiracy to commit fraud to second degree murder. The response from the black community has been one of outrage, with many taking to the streets to protest what they believe is an unjust result. A demonstration is planned at the Metro Justice Building in Downtown Miami shortly. More details as this story—"

Emilia shut the radio off, tossing her cigarette butt out the window.

"Guess I'm missing class tonight," Tina murmured, closing her journal.

"Fred tried to divide the stories up, you know," Emilia said. "When the McDuffie thing first broke, he tried to get a couple of people on it. Thought it was too much for one person. I insisted on doing them myself. And since I was the one with the direct source, they didn't have much choice."

"Those articles were great though," Tina said. "You can't blame yourself."

"I don't," she said. "It's just this entire time I've been able to stay just below the radar because I really honestly believed it would go the other way. Those lawyers spent months trying to subpoena me. I only managed to dodge them because this thing was local. This is *going* to go national now."

"Which means everybody's going to be calling the person who first reported the story," Tina said. "You."

"I almost don't want to go back to the office," Emilia said. "Actually—"

Emilia veered across three lanes of traffic to the Government Center exit.

Tina braced herself against the dashboard. "Where are we going?"

"If there's gonna be a demonstration," Emilia said. "Then we should go."

Approaching the Government Center complex, the Metro Justice Building loomed next to the PSD headquarters and the State Health Department. The Justice Building itself housed county courtrooms and the offices of the state attorney where—as Emilia pointed out—employees would be particularly despondent right now after hearing the verdict against their colleagues. Over 900 inmates awaited trial in dingy cells at the Dade County Jail further south, overlooking the Miami River.

Emilia pulled into one of the lots and parked facing the Justice Building, a giant mass of a couple hundred people already gathered at the front steps. Tina and Emilia climbed out and someone called Emilia's name. They turned to find another Metro beat writer—James Malone, his desk five feet from Emilia's—walking towards them wearing brown slacks and a faded Miami Dolphins t-shirt.

"Fred put you on this too?" he asked, acknowledging Tina with a nod.

"We heard it on the radio," Emilia said. "Decided to check it out."

"You're coming from the office?" Tina asked.

"Everybody's on edge since the news broke on the wire," he said. "The two-way started squawking right before I left." He nodded at the Justice Building. "We should probably get over there before we can't see the front."

They faced the crowd, which had grown even larger since they got out of Emilia's car. The PSD building was barely visible from their vantage point. Holding her camera, Tina followed James and Emilia towards the crowd, snapping photos of angry faces. Emilia stopped at a streetlight and pulled out her notepad, alternating between scribbling and dodging protesters barreling past her. James did the same on Tina's other side. Tina braced herself against the light pole as men, women and a few children coalesced into a knot of bodies just ahead of her. Another dozen men came up a side street, dressed in black and carrying a wooden coffin over their heads, lowering and raising the coffin in rhythm with their chant. Tina took a photo of them then another of the crowd, and another, every shutter snap revealing more people in the frame than the last. She finished the film roll and switched it out, tucking the used roll in her pocket and looking around for Emilia. Nothing but unfamiliar faces surrounded her, and a sudden pang of fear hit her in the gut. A bearded black man with fire in his eyes looked at her for a moment—frown lines creasing his forehead so deep they looked like razor blade cuts—then breezed by her with a fist raised.

"Right next to you," Emilia yelled, pushing through the crowd to Tina and the light pole. "Like a goddamn tsunami!"

Tina faced the courthouse again as clashing chants echoed through the air.

Reno Must Go!

We Shall Overcome!

A-men!

It was wrong what they did!

Can't let these crackers go!

An old black man with a ring of hair around his balding head approached the courthouse steps, facing the crowd. Tina raised her camera as the man raised his hand. He held it there and the chanting died down. When it was relatively quiet, he crossed his arms behind his back.

"The NAACP," the man bellowed, his voice distant and ghost-like. "Would like to first say that we, as an organization, are as outraged as you are by the injustice that has taken place today against our brother, Arthur McDuffie."

The crowd wailed. The man raised his hand again, waiting.

"We tried to find a speaker for this moment," he said. "But understandably, it is hard for any one person to find the right words in this situation. Therefore, we will turn to the word of God, and *pray* for the justice—"

"Fuck praying!" somebody bellowed.

The crowd erupted.

"We ain't come to pray," someone else shouted. "We gotta *do* something!"

Each guttural yell increased the collective ire, like oxygen to a flame.

Fuck yo' prayers!

Praying don't do shit!

Let's march!

Falling into a lull of disconnection, Tina snapped picture after picture.

A car turned onto the street, headed in the direction of the crowd. *Snap.*

Behind the wheel, a black woman wearing a nurse's outfit, eyes wide as she stared at the mob in front of her. *Snap.*

The car disappeared, blotted out by bodies. Tina faced another side street where a group of protesters had turned on three PSD patrol cars approaching from the south. *Snap.*

The police cars came to a squealing stop at the end of the street, blocking off the intersection. Half a dozen officers hopped out with their hands on the butts of their service pistols, facing a crowd that had grown to over a thousand.

Snap.

"They shouldn't be here," Emilia said in Tina's ear. "They're only going to make things worse."

As if on cue, somebody threw a brick.

By time Tina saw it, the thing was already in the air, flipping end over end (*Snap*) before smashing through one of the patrol windshields.

Two of the officers pulled their guns, pointing them at the crowd.

The crowd attacked.

Tina held fast to the light pole as the sea of bodies shifted like a hive of disturbed bees. Emilia grabbed Tina's shoulders, her eyes giant.

"We can't stay here!"

Tina looked around. "Where's James?"

No sooner had she asked the question, Tina spotted James. He stood a few feet from the light pole and as Tina opened her mouth to call for him, a fist smashed into his face. James went down hard, out cold before he hit the floor. Tina and Emilia pushed over to him as a wailing teenager raised a stick over his head, aiming for James.

"No!" Tina yelled, jumping in front of James. She looked the boy in his eyes. He couldn't have been more than sixteen, yet the anger Tina saw in his pupils seemed eternal. The kid seemed to contemplate bringing the stick down anyways, then spit on the ground and disappeared into the crowd.

Tina and Emilia pulled James to his feet, his eyes swimming back to life. He shook his head and grimaced, holding his hand to an eye that had already started to swell.

"What happened?" he said groggily.

"We have to go," Emilia said, pulling his arm. Tina grabbed his other arm and they staggered a couple of feet towards the parking lot. A sudden, loud crash brought their attention back around. One of the PSD patrol cars skidded across the sidewalk on its roof. A cheering group of protesters nearby moved on to the next patrol car, swamping each side and rocking it back and forth. Something whistled past Tina's ear—close enough for her to feel the wind— and a bottle smashed into the concrete next to her feet. Glass pellets bounced off her jeans. She turned to see who threw it but the crowd had grown even thicker, the perpetrator disappearing into the throng.

Pulling James against the flow, they cleared the thickest part of the crowd and made for Emilia's car. They leaned James against the hood and Tina raised her camera once more, taking a panoramic shot of the scene outside the courthouse. From this distance, a single chant roared above all others.

Jus-tice! Jus-tice! Jus-tice!

Emilia grabbed Tina's elbow. "Forget the photos. We need to get back to the office, now!"

Tina glanced once more at the spiraling situation then helped Emilia get James into the car.

13.

Cruising south on 95, Rusty glanced over at his brother as Lenny turned to his friend Matt in the back seat.

"Bullshit," Lenny said. "They don't get that big."

"They do," Matt said. "Might've been bigger actually."

"You're so full of crap."

"Guys, c'mon," Rusty said. "Enough, you've been at it the entire drive."

"How big was that grouper, Russ?" Matt asked.

Rusty glanced at Lenny, winking. "I'd say it was *maybe* three feet."

"See?" Matt said, sticking his tongue out at Lenny.

"Three feet is not that big," Lenny said.

"Yes it is."

"How about some music!" Rusty yelled, grabbing a tape from his glove compartment. He pushed it into the 8-track and a familiar tune started.

"All you ever listen to is country," Lenny said, rolling his eyes.

"It's Kenny Rogers," Rusty said, taking the NW 6th avenue exit off I-95 and turning right on MLK Blvd. "What's wrong with Kenny Rogers?"

"He's alright," Lenny said.

"Okay then," Rusty said. "What does a 15-year-old listen to these days?"

"Pink Floyd," Matt said.

"Blondie," Lenny said.

"God, Debbie Harry," Matt said.

Lenny let out a groan of ecstatic approval. "Debbie Harry."

"Figures," Rusty muttered. "But can you appreciate other types of music?"

"Not country," Lenny said.

"Come on Len—have you two even heard this one before?"

They both stayed quiet.

"It's called 'Coward of the County,'" Rusty said, raising the volume. "He's telling a whole story here. That's hard to do in a song."

"What's it about?" Matt asked.

"This guy everybody thinks is a coward because he never wants to fight," Rusty said. "They're always making fun of him, calling him yeller."

"Yeller," Lenny said with a smirk.

"But he's just got this code, you know?" Rusty said. "Because his dad died in prison and made him promise not to be like him. So he doesn't fight."

"That's it?" Lenny said.

"No," Rusty said, pointing at his ear and turning the volume up. "Listen."

The three of them listened, cruising through the deepening dusk. They stopped at a light on 10th ave and the song faded to an end.

Lenny shook his head. "I don't get it, what happened?"

Rusty sucked his teeth. "You weren't listening."

"I was," Matt said. "Some guys messed up his lady so he found them at a bar and gave 'em the business."

"In the process *breaking* his promise to his dad," Rusty said. He pushed Lenny's shoulder. "But for a good cause. Because—" Rusty broke into a high, twanging sing-song voice. "—'*Sometimes you gotta fight when you're a man.*'"

Rusty grinned at Lenny and Lenny grinned back. The light turned green and Rusty pulled off. They were just passing 12th avenue when a giant piece of concrete appeared in the air in front of the car. Rusty stared at it confused until it hit, shattering the windshield and landing in the passenger seat right in Lenny's stomach, knocking the wind out of him. Rusty let out an involuntary yelp, the car swerving at 40 mph and skidding across two lanes of oncoming traffic. They went down a side street as Rusty wrestled with the wheel. The front tires hit a curb and the truck bounced onto the sidewalk. Too late, Rusty saw the large eyes of a small black girl—couldn't be more than twelve— standing frozen in front of the hood. Then she was in the air, the truck squealing into a newspaper dispenser. The girl flew into the side of a concrete apartment building and hit the wall hard, leaving behind a smear of blood as she slid to the ground. Rusty's truck came to a halt near a stop sign, the fishing gear and cooler in the truck's bed flying out into the middle of the street.

Rusty shook himself, his head pounding. Next to him, Lenny pushed the heavy piece of concrete off his lap. Blood stained his t-shirt. He glanced back at Matt, who'd been tossed and now lay hidden in the footwell between the front and back seats. Rusty turned to Lenny, leaning over to check his brother's injuries as the truck's doors flew open and rough hands yanked him out, tossing him to the ground next to his truck. He hit the concrete and the air burst from his lungs. Twisting around to find his brother he found instead what had to be a hundred black faces. He tried to focus on individuals and saw men, teenagers, children, toddlers even, held back by mothers who stared at Rusty with both anger and horror. An old man with a cane walked over to Rusty's truck and busted out the driver's side window, the glass pebbles littering the concrete by Rusty's head. The sky disappeared and Rusty looked up at a kid who seemed no older than Lenny, holding a giant rock above his head.

"Guys," Rusty said, his voice raspy. "I don't know what happened but—"

"Motherfucker killed that little girl," somebody yelled.

"It was an accident!" Rusty said and the kid with the rock hit him right in the face.

The impact seemed to be a signal, the explosion of pain followed by a flurry of arms and legs and rocks assaulting Rusty from every direction. He twisted around to push himself up and a sledgehammer of pain hit him in the ribs, sending stars sailing across his vision. He tried again to push himself up and another blow caught him on the other side, forcing a guttural scream out of his ragged throat. The edges of his vision faded, the colors returning at a leisurely pace as somebody dragged him into the street. He caught a glimpse of Lenny on the other side of the truck. Matt remained in the truck, not yet noticed by the mob. A half dozen men held Rusty's brother against the side of the pickup with his arms stretched wide, punching and kicking and hitting him with rocks and pieces of wood.

"No, please," Rusty screamed. "He's just a kid!"

Another blow to the gut dropped Rusty again, Lenny disappearing from view. Rusty gave up fighting the relentless fists and feet and projectiles, curling into a ball and trying unsuccessfully to protect his core.

It was then Rusty realized he was about to die.

The sheer terror of the knowledge hit him and his body went rigid. The blows continued. One of his attackers walked to the curb, snatched a broken chunk of concrete from the sidewalk, and walked back over to him. Rusty watched through one eye, the other swollen shut. From his peripheral, he noticed the back door of his truck open, Matt slipping out and taking off running down the street, disappearing from view a moment later. Rusty opened his mouth to say something as the man holding the concrete slab stood over him, the slab raised over his head. The others screamed for him to do it. The man bent his knees, his puffy, disheveled afro shiny with sweat. Face shrouded in shadows, only his eyes were visible, piercing.

"Goddamn crackers," he said, then slammed the concrete slab down.

An hour later, when the beatings had stopped and Lenny and Rusty lay still on the sidewalk, a Liberty City derelict most people knew as Doughman walked up to Rusty and placed a red rose in his broken mouth. Taking a step back, Doughman studied the rose like a sculptor surveying his work. Satisfied, he nodded and whistled his way towards the fires growing in the distance.

14.

Tommy glanced out the window at the small crowd gathered at the courthouse's front steps, turned a corner and watched the crowd disappear. He pulled into the parking garage at the Omni Hotel on Biscayne and parked on the second floor, the BMW parking two spots over. Inside the hotel, Tommy and Luchi and Luchi's other men headed past the concierge to the restaurant, walking over to a large round table in a section by the bar where a handsome man with slicked-back hair and a pleasant face sat alone. He wore a black button-down tucked into gray slacks, the sleeves rolled up. On the table in front of him was a black, beaded cowboy hat. Four men stood against the wall behind him, wearing black suits with telltale bulges under their arms.

Luchi approached the table with a grim expression, as if this were a funeral proceeding. Tommy and company stood back, staring at the other men standing against the opposite wall. Luchi motioned for Tommy to take a seat as a waitress walked over and placed glasses of water around the table, walking off without a word. Tommy hesitated then sat down, sipping one of the waters.

"Don Pepe," Luchi said. "Lo siento mucho por esta situación."

Pepito nodded. Luchi glanced at Tommy. The sight of uncertainty in his eyes dropped Tommy's stomach to his asshole.

"Vamos a ver que paso," Luchi added.

"Qué paso?" Pepito said. "What happened is my shipment was stolen."

"We are sorry for di mistake, Don Pepe," Luchi said. "But di shipment is not stolen. It is taken, by di police."

"Was it?" Pepito said. "My men have checked the papers, the news. There is no report of seizures. How do I know you have not just stolen the package and *claimed* it taken?"

"I do not know why—" Luchi cut himself off. "Dis is a error. Bilsner—"

"Yes, Bilsner," Pepito said. "The leader of your pilots that you cannot seem to find."

"I'm right here."

Tommy and Luchi turned to Mike Bilsner approaching from the lobby, wearing a stained button-down and chinos, the gap between his two front teeth displayed prominently in his grin.

"I'm late, I know," he said, taking a seat next to Tommy. "My apologies. *See-en-toe*, as y'all like to say."

Luchi glared at Bilsner, leaning back in his seat and crossing his arms.

Bilsner looked around the room. "Alright now," he said, holding up his hands. "Let's all just take a breath."

"Where is my shipment, Mr. Bilsner?" Pepito said.

"Sitting in an evidence locker, my best guess," Bilsner said, glancing at Luchi. "You didn't tell him?"

"Qué mierda," Pepito muttered. His men grew restless, hands close to their waists. "And where is this pilot, who drops my product right where the police can find it? Eh?"

"Right now he's making sure we can keep flying," Bilsner said, clearing his throat. "With all due respect, he did what he was supposed to do."

"If he does what he is supposed to do," Pepito said. "My shipment will be where it is supposed to be. Not in a 'evidence locker,' as you say."

"Okay, so you're pissed your shipment got snatched," Bilsner said. "I get that, that's obvious. I'd be pissed too. But you gotta understand we did everything by the book. Scoped the spot out two weeks beforehand, never saw nobody out there. Dropped the bags exactly where your guys told me to and did it in the middle of the night." He opened his palms, shaking his head. "I mean, shit like this just happens sometimes. It's a freak accident."

"Freak accident," Pepito said, pursing his lips. "And why is this freak accident not in the papers? Where is your proof?"

"Of course," Bilsner said. "Figures that's what got y'all underwear in a bunch. Account-a-bil-i-ty." He reached in his back pocket and Pepito's men tensed. Bilsner produced a torn piece of newspaper, sliding it across to Pepito who picked it up.

"Naples Daily News," Bilsner said. "Morning edition."

Pepito looked the paper over, glanced at Bilsner then handed the paper to Luchi. Luchi gave it a perfunctory scan, sliding it to Tommy.

"Qué dice?" Luchi said.

Tommy skimmed through the article. "Authorities seized a shipment yesterday out in the Everglades." He looked up at Pepito. "Says they recovered 235 kilos."

"Two hundred but who's counting, really?" Bilsner said.

"La policia," Pepito said, smiling. "They love to exaggerate."

"Helps them get funding," Bilsner said, taking the article from Tommy and sliding it back to Pepito. "You really think about it, we're kind of the reason they have jobs in the first place. They should be thanking us."

Pepito laughed and the tension in the room dissipated. Tommy took a deep breath, unclenching his asshole.

"Very good," Pepito said. "These things, they happen. These, eh—how you say? Freak accidents?"

"We ain't the only ones," Bilsner said. "Shit's the Wild West out there. Talked to my guy out at Tamiami, says last week two planes crashed into each other right near where our stash got taken. Six people dead, including both pilots. Three hundred keys between the two of 'em. Coast Guard won't even fly at night anymore, too many planes going under the radar."

"Yes, but we must not let this interrupt business, so—" Pepito clapped his hands together. "—We will fly more in a week. This is good?"

"Works for me," Bilsner said, nodding at Luchi. "If it works for him."

Luchi and Tommy nodded. Bilsner stood, shook Pepito's hand, patted Tommy on the shoulder then walked out.

"Y tú, El Gringo?" Pepito said.

Tommy raised his eyebrows. "Me?"

"Sí," he said. "You are sitting at the table. What are your thoughts?"

"My thoughts?" Tommy said.

"About this freak accident."

Tommy took another sip of water, cleared his throat. "It's like Bilsner was saying," he said. "Shit happens."

Pepito glanced at Luchi and smiled, his teeth white and shiny. "You do tell me, eh?" he said. "El Gringo con los cojones de acero."

"Gringo Cubano," Luchi said.

"Cubano?" Pepito said, his smile fading. "Tú eres Cubano?"

Tommy glanced at Luchi. "Um…yes?"

"We do not do business with the Cubans," Pepito said. "They are—eh, not so trustworthy."

"I'm Cuban by birth," Tommy said quickly. "Moved to the states when I was a kid, lived here my whole life."

Pepito nodded. "Luchi tells me you are family."

Tommy forced a smile. "My wife's his niece."

"Bueno," he said, grinning wide. "Este es un buen negocio para familias."

"Yup," Tommy said, his lips thinning around his smile. "Always wanted a family business."

Pepito nodded, eyeing him some more. "And you went to university here?"

"University of Miami," Tommy said. "Bachelor's in accounting."

Pepito tossed Luchi an approving wink, patting Tommy's arm across the table. "Luchi is a good man. He says you are a good man, so you must be a good man." He raised his hand and motioned for the bartender. The woman stopped wiping glasses and walked over. Pepito ordered a round of aguardientes and some ceviche and the bartender left, Pepito relaxing in his seat.

"I have a solution to the lack of cash flow caused by this most recent failure," he said. "Another thirty keys need to be moved from an associate distributor who is—" Pepito paused, looking up at the ceiling. "—not an option anymore. This happens. But I must leave back to Colombia tomorrow, so I will need you—" He pointed at Luchi, then Tommy. "—to take care of it."

Tommy glanced at Luchi, sweat prickling the back of his neck. Luchi nodded and reached across the table to shake Pepito's hand, thanking him— thanking *him*—for the opportunity. Tommy's stomach sank.

Pepito shifted his attention again to Tommy, studying his reddened face.

"You are good with this, Gringo Cubano?"

Tommy forced a nod. "Yes."

"Of course," Pepito said. "Who is not okay with making more money?"

Tommy opened his mouth to respond but the waitress interrupted with the shots, dropping one in front of each of the seated men. She dropped her tray off at the bar and disappeared back into the kitchen.

"So, Gringo," Pepito said, touching his shot glass. "You enjoy Cali?"

"Yes," Tommy said. "Very much, it's a beautiful city."

"And you met our chef, no? Fernando?"

"We spoke," Tommy said.

"He is a funny man, no?"

"Uh…yeah," Tommy said. "He, uh—he knows what he's doing."

"Yes," Pepito said. "Fernando is very good at his job. We must all be good at our jobs if we are to stay on top, sí?"

Tommy nodded. Pepito leaned back in his seat. "You must visit my father's ranch sometime," he said.

Tommy took a deep breath then stood with his shot glass raised, looking Pepito in the eye. "It would be an honor."

"Yes, an honor it is," Pepito said, standing and placing his black cowboy hat on his head.

Luchi followed suit, raising his glass in unison with Pepito.

"To no more freak accidents," Pepito said.

"No more," Luchi said.

Tommy stayed quiet, raising his glass higher. They knocked the shots back and the aguardiente—the fire water—burned the whole way down.

15.

Stopping at the light on 60th and 12th, Ralph squinted through the smoke at the silhouette of a crowd due south. The light turned green and he coasted through the intersection. A dozen people stood at a gas station on the corner. Others across the street lounged outside their apartments. Ralph pulled the car over to the curb and motioned for the walkie on Terry's hip. Terry handed it to him and Ralph turned the volume up, scattered calls coming across the channel.

Unit 260, just got a bottle thrown at me on 62nd street and 16th.

"Four blocks over," Terry said.

"That's Morrison," Ralph said. "He can handle it."

Unit 211, just got a window blown out by a rock at 76th and 15th ave.

Unit 254, large crowd of negro males at 65th street and 18th avenue throwing shit at passing cars.

This is Lieutenant Johnson, all PSD patrol units are ordered to stay out of Liberty City. Repeat, stay out of Liberty City.

"Too late for that," Ralph said.

All available units head to 7th avenue and 62nd street. Keep all white westbound motorists out of Liberty City. Repeat, all white westbound motorists.

"Subtle," Terry said.

Attention all units—

Terry and Ralph stared at the walkie, waiting for it to speak again. It didn't. Ralph turned it over.

"It's dead," he said.

"Shit," Terry said. "I thought it was charged."

Ralph leaned his head back. "Wouldn't be a problem if they hadn't taken the damn things out the cars in the first place." He glanced outside, an electricity in his eyes that wasn't there a moment ago. "We're cut off."

Two blocks west smoky shadows crossed the street. The air smelled of burnt rubber, Ralph's eyes watering. A bead of sweat appeared on his forehead. He touched the pistol in his shoulder holster.

"Cover me," Ralph said, opening the car door. Terry followed suit, both men stepping into the street as Ralph waved at some approaching headlights.

"It's Weis," he yelled.

The car pulled over behind Ralph's and the driver's window rolled down, Detective Richie Weis peeking out at them.

"Fellas alright over here?"

"Walkie just died," Ralph said. "You got a radio in there?"

Weis held up a black receiver. "Checking the channels now."

Ralph leaned in the window, Terry posting up behind him. Weis turned the radio up, the static calls growing more agitated by the second.

Unit 234, we're going to lose this spot if we don't stop that traffic on 62nd.

Unit 287, building on fire at 73rd and 13th, crowd blocking units from access.

Unit 216, someone busted in one of the windows at Norton Tire, smoke is just pouring out the back.

"This escalated quickly," Terry said.

"Why they would release the verdict today is beyond me," Weis said. "Everybody's home bored. What the hell did they think was going to happen?"

"Hindsight's twenty-twenty," Ralph said.

"It's simple logic," Weis said. "If they had any fucking clue what the temperature is around here."

Reports of two white males down at 62nd and 13th, a dispatcher squawked. *Repeat, two men down, heavy crowd, witness says they're beating them.*

"That's around the corner," Weis said.

Ralph and Terry hopped back in his car, following Weis to 13th where they turned left and screeched to a halt. Half a block south, a swarm of people stood around a crashed pickup truck. Smoke rose from the truck's hood, a battered newspaper dispenser lying near the crushed front fender. Surrounding the truck, the crowd congregated on a single point near the sidewalk. Across the street, people stepped out of their apartments to watch the spectacle. A sliver of space opened in the crowd, enough for Ralph to squint through the smoke and see two bodies lying in the street. Ralph watched as a kid no more than fourteen walked up and stabbed a small pen knife into one of their abdomens. The crowd cheered and several people started kicking them.

"Think we should tell Weis to call for back up," Terry said, a distinct quiver in his voice.

Ralph opened the car door and climbed out, pulling his pistol. A hand dropped on his shoulder, Weis stepping up next to him. Terry climbed out the passenger side with his gun cocked.

Pointing his gun at the sky, Ralph pulled the trigger.

The deafening report got the crowd's attention, half of them running in the other direction. The other half backed away from the truck, watching Ralph and Weis like wolves. Before Ralph could consider what he was about to do, he headed towards the bodies, gun held down at his side. Terry and Weis called after him. Halfway to the crashed pickup truck a gunshot rang out behind him, then another. Ralph spun around, expecting Terry and Weis with their service pistols raised. Instead, muzzle flashes sparked from the surrounding apartment buildings. Ralph dropped to his stomach. Bullets pinged off his and Weis's cars, off the surrounding sidewalk, off the crashed truck and banged up newspaper dispenser. Ralph crawled to the pickup truck, ducking behind the smoking hood. The bullet flashes from the apartment windows stopped. Weis duck-walked over to him and the flashes started again, Weis diving next to Ralph.

"Where the fuck are those coming from?" he yelled.

Ralph pointed at the apartments. Other projectiles pelted the area as well, kids standing on the apartment roofs throwing whatever they could get their hands on. A rock landed a foot away from Ralph and he pulled Weis closer to the truck, looking behind the other detective.

"Where's Terry?" Ralph said.

Ralph and Weis both peeked around the truck's crushed front fender. Terry stood in the middle of the street, staring blankly at the apartments. Bullets ricocheted off the concrete around him.

"Terry!" Ralph yelled. Terry didn't move. "Terry, get the fuck over here!"

Terry didn't even look in their direction. His eyes pointed straight ahead, wide and blank. Ralph looked at Weis but Weis was staring at the bodies in the street, his eyes haunted. Glancing over, Ralph understood. The two dead men lay a couple of feet away from each other, both their lips split to the gum, eyes so swollen the slits were no longer visible. Noses lumps of ground meat, missing skin where their eyebrows should be. Every appendage seemed bruised and broken, torso, legs and arms disfigured beneath their clothes. Their hands were purple, the fingers crooked. One man's shattered femur had ruptured skin, piercing through his pants leg. The other had a visible dent in the back of his head, like a plastic ball kicked too hard.

"Holy shit," Ralph said, his voice barely audible above the gunshots and yelling. "What the fuck did they do to them?"

"I don't know," Weis said. "But we can't leave them here."

A cracked piece of the sidewalk lay in front of the pickup truck under an overshadowing oak tree, one of its corners glistening with blood. Ralph crawled towards it and a bullet pinged off the edge. He scooted back to the truck.

"We gotta get them," Weis yelled. "You take one, I'll take the other."

Ralph nodded and moved to grab one of the men, the bodies jumping as small caliber bullets hit them. Ralph and Weis ducked back behind the truck. Ralph looked out at Terry, still frozen in the middle of the street. He opened his mouth to call him again as a rock flew into the side of Terry's head. Terry dropped like a bag of cement.

"Terry!" Ralph yelled, pushing Weis. "Pullman's down!"

Weis looked at the knocked-out detective and cursed. The muzzle flashes from the window paused again, the silence lasting just a second before a chatter of gunshots rang out in the distance, on another block. Distant screams erupted then faded away. Sirens wailed from everywhere all at once. Orange flames danced through the smoke in both directions on the avenue.

"We gotta get Terry," Ralph said.

Weis looked at the broken men on the ground. "Fuck!" he yelled. "We can't just leave them here!"

"Look at them!" Ralph said. He pointed at Terry's lifeless body. "We've gotta get Pullman out of here."

Weis took a deep breath and nodded. Ralph glanced at the two dead men then he and Weis crawled over to Terry. Ralph waited for the gunshots to resume. A few pinged off the truck behind them. They reached Terry without getting hit and Ralph was thinking them lucky when he saw two teenagers standing next to Weis's car, a rag sticking out of the gas tank. One of them sparked a lighter and recognition washed over Ralph's face.

"Weis," he said, pointing a shaky finger as the kids took off running.

Weis turned and the back of his car exploded, the blast knocking them both on their asses. Terry stirred from his unconscious state.

Weis jumped to his feet. "What the fucking hell!" he yelled. "They blew up my goddamn car!"

Ralph pushed himself up and grabbed Weis's shoulders, spinning him around. Weis's face was dirt-streaked, eyes crazed.

"We have to get out of here," Ralph said. "Help me with Pullman."

Weis squeezed his eyes shut and nodded. Grabbing each of Terry's arms, they pulled the groaning detective to his feet and helped him to the car. Ralph tossed their cold Jumbos lunches out into the street and helped Weis get Terry in the back seat. The gunshots from the apartment windows stopped. The crowd that earlier had backed off the two dead bodies crept back in view, shadowy silhouettes surrounding the crashed pickup truck.

Back behind the wheel, Ralph put the car in reverse and slammed on the gas, doing a one-eighty and speeding back towards the intersection.

Terry stirred in the backseat. "What happ—"

"Quiet," Ralph said. "Lean your head back, we gotta get you to a hospital."

"What happened with those bodies?" Terry asked, his voice slurring.

"You almost fucking became one yourself," Weis yelled, spinning around to face Terry. "What the fuck was that back there?"

"Easy," Ralph said. "Guy's never seen combat."

"Fucking has now," Weis spit, slamming his palms on the dashboard. "Fuckers blew up my fucking *car*."

"We gotta get Pullman to the hospital," Ralph said. "Then head to the precinct, tell them what's going on."

"No, no hospital," Terry said, holding a hand to his head. "I'm fine."

"You most definitely are not," Ralph said.

"All due respect, sir," Terry said, looking at Ralph through the rearview mirror. "There's more important things to deal with right now."

Ralph stared at his partner and shook his head, speeding towards 14th street. He was half a block away when he let off the gas, cruising to a stop at an intersection on 15th. Ralph's eyes reflected the flames shooting out of the Justice Building's lobby. Putting the car in park, he stepped out and climbed on the hood to see better. A patrol car burned a block away.

Weis slammed his hand on the car horn. Ralph looked down and Weis pointed straight ahead, where a group of people had broken off from the larger crowd surrounding the courthouse and started running at them.

Sliding off the hood, Ralph got in the car and threw it in reverse, twisting around to look out the rear windshield as they sped towards the I-95 Government Center exit. The crowd drew closer, the mass of enraged faces seeming monstrous reflected against the ever-present flames. The car gained ground and they hit the ramp backwards at fifty miles per hour, the rear bumper narrowly missing a wall. At the highway, Ralph slammed on the brakes and put the car in drive, speeding forward a hundred feet before squealing to a stop in the breakdown lane. He hopped out and ran to the wall, looking out from the overpass at the scene, dimly lit in the fading twilight. Thousands of people crowded the streets. At least a dozen flipped police cars were on fire. A mob streamed in and out of the PSD precinct, smoke pouring from every window on the first floor.

Weis walked over and the crack of a rifle dropped them both to their knees.

"That was high caliber," Ralph said.

"Headquarters is gone," Weis said. "We have to get out of here, find somewhere to regroup."

Ralph's eyes lit up and he grabbed Weis, dragging him back to the car.

Speeding south, he pulled off at the next exit, onto Miami Avenue.

Weis braced himself against the dashboard. "Where are we going?"

Ralph glanced at Weis. "You're always talking about how good Emilia Brathwaite is at her job."

Weis looked at him. "What the fuck's that got to do with this?"

"Tribune's got radios," Ralph said. "Let's go see your mentor."

16.

Lying on a bench near the TVs, James placed a wet towel over his face, hiding the knot on his forehead. Tina sat with Emilia near a row of brand-new video display terminals. One of the secretaries walked over, handing Emilia a stack of yellow slips.

"The line's been ringing off the hook for you," she said.

Emilia glanced around the hysterical newsroom, the individual rings of each phone no longer discernible, only the discordant sound of them all going off at once. "Sounds like I'm not the only one."

"Most of it's people getting a busy signal from the main line and just dialing any desk they can get a hold of," Karen said. "They all want to talk to you."

"You *are* the one who wrote the articles," Fred said from his office door. Behind him, the row of TVs near the break area flashed images of buildings on fire, helicopters hovering near rising towers of black smoke. Fred glanced at James lying on the bench. "Is he okay?"

"He says he's fine," Emilia said. "Just a headache. Tried to get him to the hospital but—"

"I'm not going to a hospital during a riot," James said, his voice muffled beneath the towel.

"How about you two?" Fred said, looking from Tina to Emilia.

"I'm fine," Emilia said.

James sat up and removed the towel from his face, revealing a purple bruise above his left temple. He looked confused for a moment, then lay down again and put the towel back.

"He really should get that checked out," Tina said.

"He's probably right about the hospital," Fred said. "Judging by the radio calls, emergency room's a madhouse. I do not understand why you all decided to go this alone."

"It happened really quickly, Fred," Emilia said. "If we weren't there we wouldn't have been doing our jobs and then I'd have had to hear you bitch about that. And my pieces did not cause a riot, if that's what you're insin—"

"I'm not," Fred said, holding his hands up. "I'm just saying, between today's verdict and what's going on outside right now, the country's attention is on Miami now. And *you* broke the original story. People want to hear your take on things."

"And you?" She stared at him. "Do *you* want to hear my take, Fred?"

Fred crossed his arms. "My suggestion is don't respond to anything until this situation is under control. Have a talk with legal, see what they think."

Tina felt an itch on the back of her arm and scratched. The itch turned painful, and when she looked at her fingers, bits of red stood out beneath her nails. She twisted her arm around to stare at a two-inch gash just below her shoulder. A bloody hole stained the back of her shirt sleeve.

Emilia glanced over at the cut. "That happened out there?"

"I guess so," Tina said. The area surrounding the cut was starting to bruise. "I guess one of those bricks grazed me. I didn't even notice."

"The two of you should've never been out there alone," Fred said.

"You've voiced your sentiments, Fred," Emilia said. "We get it."

"I got some good shots at least," Tina said. "And we're safe now. I think."

"Have we heard anything from PSD?" Emilia asked.

"Just talked to the fire inspector," Fred said. "Said it's like they're trying to burn down the whole north side of town."

Tina stared at the row of video terminals as people shrieked into phones and radios throughout the newsroom. At a desk by the elevators, the police scanner spit out a steady stream of codes, reporters standing nearby with pens jotting down notes.

Another secretary walked over, nodding at Tina. "It's your mother."

The hairs on the back of Tina's neck stood up. She hurried over to Emilia's desk and grabbed the phone.

"Mami?"

"Mija," her mother said. "Donde estás?"

"At work," Tina said. "Are you okay? Is anything happ—"

"Mija, we see on the news the fires," her mother hissed, drowning Tina out. "You must come home."

"I can't leave, Mami," Tina said. "I'm still working. And I don't think I should be out on the street right now anyways. I'm safer here."

"Your brother called, asking what is going on," her mother said. "I don't know anything but what I see on the news."

Behind Tina, Emilia yelled, "*They're in trouble!*"

"It's a riot, Mami," Tina said. "That trial, the McDuffie trial. People are really mad about the verdict. Fern called?"

"*Sí.*"

"How is he?"

"I don't know," she said. "We didn't talk long."

"I haven't heard from him in like four days," Tina said. "How is he? He had an interview, did he get—"

"I knew you should have never taken this job," her mother spit. "You need to come home now. This is not safe."

"I'm okay, Mami," Tina said.

"Come home now."

"*No,*" Tina barked. She took a deep breath, clenching her teeth. "I'll call you back when I know more. Te amo."

Tina hung up before her mother could respond.

Emilia tapped her on the shoulder.

"Just got off the radio with Klinger and two of your people from photo," she said, motioning for Tina to follow.

Tina's eyes went wide. "Are they okay?"

"They're almost in the employee lot," Emilia said. "They got attacked."

Tina followed Emilia and a security guard to the elevators, Fred on their tail. The elevator doors opened downstairs just as a car rolled up to the entrance. Every window on the vehicle was shattered, a constellation of bullet holes and rock dents peppering the sides. The car rattled to a stop and three people jumped out: the beat writer Klinger and two photographers, Brian and Molly. The security guard unlocked the Tribune doors and the trio ran over, stumbling to the reception benches.

"There's hundreds of people in the street," Klinger said. "On every block. They started hitting us with rocks and—" He took a deep breath. "The gunshots started right when we were trying to get out."

"We barely made it," Molly said.

"Fucking insanity," Brian said, plopping down on the floor.

"I should lock back up," the security guard said. "Maybe—just an idea, but I could go down to the cafeteria and grab some oil, pour it down that hill so nobody can climb up."

"That cannot be the extent of our security," Emilia said.

The guard shrugged. "Might help."

Emilia pointed outside. "Somebody else is coming."

The room tensed as a blue Plymouth pulled into the lot, stopping outside the building. Two men in suits hopped out, opening the back door and pulling out a third hobbled man. Tina felt a sense of recognition just as Emilia yelled.

"It's Sergeant Williams." She motioned to the security guard. "Let them in."

The guard opened the door and the detectives limped in, depositing their injured companion on a reception bench.

"God, what happened to you guys?" Emilia said.

"He got brained pretty good," Williams said, nodding at the stunned detective on the bench. "Whole city's gone insane."

"We were at the Justice Building," Tina said. "Saw it all start."

"You two were *there*?" Williams said, looking from Tina to Emilia with disbelief. He shook the question off. "I'm not even talking about that. Liberty City's on fire."

"Probably a pointless question," Emilia said. "But what are you doing *here*?"

"Our walkies died on patrol," Williams said.

"So they got on my radio," the detective next to him said, his first words since entering the reception area. His voice was gravelly. "Got a call about some bodies, showed up and got fucking attacked." As he spoke, he reached in his pocket and pulled out some cigarettes, the pack crumpled almost into a ball. He opened the top and flecks of tobacco fell out, the cigarettes ruined. He sucked his teeth, throwing the pack against the wall. "Fucking ambush."

"Some kids blew up his car," Williams said.

"They *what*?" Emilia yelled.

"With our only radio inside," Williams added.

"Trust me," the pissed-off detective said. "That's the least of it."

"We need to get in contact with the other precincts," the dazed detective said, sitting up. His face was red, attractive in spite of his condition. A ruggedness that seemed both experienced and youthful. He locked eyes with Tina and something stirred in her stomach. "Gotta call for backup. If we can use your radios. Please."

"Governor's gotta call the National Guard in on this one," Williams said. "We're outnumbered here."

Emilia glanced at Fred and Fred shrugged.

"Right this way, detectives," he said, motioning towards the elevator.

17.

Leaning against Luchi's Mercury, Bilsner grinned at Luchi and Tommy as they approached. His smile disappeared when Luchi balled his hand into a fist and let a jab loose right into the man's stomach. Bilsner fell to the ground gasping, pushing himself up and coming face to face with a sleek black pistol. Luchi glared at the man from the other side of the trigger.

"When I call," Luchi said. "You pick up the phone. Sí?"

Bilsner stared at the gun, fear crackling in his eyes. He nodded.

"Good," Luchi said. "Now go. Get ready the next plane."

Bilsner glanced at Tommy and walked off holding his stomach, climbing in a car a few spots over and pulling out of the garage. Luchi put his gun away as his men loaded the duffel bags into his car then retreated to the BMW two spots over. Tommy climbed behind the wheel of Luchi's car, glancing at the duffel bags in the backseat. Starting the engine, Tommy pulled out of the parking garage with the BMW behind.

Turning onto 14th, the crowd Tommy had noticed near the justice building appeared again, quadruple the size it was a half hour ago. He watched them curiously as he pushed the car back towards US-1. He stopped at a red light and Luchi tapped him on the leg, wrinkling his nose.

"Tú cara," he said. "Porqué?"

"Nothing," Tommy said.

"You do good," Luchi said.

"I didn't do anything," Tommy said, pulling through the intersection.

"Exactamente," Luchi said.

They headed towards Morningside with protesters spilling out onto the street at every red light. Tommy studied the pockets of crowds as he guided the car around them.

"Pepito, eh?" Luchi said.

"Yeah, he's something," Tommy said. "I'm just glad Bilsner showed up."

"Pinche Bilsner," Luchi said, his expression darkening. "He is a lucky man."

"He's right, you know," Tommy said. "If these cops really wanted to cause chaos, all they'd have to do is stop reporting busts. Everybody would end up killing each other."

"This is true," Luchi said. "Thank di gods di pinche police must put in reports for everything."

"They do love bragging."

Luchi grunted and reached for the radio, scrolling through newsflashes before finding a station playing Donna Summer's "Hot Stuff." A bulletin broke in halfway through the song and Luchi sucked his teeth, turning the radio off.

"Something's going on," Tommy said as they passed more protesters.

"Los negros," Luchi said. "They are upset di cops kill di man." He glanced at Tommy. "Pepito says you will visit di Moreno ranch. Dis is a honor."

"I am honored," Tommy said.

"Di Morenos only invite friends to di ranch."

Tommy nodded, keeping the car steady and staring out at Biscayne stretching ahead of them. The air grew hazier as they coasted north. A few blocks west, a column of black smoke twisted towards the sky. They approached another intersection of protestors, this group blocking off the entire street. Tommy turned right, headed towards the ocean to detour down an alley. He stared at the crowd as they disappeared in the rearview, catching sight of one cardboard sign:

Justice.

"Verdict from the trial must have come in," Tommy said. "I'm guessing the cops who killed that black guy got off?"

"Maldita policia," Luchi said. "Dey are also corrupt in Colombia." Luchi paused. "But dere we buy dem."

"That's…definitely a solution," Tommy said.

"Los negros," Luchi said. "Dey sell di coke better."

Tommy raised an eyebrow. "I didn't know it could be sold better."

"Sí," Luchi said. "Dey cook it. Very popular. I want to sell dem more."

Tommy glanced at the protestors again. "They cook it?"

"Sí," Luchi said. "We will sell to dem and make much more."

Turning onto Tommy's street, they pulled to a stop in front of his house with the BMW trailing behind. Tommy killed the engine and nodded at Luchi, reaching for the door. Luchi grabbed his arm.

"You do good today, Tommy," he said, reaching in the back for the duffel bags. A zipper opened and closed then Luchi settled back in his seat, holding out two brown wrapped packages the size of bricks. "Un regalo."

"Luchi," Tommy said, staring at the packages. "All due respect. I'm not bringing those in my house."

Luchi leaned over and placed the two packages on Tommy's lap, patting Tommy's leg. He looked out the passenger window, pointing at the front gate.

"Dis is your house, sí?" he said. "Tú y Clara?"

Tommy nodded. "Yes."

"But Clara and you do not have dis house without me," Luchi said, pointing first at himself then at the bricks in Tommy's lap. "Without dis. No?"

Tommy looked at the packages. They felt heavier than they should.

"No," Tommy said. "We wouldn't."

"No," Luchi said. "So you take dese. Dis is not asking much, no?"

Tommy looked into Luchi's eyes and saw the same thing he always saw when he looked at the man: nothing. An emptiness that reminded him of a paper he'd read in college on the Cygnus X-1, the first black hole discovered.

Tommy touched the packages. They felt like overstuffed bags of flour.

"I guess not," he said.

"Tommy," Luchi said. "Dis is nothing." He pointed at the bricks. "This is *money*. I am giving you *money*. We will make more and more *money*." He grabbed Tommy's shoulder. "La Compania, you and me. We will run Miami, no?"

Tommy forced a smile, nodding. "Nothing wrong with a little money."

"Exactamente," Luchi said.

Tommy opened the car door and stepped out with the bricks under his arm. Luchi scooted over to the driver's seat. He held up a hand as Luchi tapped the horn and pulled off, the BMW following. The taillights dwindled to nothing. Tommy looked up at the purple sky, at the smoke trails dampening the horizon, helicopters floating around them like flies. Bouncing the packages in his hand, feeling the heft of them, he headed up his walkway.

Inside, the house was quiet. Tommy tiptoed across the living room, checking around the TV stand, the bookcase in the corner, the stereo on the back wall. Walking over to the sound system, he opened the cabinet and peered in. There was a bit of empty space behind the record player. Tommy moved it, shoved both of the brown packages in then adjusted the player so it rested in the same spot of dust it had been sitting in.

Closing the cabinet, Tommy relaxed a little. He walked down the hallway to the first door where his son lay in bed, the green glow of his nightlight illuminating the room. He found Clara in Lorena's room standing over their daughter's crib. Walking up behind his wife, Tommy hugged her. Clara pressed her butt against him, leaning her head back against his chest.

"How'd it go?" she whispered.

"Fine," Tommy whispered back.

"You hungry?"

"Definitely not," he said. "Could use a drink though."

"I'll join you," she said, grabbing his hand and leading him back to the living room. Tommy sat, tensing as Clara passed the record player on the way to the bar. She filled two glasses with ice from the cooler and poured some whiskey in each, heading over to the couch and handing one of the glasses to Tommy. She tapped hers against his and took a sip.

"Now how did it *really* go?" she asked, sitting and placing her glass on the coffee table.

Tommy finished half his drink before dropping his glass next to hers. "Alright, I think," he said. "Was touch and go there for a moment."

"How so?" she asked. Tommy said nothing and she put a hand on his knee. "You said."

"I know."

"We'd talk about everything."

"I know," Tommy said. "I just—"

"What happened?"

Tommy sighed then relented. He told her about the lost shipment, the tense meeting with Pepito, the invitation to the Moreno ranch. He left out his last interaction with her uncle, trying *not* to look at the record player.

When he was finished, Clara let out a long breath. She took a huge sip of her drink, put the glass down and grabbed Tommy's hands, squeezing them.

"At least he likes you," she said. "They all seem to like you, actually."

"I don't know what to do," Tommy said. "This has gone so far."

"Options," Clara said. "You always said we should look at our options. No matter how bad things might seem, there are always options." She touched his chin, forcing his eyes up. "And you were right."

"Okay," Tommy said. "So what are our options now?"

"You can keep doing this," Clara said. "See where that goes."

"Luchi is going to get caught," Tommy said. "And at this point if he gets caught, we go down with him."

"Or," Clara said, holding up a finger. "We can run. Take what we've got and leave. You've made a lot, we could just—disappear."

"They'll kill us."

"Tommy, he's my uncle," Clara said. "He wouldn't—"

"The people he works for will track us down along with everybody we care about," Tommy said. "Including the kids."

"Fine," Clara said, holding up another finger. "A third option."

Tommy sat back on the couch, saying nothing.

"Stop being just his driver," she said. "Help him get better at what he does. So he *doesn't* get caught."

Clara's words hung in the air.

"And how exactly am I supposed to do that?" Tommy asked.

Clara lay her head against his chest. Her hair smelled of lavender. "You're one of the smartest men I know," she said.

"You sure about that?"

"I thought we were going to die in New York," she whispered. "I thought he sent us up there because he couldn't do it himself. Just hiding us until he could get somebody else to do it."

Tommy pulled her chin up, looking her in the eyes. "I told you that wasn't going to happen."

"And it didn't," Clara said, putting a finger against his chest. "Because of *you. You* got us back here, *you* turned this into opportunity. And *you* will figure this out."

"Your faith might be a little misplaced," Tommy said. "Half that was luck."

"I wouldn't have married you if you were just lucky," she said. "Give me more credit than that."

Tommy gulped the rest of his drink. Peering down at the top of his wife's head, he listened to the symphony of crickets outside. Clara's breathing slowed, as did his, until their chests were rising and falling in unison. He tightened his arm around her shoulders, staring at the blank TV screen. His reflection stared back, blurry and distorted.

"Do you remember the day they shot Kennedy?" he asked.

Clara looked up at him, confused. "Um—of course, yeah."

"Where were you?"

"Elementary school," she said. "Second grade. It was all over the news. Our teacher started crying, a bunch of parents picked their kids up." She paused. "I remember it vividly. Why, don't you?"

"No," he said. "I don't remember what I was doing at all actually."

A heavy knock at the front door startled them both. Tommy eased out from under Clara, standing cautiously. He held up a hand for Clara to stay back but she ignored him, clinging to his pants' waist.

"You expecting somebody?" Tommy whispered.

"No," she said. "You?"

"Definitely not," Tommy said.

He reached for the baseball bat behind the door, gripping it in his right hand as he placed his left on the wall to steady himself, peering through the peephole. A man stood on the other side, holding a black duffel bag and looking out at the large front yard as if he were lost. He paced a little, limping on his right leg. He seemed familiar, though Tommy couldn't pinpoint where he knew him from.

Motioning for Clara to step back, Tommy raised the bat and unlocked the door, opening it. Tommy and the man locked eyes and the man's mouth opened into a gap-toothed grin.

"Tomas," he said.

The bat fell from Tommy's hand, clattering to the ground. Tears welled in his eyes, his mouth parting to let out a strangled breath. He coughed, putting a hand to his chest.

"Adán?" he whispered.

The man nodded, grabbing Tommy and pulling him in for a hug. They gripped each other, Tommy's chest hitching as he let out a sob. They took a while to let each other go, studying each other's faces.

Clara stared at them with her own mouth hanging open.

"Tommy," she said.

Tommy turned to his wife, his nose and eyes a mess of tears. Just past Clara, a sleepy Adam stood hiding behind a dining table chair. Tommy crouched, motioning for his son to come to him. Adam ran over, staring up at the strange man in the doorway. Tommy picked up his son.

Tears beaded at the corners of the man's eyes. "Tu hijo?" he said.

Tommy nodded, coughing and laughing at the same time. "Adam," he said. "Su nombre es Adam."

The man blinked hard, tears spilling down his cheeks.

"Tommy!" Clara barked.

Tommy startled, turning to his wife.

Clara motioned from the stranger to him. "What is happening right now?"

"It's Adán," Tommy said, looking at the man as if he could up and disappear at any moment. "My brother."

The three adults stood with almost photographic stillness as Adam sucked his thumb and lay his head on his father's chest. The distant sound of helicopter rotors floated over from the stacks of smoke rising to the sky.

"You have a fucking *brother*?" Clara yelled.

18.

The shirtless sniper steadied his rifle on the edge of the roof, his skin as dark as the barrel. A SWAT van turned onto the avenue, stopping just short of where the two dead men were still being beaten. Rig could see the whites of the cops' eyes in the front seat. Sitting on a concrete block, he passed the box of Milk Duds to Otis.

"Fuck they think they 'bout to do?" Otis muttered, shaking a couple of chocolates into his hand.

"This is wrong, man," DJ said, his eyes hollow.

"Fuck them crackas," Otis said.

Rig watched the bodies of the two dead men, his stomach twisting in a knot as they bounced through the attacks. A man holding a .25 automatic walked over and unloaded the clip. Another man picked up the damaged newspaper dispenser and used it as a sledgehammer, the body twitching on impact. Right before the SWAT van arrived, a green Cadillac had turned onto the street and rolled slowly over each dead man, reversing back over them again before driving off.

A toddler sat out on the front porch of one apartment with his mom, watching the action. Almost all the apartment windows had faces pressed against them, expressions ranging from elation to fear. The crowd noticed the SWAT van and some of them wandered off.

"Naw we ain't done," Otis said. Picking up a loose brick, he walked across the street, stopping at the closest body. Staring right at the SWAT van, Otis slammed the brick into the dead man's neck. The crowd erupted in cheers, some of the wanderers returning to resume the beating. Otis dropped the brick and walked back over to Rig and DJ, eyes remaining on the SWAT van.

Rig looked down at the clumps of small rocks in his fist. He uncurled his fingers and they fell to the ground.

The SWAT van idled as three cops jumped out in riot gear. The crowd started pelting them with projectiles. The sniper on the roof looked through his scope and pulled the trigger, the blast ringing in Rig's ears. The bullet pinged off the SWAT symbol, the cops ducking behind the van. Gunshots sparked from apartment windows. One of the officers reached in the van and put it in neutral, the three of them using it as moving cover, pushing towards the small crowd still surrounding the bodies. The cops screamed with guns raised and the crowd relented some, backing away from the crashed pickup. Reaching the bodies, the SWAT team loaded them into the back of the van then took off back towards 62nd street. The sniper followed them with his rifle, firing a shot that sparked off the van's bumper.

"Come on," Otis said, jumping up and ducking through the Crystal Palaces courtyard. Rig followed behind him with DJ, trying to keep hidden from his apartment where he assumed his mom was one of many standing outside watching the deteriorating conditions. Rig, Otis and DJ came out on 61st. Flames shot out the window of a business property at the end of the block, while straight ahead a group of people sat in a circle playing guitars and drums and singing gospels. DJ and Rig ran past them after Otis.

At the intersection, protesters spilled off the sidewalk, throwing rocks at cars. One connected with a station wagon and the car skidded off the road, smashing into an abandoned auto shop. The crowd descended and yanked three white people out, their bodies disappearing beneath the writhing mass of attackers. At the shopping center on 62nd, another crowd gathered outside a building on fire. People with all manner of battering rams smashed through windows and climbed into stores. KC's Beauty Shop—where Rig's mom worked—was locked up with a metal garage door pulled down over the storefront. Same with the pharmacy next door, the only two places on the block not being raided. At 62nd and 7th, protesters a hundred deep filled the intersection, stopping traffic. Around them, people ran across the street with full shopping carts.

"Bet they ain't see this shit coming," Otis yelled at the sky, pulling a small white joint out of his pocket. "Fucking pigs *gotta* quit fucking with us now!"

A man pushing a shopping cart filled with shoeboxes appeared at the corner, approaching the boys with one box held in the air.

"Ten dollars, young bloods," he said.

DJ and Rig waved him off. Otis put the unlit joint behind his ear and walked over to the man, peering inside the shopping cart.

"Da fuck are these?" Otis said. "Fuck outta here with this cheap ass shit."

The man glared at Otis and shoved the rattling shopping cart down the street. Half a block ahead, a group of teenagers crowded around a body on the ground, stomping the person out. Helicopters drifted near one of the many spirals of smoke dotting the Liberty City skyline. A patrol car turned onto 62nd and squealed to a stop near the mob at the intersection. Two uniformed officers jumped out, guns drawn. The crowd turned on them, bats and sticks raised. The cops hopped back in the car and sped away.

"Everybody on the come up but us," Otis said, pulling some matches out of his pocket. He lit the joint and puffed until the tip turned bright red.

"This shit is crazy," DJ said in a low voice.

"Everybody's lost their fucking minds," Rig said.

"Or *found* 'em," Otis said, his voice hoarse with smoke. "All our mamas and daddys and all *they* mamas and daddys, they done got all these crackas used to black folks bein' on this yessir massah bullshit." Otis puffed his chest out and screamed in the direction of the mob. "Ain't no yessir massah in here no mo'!"

Otis handed DJ the joint. DJ hesitated then puffed it twice, holding it out to Rig. Rig took it, studying the bright red cherry at the end.

"Ain't you say yo' Pops got locked up for this shit?" Otis said, shaking Rig's shoulder. His eyes were blood red.

Rig nodded, staring at the joint. The paper felt brittle in his hands.

"That's funny as hell," Otis said, cackling. "Yo' pops locked up for that shit, now you smoking the shit, while the whole 'hood getting' burnt to shit."

Rig put the joint to his lips and inhaled. The smoke hit the back of his throat like lava and he doubled over coughing. Fifteen seconds of this and Otis clapped a hand across his back, hooting and hollering.

"Ol' virgin lungs over here!" he yelled.

"Holy shit," Rig said, face puffy, nose runny, eyes teary. "Goddamn."

"That's what I'm calling this shit," Otis said, taking another hit of the joint and holding it up in the air. "Goddamn. Like 'Goddamn, this the best Goddamn weed on the Goddamn planet.'"

Otis handed the joint to DJ, who took a small hit and held it out to Rig again. Rig took it and hit it one more time, the smoke not as intense. He held it in for a five-count then exhaled a cloud that expanded as it faded into the sky. Staring up at the streetlights, the haze surrounding them grew a wider range of colors, the night sky a kaleidoscope of patterns. Rig handed the joint back to Otis and stared at the lights. Otis finished it and dropped the roach.

"Yo, there go Black," DJ said.

Otis turned towards his uncle outside an electronic store. He took off running across the street towards the shopping center where a meat market was on fire, as was a furniture store and an Army-Navy store. The U-Totem on the opposite corner had all its windows smashed out, same with Pantry Pride Supermarket across the street. Flames shot out the top of a lighting store, the Harley Davidson dealership down the street missing all its display bikes.

The boys ran up to the electronics store, the front door and windows caved-in. Three men standing outside turned to them. Two had masks pulled down over their faces. Black's mask sat bunched up on his forehead. All three men carried shotguns.

"Fuck y'all doing out here," Black said, smacking Otis lightly on the back. "Y'all ain't heard? These streets ain't safe."

"For who?" Otis said, grinning. "For *them* maybe."

Black laughed and motioned them over, pointing at a car parked up on a curb next to the store. Another masked man stood near the open trunk. "Y'all go check out the merchandise," he said. "If you can carry it, you can take it."

Pulling his mask over his face, Black followed his men into the store. Gunshots rang out from the street. DJ and Rig ducked. Otis stood tall, his eyes filled with glee.

"Y'all stand up," he said. "Ain't nobody after us tonight. We after *them*."

At the car, the masked man stood back as Otis approached. Otis dapped him up. The man looked at Rig and he recognized Black's friend Talvin behind the mask. Otis rummaged through the bounty, motioning Rig and DJ over. The boys joined in, digging through the scattered items. Rig found a Sony Walkman. DJ pulled out a record player.

Otis grinned at him. "You 'bout to earn yo' name."

DJ laughed, the gesture bringing a smile to Rig's face. Otis grabbed Rig's shoulders, squaring him up. He did the same to DJ then faced the trunk again.

"If we goin' be a crew," he said, glancing at Talvin. "Like you and Black and 'em, we gotta look fly."

Otis dropped three shoe boxes on the ground, handing a couple of outfits out to DJ and Rig. Rig held up a pair of Dickies shorts.

"Pay dirt, nigga," Otis said, moving the clothes to the side to show the sneaker boxes. "Foxes for y'all. BK's mine. We 'bout to look fresh as *fuck*."

Rig opened the shoebox and pulled the brand-new pair of shoes out, taking off his own duct-taped rags and tossing them in the grass. He pulled the laces out and ran them through the shoes then slipped them on, tying the laces tight. He stood and stared down at the jet-black high tops. When he looked up, tears sat in the corner of his eyes.

Otis found an errant shopping cart and dumped their possessions in, saluting Talvin as he pushed it towards the sidewalk. They were walking back towards Otis's place when Rig heard somebody yelling. He looked back to find Marquise and his cousin Day-Day standing across the street. Marquise's nose was still crooked, a sight that conjured an animalistic sensation within Rig. The moment he laid eyes on the other kid, Rig felt like tearing off his shirt and barking like Black's dog Booze, a feeling amplified by the fact that his head felt like it was about to float away.

Marquise said something Rig couldn't hear over the helicopter blades and gunshots and chants. Judging by the other boy's expression though, his words were not in good faith.

Rig dropped his shoebox and clenched his fists. Marquise motioned for him to cross the street but before Rig could move, Otis ran past him carrying a piece of concrete the size of a football. He pitched it at the boys, the projectile hurtling through the air and hitting the curb at Marquise's feet. Marquise jumped back, screamed something unintelligible. A second later an old Monte Carlo flew through the 9th avenue intersection and smashed into a parked Impala sitting in the street right between the two groups of boys. The car spun out and Rig dove back to the sidewalk, the front bumper narrowly missing him. The Monte Carlo came to a stop, smoke spilling from under the hood. The driver's door opened and a young black guy stumbled out, looking at each of the boys before taking off running south. Rig, Otis and DJ faced the opposite side of the street again, but Marquise and his cousin were gone.

"Bitch ass niggas," Otis said, walking back over to the shopping cart.

And suddenly, Rig found all this—the riot, the looting, the beef with Marquise and his crew—funnier than anything he'd ever heard or seen or experienced before and he broke into hysterical laughter. Otis and DJ raised their eyebrows at him, glanced at each other then started laughing too. Soon the three boys were hooting as they pushed their new possessions down the street.

A block away from home, Rig stopped, turning to DJ. "Gimme a tune."

Smirking at Otis, DJ put his hands up to his mouth, blowing a beat into the cups of his palms.

Rig closed his eyes, nodding to the rhythm, foot tapping on the sidewalk. Behind him, Otis whooped in time with the beat as Rig opened his mouth.

> *Y'all need to show some respect 'fore you get checked and wrecked*
> *Ain't gettin' none of our time unless you rep da set*
> *Standin' at an intersection in da fuckin' projects*
> *Starin' at a murder scene and wearin' brand new kicks*
> *Know what I mean? Listen to the rhymes I spit*
> *While I'm leanin' off this weed, peep da fresh outfits*
> *With my nigga O-dawg call him Rocky too*
> *And da DJ of the crew kickin' beats dat's sick*
> *Dat's it.*

Otis grabbed Rig's shoulders, bellowing in his ear.

"My nigga *spittin'*!"

"Shit was tight," DJ said, dapping Rig up.

"Been writing some," Rig said, his eyes dreamy and faraway.

"You definitely getting' better, bruh," DJ said.

"Gotta get you battlin' these niggas at the park," Otis said.

"For real," DJ said.

"And you need to learn how to use that shit," Otis said to DJ, pointing at the turntable in the shopping cart.

DJ walked over and pulled the box out, glancing around at the smoky night. "I gotta get home, check on Mama." He grabbed the shorts and t-shirt with his free hand. "I'ma hit y'all up later, be easy."

"Fo' sho," Otis said.

DJ dapped them up then walked off towards his house two blocks over.

Rig and Otis headed in the opposite direction with the shopping cart.

"You ain't got no brothers, huh?" Otis asked.

Rig glanced at him, shaking his head.

"Sister?"

Rig shook his head again, swaying on his feet. "Mama was supposed to have a baby last year but she lost it. Doctor said she can't have no more."

"Damn," Otis said. "How long yo' pops up for again?"

"Three years," Rig said, touching his temple. His head felt filled with helium. "He got parole in two."

"So you know him," Otis said, letting the shopping cart roll to a stop. "Like he been around? Before he got sent up?"

"He did a couple years in Jacksonville," Rig said, leaning against the shopping cart. "Ain't come back 'til right before we moved out here."

Otis whistled. "Mine been locked up since way back," Otis said. "Gun charge, ain't getting out no time soon. Mama make us go visit him sometimes."

"I hate them visits," Rig said, his brain bigger than his head.

"Me too," Otis said, rubbing his cheek and looking up at the sky. "I ain't never getting locked up. Ain't trying to be in there with all them sad ass niggas."

"That shit is sad," Rig said, closing his eyes. "Like there ain't no hope."

"Shit, I got hope," Otis said. "I'ma play for the Dolphins, be like Mercury Morris. NFL don't be taking niggas been to the pen."

"That'd be cool," Rig said. "Real cool. O-dawg on the Dolphins."

Otis smiled. "What you tryna do when you get up outta here?"

Rig opened his eyes, frowning. "Never really thought about it."

Otis nodded. "I feel you."

Rig giggled, rubbing his face. "This shit's crazy," he said, wiping the corners of his mouth. "Goddamn, for real."

"Man, take yo' high ass home," Otis said, shoving Rig.

A sudden explosion nearby startled the boys. They turned to a cloud of gas spreading in their direction. It reached them and Rig's eyes started watering, his throat on fire.

"What the fuck!" he coughed.

"Tear gas," Otis yelled. "Get to the crib, I'll hold yo' shit. Hit me up later."

Rig coughed and waved at him, taking off running, spitting fire as he pushed away from the expanding cloud. He stumbled around the corner to his block, cutting through some clotheslines to the courtyard where residents of Crystal Palaces stood outside holding wet cloths over their mouths and noses, conversations buzzing.

Standing across from his apartment, Rig froze, eyes red, his nose a puddle of snot. His mother and aunt sat outside on the front steps, Mrs. Anselbery standing behind his mom rubbing her shoulder. His mom puffed on a cigarette in one hand, clutching a pack of Virginia Slims in the other. Light shone off her wet cheeks, her eyes streaming tears though her expression was filled with nothing but anger. She spotted Rig and jumped up. Didn't move off the steps, just glared.

Rig thought about turning and walking away. Floating away. The thought warmed him. He pulled his crucifix from under his shirt and tugged on it.

Dropping his chin, Rig sighed and trudged the last few yards back home.

Deadliest Riot Day Claims 10 Lives, *May 18, 1980*

Cuban Refugee Wave Passes 51,000, *May 18, 1980*

Miami Riot Damage Toll: $100 Million, *May 20, 1980*

Record Cocaine Haul Seized: Car Trunk Sags with 410 Pounds, *May 21, 1980*

Study Sees Florida Banks Poised for a New Boom, *June 2, 1980*

Cuban Sealift Sailing to Calm Conclusion, *June 12, 1980*

Demoralized Miami Police Feel 'Nobody Cares', *July 17, 1980*

Leaky Cocaine Packets Kill Smuggler, *August 7, 1980*

1980 Miami-Dade's Deadliest Year—362 Homicides, *September 6, 1980*

Angered Miami Citizens Taking the Law into Own Hands, *September 6, 1980*

The Latinization of Miami, *September 21, 1980*

Dolphins Beat Saints for Third Win in a Row, *September 29, 1980*

Ronald Reagan Wins in Landslide, *November 5, 1980*

Anti-Bilingualism Measure Approved in Dade County, *November 5, 1980*

Murder Score—Six in 12 Hours, *November 18, 1980*

Hurricanes Rout #18 Gators in Gainesville 31-7, *November 30, 1980*

Reagan's Shooter Identified as John Hinckley Jr., *March 31, 1981*

PSD Officers Suspended in Rape Case, *May 1, 1981*

Emilia Brathwaite, Miami Tribune, Metro

Two officers accused of ignoring a rape victim and helping her attackers have been suspended, according to Public Safety Department Captain Lawrence Paschal. The Dade County State Attorney's office is working with PSD to investigate the actions of the two officers during the incident that took place early Monday morning. On Thursday, Captain Paschal ordered 30-day suspensions for Mark Patterson, a 35-year-old officer with seven years' experience on the force, and Jerry Leland, 40, an officer for ten years who is also a Vietnam veteran. Captain Paschal has also expressed a desire to have the officers dismissed, a move requiring approval from the Police Board.

"There is no room for this kind of behavior," Captain Paschal said. "To think that people will associate this with the entire department is disheartening. The actions of these officers were outrageous and disgraceful."

The two suspects—James Nieves and Timothy Boor—were apprehended late Tuesday evening and have been charged with rape, sexual assault, aggravated kidnapping, unlawful restraint, and robbery. Both are being held in Dade County jail on $100,000 bonds.

The victim is a 24-year-old pharmacy tech who spoke with the Tribune on the condition of anonymity. She says she was walking home when a white van pulled up outside of her apartment building. Two men jumped out and forced her in at gunpoint. They then drove to an abandoned lot in West Kendall and proceeded to beat and rape her.

At some point, the accused officers arrived in their squad car. The suspects exited the van, ordering the victim to stay quiet and hidden. As soon as they left her, she climbed into the front seat and opened the driver's side door, running over to the officers for help.

"The policemen were just standing there talking to them," the victim stated. "So I ran up and told them what they'd done to me, tried to show them the cuts and bruises but they ignored me and told me to go sit in their squad car. They wouldn't even look at me. They just kept joking with the guys who had just raped me, and then they let them go."

After releasing the suspects, the officers drove the victim to a friend's house where the victim's friend dialed 911 and asked for different police officers to respond to the crime. The suspects were later apprehended shoplifting a convenience store.

"They never even asked me my side of the story," the victim added. "They just had no interest."

Neither of the suspended officers was available for comment.

Miami the New 'Capital' of Latin America, *May 15, 1981*

Amid Turmoil, PSD Rebranded Metro-Dade Police Department, *July 21, 1981*

Part Three: Icarus
Monday, September 7, 1981

"Por la esquina del viejo barrio lo vi pasar,
Con el tumbao' que tienen los guapos al caminar,
Las manos siempre en los bolsillos de su gabán,
Pa' que no sepan en cuál de ellas lleva el puñal."

Willie Colon, Ruben Blades, "Pedro Navaja"

"Cel-e-brate good times, come on!
It's a celebration.
Cel-e-brate good times, come on!
Let's celebrate."

Kool & The Gang, "Celebration"

1.

Santi stepped out the double doors into the Arrivals lot at Miami International, inhaling the heavy scent of humidity and car exhaust. He held up a hand and a cab braked fast, pulling to the curb in front of him. Opening the back door, he tossed his duffel bag across the seat and climbed in.

"Paradisa Hotel," he said. "En la playa. Por favor."

The cab driver pulled off. Santi grimaced, palming his distended belly.

The sun beamed just above the horizon as the cab headed east. Santi pressed his face to the window, studying the scenery. In the distance, a cluster of skyscrapers partially blocked Biscayne Bay, glistening and dotted with boats of all sizes. The Macarthur Causeway took them past the Port and a docked cruise ship, the colorful sky contrasting with the palm trees lining the median. They passed Star Island, the expensive homes shrouded in decadent landscaping. On Alton Road they slowed for traffic, cars jamming the lanes in both directions. Santi read the street signs to himself as they passed: *Meridian, Euclid, Washington* to *Collins* where the cab took a left past food shops, hotels and clothing stores. The alleyways brimmed with homeless. Santi frowned when he saw their greasy faces, then they were gone and the sky was bright again.

They approached a pharmacy and Santi tapped the back of the driver's seat. The man pulled over. Santi dropped a ten next to him.

"Espera aquí," he said. "Cinco minutos."

The man nodded and Santi hopped out, running into the pharmacy. He returned with a plastic bag of items, his forehead dripping sweat as he dropped it on the seat next to him. He swiped his face with his shirt. A few intersections later the cab stopped outside the Paradisa Hotel. Santi gave the driver a twenty, grabbed his bags and climbed out. He looked up at the square building and smiled, his teeth grinding.

Checking in at the front desk, Santi took a room on the second floor with a balcony, paying for the night with a hundred dollars cash. Sweat dripped off his nose onto the paperwork as he signed. He took the key from the front desk attendant and headed for the stairs, the veins in his temples standing out.

Stopping short of the stairwell, he turned and walked back to the front desk. The attendant slipped a bookmark in his novel and set it aside.

"Plees," Santi said, clearing his throat. "Qué cuarto?" Santi's left eye twitched for a second. "Eh—di room?"

"You're in 204," the attendant said. "You need me to show it to you?"

Santi nodded. The attendant came around the reception counter and Santi followed him up to the second floor. They approached a room and the attendant took the key from Santi's shaky hand, unlocking the door and leaving the key hanging. He tossed Santi a raised eyebrow as he walked away.

Locking the door behind him, Santi dropped his duffel bag and pharmacy purchases on the queen size bed. He twisted the window blinds open and stepped out onto the balcony, looking past the rows of buildings to the bit of ocean visible down a side street between two other hotels. The waves crashed, pale figures lying out on the sand. Santi's eyes blurred with sweat. He fluffed his collar, then took the shirt off altogether, stepping back inside and tossing it on the bed. He pulled a slip of paper out of his pocket and grabbed the beige phone on the nightstand, willing his fingers to stop shaking as he pressed each button. The phone rang three times then clicked.

"Dile a Luchi," Santi said. "Que Santi está aquí."

Santi listened to the voice on the other end then hung up. Closing the balcony door, he messed with the AC unit until a blast of air hit him in the face. His head twitched to the left, eyes fixing on a spot above the balcony door. He reached a hand out to touch nothing.

Shaking himself, Santi walked over to the pharmacy purchases, dumping the items on the bed: two enemas, two bottles of laxative, a package of pitted prunes. Reaching for the laxatives, a sudden belch escaped his lips. Santi grabbed his stomach, making it to the toilet in time to hack up a stream of yellow bile. He dry-heaved for a solid thirty seconds then fell to the ground a sweating pile of shaking limbs, grimacing and sniffling. His right arm twitched. He tried to hold it down and it shook harder. He struggled to push himself up and fell back to the floor. Crawling to the door, Santi coughed more bile up onto the bathroom tiles, smearing it across his chest as he scratched his way over to the dusty carpet. He reached the bed and grabbed for the laxatives, knocking a bottle to the ground. Picking it up, he rolled onto his back and pried at the lid. He twisted and pulled, grunting through gritted teeth until a giant convulsion hit. Santi twitched once, twice, then exhaled, the air seeping out of him like a stabbed car tire, his eyes open and lifeless.

The phone rang and rang, twenty times before it stopped, the echo lingering for a few seconds before fading to silence.

2.

Rig's running full speed away from something large and shadowy with a rumbling growl and a hyena cackle and it's catching up to him with a long claw that touches his shoulder and—

The bell rang and the entire class jumped up from their seats. Rig picked his head up off his desk, a line of dried spit trailing down his cheek. He wiped it with the back of his hand.

"Remember the homework for tomorrow," Mrs. Crawford yelled. "Romeo and Juliet, act two! There may or may not be a pop quiz!"

Scattered groans from the crowd as they cleared the room. Rig stood and was almost out the door when Mrs. Crawford called him to her desk. He trudged over and the teacher opened a drawer, pulling out some stapled sheets of notebook paper filled with familiar scribble.

"I read your essay," she said.

Rig said nothing, staring at the paper, a large red letter *A* stamped at the top with a circle around it.

"It was very well written," she continued.

"Thanks," Rig said.

"I do have some concerns though," she said.

Rig stayed quiet.

"About the subject matter," she added. "There are a lot of…" Mrs. Crawford flipped through the essay then placed it back on her desk. "…*Violent* images here. The part about your dad going to jail is particularly vivid."

"Am I in trouble?" Rig asked.

"No, definitely not," she said. "I'm just—"

Mrs. Crawford paused. Rig stared at her. She sighed.

"Is everything okay at home?" she asked.

"Yeah," Rig said.

"You sure you don't need help with anything? Maybe just talk about stuff?"

"I'm good," Rig said.

Mrs. Crawford nodded, pursing her lips and handing him the paper. Rig took it and walked out of the room.

Around the corner he found a trashcan and dropped the essay in.

Weaving through the crowded hallway, Rig dapped up a couple of people walking in the opposite direction. A commotion started behind him, two boys standing face to face in front of a row of lockers.

"Fuck you said 'bout me nigga?" one of them yelled.

"You smell like a dirty ass fucking Haitian," the other kid yelled back.

The first boy threw a punch and then they were on the ground, one wailing while the other yanked his shirt over his head. Within seconds a cop and security guard pushed through the crowd, grabbing the boys and slamming them against the wall.

Rig felt a hand on his shoulder, a brown kid sliding up next to him. The kid stood with his thumbs crooked in the straps of his book bag, pimples covering the area under his bottom lip.

"What's happenin', Eric," Rig said.

"Nothin' much," the kid said, slapping Rig's outstretched hand and looking around covertly. "You got anything today?"

"Yeah," Rig said. "You got cash?"

Eric nodded and followed Rig around the corner to a secluded bathroom. Rig opened the door and a trio of boys walked out. He waited for them to pass then ushered Eric inside, locking the door behind them. He checked the stalls, the last door wide open with a toilet filled to the rim with shit. Rig wrinkled his nose, closing the stall and taking off his book bag.

"How much you need?"

"Lemme get three," Eric said.

"Six for five," Rig said.

The kid pulled five crumpled dollar bills out of his pocket. Rig smoothed each bill out on his palm then slipped the folded wad in his pocket. He opened his bag and pulled out a plastic sack filled with a dozen joints, pulling out half the sack and handing them over. Eric carefully slid the joints into his pockets, backing towards the bathroom door.

"Yo, where you getting the money for this shit?" Rig asked.

Eric hesitated, a lightning flash of fear coursing through his eyes. "My boys." He held his hands up. "I know you said not to say nothin'. And I didn't, I swear. I just told them I know a guy. They don't know it's you."

Rig nodded. "Go ahead and tell 'em," he said. "If y'all wanna make some real money, let me know. Looking to expand the business."

The fear in Eric's eyes fizzled out. "Really?" he said, cocking his head to the side. "I mean—yeah. I'll talk to them."

Rig nodded, stuffing the sack of joints back in his bag. Eric unlocked the door and hurried out and Rig found himself alone. He stared at his reflection, forehead greasy, hair hanging limp to his shoulders. Pulling his chain and crucifix out from under his shirt, he studied the gleam in the overhead lights. Tucking it back, he zipped his bag closed, throwing the strap over his shoulder and splashing some water on his hands. He wiped them on his shirt then headed out, down the hallway to the school's front doors.

Outside, the sign for Winslow Junior High stood atop a pillar at the corner, next to the sign for Holydale Church. Students milled about, a couple of yellow buses idling at the curb. Rig spotted DJ sitting on a bench near the sidewalk, bouncing side to side with headphones over his ears. DJ saw him and pulled the headphones down, pointing across the school's courtyard at Otis standing with three girls, his arm around one of their shoulders. Rig walked over, DJ following. One of the girls noticed Rig and smiled, moving a strand of hair out of her eyes, flecks of green in her dark pupils. Rig's eyes drifted down to her shorts, the hem ending a half-inch below her butt.

"Hi, Rig," she said.

Rig smiled. "What's happenin', Keisha."

Next to Keisha, Otis had his mouth against Tasha's neck. Tasha giggled, slapping his chest. The third girl in the trio stood to the side, holding her textbooks against her chest. She glanced at DJ. DJ smiled back, said nothing.

Rig elbowed Otis. "Let's roll," he said.

"What y'all doing later?" Otis asked the girls.

"Nothing," Tasha said.

"We heading to the park," Otis said. "Y'all coming?"

"I gotta ask Mama," Tasha said.

"Tell her you goin' with them two," Otis said, motioning to her friends.

Tasha looked at them. "Y'all down?"

Keisha eyed Rig. "You goin'?"

Rig nodded. "Yeah, I'll be there."

Keisha smiled again, tucking the same strand of hair behind her ear.

The third girl said nothing.

"Sam?" Tasha said. The girl stayed quiet. "Samantha!"

Samantha looked up, startled, as if noticing for the first time that she was surrounded by people. Tasha raised her eyebrows and Samantha shook herself.

"I don't know," she muttered. "I've—I got homework."

Tasha glared at Samantha then planted a kiss on Otis's cheek. "We'll see y'all out there."

The girls waved goodbye and walked away, Tasha reprimanding Sam.

Rig slapped the back of DJ's head. "Why you ain't say nothin'?"

"To who?" DJ said, flinching away.

"Fuck you think, nigga?" Rig said, reaching to slap him again. "Sam."

DJ dodged Rig's hand, taking a few steps back. "Fuck'm I supposed to say."

"She shy, bruh," Otis said. "You gotta talk to her first."

"Whatever, man," DJ said. "I'll say what's up at the park."

"Better make yo' move, nigga," Otis said, smacking his palm against DJ's stomach. "Or I'ma bag her *and* Tasha."

DJ feigned a punch at Otis's head and Otis side-stepped, the two slap-boxing next to some benches. Rig watched with amusement until one of the security guards by the school entrance blew a shrill whistle.

"Y'all stop that shit!" he yelled.

"Fuck you, Maclin!" Otis yelled back.

"Get the fuck out of here, Otis!" the security guard hollered, pointing at the street. "You and DJ don't even go here no more! Y'all trespassing!"

Otis held up both his middle fingers and danced backwards to the street. Rig gave the security guard an apologetic smile and shrug, following his boys.

"Fuckin' Maclin," Otis said. "Can't stand his bitch ass."

"He used to catch me in the hallway every morning," DJ said. "Ten seconds late, this nigga still sending yo' ass to detention."

"Y'all need to chill," Rig said. "Maclin ain't all that bad."

"Oh alright, cool, so tell me," Otis said, dropping a hand on Rig's shoulder. "How long you been sucking his dick?"

"Fuck you, nigga," Rig said, pushing Otis away.

"Naw, fuck *him*," Otis said.

"Maclin's cool, bruh," Rig said. "Copped two joints off me this morning."

Otis froze, looking at DJ. "Did this nigga just say he sold to Maclin?"

"He goin' holla at me next week for more," Rig said.

"My *nigga*," Otis said, slapping Rig on the chest.

"Told you I don't need yo' ass," Rig said. "Got Winslow locked up."

"Hell *naw*," Otis said, letting out a whoop. "Maclin smoking that *dank*! Same nigga wanted to kick me out last year. 'Bout to take *his* bitch ass out."

Rig's smile disappeared. "What?"

"Getting' that nigga by end of the week, watch."

"O, come on man—"

"School find out he smoke that shit," Otis said, talking to himself now. "He gotta be out."

"Whoa, bruh, chill," Rig said. "I ain't trying to take the man's job."

"I am," Otis said.

Rig sucked his teeth. "He ain't even all that bad, O."

"Says who?" Otis said, spinning on Rig. "You?"

The two boys stared each other down. DJ watched from a few feet away, looking bored.

Rig sighed, rolling his eyes. The tension diffused.

"Be smart, bruh," he said. "We can use that nigga. What about, like—what about when I gotta get shit past the metal detectors?"

Otis squinted at him. "You a smart muhfucka, you know that?"

"Yes, in fact, I do," Rig said.

"*Yes in fact I do*," Otis echoed mockingly. "Ol' boujie ass nigga."

Rig pushed Otis and Otis bounced into DJ with exaggerated impact.

DJ rolled his eyes. "Y'all sound like y'all married."

"Fuck you, nigga," Otis said, reaching in his pocket and pulling out a joint. He sparked it up and took a long drag, passing it to Rig. Rig hit it twice and passed it to DJ. They walked by another church, a large black man out front watering a plant. He looked up at the boys and Otis took the joint from DJ, sucking in a lungful and exhaling a giant cloud in the church's direction. The man kept staring, expressionless. Otis waved him off, skipping past an apartment with a panting pit-bull chained to a water faucet, *Stop Killer Cops* spray-painted on the side of the building in dark red graffiti.

Crossing from one building to the next, an echo drew their attention. Deep in an alley, an older girl wearing red heels and a short black skirt faced a man leaning up against a wall between two windows. The girl sat crouched on her knees, her white shirt unbuttoned down to the middle of her chest. The man— late-thirties, maybe older—tilted his head back and let out a soft moan, the girl's head bobbing up and down on his lap. The boys stared until the man looked over, startled.

"Fuck y'all staring at?!" he yelled.

The girl looked at them too, her eyes droopy and glazed over. Rig and DJ shook their heads and kept walking. Otis stared. The girl went back to work and the man forgot about them, tilting his head back. Otis jogged after his boys.

"I know that bitch," he grumbled, picking up an empty beer bottle from the gutter and tossing it at a boarded-up building. The bottle exploded.

"Who that?" Rig asked, holding the joint out to DJ.

"Shirley," Otis said. "Went to Jackson with my sister."

"How old she is?" DJ asked.

"Shit…seventeen?" Otis said, finishing the joint. "Eighteen, maybe."

"Niggas don't even be lookin' for a room these days," DJ muttered.

"For real," Rig said.

"Her mama stay next to us," Otis said.

"Her mama ain't got no job?" DJ said. "She gotta be out here doing that?"

"Only time I ever seen her she out on the front steps smoking cigarettes," Otis said. "Don't talk much." He glanced back at the alley. "Shirley used to work over at Jumbo's."

They walked in silence for a block.

"What'd Black say?" Rig asked.

"He got an ounce for us," Otis said. "Two more if we sell it by Monday."

Rig whistled. "Monday?"

"Ain't nothin', bruh. Move most of it at the park later, sell the rest at school." Otis chuckled. "Northwestern niggas love that dank."

They cut through an empty weed-covered lot, a thick clump of bushes drawing Rig's attention.

"What coach say 'bout you playing this year?" DJ asked Otis.

Rig stepped past the bushes and froze.

"Fucking grades, man," Otis said. "They *killing* me with that shit."

Rig noticed the man's boots first, scuffed, faded, the laces untied, his legs splayed beneath him on the dented concrete. His milky eyes stared at the sky, the mouth beneath them wide open. His shirt looked sticky, the entire front stained brown, a bullethole in it at chest level. Rig saw through it to the puckered flesh where the bullet had entered. The dead man's dark skin held a grayish tint. Flies buzzed everywhere.

Rig took a step back, bumping into Otis and DJ behind him. The other two boys noticed the dead body and froze. Time stood still until a passing car gunned its engine and they all jumped.

"Maaaan, I ain't trying to see this shit," DJ said, staring miserably.

Otis pushed him. "Quit being a bitch," he said without conviction.

"I ain't."

"Like you ain't seen a body before."

"Not this close up."

"That's right," Otis mumbled, crouching over the dead man. "You ain't come to Dadeland with us that day."

Otis patted the dead man's pockets, finding a wallet. Rig opened his mouth to protest but nothing came out. Otis took a thin gold bracelet off the man's wrist, checked his shoes then backed away.

Rig looked around. "We should tell somebody."

"Hell naw," Otis said, nodding past Rig's head. Rig looked over at an apartment across the street where an old woman with tufts of gray hair looked at them out her second-story window.

"I ain't trying to see no police right now," Otis said, reaching in his pocket and pulling out another joint. "Let's roll. Fucking up my high."

Otis walked away, leaving DJ and Rig standing over the body. Rig touched DJ's shoulder and DJ flinched, looking at him with watery eyes.

"Quit staring at it," Rig said.

DJ shook himself, forcing a smile. "Like you ain't, nigga," he said, then walked after Otis.

Rig stared into the dead man's eyes for another couple seconds then followed his friends.

3.

Tommy had heard the story many times over the last year yet the revelations still surprised him.

Like how he was born in Oriente, same province as the Castros.

Like how his mother died of a heart attack two years to the day after he left, making the lasting image of her handing him a bag and pushing him towards a line of children boarding a plane (*te veré pronto*) that much more agonizing.

Their father, Adán informed him, had died in Presidio Modelo, one of the last inmates to be housed in the panopticon prison before the hunger strikes and rioting and overcrowding led Castro to close it down in '67. Adán's mother succumbed to cancer not too long after, he told Tommy, which was also when Tommy found out they were half-brothers. Their father had three families (*de que sabemos*), though he and Tommy were the only offspring (*de que sabemos*).

Watching his own mother shrivel away those last few months, Adán began thinking of her disease as a reflection of the country at large. Adán used to skip school and run errands for the prostitutes at San Miguel de Padron. When Castro took over, the hookers disappeared, as did much everything else fun in the city. Orphaned at fourteen, Adán got into some trouble and was presented with the age-old choice of jail or military service. Logically, he chose the latter, and was good at it too, he told Tommy. Real good, moving up the ranks, getting in with the type of crowd that could make life manageable in El Jefe's world. Then, one day, he's chauffeuring some officers to a meeting and a first lieutenant makes an offhand joke at his expense, something about black beans and Adán's dark skin.

He was having a bad day, Adán admitted. Which is why he broke the first lieutenant's jaw.

Six months in jail and a dishonorable discharge later, Adán thought himself lucky when he landed a gig driving an aspirin bus in Havana, hitting stops around the city once every four hours. Still, those days were tense. Between army, police and the CDRs (neighborhood defense committees), there was always somebody prying for information, hoping to appease government officials if not Castro himself. Adán kept his head low and worked but at least once a day he'd catch himself spinning around to look behind him, that feeling of eyes in his direction as real as the shiver running up his spine.

One morning last spring, Adán walked out of his apartment to find a tall man in a bleached white guayabara and expensive sunglasses standing right outside his door. The man stared at him, smiled, and walked away. Adán walked back in his apartment and packed a bag.

A week later, Tommy's brother sat in a bus with five other men outside the Peruvian embassy in Havana. The driver gunned the engine, put the bus in gear and sped towards the complex. Cuban guards manning the gates fired their rifles, bullets piercing the windshield and sides of the bus. Two hit Adán, one in his leg, one in his right butt cheek (he proudly showed Tommy the scars one day, despite Tommy's protests). Still, the driver floored the gas, the embassies front gates crushing under the wheels. They came to a stop fifty feet inside, Adán bleeding as he and the other passengers stormed out of the bullet-ridden van, screaming for asylum. The Peruvian ambassador was still carrying the napkin from his breakfast when he ran outside.

Castro's response was immediate: return the six Cuban citizens. Now.

Peru declined.

So Castro told his guards to retreat, leaving the embassy's gates vulnerable.

Within three days, ten thousand asylum-seekers crowded the embassy's grounds. Not a patch of the complex's spacious green lawns was visible. Men hung from mango tree branches and slept pressed against each other on the hard floor. Adán's injuries landed him in the embassy's hospital, where Castro's attempts to get him back were repeatedly thwarted by the Peruvian ambassador.

One day, in a move of pure pettiness, Castro ordered his troops to hand three thousand meals through the embassy gates to the ten thousand people on the grounds, leading everybody to fight for scraps. People ate boiled mango leaves. Someone caught the Peruvian ambassador's cat and roasted it over a fire.

On a Friday night, just over a week after Adán's arrival, the electricity in the embassy went out and Castro appeared at the front gates like an apparition, unaccompanied by guards. Adán saw the bearded figure from the window of his hospital room, said he'd never in his life been as scared as he was in that moment. Castro spoke with the Peruvian ambassador for a few minutes then walked the two acres of bodies, making note of the amenities: three bathrooms, a dozen beds, thousands suffering through dysentery in darkness. He walked out the front gate ten minutes later without a word.

Another week passed and five more cats died. Hundreds were forced to sleep in their own shit and urine. Adán got through the worst part of an infection, saving his leg. Then, one afternoon, buses showed up outside the embassy. Adán and the other asylum seekers climbed on and sat through the rumbling trip to Mariel Harbor. When asked, Adán picked the largest ship he could find and arrived in Key West among eight hundred. He was processed in a crowded hangar, given a set of clean clothes, a check for a hundred and twelve dollars and a couple of nights in a hotel on South Beach.

Adán paused and turned up the volume on the radio, a Cuban man yelling about something through static.

"He say di democrats love Castro," Adán said.

"I don't think anybody *loves* him," Tommy said.

"No sé," Adán said.

Tommy shook his head. "I still don't get how you found me."

Adán frowned. "Di phone book. Easy."

"It's just crazy," Tommy shook his head. "The whole fuckin' story."

"Ju no see crazy," Adán said, smiling. "Dat is nothing."

Ahead of them, one of Luchi's men leaned against the hood of a blue BMW, two others inside the car. To the right, a brand-new high-rise rose into the sky. Luchi appeared in the lobby with a short round man trailing him. They stopped and shook hands. Tommy noted the two giant suitcases Luchi's men had lugged into the building had not come back out. Pushing through the lobby doors, Luchi walked towards Tommy's car.

"You know, you really don't have to do this," Tommy said. "I told you, I'll take care of everything until you figure—"

"Ju know es no mi first time en Miami," Adán said.

Tommy looked over at him, frowning. "What?"

Luchi slapped a hand down on the top of Tommy's car, startling Tommy as he climbed in the back seat. Tommy stared at his brother. Adán held a hand up, smiled and shook his head.

"Paráte," he said, his voice low.

"Let's go," Luchi said, smacking the back of Tommy's chair.

Tommy looked away from Adán and pulled off, Luchi's men following.

They drove north a bit and turned into a motel near I-95, half a dozen loiterers scattering when they saw the newish cars enter the lot. Tommy parked and left his car running. The BMW pulled in next to him and the men in the backseat climbed out, walking over to two identical black sedans parked next to each other. The Sedans pulled out of the lot and Tommy followed them north to 125th street, the BMW's headlights in his rearview the entire time. Tommy lit cigarette after cigarette as he drove, tossing glances at his brother. Adán either ignored him or didn't notice, Tommy couldn't tell.

Turning into a middle-class neighborhood in North Miami, the sedans drove up to a house with a double car garage that opened as they entered. Tommy waited for the cars to park and the garage door to close before he pulled into the driveway, shutting off the engine. He reached for the glove compartment between Adán's legs, opening it and pulling out a spiral-bound notebook. Luchi climbed out the backseat.

At the front door, Luchi knocked and waited. Tommy and Adán stood behind him. Footsteps approached and the door opened on a gray-haired, dark-skinned Hispanic woman wearing a navy-blue dress that flared past her knees. She did a fair impression of a curtsy then leaned against the doorframe.

"Welcome, gentleman," she said in a thick accent. "Entre, plees."

Luchi walked past her without a word. Tommy and Adán looked at each other then followed him inside.

4.

Tina clipped the last print up to dry, the red light overhead casting bloody shadows across her face. Wiping her hands with a nearby towel, she walked the photo line, stopping at one with a fingerprint smudge in the bottom right corner. The white marks coiled around the face of an irate middle-aged white man in a frumpy shirt and sagging khakis, shouting at a podium with a finger pointed at something out of view. Tina plucked the photo from its clip and tossed it in the trash. Wiping her hands again, she sat down and unwrapped her tuna sandwich, grabbing her notebook and a pen from her purse.

An hour later, Tina walked out of the developing room with the finished prints in an envelope. A normal level of mid-morning buzz hummed amongst the photographers and reporters as she walked over to her desk near the elevators. She grabbed her purse and camera bag from her chair just as her desk phone rang. Picking it up, she gave her name and position.

"I swear to God I just saw a bird the size of a fucking dog," the voice on the other end said.

Tina smiled. "Hi, Fern."

"No lie," her brother said. "A fucking flying Labrador."

"It'll be an elephant by the end of the day," she said. "Aren't you supposed to be working?"

"A bartender's Saturday is you regular folks Monday," he said.

"Okay so you're bored, got it," she said.

"How dare you," he said. "No, I am not calling my sister because I am bored." He paused. "Though I am bored, but that's neither here nor there. I am calling because I just got a message on the machine from our dear mother."

Tina's smile faded and she rubbed her forehead, squeezing her eyes shut. "What's her problem now?"

"I don't know," Fern said. "You tell me. She just called and said she's going to San Juan tomorrow, doesn't know when she'll be back."

Tina's eyes flew open. "Wait, what?"

The humor faded from Fern's voice. "You don't know about this?"

"No, I don't," Tina said. "We literally just ate breakfast together."

"And she didn't mention it?"

"No, she didn't mention it. She spent the whole time bitching about you."

"*Me?*" Fern said. "What the hell did *I* do?"

"She's never gonna get over you moving," Tina said. "Especially to Orlando. Jersey, maybe but—"

"I'd die before I go back to Jersey," he said. "Anyways, the way things are going around here she might get her wish. All of a sudden everybody wants to drink at home, barely made rent last—"

"She said she's going to San Juan?"

"That is correct."

"And she didn't say why?"

"Also correct."

Tina looked out the window at the bay. "What the fuck."

"My sentiments exactly."

"Let me talk to her," Tina said. "Find out what's going on. I'll call you later, give you the update."

"Please do," he said. "And it sounds like you need a day off too, sis."

Tina wrinkled her nose. "Why?"

"I can hear it in your voice," Fern said. "I know you, you're probably killing yourself at that place to avoid going home. Try and relax."

"I will when you have a conversation with mom that isn't through an answering machine," she said.

Fern chuckled. "Touché."

They hung up and the phone was barely in its cradle before it rang again. Tina picked it up and Emilia spoke before she could say hello.

"You still shadowing me on this interview?" she said, chattering reporters in the background. "Heading to the parking lot now."

Tina grimaced. "Shit."

"We can reschedule if you want."

"No," Tina said, glancing at her folder. "I'll meet you at your car."

Emilia gave an affirmative and clicked off. Tina headed to one of the office doors on the back wall, knocking and stepping inside. A man with a head of shaggy blonde hair and large bifocals sat with photos spread out on the desk in front of him. Tina placed the folder on the edge of his desk. He gave it a cursory glance and returned to the photos.

"These are…" he said.

"City council session."

"Solid," he said, leaning back in his seat and looking up at her over his glasses. "Nice work on that North Beach fire by the way."

"Thanks," Tina said. "I'm headed out, got that thing with Emilia."

He shook his head. "The two of you are straight out of *Bosom Buddies.*"

"What can I say?" Tina said, tucking a curl of hair behind her ear. "People just love having me around."

"Get outta here," he said, shooing her away.

Downstairs, Emilia sat smoking behind the steering wheel in her Caprice. Tina climbed in the passenger seat and Emilia pulled off, headed west towards I-95. They hit the highway and Emilia handed her a cigarette, Tina lighting up as "Slow Hand" started on the radio. Leaning her head into the wind, Tina put the cigarette to her lips, blowing a cloud of smoke out the window. The blue sky shined above, sprinkled with tufts of clouds. "Slow Hand" ended and "Jessie's Girl" began. Emilia made a face and turned the volume down.

"So tired of this song," she said. "It's on repeat everywhere I go."

"They played it at least twenty times at the bar the other night," Tina said.

Emilia glanced over at her. "The bar, huh? Who'd you go with?"

"You know who I went with," Tina said, rolling her eyes. "Ralph was there too. He asked about you. You should have come."

Emilia shook her head. "Sergeant's been a train wreck since his separation. I want no parts of that. How's it going with Terry?"

"Good," Tina said. "He's nice."

"Nice?" Emilia said, lowering her voice and wiggling her eyebrows.

"If you're asking what I think you're asking," Tina said. "Yes, Terry has been a total gentleman."

"No cop is a gentleman," Emilia said.

Tina smiled. "In public at least."

"You devil!" Emilia said, slapping Tina's arm and smiling. "God, what I would give to be 23 again."

"You make it sound like you're some grandmother," Tina said. "You do realize you're hot, Ms. Brathwaite."

Emilia laughed. "If you mean sweaty then yeah."

"Come on," Tina said. "You're telling me there hasn't been anybody on your mind all this time I've known you?"

"Does Sparky count?"

"No," Tina said, laughing. "He doesn't."

"Why not?" Emilia said. "I sleep with him every night, feed him, bathe him, walk him. Sounds like marriage to me."

Tina rolled her eyes, glancing out at the passing houses and businesses to the east of the highway, many still showing signs of last year's riot. A tickle in her nose grew to irritation and she sneezed, a string of snot coming out.

"Gesundheit," Emilia said.

"Shit," Tina said, covering her face.

"Glove compartment."

Tina opened the glove compartment and grabbed a wad of napkins, the gleam of metal catching her eye.

She looked over at Emilia. "Since when do you have a gun?"

Emilia glanced at it, staring for a moment as if the gun had appeared out of nowhere. She shook herself. "Couple of months now," she said, focusing back on the road.

Tina closed it away. "I thought you were against them."

"I am," Emilia said. "I don't want to have one. Don't even plan on using it. Just…you know. Peace of mind."

Tina said nothing.

"It's ever since that fucking police union meeting," Emilia muttered. "Ralph got in my head. And Birch, the M.E. On TV telling everybody they should arm themselves. Felt almost…I don't know. Obligated."

Tina looked out the window again as "Endless Love" ended on the radio and a news bulletin broke in. Tina reached over and turned down the volume.

"For somebody who works for a newspaper," she muttered. "I'm really getting tired of hearing the news."

"You know what I'd like to hear?" Emilia said. "More about Puerto Rico."

"Apparently my mom's heading there tomorrow," Tina said.

"Really?" Emilia said. "Lucky her, what for?"

"No sé," Tina said. She blinked and looked over at Emilia. "I mean, I don't know. She didn't tell me. Didn't even tell me she was going. I had to hear it from my brother."

"Wait," Emilia said, frowning. "Don't you live with her?"

"Exactly."

"Yikes," she said. "Looks like you've got a conversation ahead of you."

"Not looking forward to it," Tina said. "San Juan probably looks so different now. Seven years since I've been. I miss my grandmother."

"Never knew my grandparents," Emilia said.

"On either side?"

"Mom's mom died when she was twelve, and she never knew her father," Emilia said. "She had me at 17, my sister at 19. Dad was a gambling addict, left not too long after Sara was born. Don't really know anything about his side."

Juice Newton's "Queen of Hearts" started on the radio.

"You know, when you told me you were born in Jersey," Tina said. "It felt like…I don't know, like I was destined to meet you when I did."

Emilia raised an eyebrow. "You believe in that? Destiny?"

Tina paused. "Never really think much about it. I mean, I was raised Catholic. So—kinda?"

Emilia patted Tina's leg. "I'm glad we met too. Just wish it'd been under less violent circumstances."

"Holy crap, the Dadeland shooting." Tina touched her forehead, chuckling. "I almost forgot. How do you forget something like that, huh?"

"A lot's happened since then," Emilia said.

"City's changed so fast," Tina muttered.

"I always wanted to ask," Emilia said. "That day. Why'd you run towards the gunshots?" She looked over at Tina. "Everybody else was running away yet there you were with your camera."

Tina paused, giving the question some thought. "I—don't really know actually," she said. "It was just instinct, I guess."

"Best skill to have in this job, let me tell you," Emilia said. "To be honest, I wasn't surprised when you told me you were from Jersey."

"Really?"

"Been noticing coincidences like that my whole life," she said. "Used to unnerve me, felt like somebody was dictating my life or something. Like I'm a character in somebody else's story."

"Yeesh," Tina said. "Creepy."

"I try to just appreciate the intricacies of life now," she said, smiling at Tina. "Like I appreciate our work-friendship."

"Awww," Tina said, sticking out her bottom lip. "I hate you too, Emilia."

They laughed and Emilia turned up the radio. The lanes widened and the traffic density thinned out. Exiting the highway, they drove west another mile, turning onto a non-descript street with apartment buildings lining both sides. Emilia slowed the car down.

"So I told you this was going to be a heavy interview," she said, staring at one of the complexes.

They parked and Tina looked up at the building. "Yeah?" she asked. "You didn't mention who it was."

"Partly because I thought you wouldn't want to come," Emilia said, sheepishly. "It's Mikayla Lawson."

Tina knew the name but couldn't pinpoint the source.

Emilia turned off the engine. "Story from a couple of months ago. Little girl. Cop. Backseat."

Tina's eyes widened and she looked again at the apartment building. "Shit."

Emilia opened the car door. "Her mother finally agreed to talk."

5.

Ralph shot up in bed, his naked body drenched. The cold sweat against his skin drew a violent shiver. The image of a machete coming at his head lingered and he pulled his knees up to his chest, hunched over and sniffling as the nightmare faded. A sharp pain jabbed behind his left eye and he touched the back of his head, grimacing as the hangover took hold. Looking around the sparsely furnished efficiency, he smacked his lips and wrinkled his nose at the rank taste of old whiskey.

Something shifted on the bed next to him and Ralph swung around, staring at the naked body lying with sheets tangled around her midsection, her butt and upper back bare. Her skin looked soft and unfamiliar. Tufts of curly brown hair shrouded the pillow around her head.

Ralph leaned back against the headboard, staring at the ceiling, veins throbbing at his temples. The phone on the nightstand trilled and the woman next to him stirred, letting out a soft groan. Ralph snatched the phone up.

"Williams," he said, his voice hoarse.

"You up?" Terry said.

Ralph pushed himself back to a sitting position. "Yeah. What's happening?"

"Meet you at the morgue," he said. "Patrol picked up a John Doe at a hotel on Collins last night."

"So let the Beach handle it."

"They're backed up."

"And we're not?"

"Don't know what to tell you, Sarge," Terry said. "We're up."

Ralph squeezed his eyes shut. "Give me twenty minutes."

"I'll be there," Terry said, and the line clicked.

Ralph put the phone down and the bed shifted. He looked over and the woman smiled up at him, rubbing her sleep-filled eyes.

"Hey, stranger," she said.

Ralph climbed out of bed and pulled on his boxer briefs. His pants, shirt and shoes lay in a pile near the front door. Ralph stared at them until the woman cleared her throat. Throwing her a quick glance, he picked up his clothes and sat on the edge of the bed. The woman pushed herself up, holding the sheets over her chest. The morning sun streamed through a single window, giving Ralph a good look at her face: late twenties maybe, full lips, big brown eyes and high cheek bones. The type of face TVs and movies tend to love. She smiled, then pouted and touched her forehead.

"You want to go grab a coffee or something?" she asked, her voice high-pitched. "I definitely need a cup."

"Can't," Ralph said. "Gotta get to work."

"*Detective* work?" she said.

Ralph squinted at her. "Yeah," he said, dropping his shirt and pants on the bed. "Something like that."

"So rad," she said, twirling a strand of hair around her finger. "Am I gonna see you again?"

Ralph turned to face her. "I don't know your name."

She shrugged. "I don't know yours either. Makes it kind of fun, huh? Add a little mystery?"

"Just because something's mysterious doesn't make it fun," Ralph said. "You do this all the time? Find strangers and take them home without knowing their name?"

Though the smile remained on the woman's face, the gleam in her eyes faded. She clutched the sheets tighter to her chest.

"I mean, I don't make a habit of it," she said. "You just seemed nice and I thought we could—"

"Seemed nice," Ralph said. "Seemed nice. The amount of women in this city meet a guy 'seems nice,' next thing you know I'm the one has to figure out who gutted them, or slit their throat, or left them raped in a corner of some alley crying because she had no clue what type of guy she trusted with her body like, tell me something—" Ralph hopped off the bed, leaning in close to her. "—Does that sound *nice* to you? Does that sound *fun?*"

The woman's smile disappeared, her cheeks flinching with every word Ralph spit. Ralph stalked over and snatched up the thin pile of clothes on the floor beneath her hanging feet—a blue dress, some black lacy panties with a matching bra. He tossed them at her.

"I need you to leave," he said through gritted teeth.

The woman gathered her clothes. Ralph walked into the bathroom, closing himself in. Leaning against the door, he relished the cool white paint on his forehead. She shuffled around the room for a moment before the clack of high heels tracked a path towards the front door. Ralph listened to the door squeak open, waiting for it to close.

"You're an asshole, *Ralph*," she yelled. "In case you actually want to know, my name's Carol. Like I fucking told you *last night.*"

The door slammed shut. Ralph turned and stood in front of the mirror, studying himself—the scruffy beard, bloodshot eyes, disheveled and thinning hair. Then his stomach turned and he dropped to his knees, puking into the toilet bowl.

Twenty minutes later Ralph climbed out of his car with a lit cigarette between his lips, approaching a newspaper vending machine across from Jackson Memorial Hospital. He dropped a quarter in and grabbed a copy, about to turn back to his car when he noticed something in a nearby alley between a pharmacy with tinted windows and a furniture store. A few somber stares met his from the alley shadows. Ralph counted two men and a woman, all dressed in rags. The woman dozed on a bed of trash bags, one of the men holding a tattered Army beret while the third man held a pipe up to his mouth, flicking a lighter over the bowl. Ralph smoked his cigarette down to the filter, staring at the group until their faces blended back into the shadows.

Tossing the cigarette butt, he climbed back in his car and pulled off.

6.

Short with bushy mustaches and afros, dark shades covering their eyes, Luchi's men looked nearly identical to him and each other as they dropped the duffel bags in the living room and headed back to the garage. Tucking his notebook under his arm, Luchi opened one of the bags to reveal dozens of football-shaped packages covered in black duct-tape with writing on them. He opened the other three bags and the room filled with a chemical scent reminiscent of a hospital. The woman who'd greeted them brought four bottles of vinegar from the kitchen and set them down near the bags, spraying a lemon air freshener around the room before perching on the edge of the couch, legs crossed, palms on her knees. The lemon scent made Tommy's eyes water and his stomach turn. In his head, he heard two bricks smashing together.

Adán nudged him, nodding at the woman.

Luchi noticed the gesture and smiled.

"That is Magdalene," he said. "Her family and my family know each other—" Luchi made a flinging motion over his shoulder. "—Generations. Conozco a sus hijos, a sus nietos, a sus sobrinas y sobrinos. I know all the names of her family, where it is they live. We make much from this house, so Magdalene cares for it. And I care for her family."

Adán nodded at the packages in the bags. "Qué son esos dibujos?"

"They're labels," Tommy said. He picked up one of the packages with *CIA* written on the side in red ink.

Adán raised his eyebrows, lowering his voice. "Ju work for espías?"

"No," Tommy said, smiling. "En Español, cia."

Adán wrinkled his nose.

"La Compañia, parce," Luchi said, waving his hands around the room. "Los que están pagando todo esto mierda." Luchi nodded at the package. "La cia is for them."

Tommy picked up another package with a square patch of tape on it colored light brown.

"Qué color?" Tommy asked.

Adán smirked, saw Tommy was serious and frowned. "Marrón?"

Tommy nodded. "For Los *Morenos.*"

"Ah," Adán said.

Luchi's men returned with two more duffel bags, dumping them next to the others and retreating to the kitchen. Luchi opened these up too, revealing more packages. A knock at the front door brought Magdalene to her feet. Tommy glanced out the front window at Bilsner standing on the porch wearing jeans and a Rolling Stones t-shirt.

Magdalene opened the door with her practiced ritual. "Welcome. En—"

"Yeah, hey, what's up," Bilsner said, walking past her to the living room. "You guys ready?"

"Come," Luchi said, dropping his notebook open on the floor. He dumped the packages out of each duffel bag and separated them into six coded piles, jotting numbers down in his notebook. Finishing his count, he handed Tommy the notebook. Tommy turned to Adán.

"This part's insurance," he said. "Accountability. I know it seems redundant—pointless. But we all have to sign off." Tommy motioned towards the packages. "Help me with the recount."

Adán nodded and crouched next to the piles, calling out codes and numbers. Tommy checked them against Luchi's scribble then handed the notebook back to Luchi, who ceded the floor to Bilsner. Bilsner gave each package little more than a perfunctory glance, jotting on a piece of paper.

When Bilsner was done, Luchi motioned for everybody to take a step back, nodding at Magdalene who picked up a pen and legal pad from the coffee table, dashing checkmarks as she walked the piles with an ever-present smile on her face. Finishing, she signed the bottom of the legal pad and handed it to Luchi. Luchi signed it too then handed her back the pad, nodding at the two men standing in the kitchen. Like woken sentries they walked over and dumped each coded pile into separate duffel bags. Three of the bags went to a room in the back of the house, the other three out the front door.

Bilsner closed his notebook and shook Luchi's hand, patting Tommy and Adán on the shoulders.

"Another job well done," he said. "I'll call when we're ready to go again."

Bilsner nodded at Magdalene and left.

Adán shuffled his feet. "El baño?"

Magdalene motioned for him to follow her, taking him down a hallway.

Luchi's men returned to the living room and Luchi pulled them to the side. Tommy took a seat on the couch, staring at the crucifix hanging above the front door. Luchi finished talking and his men headed back to the garage, the door outside rumbling open.

Luchi joined Tommy on the couch, patting him on the knee.

"Why do you lie?" he asked.

Tommy looked over at him. "Excuse me?"

"When we meet," Luchi said. "Years ago, I ask you if you have brothers or sisters. You say no."

Tommy glanced at the hallway. "Honestly, I thought he was dead."

Luchi laughed, a genuine one. "I like Adán," he said. "He is like you only—only not so American, eh?"

"Luchi—"

"And you are a good man, so." Luchi shrugged.

"We talked about this," Tommy said. "You said I could ease him in."

"Yes, but if he will learn," Luchi said, shaking Tommy's shoulder. "He must learn how you learn. How we all learn. By *doing*. He will come with us for the next part too."

Tommy squeezed his eyes shut. "This wasn't the plan."

"It is now the plan."

"This wasn't the plan," Tommy said, forcing his voice steady. Adán and Magdalene's footsteps came down the hall. "We made a *plan*. We let him in—"

"Tomas, you are in or you are not in," Luchi said, patting Tommy's cheek. "There is no other way. You know this. He will come, and you will both drive."

Tommy resisted the urge to recoil from Luchi's hands, his skin warm and rough. Magdalene and Adán reappeared, Adán looking from Luchi to Tommy curiously. Luchi stood up, holding his arms out towards Adán.

"You will drive por la siguiente parte."

Adán's eyes widened and he looked at Tommy. Tommy gritted his teeth, forced a nod. Adán stood up straighter.

Saying goodbye to Magdalene, the three men headed outside and piled back into Tommy's car.

7.

Black rented the apartment a couple of months ago and converted it into a workshop, stocked with equipment. Two folding tables stood in the center of the living room with half a dozen flat metal chairs. Piles of white rocks sat on the table in front of three women holding razorblades, scraping chunks off into plastic baggies and dropping them into the cardboard boxes sitting by their legs. The women wore black shower caps, pink tank tops and baggy underwear. The air smelled like a hospital. Rig wrinkled his nose, leaning against the kitchen sink, Otis and DJ nearby. Talvin sat on a stool by the counter reading a book. Black sat behind his desk in the corner of the living room with a brooding look on his face. He glanced over at Rig.

"Otis tell me you speak Spanish," he said.

Rig shot Otis a glance. "A little."

"Where you from?"

Rig looked confused. "Here," he said. "Miami."

"Naw, Blood," Black barked. "Where yo' *peoples* from? Ain't no niggas from 'round here, we all was *brought* here. Remember that."

"His mom's a yardie," Otis said.

"A yardie?" Black relaxed a little, chuckling. "You feeling right at home with this ganja shit then."

Rig shrugged.

"Where yo' Pops from?" Black asked.

"Nicaragua."

"So you is a chico," Black said. "A yardie chico. No wonder yo' ass so yella. You got more fam 'round here, Rig?"

"My aunt," Rig said, smirking. "But she's a chica."

Black furrowed his eyebrows. "Fuck's that supposed to mean?"

"Chic*a*'s Spanish for girl," Talvin said without looking up from his book. "Chic*o* means boy."

Black squinted at Rig. "So I call you chico," he said. "I'm just calling you 'boy' in Spanish?"

Rig nodded.

"Sound better than boy though," Black said. "Some cat walk up to me like 'What up, *Boy'* I'm 'bout to swing on the nigga. 'What up *Chico'* though. Got a ring to it." Black switched focus to Otis. "Yo' mama got that box I left?"

"Yeah," Otis said. "Good lookin' out."

"Found out who robbed y'all," Black said. "Ain't goin' be a problem with them particular niggas no more. But y'all need to stop leaving y'all windows open at night."

"It's hot as hell in there," Otis said.

"Turn on a fan."

"We do, it just be blowing hot ass air all—"

"Shut yo' boujie ass up, nigga!" Black yelled, snapping his fingers to get Talvin's attention. "You and yo' mama keep playing. Y'all asking for that shit."

Talvin looked up and Black nodded at the back room. Closing his book, Talvin stood and disappeared, returning with a scale, a tattered blue notebook and a clear garbage bag filled with weed. He sat back on his stool and laid everything on the counter, opening the notebook to a blank page. Looking over at Otis, Talvin pointed at one of the kitchen cabinets.

"Gimme some of that wrap in there."

Otis opened the cupboard and pulled out a roll of cellophane, handing it to Talvin. Talvin peeled off a length and laid it flat on the counter. Shoving his hand in the garbage bag of weed, he placed a few buds on the scale, studied the numbers and jotted in his notebook then tossed the bud on the plastic and dug out some more.

Black watched the women at the tables with a glowering expression.

"What up, Unc'?" Otis asked. "You look heated."

Black shook his head. "Just—Jimmy, man."

Otis frowned. "Jimmy?"

"Fucked up how they did him," Talvin said.

"What you mean?" Otis said. "I saw him yesterday down the street. In his church clothes. Sun was 'bout to go down."

Black shook his head. "Every week this nigga out there watching Pastor James' sermon, go sin his ass off da same night."

"What happened?" Otis asked.

"They took his ass out," Talvin said.

"For *real?*" Otis said, his eyes going wide. "Where?"

"Ballpoint's," Black said. "Knew exactly where to find Jimmy's ass on a Sunday night."

"Jimmy *stay* at Ballpoint's," Talvin said.

"Nigga just walked up in the joint and stabbed him in the throat," Black said. "Right in front of everybody."

"Who did it?" Otis said.

"Don't know yet. Ain't nobody talking."

"What for?"

"Coulda been anything," Black said, standing and joining them in the kitchen. "Jimmy weren't short on enemies. But gettin' that nigga on a *Sunday*? Ain't supposed to do work on Sundays, bruh. Just—them's the rules."

"Ain't have to do the man like that," Talvin said.

"Niggas mad disrespectful these days," Black said. "Shit ain't the same."

"And then Po'boy's dumbass," Talvin muttered.

"Naw, they got *Po'boy*?" Otis said.

"Not yet," Black said. "But they 'bout to."

Otis frowned. "Who? For what?"

"Nigga shot a pig," Talvin said. "Got his ass on camera."

The boys glanced at each other.

"Shit," Rig said.

"Damn right, shit," Black said.

"What you goin' do?" Otis said.

"Not a damn thing," Black said. "Been draggin' that nigga 'round since junior high. He ain't gettin' away from shooting no cop."

"Po'boy in too many pockets anyways," Talvin said. "Depend on too many people for his livelihood."

"Ain't lyin' there," Black said, clamping a hand down on Otis's shoulder. "That's why I be telling you, O. Make your *own* way. You ain't supposed to be workin' for *nobody* but yo' *self*. Ya feel me?"

Otis nodded, glancing at the women at the tables. "Be a whole lot easier you let us in on that."

"I told you I don't want you mixed up in that shit," Black snapped, looking over at the tables. His eyes glazed over and he stared at the ground. "Not yet."

"Here," Talvin said, twisting the cellophane around a ball of weed. He handed the package to Otis and picked his book back up. Otis shoved the ball in his bag.

"Don't be telling yo' mama 'bout none of this shit," Black said, walking to the front door with the boys behind him. "I ain't trying to hear her mouth."

Otis shook his head. "She don't know nothin'."

"Good," Black said. "Y'all be easy. And keep this nigga Chico around." He winked at Rig. "Cuban's own Miami now. We goin' need his ass."

Dapping Black up, the boys walked out of the apartment and around the corner towards Otis's house. They stepped onto the pock-marked sidewalk leading up to the front door just as Otis's mother—Miss Marjory Lawrence—raised a pearl-white .22 and pointed it at an old man backpedaling away from her with his hands up. The man wore faded jeans, a Dallas Cowboys t-shirt and a look of pure terror.

"Come 'round here again," Marjory yelled. "Come near my muhfuckin' daughter again, Claude! I swear to God I'll shoot yo' dick off!"

The man shambled off. Otis walked up behind his mother and touched her shoulder. Marjory wheeled around with the gun still raised.

Otis jumped back. "Relax, Mama!"

"Boy, don't tell me to relax," she growled, lowering the gun.

"What happened?" Otis asked, staring after the man as he disappeared around a corner.

"Claude's nasty ass out here sniffing after yo' sister," she said.

"Toya?" Otis looked confused.

"Nigga ain't nobody tryin' to mess with Toya's pregnant ass," his mom snapped. "Melly. Caught him out here trying to take her for a walk. Or so he out here sayin'."

Otis's expression darkened. "But she's seven."

His mother scowled at him.

Otis pointed at the pistol in her hand. "Where you get that?"

"None of yo' damn business," she said. "And don't let me catch y'all with one of these in my house, hear me?"

They all murmured acknowledgment, Otis looking back at his friends and rolling his eyes. Marjory held the front door open and the boys trudged over. Tripping on a crack, Rig stumbled onto the square patch of grass in front of the garbage bin against the side of the apartment. Marjory swatted him on the arm.

"Stay off my grass," she said. "I done told you."

"Sorry, Ms. Marjory," Rig said.

"Sorry don't help," she grumbled. "Just don't do it."

Inside, Marjory stuck her gun under a couch cushion and walked down the hall, disappearing into her room. Muffled voices conversed for a moment then she came back out, sitting and picking up the copy of Essence magazine lying on the floor. The bathroom door opened and Latoya, Otis's older sister, waddled out swinging a purse over her shoulder, the dark skin of her swollen belly poking out beneath her pink shirt. Otis barely acknowledged her, dropping his bag on the counter and pulling out the ball of plastic-wrapped weed.

"Headed to work," Latoya said.

"Pick up cigarettes when you coming back," Marjory said.

Latoya sneered. "You got money?"

"Girl, pick me up some goddamn cigarettes," Marjory said. "I'll give it to you when you get here."

"Same thing you said last time," Latoya grumbled.

"Quit back talkin' 'fore I smack you upside yo' head."

Latoya rolled her eyes and headed for the door, opening it just as a man on the other side was raising his hand to knock.

"Craig out here," Latoya yelled back over her shoulder.

Otis snatched up the weed, shoving it back in his bag and zipping it closed. Craig stepped to the side for Latoya then peered in the apartment.

"Hey y'all," he said, waving.

Marjory dropped the magazine on her lap. "What you want?"

Craig stepped inside and closed the door behind him. Melissa, Otis's little sister, poked her head out of the bedroom, braided pigtails bouncing, ketchup stains on her blue t-shirt .

"Craig!" she yelled, running towards him.

Marjory jumped up and intercepted her daughter, glaring at the man who wore overalls and a sheepish grin.

"What you want?" she repeated.

Craig's shoulders dropped. "Can we go talk somewhere? Alone?"

"Ain't got nothing to talk about," she said. "Not with you."

"Margie."

Marjory widened her eyes. "Yes?"

"I just want to explain."

"Don't need no explanation," she said.

"Marjory."

"Not from you," she said, ushering Melissa back down the hallway. "Not from *any* of y'all sorry ass niggas."

"Margie—"

"You got a stutter?" she said. "Quit calling my name!"

"I just—"

"You *just* need to get outta my place," she said. "I told you last time, I don't want you 'round here."

"You ain't even trying to hear what I got to say?"

"No, nigga!"

Craig jabbed a finger at her. "You know what? *This* is why." He glared at her, the couch, the TV, the boys in the kitchen. "*This.*"

"Go on then!" she said, hands on her hips as she followed Craig to the door. "Bunch a bastards, all of y'all. Ain't one decent nigga in this city, not *one*."

Craig opened the front door and stormed past a woman walking up the concrete path towards the apartment. Wearing a conservative navy-blue dress, the woman jumped out of Craig's way, looking at Marjory with concern.

Marjory threw her hands up. "I mean damn, am I goin' get a visit from Jesus today too?" She left the door open and retreated to the couch. "Can't get no goddamn peace."

The woman in the blue dress stepped inside and closed the door, purse on her shoulder with a folder tucked under one arm. Her face was thin and angular, her eyes a bit slanted, her skin the color of the caramel treats Marjory kept in a glass container on the kitchen counter.

"Hi Otis," the woman said, walking into the kitchen and smiling at the boys. "How have you been?"

Otis smiled back, displaying a rare moment of shyness. "Good," he said. "How are you, Ms. Carmen?"

"Boy, stop," Marjory snapped. "She ain't got time for yo' nonsense."

"It's okay," Carmen said. "I'm good, Otis. And who are these gentlemen?"

"My friends, Rig and DJ."

"Nice to meet you, Rig and DJ," she said looking back at Marjory. "And how are you making out today, Marge?"

"Fine," Otis's mom said, picking up her magazine. "Fine now, told you I was fine last time you came out here, goin' be fine tomorrow. We all fine."

"I'm sure that's true, Marg—"

"Don't know why y'all gotta keep coming all the time asking the same damn questions." Page flip. "We fine."

"I have to do these visits, you know that," Carmen said, surveying the apartment. "It's my job."

Marjory sucked her teeth.

Carmen sighed. "I also do it because I care."

Otis's mom flipped another page, grumbling under her breath.

"I know how hard it must be," Carmen said. "Taking care of children while also trying to take care of—"

"Listen, Ms. Carmen," Marjory said, dropping the magazine on her lap. "When you walk outta here, you goin' go to a bunch a other people live in projects look like this one, say the same things you always saying to me, then you goin' go home and feel bad for 'bout a hour 'fore you make yo'self some food and probably take a bath and shit, watch some TV, right? And guess where I'ma still be?" Marjory looked back down at her magazine. "Go on 'head and do your check and get the hell out my place."

Carmen faced the boys, a sadness in her eyes that made Rig's stomach sink. She flashed a smile at them and pulled the folder from under her arm, grabbing a pen from her purse. Walking the kitchen and living room, she scribbled on a paper inside the folder then made her way down the hall, looking in first the bathroom then the single bedroom at the end. She disappeared inside and Rig caught snatches of conversation drifting from the room.

Walking back into the kitchen, Carmen dropped her folder on the counter and made some more notes. The boys stood there, waiting. Carmen raised her nose and sniffed the air, glancing at Otis and his backpack. Otis played with his fingers. Carmen looked at Otis's mother. Marjory continued flipping through her magazine. Shaking her head, Carmen closed the folder and offered the boys a quick wave, heading for the door.

The moment Marjory was gone, Otis's mother dropped the magazine, hopped over and threw the lock.

"Uppity bitch," she grumbled, turning back to the boys. "Think 'cause she all college-educated from New York she better than everybody."

Otis rolled his eyes over to Rig, nodding at the hallway. The three of them headed to the back room where Melissa lay on a mattress coloring. Otis gave her a hug and guided her to their mom, planting her in front of the TV.

Returning to the bedroom, Otis closed the door and pulled a polished piece of wood the size of a skateboard out of the closet. He laid it on the ground next to the mattress and opened his book bag, unwrapping the ball of weed and dumping the contents on the slab. Flecks of shake fell in a green layer of dust around the large buds. Otis pulled a stack of thin boxes out of the bag's smaller pocket, each of them imprinted with the letters J O B in Victorian-era font. He tossed a couple of boxes at Rig, some to DJ.

"I wanna get a hundred outta this," Otis said, studying the pile. "So we each gotta roll—" Otis looked at his fingers.

"Thirty-three," Rig said. "Times three is ninety-nine. One of us gotta roll thirty-four."

"Yeah," Otis said, settling into a cross-legged position. "Thirty-three from each of y'all, I'll do thirty-four. Gotta get it in before it get dark so hurry up."

"I told you I ain't selling this shit, O," DJ said, staring at the boxes of papers. "That's y'all thing, I'm good."

"You goin' smoke the shit though, right?" Otis snapped. "You wanna smoke, start rolling."

DJ glanced at Rig, sighed and plopped onto the ground.

Breaking the weed up by hand, the boys worked until they each had a pile of shake in front of them. They pulled thin sheets of paper from the boxes and sprinkled weed on them, rolling the papers up and licking them closed, twisting the ends. They repeated this process while Otis cracked jokes that sent the trio into fits of laughter. An hour later, the wooden board was cleared, a hundred joints lying in a pile on the carpet. Otis pulled a slew of small manila envelopes from his bag, dropping them on the floor.

"Professional, my nigga," he said, handing envelopes to each of them. "Janitor left the supply closet open the other day, snatched this shit."

Rig looked impressed. "Nice."

They placed joints inside each of the envelopes and sealed them, splitting the final load between Otis and Rig's bags. Back in the living room the boys headed past Marjory as she dozed on the couch, Melissa staring at some show on TV. They were almost out the front door when Marjory stirred.

"Otis," she said. "Let me get some a what Black gave you."

Otis sucked his teeth. "We 'bout to go sell it."

"Just one."

"Mama—"

"Boy, you got a roof over yo' head 'cause of me," she said, sitting up. "I ask you for something you hand it over. Now."

Otis took a deep breath and pulled one of the small manila envelopes out of his bag, tossing it on her lap. He headed back to the front door.

Marjory picked up the envelope. "And get me cigarettes on your way back!"

Otis said nothing, pushing past Rig and DJ outside. They closed the door behind them and were halfway to the sidewalk when they heard the lock click.

Turning into Jackson Memorial, Ralph passed the Emergency Room entrance and the one-story Medical Examiner's building tacked to the side. He pulled up to an AC-equipped trailer taking up half the spots in the lot, Terry's Chevy Cavalier sitting under a nearby tree. Ralph parked next to him, approaching the trailer with a fresh cigarette between his lips. He sucked it down and crushed the butt in the grass, opening the door to the thick scent of formaldehyde and decay, like a baseball to the face.

"Fuck me, that'll wake you up," he said, sniffling and shaking his head.

"Been here twenty years," a voice from the other side of the trailer said. "I can tell you, you never get used to it."

Ralph closed the door, sinking the room back into artificial lighting. Terry stood in a brown suit smoking in a corner of the trailer. At a nearby gurney, Dr. Lewis Birch donned his medical coat, hunching over a body and working with a scalpel and mirror.

"Of course you show up when he's done," Terry said, a look of disgust etched into his face.

"Got here fast as I could," Ralph muttered.

Dr. Birch looked up and gave his customary greeting: a tight-lipped nod, studying Ralph over a pair of thin bifocals.

"Sergeant Williams," Birch said.

"How's it hanging, Doc?" Ralph said.

"Poorly as always," Birch said, looking back down at the body.

A wooden desk and chair set up on the opposite end of the trailer served as the Chief Medical Examiner's office. A small sign at the edge read *A Cluttered Desk is the Mark of a Genius*. Dozens of photo slides lay across the surface, everything from accident victims to close ups of gunshot wounds. Scattered slips of paper everywhere, messages from doctors, lawyers, funeral homes, other homicide detectives checking on their cases. Books lined the wall behind the desk, above them a picture of Dr. Birch standing with the rest of the investigations committee for President Kennedy's assassination. Another picture marked his similar work for the Reverend Dr. King. Above the pictures hung a Samurai sword, a rifle, and a model figure of the Eastern Airlines Lockheed L-1011 TriStar jet—Flight 401—that crashed into the Everglades back in '72, killing 101 of the 176 people on board. A gold plaque beneath it listed the details.

"Tell me, Doc," Ralph said, pointing at the model jet. "Why do you have that? Figured you'd be the last person want something to remember it."

Birch glanced at the model, lowering his glasses to the tip of his nose. "I worked sixty straight hours on that case, Sergeant," he said. "Three days, no rest. Scrambling in and out of that wreckage trying to figure out where everybody was sitting when they passed. I believe my herniated disc was a result of that time. I couldn't forget it if I tried." The doctor focused back on the body. "So I don't."

Terry stubbed his cigarette out on a medical tray. A dozen occupied gurneys filled the truck in neat rows, all of them covered in white sheets. Ralph's breath fogged up as he approached the body in front of Dr. Birch: young male, gray skin, buzz cut hair, scar under his left eye, right ear mangled, stomach distended, jagged stitching running up the midsection.

"What's the story?" Ralph asked.

"Beach patrol got the call this morning," Terry said. "Manager of the hotel found him holed up in a room. Had a plane ticket from Bogotá and a suitcase with some pants and shirts. Couple boxes of laxatives, enemas. And prunes."

"Prunes," Ralph echoed, turning to Birch. "Any cause of death yet?"

"Acute myocardial infarction," Birch said, pulling his gloves off and dropping them in a metal trash can next to the gurney. "Or cerebral hemorrhage. Or both. As you know, detectives, Monday's our busiest day." He motioned toward the other gurneys. "Weekends tend to bring a lot of clients. Whole reason we had to rent this trailer."

"All the complaints you've got about your job, Doc," Ralph said. "Same complaints we've got about ours."

"Myocardial infarction," Terry said. "What's that?"

"A heart attack," Dr. Birch said.

"Why can't you just say heart attack then, Doc?"

"Because I'm a doctor, detective," Birch said, nodding at one of the the washing stations set up on the back wall. "The only thing I can be certain of right now is *what* killed him."

Ralph followed Terry and the doctor to a stainless-steel sink, peering inside at dozens of tiny yellowish balloons covered in bloody goo.

"Again with the condoms," Ralph said, shaking his head. "That's a lot more than last time."

"Sixty-eight to be exact," Birch said. "Double-wrapped in thirty-four packages. Roughly three quarters of a pound total. I pulled fourteen of them out of his small intestine alone, most of them ruptured."

"So what killed him then," Terry asked, winking at Ralph. "The condoms or the coke?"

Birch rolled his eyes over to Terry. "Do you know what cocaine does to someone when ingested at these levels, Detective?"

"Apparently that," Terry said, nodding at the body.

"It paralyzes you first," Birch said. "In his case, it would have rendered his intestinal tract useless. Impossible for him to pass *anything*, much less these."

"Explains the laxatives and enemas," Ralph said.

"And the prunes," Terry said.

"My guess is he died painfully," Birch said. "Terrified and out of his mind."

"Nobody told him to swallow a pound of cocaine," Terry said.

"No ID?" Ralph asked

Terry gave him a look. "What do you think?"

Ralph sighed.

"This is the fourth one in the past month," Birch said. "The others still haven't been claimed. My guess is he'll go the same route."

Ralph returned to the gurney, the dead man's lips cracked and peeling.

"Definitely a trend here," Ralph said, turning back to Birch. "You pegging this self-inflicted?"

"Seems so to me."

"Then we're done here," Ralph said.

Terry clapped his hands together. "Hallelujah. Was not looking forward to that paperwork."

"You'll let us know if anything else comes up," Ralph said to the doctor.

"Always do," Birch said.

Ralph opened the trailer door and stepped out. Terry paused in the opening to look back at the doctor as Birch lifted a sheet over the dead man's face.

"Quick question," Terry said. "What's gonna happen to him? When you're done, I mean."

Birch looked confused. "I don't follow."

"What do you do with the bodies don't get claimed?"

Birch nodded. "Jackson works with UM's med school. Those auditoriums upstairs are for surgical lectures. Instructors use unclaimed cadavers for anatomy lessons."

Terry glanced at the gurney again and shivered, following Ralph out.

Outside, the day's humidity sucked the cold right out of them, Ralph swiping sweat from the back of his neck. Terry pulled out his cigarette pack and shook two into his palm, handing one to Ralph. Leaning against the side of the make-shift morgue, they smoked and listened to the afternoon hum of Miami.

"You alright?" Terry asked.

"Yeah," Ralph said. "Why?"

Terry puffed his cigarette. "Sounded off when I called."

"Just woke up," Ralph said putting on his sunglasses.

Terry nodded. "You eat yet?"

Ralph smiled. "Nope."

"Good," Terry said, clapping Ralph on the back. "I'm starving."

9.

The door opened on a thin black woman wearing a blouse and slacks with her hair up in a tight bun, her forehead and cheeks lined with faint wrinkles. Clinging to her side was a little girl who bore a strong resemblance.

"Ms. Lawson," Emilia said, holding out a hand. "Emilia Brathwaite."

"Oh, yes," the woman said, shaking Emilia's hand. She glanced at Tina standing by Emilia's side, focusing on Tina's camera bag and placing a hand on the little girl's head. "I don't want her face in the newspaper."

Tina glanced down at her bag with surprise, as if it had just appeared there.

"No, I'm sorry," she said, holding up her hands. "I honestly didn't even realize I brought it. Force of habit. It stays in the bag."

"Okay," Ms. Lawson said, nodding and stepping aside. "Please, come in."

Tina and Emilia walked down a short hallway to the living room. Ms. Lawson sat on a brown chair, her daughter curling up by her feet. Emilia and Tina sat on a couch across from a large wooden TV showing a cartoon Superman flying over a building. The character's voices sounded faint and tinny, the volume low.

Ms. Lawson's daughter studied Tina and Emilia.

Tina smiled at her. "Hi, Mikayla."

Mikayla said nothing. Her mother touched the side of her face.

"This shouldn't take too long," Emilia said.

"It's fine either way," Ms. Lawson said. "Can I get you anything to drink?"

"I'm okay," Tina said.

Emilia cleared her throat. "Water, please."

Ms. Lawson stood and walked into the kitchen with Mikayla on her tail. She returned a moment later, placing a glass of water in front of Emilia on the coffee table. Emilia thanked her and took a sip. Ms. Lawson returned to her seat with Mikayla curling back up at her feet like a timid cat. Tina took out her notebook and a pen.

"So, Ms. Lawson," Emilia said.

"Please," Ms. Lawson said. "Sheila."

Emilia smiled. "Sheila. An interview like this is fairly simple, but I'll outline the process anyways. I'm going to start by noting your account of what happened—anything you can remember about that day—then I'll follow up with some questions for clarification." She glanced at Mikayla. "If that's okay with you, of course."

"Yes, okay," Sheila said. "We can do that."

Emilia flipped to a blank page in her notebook.

"Let's start at the beginning," she said. "What happened to Mikayla?"

"She was violated by a police officer," Sheila said, a fire blazing in her eyes. "He used the fact that he *was* a police officer to violate my daughter."

Both Tina and Emilia's pens scratched across paper.

Emilia looked up at Sheila. "I'm sorry, Ms. Law—Sheila. I'm going to need a lot more details to do this story—" She glanced at Mikayla again. "—I mean, to do *her* justice."

Mikayla's mother looked down at the floor, saying nothing for a moment. When she looked up, her eyes were brimming with tears.

"She was walking home from school," she said. "She used to love walking home from school. I didn't let her right away, when she first started asking. She was too young, you know? She only eleven now. Even younger at the time. But she insisted. Said Mama, this year—her last year in elementary—said, Mama, I want to—"

Sheila's voice cracked. She swallowed thickly, looking at her fingers.

"She wanted to be grown," she said. She looked down at her daughter, who sat fiddling with her shirt. "Kayla, you want to go play in your room?"

Mikayla shook her head furiously.

Her mom nodded, folding her hands on her lap. She spoke again with a steadier voice.

"She said he was wearing his uniform. Only reason she listened to him. She know not to talk to strangers. 'Specially all these children been going missing lately? I—" Sheila wrung her hands together. "He told her somebody reported her for stealing money from another student at school. Said she had to sit in the back of his car while they figured out what was going on. So she went in the back. And he got in and drove her out to a field somewhere, and—"

Sheila's mouth snapped shut. Standing, she walked over to the television and turned the volume up. Mikayla looked over at an image of Wonder Woman swinging a lasso.

"Keeps her mind occupied," Sheila said, taking her seat again.

"I understand," Emilia said, studying her notes. "I'm sorry but are there any other details you can recount? I know this is hard, but it's necessary."

"Yes, I know," Sheila said, taking a deep breath. "He drove her out to some field somewhere, climbed in the back of the car with her. She say he touched her over her underwear, asked her to take 'em off. That's when she started crying." A tear ran down her cheek. "He didn't stop 'til she started crying, then he dropped her back where he found her and drove off." Her nostrils flared. "Asked her if they could still be *friends* before he left."

Emilia scribbled. Tina dropped her pen in her journal, studying Mikayla. The girl seemed oblivious to their conversation, her eyes studying the TV.

"Okay, so she comes back home and you find out what happened," Emilia said. "When? Right then?"

"No, she ain't want to tell us at first," Sheila said. "Me and her uncle had to drag it out of her. Knew something was wrong though. You just know, you know?" She glanced at Tina. "Either of y'all got children?"

Emilia and Tina glanced at each other, shaking their heads. Sheila nodded.

"You just know," she repeated. "Once she said what had happened, her uncle, my brother, he threw a fit. Wanted to kill the man, police or not. So I calmed him down then we got in the car and went down to the station."

"And what happened then?" Emilia asked.

"A couple of detectives questioned us."

"And what were these detectives like?"

Sheila looked confused. "How do you mean?"

"Were they black?" Emilia said. "White? Men? Women? Nice? Mean?"

"They were men," Sheila said. "Both of them was white. They weren't mean or nothing. They didn't seem like they was all that concerned 'bout what had happened though."

Emilia jotted. "Did you get their names?"

"One of them gave me a card," Sheila said, standing and walking over to a cabinet near the TV. Mikayla watched her go cautiously, remaining by the couch. Sheila walked back and dropped the card on the coffee table next to Emilia's water glass.

Emilia picked the card up. "Mind if I hold on to this?"

"It's yours," Sheila said, settling back in her seat.

"Now, the officer in question," Emilia said. "Did you ever have any personal interaction with him after you reported what happened?"

"No," she said.

"What about these two detectives you reported it to?"

"They just told me they was goin' take care of it," Sheila said. "Few weeks later I get a visit from two other detectives. Told me they fired the man and he wasn't goin' ever be allowed to be a cop again. And I mean—" She fiddled with her fingers some more. "I guess that's right? Sure don't feel like it."

"It isn't," Emilia said. "The officer's name is Billy Wallace James, and he was not fired, they allowed him to resign. And he never lost his badge. Technically he can work as a cop in any other county if he wants."

The woman's face went blank. "But they said—they charging him, right?"

"The case is currently closed," Emilia said. "He got probation."

Sheila looked at the TV, the cartoon images reflecting off her wet eyes. "It's not fair," she said.

"That's why we're here," Emilia said. "Anybody that I can prove helped cover this up will make it into this article. Then maybe we can see some justice."

Cheeks glistening, Sheila looked at Emilia and forced a smile. "Thank you," she said. Taking a deep breath, she nodded.

As they spoke, the TV switched to an ad for Tide, two women competing in a wash-off with Tide beating out the "other leading powder."

"*Women trust Tide,*" the jovial voiceover said as the commercial ended. "*It's the best detergent on American soil.*"

10.

All Tommy's gotta do is sit and wait in the driver's seat of his car chain-smoking cigarettes.

So he sits and waits and waits and waits until this big black sedan pulls into the Denny's lot and parks next to him. The man driving the sedan gets out, walks over and hands Tommy some keys. That man then walks down the street and disappears. Tommy smokes his cigarettes and watches the man leave and he doesn't like any of it. Never mind that he's helping see it through; doesn't mean he's gotta like it. Yet he's going through with it anyways because—what choice does he have, really?

The answer to that, of course, is none.

So Tommy smokes his cigarettes and waits and checks the mirrors and he fucking *hates* how this is going down. He hates even more that his brother is involved but, then, what can he do about *that*?

Again. Nothing.

So Tommy joins his brother and Luchi as they get out of the car and walk inside the Dennys, taking a booth near the back. Tommy orders coffee and Luchi orders eggs with cheese and bacon and Adán orders a milkshake—swear-to-God a fucking strawberry milkshake with this big shit-eating grin on his face as he hands the waitress back the menu.

Tommy wants to say something. He's *itching* to say something.

Instead he watches.

He watches Luchi, he watches his brother, he watches the other patrons in the diner. He watches the servers, he watches the cooks, he watches the manager as he makes his rounds, greeting each table with a toothy smile and a handshake. He watches a second of the news report on television about a recent bust, an image of smiling cops surrounding a table covered in white bricks. He watches the cars outside, he watches the people outside. He watches a beat-up brown Benz and another big black sedan pull into the lot and park a few spots down from his car, which makes it four cars total now involved in their rendezvous. The drivers of the Benz and second sedan climb out and walk in, joining Tommy and company.

Luchi and the man from the brown Benz embrace while Tommy avoids the unwavering stare of the sedan's driver, a round man with beady eyes and a thick mustache. The waitress brings Luchi his food, places Tommy's coffee in front of him and hands his brother a giant strawberry milkshake. Luchi and the man from the Benz talk about how hot it is, about the hurricane that just missed the city, about the last time they were in Colombia, how bad things are getting between La Compañia and the government.

After small talk, the man from the Benz hands Luchi a key, which Luchi hands to Adán. Adán sucks down the rest of his milkshake and walks out, climbs in the sedan that Beady Eyes pulled up in and drives away. The man from the Benz and Luchi talk some more. Luchi does that thing where he tells everybody where Tommy and Adán were born and suddenly the man from the Benz is asking all sorts of uncomfortable questions. Tommy responds with a series of nods and grunts until Luchi hands the man a set of keys, which the man hands to Beady Eyes. Beady walks out, climbs in the other black sedan and drives off. Small talk resumes.

After twenty minutes, the man from the Benz checks his watch and pulls a roll of bills out. He drops a twenty on the table and excuses himself, walking out and driving away. Tommy and Luchi wait until the Benz is out of sight before leaving the restaurant and climbing back in Tommy's car. Luchi gives Tommy directions to a nondescript house in Miami Lakes and they drive there without incident, pulling up as Adán is walking down the driveway to the street. He hops in the backseat behind Tommy. The black sedan he drove here is nowhere to be seen.

The entire exchange takes just over an hour. Tommy's proudest to have not puked through it all.

Back at Tommy's house, Luchi's car is parked in the driveway next to a half dozen other cars. Tied to Tommy's mailbox, a bouquet of blue balloons bounces around in the wind. Adán climbs out and Luchi opens the passenger door and Tommy's about to head inside too when Luchi grabs his arm. Adán pauses by the front gate to Tommy's property, looking back at the two men. Tommy motions for him to head inside, then closes the car door, glancing at Luchi. Luchi frowns at him.

"Your face the whole day," he says. "Like you are drinking bad milk. What is the problem?

Tommy hesitates, calculates his response. "Can we talk?" he says. "But I mean like, candidly?"

Luchi says nothing.

"Honestly," Tommy says. "Can I speak honestly."

Luchi gives him a slight nod.

"I respect what you do," Tommy says. "That's first of all. This should all be impossible but you're making it possible, which is admirable." Tommy takes a deep breath. "But you guys are going to get arrested doing shit this way, and I can't have that. Especially with my brother coming on."

Luchi wrinkles his forehead. "What are you talking about, Gringo?"

"I'm not going to jail," Tommy says. "And I'm pretty sure you don't want to go to jail either. And we are going to go to jail if we keep operating like this. But." Tommy holds a finger up. "If you give me a chance, I can come up with a better process than this."

Luchi stares at him long and hard. Tommy steadies his breathing.

"Mírate," Luchi says, laughing and slapping Tommy on the chest. "What did I tell you? You have the brains, eh? Gringo Cubano. Sí. Yes. You are right."

"Don't hand out trophies yet," Tommy says, rubbing his chest. "I haven't worked it all out. But I will."

"I know you will, parcero," Luchi says. "Tenemos trescientos en camino, próxima semana. I must travel to Cali so you will take care of it." Luchi shakes Tommy's shoulder. "You will make the process better, no?"

Tommy's mouth goes dry. "Three hundred keys?"

"Sí"

"By next week?"

"You will meet with Bilsner, make the arrangements," Luchi says, looking at the house as Adán steps inside. "You are good at this, I know this. And tu hermano, Adán. He is yours to watch. Sí?"

Tommy nods and Luchi pushes the passenger door open, putting a foot out. He turns back with gleaming eyes.

"You will do great, Tomas," he says, then heads towards the house.

Tommy watches him until he's through the front door then climbs out of his car and walks to his front porch, pausing to stare up at the fading sun in the clear sky. He takes some deep breaths and forces a smile on his face and it hurts his cheeks but he keeps it there anyways as he opens the front door and happily greets his family.

11.

Wind whipped through the open windows, the cherry of Emilia's cigarette bright red. She dragged it to the filter and tossed the butt out the window.

"He needs a name," she said. "Like these other assholes. A moniker. Like the Boston strangler. The pillowcase rapist. The zodiac killer." She paused. "The rapist pedophile copper."

Tina gripped the door as Emilia squeezed between two cars, speeding towards the 1st avenue exit.

"You think he did it to others?" Tina asked.

"It's usually the case with people like that."

Tina stared outside. "I can't even…"

"And this whole fraternity," Emilia said. "This bullshit unwritten rule that none of them can ever cross the blue line. How can you work with somebody who's done something like this? How can you *protect* that person?"

"They probably don't think it actually happened," Tina said. "They talk to each other more than the victims. He could have convinced them it was a lie."

"The worst part is this article probably won't do anything," Emilia said. "Used to be we'd publish something and it would shake things up, make people *have* to respond. Nowadays it's like nobody cares about real news, just want to crap all over it like it's not our *job* to report. People are so in their own little worlds, no sense of—of *community*."

"People care about the news, Emilia," Tina said.

"For how long?" Emilia said. "Attention spans are disappearing. All people want now is their blessed CNN, MTV, just—" She took a deep breath "—all flash and no substance. Did you hear about this new one coming out? What is it—Entertainment Tonight?"

"I saw a commercial for—"

"Why?" Emilia snarled. "Why are they making an entire show for entertainment news? Is it really *that* important? Do people really want to hear that shit so much they need a TV station devoting entire slots of airtime to it?"

"I don't think they'd make it if people didn't want to watch," Tina said. "They test things like that, don't they?"

"It's all just so ridiculous," Emilia said. "There's so much bluster out there now, real stories get buried beneath—" Emilia smacked the steering wheel. "The princess's wedding! You know she was in the news cycle longer than Reagan getting shot? Our president got shot, and people care more about a wedding's got nothing to do with us or this country. Did you see her face?"

Tina glanced at her. "Princess Diana?"

Emilia smacked the steering wheel again, then held a hand up apologetically. "Sorry. It's just—Mikayla's face. She looked so young, so…"

"Innocent," Tina said.

Emilia pulled into the Tribune's employee lot and parked, leaving the engine running. Leaning back in her seat, she looked outside at the bright blue sky. She spoke without preamble.

"I was fourteen," she said. "It was a Wednesday. I was walking home from school back in Jersey, just got to our apartment and our neighbor—" Emilia looked down at her fingers. "—He was always nice to me. Before that day."

Tina leaned against the passenger door and waited.

"My mother was home with my sister," Emilia continued. "She was sick, the flu or something. It's weird, because I think that's the only reason I agreed when the guy asked me to help him move his couch. I must have figured since they were home—literally, they were a couple of feet away—nothing bad would happen." Emilia paused. "He tried to keep his hand over my mouth, but I shook it off. My mom heard me scream and ran over, caught him in the act." Emilia chuckled. "She hit him over the head with a frying pan, straight out of a cartoon. The sound it made, the way his eyes rolled back." Her smile faded. "I remember his face more than anything."

They both stared at the sky for a moment. In the far distance, dark clouds rolled in from the ocean.

"It was pretty easy for the state to prosecute," Emilia said. "There was evidence everywhere, and my mom an eyewitness. Aggravated sexual assault gets you twenty years max in Jersey."

"How many did he serve?" Tina asked.

"Five," Emilia said. "He got out in '70, still lives on the same street."

"At least he did some time," Tina muttered.

"That's what always gets me," Emilia said, her voice strained. "I'm one of the 'lucky ones.' They got the guy and he paid for it, so I'm one of the lucky ones." She laughed coldly. "I've never felt so unlucky in my life."

Anger flared up in Tina then, brighter than she'd ever felt before. In an instant she had the intense desire to destroy something, anything. Rip the world in half and watch it burn. She clenched her fists in her lap until her nails dug into her palm, listening to Emilia's shallow breaths next to her. The words were out of her mouth before she even realized she was speaking.

"I told you the reason we left Puerto Rico was my dad," she said.

"Yeah," Emilia said. "Navy, right?"

"That's just part of it." Tina took a deep breath, looking out the window. "I had an uncle, Tio Raul, my mother's half-brother on her father's side. Like ten years younger than her. I mean—" She shook her head. "I guess I *have* an uncle, not like he's dead. I don't know how old I was. We left when I was six and it happened before that but I don't remember how long before. I want to say I was five."

Emilia stared at Tina with no expression. For some reason this helped.

"He was a teenager," Tina continued. "I've always just—I told myself that part means something. He was like fifteen. One day my mom had to take my brother to the doctor in town so she asked him to watch me. And he did, but he also made me…you know." She looked out the window.

Emilia put a hand to her mouth, her skin going gray. Tina closed her eyes.

"Sometimes—I don't even know how it's possible, but sometimes I forget. Or it gets…hazy. You know how your earliest memories are kind of fuzzy? It's like that." Tina sighed. "Only I wish it was fuzzier."

Distant thunder registered like a phantom echo.

"I've never told anybody but my brother," Tina said.

"I wish I'd known," Emilia said. "You didn't have to come today."

"No," Tina said. "I'm glad, actually."

"What happened to him?" Emilia asked. "Your uncle?"

"Nothing," Tina said. "My mom figured out something was up, I don't know how. Guess it's like Ms. Lawson said. They just know. She got really adamant after that about my dad getting us to the states."

"Good move," Emilia said.

"She always stuck to the Navy story though, acts like the whole thing with my uncle never happened." Tina dropped her head. "Can't help feeling guilty sometimes. Like I'm the reason our whole family got separated."

"You aren't the reason for any of it, stop that thinking," Emilia said. "For the longest time, I was convinced I'd done something wrong. Like maybe I led him on, gave him the wrong impression." Emilia squeezed Tina's shoulder. "It's not my fault, and it's not your fault."

More rumbling thunder, though the dark clouds were still well out over the ocean. Tina and Emilia smoked another cigarette. They finished and dropped the cigarette butts outside. Looking at each other, an unspoken exchange occurred and the women reached across the middle console, embracing. They hugged until another rumble of thunder vibrated through the car, then they got out and walked inside.

12.

Ralph brought the coffees over to a row of tables where a mix of detectives and uniforms surrounded Captain Murphy. He dropped a cup in front of Terry and took a seat as one of the patrols wrapped an update on the investigation into a recent string of robberies.

"Nice work, Stephens," Murphy said, turning to the crowd. "Just to reiterate, these briefings are for us to reset. A moment where each squad can keep the other squads updated on their cases, what scenes they've investigated, etcetera." He held up a folder. "Switching gears. Looks like the state attorney's office has finally removed the proverbial stick from their asses and given us information *without* the need to extract teeth."

A chuckle coursed through the room.

"Get your requests in now, while they're feeling generous," Murphy said. "Last thing, a reminder. The Mayor's Office is pushing the non-lethal agenda. We don't need anybody at city hall coming down here and getting on us anymore than they already have so avoid lethal force at all costs. Chokeholds, arm bars, whatever you need to incapacitate. Do not draw your weapon unless absolutely necessary. Dismissed."

The grumbling group of officers disbanded.

Back at their desks, Terry plopped down on his chair and started flipping through a small white booklet. Ralph took off his coat and draped it over his seat, pulling at his collar and scowling at the air vent above his head.

"Goddamn AC's broken again," he said, swiping his forehead.

"Weis said won't be fixed 'til next week," Terry said without looking up.

Ralph sucked his teeth, looking over at Captain Murphy's office window. The space inside was undecorated save for a poster on the back wall of a hand holding a gun, the barrel a large black dot in the center of the frame. The caption: *Miami. See It Like a Native.*

"At least we don't have to notify next of kin," Terry said. "On the mule."

"Would've been your turn," Ralph said.

"Then thank you, John Doe," Terry said, smirking and holding up a small booklet to Ralph. "You see this shit? You came late. Murphy said city council's scared we might set off another riot, what with all these Cubans now. So they're handing out language manuals to patrol. Bunch of translations for shit, like—" Terry flipped through the booklet, pausing on one page and following with his finger. "—Dee-tent or despair-air. Means stop, or I'll shoot."

"You serious?" Ralph said.

"Probably just butchered it to hell but, yeah." Terry handed the booklet to Ralph. "That's where we're at."

Ralph took the booklet and opened it to a random page. "Sue-alta el arma. Drop the gun."

Murphy stuck his head out of his office, looking at Ralph and Terry. "Williams, Pullman," he said. "Conference room. If you see Weis and Ace tell them to meet us there." He squinted, searching the bullpen. "Where's Bats?"

"Grabbing a donut," Terry said.

"Of course," Murphy muttered. "Get him, please. And Cole." He glanced at his watch. "Five minutes."

"I think I saw Cole by evidence on my way in," Terry said, standing.

"I'll get Bats," Ralph said.

The detectives separated, Ralph going for the door and almost running somebody over as he pushed through. He grabbed the guy before they both fell, saw the man's face and smiled.

"Mark," Ralph said. "You're back, how's the kid?"

"Good," he said, scratching his neck. "Actually, glad I ran into you, Sarge. Wanted you to hear it from me first."

Ralph frowned. "Hear what?"

"I'm out," the detective said. "End of the month."

"Out?" Ralph said. "Out where?"

"Clearwater," he said. "Department over there's growing, they need men." He looked Ralph in the eye. "Plus Miami…the city lately's just been…"

Ralph nodded. "I hear you."

"And with the baby now…"

"I hear you, Mark."

The detective nodded, smiling. "Boys're gonna throw a party though," he said. "You know how they are. We'll tie one on to celebrate."

"You bet," Ralph said, clapping the detective on the shoulder just as Robert "Bats" Paulter jostled around the corner holding a cup of coffee in one hand and a glazed doughnut in the other.

Ralph jutted his chin towards the door. "Murphy wants us in the bullpen."

Nodding, Paulter followed Ralph down a hallway to a small room. Inside, Murphy stood up front next to a man Ralph had never seen before. Across the room, the rest of Ralph's unit sat in a line of chairs: Terry next to Richie Weis next to Alice "Ace" Wilson—Weis's partner—next to Frederick "Cole" Coleman. Ralph and Bats took a seat off to the side, Bats taking a bite of his donut and chasing it with some coffee.

Up front, Murphy's face was drawn, the wrinkles on his forehead much more prominent than when Ralph first met him. The man next to him was younger, around Ralph's age, brown-skinned with thick black hair. He wore a tailored suit.

"There are some changes coming," Murphy said. He shook his head. "Not coming. Already here. Bensinger's out as the DEA liaison." He glanced at the other man. "Care to introduce yourself?"

The man smiled and unbuttoned his jacket, taking a step forward and scanning all their faces.

"My name is Eduardo Velez," he said. "But most people call me Eddie." He glanced at Murphy, gave a thin-lipped smile. "And I like to think of myself as a little more than a DEA liaison. I've spent the past decade cultivating relationships with all the agencies and, as such, I am here to make sure you all remain in the know, coordinated on a local and federal level. DEA, FBI, CIA, whatever three letter acronym you fancy."

"CIA?" Ralph said.

"Yes, CIA," Eddie said. "We are all operating under the assumption that this recent uptick in violence is directly correlated with the influx of cocaine from other countries, specifically through the City of Miami."

"Ya think?" Ace muttered behind Ralph.

"Why now?" Bats said. "Shit's been hitting the fan for months. *Years*. Got busts every other day and there's still more on the streets than ever."

"Which is why we're shifting tactics," Murphy said. "In addition to continuous monitoring of all shipping and transportation flags, we're gonna start going after the money."

"And how're we planning on doing that?" Ralph asked.

"Good question," Eddie Velez said, walking over to a chalkboard near the back of the room. He wrote the number four in thick white lines, then a seven, a five, and several zeros. He added some commas then dropped the chalk.

Dusting off his hands, he faced the group again, pointing at the number on the board. "Miami's Federal Reserve reported nearly five billion dollars in surplus last year." He paused. "That's more than all the other federal reserve branches in the country. Combined."

Terry whistled.

Murphy stepped froward. "So, in addition to operating under the assumption that the string of murders this past year are due to the steady stream of coke into the city," he said. "We are also assuming that any outrageous cash transactions are the aftermath of a felony."

"Find the money and work backwards," Eddie said. "Much shorter trip to the same destination."

"Makes sense," Ace said.

"State trooper buddy of mine stops a car yesterday for running a toll," Bats said, chewing on some donut. "Guy's got sixty grand cash in a duffel bag just sitting open on the passenger seat. Couldn't speak a lick of English, driving a brand-new Benz."

"So many stories like that," Weis said, crossing his arms. "Makes me wonder how many of them got cash on 'em when they get pulled over and we just never hear about it."

A couple of the detectives snickered.

"What's this got to do with us?" Ralph asked. "Last I checked we're homicide, not accounting."

"Another good question, Sergeant," Velez said. "President Reagan has tasked the VP and Mullen, the new DEA head, to start a joint task force based out of this area. They're bringing everybody in: ATF, DEA, FBI, customs, state all the way down to local. Minimum of seven bodies per agency, assigned to various regions around the county. Even got the IRS in on it."

"That's what's really got the fire under they asses," Cole said, looking around the room. "Uncle Sam saw all that bread, wondering where his piece is."

"Always gets his piece," Weis muttered.

"Which brings me to Williams' question and the reason I've called you all here today," Murphy said. "Every precinct in the county's being asked to put up qualified and experienced detectives for this task force." He paused, glancing around the room. "I've nominated you all."

The roomful of detectives went quiet.

Bats raised his hand. Murphy nodded.

"This mean more overtime?" he said. Murphy gave him a look and more chuckles floated around the room. Bats smiled. "Seriously though. What we gotta do different?"

"Nothing, for now," Velez said. "You guys are already doing the job, now you're just getting support. But you will start to see some changes around here over the next couple of months. New faces, new assignments."

"But we're still homicide," Cole said. "Right?"

"Yes, Detective," Murphy said. "You still work for the homicide department, you'll just be—refocused."

"You think this is going to work?" Ralph asked. "Agencies aren't really known for working well together."

"Which is another reason I've chosen this group," Murphy said. "Through our local task force, you all have shown a common desire over the past couple years to handle situations smartly, with a focus on getting results. You need to bring that to this new joint task force. I need you to work with Agent Velez and our other liaisons. No inter-department bickering, no withholding information, none of that high school bullshit."

"We are all in this for the same reason," Velez said.

"Which brings us to our main target at the moment," Murphy said.

He approached the board and flipped it away from the chalk-written number to reveal a pinboard with a single photo of a woman tacked in the middle. The woman was hefty, standing outside a house wearing a black dress, sunglasses and red lipstick, pink blush on her cheeks.

"Giselle Benitez," Murphy said. "It's been six months since we picked up her scent, yet we've gotten no closer to pinning her down."

"To be honest, Lieutenant," Bats said, raising his hand and dropping it in one motion. "Every time we get close to any of her associates they either disappear or turn up dead. And she's always got an alibi. Her kids, or her second or third or fourth fifth husband—"

"Whichever one she hasn't gotten rid of yet," Cole said.

Bats nodded. "The woman's paranoid as hell."

"Me and Ace tracked two of her guys," Weis said, standing with a folder in his hands. "Took hours. Kind of like them for that ritual murder in Allapattah last month"

Weis walked up to the bulletin board with Ace behind him, pinning two photos on either side of Giselle Benitez's. The photo on the right showed a tall, thin Hispanic man with long brown hair getting into a blue BMW, his head twisted around for a perfect camera profile. The photo on the left showed another shorter Hispanic man with an afro and bushy mustache walking down the sidewalk with a duffel bag slung over his shoulder.

"On the right," Weis said. "Hernan Lizandre, aka Hernito." He pointed at the picture on the left. "This guy is Conrado Fernandez, aka Luchi. We haven't figured out yet who or what exactly they are to Giselle, but they're both regularly getting through her security, more than anybody else."

"Got a CI says one or both of them are her primary hitters," Ace said, pointing at each photo. "He knew some of the details from Allapattah we didn't give the press—the cross and the dead chicken in particular. Nothing concrete but good a lead as any."

"Good work, get more eyes on them," Murphy said. "The rest of you, dig deeper. By all indications, Benitez is the number one player in town right now. It's safe to assume she's behind most of these hits. I want her head."

Velez nodded at the room and followed everybody as they headed out. Ralph was almost through the door when Murphy called his name, motioning him over. They waited until the room emptied then Murphy stared at Ralph for a while.

"What, Danny?" Ralph said, shuffling his feet.

"You look like shit."

Ralph looked down at his wrinkled shirt and pants. "Fair enough."

Murphy swiped the corners of his mouth. "You talk to Amanda lately?"

Ralph took a seat. "About Mikey, yeah. Picking him up tonight."

"How about you two?" Murphy said. "Talk about that yet?"

Ralph smirked, shaking his head. "She said—um, she's not ready to talk." His smile disappeared and he clenched his jaw. "Not fucking ready, she said."

"You smell like the inside of a whiskey barrel, Ralph," Murphy said. "It's coming out of your pores. Listen—" He clamped a hand on Ralph's shoulder. "—You *know* I know what you're going through right now. You were there."

"I know," Ralph said.

"So, you also know there's another side to this." He let go of Ralph's shoulder. "Nothing's ever worth giving up. Not your life, not your future. Get some sleep tonight. Come in sober tomorrow or take the day off."

Murphy stood and walked out, leaving Ralph staring at a wall.

Back at his desk, Ralph sat with a sigh, glancing at the clock above Terry's head. Terry laughed, spinning around to face him.

"Joint task force," he said, leaning back in his chair and twirling a pencil between his fingers. "Sounds like something from a comic book."

"It does," Ralph said.

"You think it'll make a dent?"

Ralph shrugged. "Who knows?"

Terry's desk phone rang and he picked it up, his smile fading as he dropped it back down.

"Liberty City," he said, grabbing his jacket. "Body in some bushes near King Square Park."

"The shit never ends," Ralph said.

"We'd be out of a job if it did."

Ralph smiled. "Touché."

13.

The boys passed the usual clusters of Lincolns and Chevys parked outside as they headed into King Square Park. A string of men sat near the park's wooden signage, smoking cigarettes and playing cards with their car radios turned up. The boys nodded at the few they recognized as they headed towards the basketball court in the middle of the park. A couple of barbecue pits were going and the smell of chicken and hot dogs saturated the air. Boomboxes competed for dominance at opposite ends of the open air space, one blasting funk, the other Motown. Under a tree, a group of young adults swayed side to side with paper plates in hand. Old men sitting on concrete blocks played checkers nearby. Otis stopped by three boys talking under a light pole, nudged one of them and dapped him up.

"Link me before you leave," he said, patting his bag. "Got that fire."

The kid nodded and the boys moved on. Otis veered off the path a couple more times for similar entreaties before they reached the basketball court. Keisha, Tasha and Samantha sat in the grass, the girls waving as the boys approached. Rig took a seat next to Keisha, noticing another trio of boys sitting on the opposite side of the court.

Rig turned to Otis. "Who's that with Marquise and Day-Day?"

Otis sat next to Tasha, following Rig's gaze. He scowled the moment he saw the other boys. "Mikey, they other cousin."

"Ain't seen him before," Rig said.

"He stay in Rainbow Projects." DJ said, plopping down next to Samantha.

Otis nudged Rig, winking at DJ. "Chico been beefin' with them niggas since way back."

"Ain't beefin' with nobody," Rig said. "Just don't like them."

Otis laughed. "The fuck you think beef is, nigga?"

Exerting their inherent gravitational pull, the girls coaxed the boys' attention back to their circle. Tasha stuck her tongue out at Otis, smiling devilishly. DJ leaned over and whispered something in Samantha's ear and she giggled. Keisha touched Rig's leg and he looked over at her, something in her eyes making his chest feel funny, like his lungs were trying to expand outside of his body. Keisha said something and Rig nodded, his eyes flitting over to the other group of boys again, Day-Day and Marquise and the new cousin, Mikey. Mikey looked damn near Rig's size, a fact Rig found disconcerting.

The boys noticed Rig staring and shifted their attention. Cousin Mikey locked eyes with him.

Mikey puffed his chest out, sitting up straight.

The back of Rig's neck tingled.

Keisha's hand on his shoulder brought Rig back. She smiled, twirling a strand of hair around a finger. Her skin glistened. She said something else and leaned in towards him and Rig hugged her and she smelled like cocoa butter and hairspray, her hands soft against his back. She was in the middle of asking him about school when Rig felt that tingle on his neck, looking back at Marquise and his cousins again. The three of them had stood and moved closer, standing on the basketball court now within spitting distance of Rig and company. Rig opened his mouth but Otis beat him to the punch.

"Fuck y'all staring at?" Otis yelled.

"A bunch of bitch ass niggas," Marquise said, snickering and slapping his cousin Day Day's palm. He focused on the girls. "Fuck y'all doing hanging with these herbs?"

Rig stood. "Don't know what made y'all think it was a good idea to come over here," he growled.

"Rig," Keisha said, squeezing his leg. Her voice sounded far away.

"What?" Marquise said to Rig, something sinister flashing in his eyes. "You got a problem? Nigga?"

Otis appeared next to Rig, nudging his friend aside with his shoulder. "I'm gettin' 'bout tired of y'all motherfuckers."

"This ain't playtime no mo'," Marquise said. "This nigga ain't 'bout to sucker punch me up in here."

"Fuck these niggas, man," DJ said, sitting next to Samantha. "Ain't—"

"Fuck you talking to, faggot?" Day-Day barked.

"Fuck you calling a faggot, faggot?" Otis snapped back.

Rig saw it coming and reached out to pull Otis back a second too late, Otis pushing off the balls of his feet and pouncing. Cursing under his breath, Rig moved behind him, the three cousins coming at them from the other direction. Day-Day headed for Otis, Marquise and Mikey stalking towards Rig. DJ jumped up wide-eyed, fists balled at his sides. Otis threw a punch at Day-Day's head and Day-Day flinched, Otis's fist hitting his chest with little effect. Day-Day reached both his hands out for Otis's neck and Otis slapped them away, Day-Day's momentum sending them both tumbling to the grass. A couple of feet away, Marquise stepped into a swing aimed at Rig's head that Rig sidestepped, jabbing Marquise in the stomach and doubling him over. Rig got a breath in before Cousin Mikey grabbed him from behind. Twisting around, Rig broke Mikey's grip and shoved a palm into the kid's nose. The boy grunted, ducking and jamming his head into Rig's stomach, trying to pick him up. Rig's feet came off the ground a couple inches and the boys stumbled, falling onto the basketball court. Rig landed on his back, his bag crushing beneath him. Pain flared up in his shoulder and he groaned, pushing himself up with a grimace. Mikey stood across from him, swiping at a bloody nose.

"I'ma fuck you up," he said.

"Go 'head and try," Rig said, lowering his chin and raising his fists. He stalked forward and Mikey jumped at him, leaning into a swing that Rig ducked, throwing all his weight into an overhead fist just as someone yelled:

"Y'all muhfuckas quit that shit!"

The person behind the voice stepped in between the boys and Rig's punch landed on his neck. The man flinched away and let out a yell, grabbing the back of his pants' and bringing his arm back around with a black nine-millimeter pistol gripped in his fist that he pointed directly at Rig's face.

Everything slowed to a crawl as the gun came level with Rig's eyes, the barrel larger than he could have ever imagined. Paralyzed, he stared into the dark hole, wondering if it was possible anything could be any darker. The longer he stared at it the wider it seemed to get.

The man holding the gun wore a black tank top and a bucket hat, a thick gold chain swinging around his neck. A single gold hoop dangled from his left ear, his finger tense on the trigger. His eyes were electric, his pupils as big and dark as the gun barrel.

The second the gun appeared, all the cheering and jeering for the fight stopped. Half the people sitting nearby hustled to the other side of the park. Suddenly, the smoking barbecue pits were unattended. A few people stayed still on the grass, as if any sudden movement would draw the gunman's attention. Only Otis and DJ stood close by, Marquise and his crew backing off with their hands held up near their chests, eyes wide with fear.

Rig felt like peeing but he held it, focusing on ignoring the urge, using the effort to distract himself from how close the gun was to his face. He let his arms hang at his sides, standing with a wide gait. Otis stepped into view at the corner of his eye.

"Tee," Otis said.

"Don't start, nigga," the man barked, tightening his grip on the pistol. "Muhfucker just punched me in the muhfuckin' neck. I should blast his ass."

"He ain't mean to," Otis said. "You saw that shit, Tee. We was just scrappin' with these niggas, we ain't got no beef wit' you."

Tee held the gun steady. Rig stared at it, willing away the shaking fear and uncertainty bubbling in his gut. He clenched his fists at his sides and brought his shoulders back, sticking his chest out and looking up from the gun to the man's face. Tee's eyes looked wild, inhuman, red-rimmed and twitching. He and Rig stood like battle statues for an interminable amount of time. Tee squinted at him from around the gun barrel.

Tee laughed suddenly, lowering the gun to his side.

"I ain't goin' cap you, blood," he said, pushing the gun back in his pants' waist. "You a wild ass nigga, I 'preciate that. What they call you?"

Rig opened his mouth but his voice was gone.

"Chico," Otis said, walking over and standing next to Rig.

"Chico, huh?" Tee said, looking Rig up and down. "How old you is?"

Rig cleared his throat. "Almost thirteen."

"*Thirteen?*" Tee yelled, taking a step back. "*Goddamn*, nigga, *thirteen?*" He looked at Otis. "This nigga goin' be a *problem*."

"Nigga already a problem," Otis said. The relief on his face was palpable.

"Might be," Tee said, his expression serious again. "Ain't *my* problem. You ever put yo' hands on me again, for any reason, I'ma blow yo' motherfuckin' head off. Ya heard?"

Rig nodded and Tee grabbed his bag, pulling it off his shoulders. "What you got in here?"

Rig started to protest but Tee already had the bag in hand, pulling out one of the manila envelopes.

"Fuck's this?" he said, opening the envelope. His eyes went wide. "Oh shit, this nigga holdin'!"

Tee shook the contents onto the basketball court and tossed Rig's empty bookbag aside, shoving the envelopes in his various pants' pockets. He turned back to the boys, his shadow blocking the sun from Rig's face.

"You know," Tee said. "Pops always told me don't pull yo' piece 'less you ready to use it." Tee smiled. "First time I ain't listen to him."

Tee walked away, holding up his bounty as he approached a couple of men standing near the park entrance.

Rig looked around for Marquise and his cousins, but they'd disappeared. Otis glared after Tee. DJ stared at both his friends in shock, plopping back onto the grass. Slowly, the park resumed normal functions, the barbecue pits attended, people moving back to their spots on the field. The sky above the park remained blue and clear though dark clouds rolled in from the south, in the distance.

Rig walked off the court and didn't so much sit as fall next to DJ, his knees wobbly. Otis sat across from him.

"I'ma kill that motherfucker," Otis said. "Wait'll I tell Black."

"Let it go, bruh," DJ said. "Ain't fucking with Tee, that nigga's crazy."

Otis glanced at him. "Fuck says we can't be crazy too?"

Rig lay back on the grass, staring up at the sky. Otis laughed suddenly, slapping Rig's knee.

"My nigga Chico the *truth*, bruh!" he yelled, shaking DJ's shoulder.

The trio of girls walked back over to them, their eyes wide with fear.

"You saw my boy right here?" Otis bellowed. "Ain't even flinch, nigga. Ain't even *budge*. Tee put that heat in his face and Chico looked right back at him like *what?*!" He smacked Rig's chest. "That was some cold ass shit."

Rig relaxed, pushing himself up as Keisha sat by his feet. Her eyes were wide and wet.

"You okay?" she asked, her voice timid.

Rig forced a smile, cleared his throat. "Yeah, I'm good."

They were just settling back into conversation when a bunch of yelling came from the park entrance. They all turned and watched as Tee jabbed a finger at some guy's forehead. The guy jawed back and Tee pulled his pistol again, pointed it at the other man's forehead and pulled the trigger.

A loud pop sounded off and the man's body crumpled to the ground, the red spray from the back of his head floating like mist.

The park sat still for a moment, even the birds shocked into silence.

Tee stepped forward and fired another shot into the body on the ground. The dead man bounced with the impact. The second shot shattered the trance in the park, sending people screaming. Tee startled, looking around as if he'd just realized he wasn't alone. Raising the gun in the air, he fired another shot at the sky, yelling something that Rig couldn't hear over the roar of his heartbeat in his ears, like rushing water.

Sitting just twenty yards from where the dead man was settling into the grass, Rig, Otis, DJ and the girls all backed away from Tee.

Tee yelled something else inaudible, waving the gun in the air.

As he spoke, two men appeared at the park entrance, both of them holding pistols as they crouched towards Tee. The men wore suits, and Rig was just picturing the word *cops* when Tee spun around, raising his gun. He pulled the trigger before he'd even had a chance to aim, the shot going wide of the detectives into the line of cars sitting outside the park entrance. Without hesitation the detectives fired back, one of them doing so with two quick shots, the other firing wildly, pulling the trigger again and again, holding the gun with one hand and screaming through each shot until the clip was empty.

Rig ducked to the ground as a bullet hit the grass a few feet away, the vibration of it coursing through his knees. He froze at the sound, paralyzed.

Tee seemed to dance as he fell, an awkward ballet that spun him around twice before he settled to the ground. The detectives approached Tee's body, the body of the other man Tee had shot lying nearby.

A scream from behind him broke Rig from his trance. He pushed himself up with his elbows beneath him, finding Otis and the girls standing over DJ. DJ lay sprawled on his back with his legs close together and his arms spread out, face pointed at the sky. Jesus on a cross.

Rig jumped up and ran over, nudging Keisha to the side. He stood over DJ and DJ stared back up at him, his eyes lifeless. A pool of blood formed on the grass beneath his torso, a small hole in his shirt right above his heart.

Otis dropped to his knees, reaching a hand out towards their dead friend but not touching him.

Rig stared at DJ's face until it looked fake, not like his friend at all but like some artificial mask somebody had made to look like DJ's face.

Taking a step back, Rig glanced at the detectives. A patrol officer spoke in one of the detectives' ear, pointing in Rig and Otis and the girls' direction. What looked like an endless stream of patrol cars had appeared out of nowhere, cops crowding the area like ants.

Rig looked down at DJ's body one more time then, without thinking, took off running back home.

14.

Tina dropped the message slips on her desk and plopped down in her chair, grabbing her purse and pulling out a cigarette. She was lighting it up when one of the switchboard operators poked her head above the cubicle.

"Call for you, Rivers," she said. "Transferring."

Tina took a puff as the phone rang, answering through smoke.

"Rivers," she said, coughing. "Photography."

"Body found a block west of King Square Park," a voice said.

Tina frowned. "Terry?"

"Headed there now," Terry said. "Just thought I'd give you the heads up."

"Wow," Tina said. "Wow, okay. Thanks."

"See you later?" he said.

Tina smiled, her cheeks heating up. "Yeah," she said. "Definitely."

The line clicked and Tina stared at the phone dumbstruck. She dropped it down and picked it right back up, dialing some numbers. Emilia answered on the first ring.

"Brathwaite, Metro."

"Terry just called and gave me my first real tip," Tina said breathlessly. "A body. In Liberty City."

There was a long pause, then Emilia laughed.

"Sounds like you should be driving," she said. "Not talking to me."

"What?" Tina said, frowning. "No, I'm—I was calling to give it to you."

"Not very reporter of you," Emilia said. "And next time, try to keep your sources private."

"I'm still a photographer, Emilia."

"A photographer who is one month away from receiving a certificate in journalism," Emilia said.

Tina stared at the cigarette in her hand. "What is happening?"

"You just got your first official assignment is what's happening," Emilia said. "And maybe I can get caught up on some of this crap on my desk."

"But, I—" Tina's voice trailed off.

Emilia lowered her voice, chattering reporters in the background. "My advice, wait until deadline to turn in copy. Gives them less time to fiddle. I'll let Fred know you're on it."

Tina sat back in her seat, taking a deep breath. "Thanks, Emilia."

"Don't thank me yet," she said. "I see some long nights in your future."

They exchanged goodbyes and Tina hung up the phone. She was grabbing her purse to head for the elevators when the switchboard operator poked her head above the cubicle again.

"Another call, Rivers," she said. "Transferring."

Tina's phone rang and she picked it up, her mother's static-filled voice on the other end.

"Tu tío está enfermo."

"I can't talk, Mom, I—" Tina paused. "Wait, what?"

"I am going to San Juan to stay at the house," Luisa said.

"Hold on, *that's* why you're going?" Tina sat back, placing her purse on her lap. "What's wrong with him?"

"No sé," her mother said. "Tu abuela llamó."

"And you're going?" Tina said. "When?"

"Por la mañana," her mother said. "We are going to get the plane tickets."

"I can't, Mami," Tina said. "I have to work."

"Your uncle is sick," she repeated.

"You said that already," Tina said. "I have a job, Mami. I can't just up and leave. If you wait a couple of days, I can make arrange—"

"You do not have vacation?" her mother said.

"That's not the p—" Tina glanced around the office, lowering her voice. "I do, but—"

Tina let the words hanging, sighing.

"But what?" her mother said.

"*En realidad*," Tina said. "Going to San Juan is—" She squeezed her eyes shut. "I just really don't want to."

"You do not want to what?" her mother said.

"I don't want to be around him."

"Around who?"

Tina shook her head. "You know who."

"Tu tío está—"

"I heard you!" Tina barked.

A few eyes turned in her direction. Tina ducked her head, squeezing the phone against her ear. She pictured Emilia staring at the sky in her car, pictured that one detail about Emilia's mother hitting Emilia's assaulter over the head with a frying pan. The sound Emilia said it made.

A dam cracked inside Tina then, pushing to the surface something she couldn't remember ever feeling before.

"I need to hear you say it," she growled.

"Qué?"

"If you say it," Tina said. "I will go. I will go to San Juan with you tomorrow, Mami. Tonight, even. I just need you to say it."

The line filled with static for a few seconds before her mother sighed. "Say what, nena?"

"Say what he did," Tina said, her voice shaking. "To me. Say what he did to me, and I will go with you to San Juan."

"Valentina, I do not know what you are talking about," her mother said. "Tu tío está enfermo, we are going. You must come."

Tina's face cooled. Her eyes glazed over, her expression going slack.

"I have to go, Mami," she said. "I'll see you when you get back."

Tina hung up before her mother could respond.

Grabbing her purse and keys, she headed for the elevators.

In her car, Tina started the engine and gripped the steering wheel, a haunted stare on her face. Placing her forehead on her clenched fists, she waited for whatever was to come, a feeling in her stomach like approaching the edge of a cliff. She breathed quietly. Slowly, the sensation dissipated.

Putting the car in gear, Tina pulled out of the *Tribune* lot, headed north on Biscayne. Dark clouds sat in her rearview mirror, the sky ahead clear, blue and bright. Tina scanned the airwaves and found nothing of interest, shutting the radio off and listening to the hum of her engine.

Stopping at a red light, she glanced out at a couple walking down the street with their daughter. The dad held the daughter's hand as the mother hung back a few feet, watching them with amusement. The man had one of those faces that seemed older than the rest of him, speckled gray in his beard. The little girl was five maybe, wearing a long blue dress. She skipped as she walked, her dad smiling down at her with a gleam in his eye. Tina watched them until they became blurry. Touching her face, she rubbed away the tears she hadn't realized were there.

The light turned green and Tina made no move to press the gas, idling at the intersection until a series of horns sounded off behind her. A couple of cars zoomed by, the drivers screaming obscenities out the window. Tina paid them no mind, just sitting at the intersection watching the couple and their daughter turn and look back at her car and the commotion she was causing, the three of them giggling and shaking their heads. Tina watched until the family walked around a corner and disappeared, until the light in the intersection flashed from yellow to red again.

Grabbing her purse, Tina pulled out some tissues, dabbing at her cheeks. A laugh escaped her lips, bursting from her like someone gasping to the surface after being submerged in the ocean too long. She laughed until fresh tears sprang from her eyes, until the streetlight turned green again and she took her foot off the brake, cruising on towards Liberty City.

Turning the corner onto 62nd street, Tina headed towards the location Terry had told her: a block west of King Square Park. She was just passing the park when two men appeared around the opposite corner, crouching towards the entrance in combat stances. Tina's face flushed, something about the men seeming familiar. Slowing to a crawl, Tina rolled down her window, squinting. She recognized Terry with Sergeant Williams just as she noticed they both had their guns drawn.

Ralph said something to Terry, pointing at the group of cars sitting just outside the park entrance.

Swiping her eyes, Tina twisted the steering wheel and pulled the car up to the curb, next to a box Chevy. She shut off the engine and grabbed her journal and pen and was climbing out of the car when a bullet smashed through the windshield, embedding itself in the passenger headrest.

Tina screamed, shrill enough to pierce her own ears but not loud enough to overpower the subsequent gun blasts echoing through the air.

Throwing open the car door, Tina ducked out onto the grass, pressing her body up against the car as the gunshots stopped.

Tina waited for them to resume, nothing in her ears but a howling ocean, the roar of it dimming to reveal the yells coming from inside the park. She stayed curled against her car, taking deep breaths, willing her arms to release her legs, coaxing her muscles to ease the tension. She planted her palms in the grass and pushed herself up, using the car to steady her wobbly feet. Glancing at the dirt staining her jeans, she reached down and brushed at it with little effect. She looked in her car, studied the bullet hole in her windshield, the bullet embedded in her passenger headrest. She turned back to the park entrance and was about to take a step forward when her legs gave out.

Tina fell onto the hood of the car, wheezing as she slid to the ground again. She raised the pen in her right hand. It shook in her face.

Tina dropped the pen and notebook in the grass and shoved her hands under her armpits, squeezing her eyes shut. A moan shuddered her entire body, tears erupting from deep within her, a fountain of them appearing with such force, Tina felt an accompanying rush of fear, certain her sanity had cracked. She sat beside her car for five minutes, until the last of the patrol cars squealed to a stop outside the park, cops running in between the parked civilian vehicles to get closer to the violence that had just consumed the area. Tina ducked her head and made herself as small as possible and the sobs shook her.

Leaning back against her car and sucking in deep breaths, Tina stared at the darkening sky.

The flow of tears slowed and she took more air into her lungs, in and out.

Reaching up and opening her car door, she slid into the driver's seat and slammed the door closed. She adjusted her rearview mirror to show her puffy face and red eyes, staring at her reflection until she couldn't recognize the person staring back.

Grabbing the rest of the napkins in her purse, she patted her face until it was dry, then pulled out her makeup kit and retouched her foundation and mascara. She put everything back in her purse and slid it beneath the passenger seat.

Picking up her pen and notepad again, Tina took one last look in the mirror, sucking in a deep breath and letting it out as evenly as possible. She forced a wide smile onto her face and held it there for a moment, held it even though it hurt to do so. Held it until her cheeks started to quiver.

Then Tina opened the door, climbed out, and walked into the park.

15.

Crouched in front of the dead man in the bushes, Ralph used a pen to peer in his pockets. Bullet hole in the center of his chest, his eyes cold, lifeless.

"No ID," Terry said from behind him.

"Somebody around here knows who he is," Ralph muttered. "And probably knows whoever tossed him here."

Terry pursed his lips. "Thinking he was moved?"

"Seems obvious," Ralph said, standing up just as a gunshot rang out from a block away. He and Terry spun towards the sound.

"That came from the park," Terry said.

Ralph turned to the two patrols standing nearby, both with the same looks of confusion on their faces.

"Hold the scene until the techs get here," Ralph said, grabbing Terry and pulling him towards the street.

They ran to the intersection on 62nd avenue, rounding the corner and approaching the King Square Park entrance as another gunshot rang out. Drawing his weapon, Ralph ducked behind a Lincoln idling near the King Square sign, Terry following suit. Several other cars sat at the curb just outside the park, a couple of the owners ducked down behind them. One young man with an afro glanced over at Ralph, his eyes wide with fright.

Pushing off the Lincoln, Ralph crept in between the vehicles with Terry on his tail. He spotted the gunman standing halfway between the entrance and the basketball courts, waving his pistol in the air. A body lay at his feet. The park patrons who hadn't fled seemed frozen in position, watching the gunman to see what he would do next. In the distance, sirens wailed.

Ralph glanced at Terry. Terry looked back at him, wild-eyed.

"We gotta take him down," Terry said, his voice shaking.

"Careful," Ralph hissed. "There's civilians everywhere. On me."

Duck-walking past some benches, Ralph and Terry headed towards the shooter, the man's back turned to them. Focused on the gunman, Ralph didn't notice an errant potato chip bag at his feet, half-inflated with air. He stepped on it and it made a crumpling sound and the gunman spun around, raising his pistol and firing a shot wildly. The bullet flew past them out the park entrance.

"Motherfucker," Terry said, raising his gun with one hand.

The gunman sighted on Terry, using his other hand to steady his aim.

Ralph let off two shots.

The gunman hopped as the bullets hit him, pirouetting to the ground. At the exact same moment, Terry fired his gun, once, twice, three times, again and again until it clicked empty.

The shooter hit the ground and exhaled his last breath. Guns still raised, Ralph and Terry approached him and the other dead body lying a few feet away.

Holstering his weapon, Ralph reached over and pushed Terry's gun down, pointed at his side. Terry stared at Ralph's hands as he did this, his eyes haunted. A line of patrol cars pulled up behind them at the park entrance, uniforms swarming the area. Terry holstered his gun. A rush of white noise sat in Ralph's ears as he refocused on the two dead men lying in the grass. The shooter lay sprawled with his arms and legs spread wide, a puddle of blood forming beneath him. The other body lay in a heap a couple of feet to the right, a clean bullet hole sitting dead center on his forehead, another in his chest. The man's eyes stood wide open with surprise. Ralph stared at the bodies until a patrol officer appeared, saying something that Ralph couldn't understand. The man's mouth moved but no sound seemed to be coming out.

Ralph shook himself, turning his ear towards the officer.

"We've—uh, we got a situation, Sarge," the man said, nodding towards the other side of the basketball court.

Ralph glanced in that direction, and it was then he registered the echoing moans. A group of kids—two boys and three girls—stood over a third boy lying on the grass. All the girls had their hands to their mouths, which did nothing to dampen the volume of their cries. The two boys looked dumbfounded. One of them fell to his knees next to the boy lying on the ground. The other took a step back, glanced over at Ralph and Terry, then took off running. Ralph felt the urge to go after him but before he could act the kid hopped a fence and was gone.

Ralph looked down at the two dead men at his feet again.

"I think the kid's dead, Sarge," the patrol said.

Ralph stared at the patrol and tried to speak but couldn't. Instead, he turned and started towards the kids, the one boy now and the three girls and the other boy lying on the ground in a way that seemed final. Ralph felt a presence next to him and looked over to find Terry in lockstep, his mouth set in a thin grim line on his face. Ralph focused back on the kids, on the small body on the ground, his horror intensifying with every detail that became clearer.

The boy lying on the ground stared up at the sky with lifeless eyes, his mouth open. A trail of blood ran from the corner of his mouth to his ear. The other boy—short, stocky kid—pushed off the ground and jumped towards Terry and Ralph.

"You fucking killed DJ!" he spit.

"Son," Ralph said, holding a hand up and standing between the kid and Terry. "I'm gonna need—"

"I ain't your fucking son!" the kid yelled, flexing his muscular arms. One of the girls grabbed him before he could attack, pulling him off towards the basketball court. The other two girls backed away, staring at Ralph and Terry as if they were aliens.

Terry glared at the kids for a few seconds before his gaze fell to the dead boy on the ground. He glanced over at Ralph and something in Ralph's expression seemed to unsettle him, his eyes flashing with fear.

"I didn't—" he said, looking down at the dead boy again. He looked back at the other two bodies across the park before looking over at Ralph again. "—We had to."

Ralph faced the patrols roping off the scene. An M.E. van appeared near the half dozen patrol cars. Ralph was reminded of the Dadeland massacre then, the chaos of that day. Only two years ago. It seemed longer.

Ralph noticed a pretty woman in a t-shirt, dirt-stained jeans and boots ducking beneath the yellow crime-scene tape. She looked rattled, shellshocked. She also looked familiar. Ralph recognized her as she caught sight of them. She raised a hand in greeting. Ralph glanced at Terry.

"Isn't that Emilia's friend?" Ralph asked.

"Yeah," Terry said, his voice choked. He cleared his throat. "Tina."

"You call her here?"

Terry shook his head. "No."

Ralph glanced over at the group of kids. The three girls hugged each other. The short kid had disappeared in the commotion. Ralph searched the area but saw no signs of him. He took a deep breath, squeezed his eyes shut then opened them and rubbed his forehead.

"Don't give her anything," he said to Terry.

Terry frowned. "What do you mean?"

"*Tribune's* gonna have a field day with this if we let them," Ralph said. "You heard Murphy, gotta keep a lid on things moving forward. Have your fun, but do not. Give her. Anything."

Terry pursed his lips and nodded stiffly, walking towards Tina the reporter.

"Make it quick," Ralph called out. "Gonna be a ton of paperwork."

Terry looked back at him, nodded again, his eyes distant, haunted.

Ralph faced the body, studying the boy's features. Clean cut, friendly face, dead eyes fixated on the sky. Ralph stood there until the lab techs approached, took their pictures and samples and loaded the kid's small body into a small black bag, whisking it away to the wagon. Stood there until the news vans approached, setting up their cameras at the park entrance.

Stood there until it started to rain, the drops washing away the blood stains in the grass.

16.

Tommy walked inside to find his house packed with people and Clara next to a cake the size of a small table. She saw him and beamed, planting a kiss on his lips and rising up on her toes to whisper in his ear.

"You're late."

"I know," he said.

She hefted the bulky video camera into his arms. "Which means you're on camera duty."

Tommy grunted with the effort, raising the camera as his son came storming out of his bedroom like a banshee, a red towel wrapped around his shoulders. A dozen children followed, tumbling into the living room. Their parents crowded around Tommy's bar near the TV, sipping on the scotch and whiskey he kept in his liquor cabinet. Adán and Luchi stood with them, talking quietly and drinking from a bottle of Macallan. Tommy stared at them until they looked over. Both men raised glasses in his direction. Tommy forced a smile.

Clara called everybody over and the parents trailed their sugar-hyped children to the table. Tommy pressed record on the camera, focusing on Adam as they all sang happy birthday. Adam smiled through it, waiting until the final *youuu* before blowing out the candles. Tommy zoomed out to take in the entire scene, noticing one little boy with curly brown hair who seemed distraught. Peering around the camera, Tommy saw the kid holding his stomach and grimacing. He opened his mouth to yell for somebody to help just as the kid let out a belch and vomited on the floor next to Adam's seat. Adam looked down at the puke, let out a belch, then puked on the plate in front of him.

Two more sympathetic eruptions occurred before the room settled down: one of them Lorena in her highchair, the other one of the mothers, who ran off to the bathroom with her hand pressed to her mouth. Clara grabbed paper towels and sprays to clean up the mess while Tommy took Lorena to her room. He held her against his shoulder until she stopped crying, cleaned her up and lay her in her crib, waiting until she started fading before walking out and leaving the bedroom door open.

After everything was cleaned up, Clara relit the candles and resumed the celebration. Tommy rewound the camera tape to the moment before the puking episodes and started recording again. Adam blew out the candles once more with less enthusiasm. Soon though, the kids' energy was back up; everybody, that is, but the first kid to puke, whose parents talked in a corner with their son before sheepishly saying goodbye and leaving.

Adam opened his presents, gave away two duplicate action figures then stashed the rest of his bounty in his bedroom as the party died down. The last set of parents left near ten o'clock. Soon after, Luchi and Adán moved towards the door in unison. Tommy caught them on the front porch, grabbing his brother's shoulder and pulling him close. Luchi paused to look back at them. Tommy looked the man in the eye.

"I just need to talk to my brother for a sec," he said.

Luchi glanced at Adán then nodded, smiling and heading down the walkway towards his car.

Tommy fixed a sharp glare on Adán, keeping his voice low. "We need to talk about today."

Adán wrinkled his nose. "Qué pasa?"

"About the entire process," he said. "Also what the fuck was that about you being in Miami before?"

Adán gave him a tired smile and shook his head. "What is di word you use di other day?"

Tommy frowned. "What?"

"When di thing dat is happening is not what you think," Adán said.

Tommy squinted. "What, irony?"

"Sí," Adán said. "Di irony. De que, ju work for La Compañía, y ju call dem la cia."

Tommy wrinkled his nose, taking a step away from his brother. "What's that gotta do with anything?"

Adán grabbed Tommy's shoulder, shaking him a little. "We will talk tomorrow, Tomas."

"No," Tommy said, closing the front door. "We need to talk now."

Adán took a deep breath, crossing his arms.

Tommy tapped a foot against the concrete walkway. "You know I didn't ask for this."

"Lo sé," Adán said.

"I told you how this happened," Tommy said. "How we got into this. This was not a choice we made out of—I don't know what you think, fucking *desire*. We got into this out of necessity. *Survival*."

"I know dis, Tomas," Adán said. "Why are ju saying dis now?"

"Because you don't get it," Tommy hissed. "You just don't."

"No, *ju* no get it," Adán said, holding his arms out. "What ju want, Tomas? Un conserje? I pick up trash?" He pointed at the house. "Live here with ju? No yob, do nothing? What *ju* want?"

Tommy opened his mouth but nothing came out. Adán turned and walked a few steps down the pathway before turning back.

"En Cuba," he said. "Di government say where ju work, what ju work. No tienes eleccion, dey say ju work dis, ju work dis." He shook his head. "I come here for freedom."

"Adán," Tommy said. "This isn't freedom."

Adán looked up at the sky then walked over and hugged Tommy.

"Te veo mañana," he said, walking down the path towards the gate, where Luchi stood waiting. "We will talk."

Back inside, Tommy headed to the hallway, catching Clara as she was coming out of Adam's room.

"He's asleep," she whispered.

"Good," Tommy said. "I'm gonna change."

"Drink?"

"Definitely."

Clara walked off and Tommy headed to the bedroom, taking off his clothes and dropping them on a chair in the corner. He put on some pajama pants and an old UM t-shirt then walked back into the living room to find Clara holding two glasses of whiskey and the video camera.

"I wanna watch it," she said.

"Now?" Tommy said. "We just lived it."

"Please?" she said, pouting.

Tommy rolled his eyes and walked over to the TV, pulling AV cables out of the top drawer of the stand. He connected one end to the TV, the other to the camera and a fuzzy picture buzzed onto the screen, static lines streaming across before giving way to an image of their dining table and a bunch of smiling faces.

Clara watched with glee for the first few minutes. The video buzzed with static once more and the image on the screen leapt through time. Clara's expression slipped away and she looked over at Tommy.

"What happened to the puke?"

Tommy glanced at her. "What?"

"The kids puking," she said. "Where is it?"

Tommy looked at the video camera. "I recorded over it." He squinted at her. "Why would you want me to keep that?"

Clara gave him a look bordering on horror. She turned back to the TV screen and a zoomed-in image of her grinning face. A curl of blonde hair lay on her video version's forehead, her lipstick a light shade of red.

Clara cleared her throat and stood, walking off to the hallway. Tommy heard the faint click of their bedroom door closing, then silence. He sat there staring at the video until it ended and there was nothing but static on the TV. Then he watched that too.

17.

Rig stood across the Crystal Palaces courtyard from his apartment, watching through the single open window as his mother danced around the kitchen. She didn't notice him, but Rig could see her. She was singing something, steam rising from a pot of whatever she was cooking on the stove. Faint music drifted over. Rig willed himself to walk towards the apartment, to go inside and sit down and talk to his mom. It's what his dad would have wanted—expected—him to do in this situation, he knew.

Rig sat on the grass, crossing his legs beneath him.

Rig's mom finished what she was doing and closed the window. He waited for her to notice him sitting there in plain sight, but she was in her own world.

Focusing on the surrounding courtyard, Rig watched the Crystal Palaces residents taking part in their evening activities, getting in some outside time before the storm clouds in the distance reached overhead. People sat smoking on their porches and gossiping on benches. Snatches of conversation reached him, enough for Rig to know that word of what happened to DJ was spreading.

Rig closed his eyes. Behind the lids, he saw his father as he'd seen him the last time he was free. Smiling, gold chain dangling around his neck as he dug his hand into Rig's curls, shoving his head side to side.

Rig touched the crucifix hanging under his shirt. He opened his eyes and everything around him was blurry. Sniffling, he swiped at the tears as footsteps approached from behind.

"Chico," a voice said.

Rig jumped up, keeping his back turned and using his shirt sleeve to clean his face. He turned to find Otis a few feet away, his fists balled up at his sides, jaw clenched. They locked eyes and for the first time in their friendship, Rig saw doubt in his friend's gaze. Thunder rumbled in the distance.

Otis stepped forward and grabbed Rig, pulling him into a tight embrace.

The gesture surprised Rig so much he just stood there with his arms raised, looking down at the shorter boy.

Finally, Rig wrapped his arms around Otis's shoulders.

Otis smacked a palm against Rig's back, letting him go and stepping away.

"It's you and me now, my nigga," Otis said. He clenched his jaw tight. His eyes were red. "You. And me."

The back of Rig's neck tingled and he glanced back at his apartment, expecting his mom at the kitchen window staring after him, or out on the front steps with her hands on her hips and a knowing look in her eye. Instead, the apartment sat quiet. The smell of rain tinged the air and people started heading back inside. A breeze picked up. The thunder rumbled louder.

Rig turned back to Otis.

Reaching in his bag, Otis pulled out a small manila envelope, opening it and shaking a joint out into his palm. He held it up towards Rig.

Rig took a deep breath and followed his friend back towards the street.

Epilogue

Sitting in the driver's seat outside the Mutiny Hotel, Luchi gripped the Monte Carlo's steering wheel, watching as the couple stumbled out the hotel's entrance. The couple laughed, hanging off each other. The valet handed them the keys to a Jaguar and seconds later they pulled out of the circular driveway, heading west.

"Siguelo, parce," the man sitting behind Luchi said. He glanced over at Adán, sitting behind the passenger seat. "Listo?"

Adán clenched his teeth and nodded.

Touching the Mac-10 lying in the passenger seat, Luchi put the Monte Carlo in gear. They followed the Jaguar out of the grove, crossing US-1 through the Gables to Westchester and pulling up to a one-story house sitting on two acres of land. The couple waited for the automatic gate to open then drove in, parking in the driveway and climbing out. Husband grabbed a handful of his wife's ass on the way inside, a sweet gesture.

Luchi turned to the man behind him.

"Por la espalda," he said, then nodded at Adán. "Conmigo."

Grabbing the Mac-10 off the passenger seat, Luchi climbed out of the car. Adán looked at the pistol in his hand then followed suit.

Hopping the fence, Luchi headed for the front door. Adán followed him, the other man heading around back. Luchi crouched at the front porch as Adán crept up beside him. They waited until they heard breaking glass inside, then Luchi raised his right foot and kicked the front door. It shuddered in its frame but held. Adán cursed, stepping up next to Luchi.

"A las tres," he said, raising his foot. "*Tres.*"

Adán and Luchi kicked again and the lock shattered, the door falling off its hinges. They stepped in as the other man approached from the rear of the house, one arm wrapped around the wife's neck, gun held to her head. Luchi glanced around the living room.

"Y él?"

A popping sound came from the kitchen and the gunman holding the wife spun, his head snapping back, the wall behind him sprayed with chunks of blood and brain as his arms dropped and he fell to the ground. Adán dropped to the floor, raising his pistol and firing a shot at the kitchen. The bullet pinged off the side of a refrigerator.

"Chinga tu *madre*," Luchi yelled, running at the wife as she pushed herself off the ground. He tackled the woman, struggled to get on top of her then smacked her across her face with the back of his hand. The wife stopped squirming. Luchi pulled her to her feet, holding the Mac-10 to her head and shielding himself with her body.

"Le meto el plomo en la puta cabeza!" he yelled.

Nothing for a moment, then the husband walked out of the kitchen, gun raised in the air.

"Ponlo en el suelo," Luchi said.

The husband glanced at Adán, who had his pistol pointed at the man's head. The husband looked at his wife, her cheek already swelling where Luchi had smacked her.

"En el suelo!" Luchi yelled.

The husband placed the gun on the ground then stood again, raising his hands, his jaw clenched, eyes burning holes in the men. Luchi walked the wife over, crouching to grab the gun off the floor. He glanced at the dead man's body, a pool of blood spreading around his head.

"No debiste haber hecho eso," Luchi growled.

"I will do it to you too," the husband spit. "Just give me the chance."

Luchi nodded from Adán to the husband. Adán walked over, holding his gun against the man's head. The wife cried out and the husband shushed her. Luchi lowered his gun and pulled a couple of cable-ties out of his pocket. Stepping over to the couple, he wrapped one of the ties around the husband's wrist and pulled it tight. He did the same to the wife then nodded at Adán.

"Vigílalos," he said. "Voy a revisar la casa."

"You won't find anything worth dying for," the husband yelled as Luchi left the living room.

Luchi searched for fifteen minutes, clattering sounds coming from various sections of the house. He rifled through cupboards, the fridge, the pantry. He walked into each of the couple's two bathrooms and checked the medicine cabinets, the linen closet, the showers. In their bedroom he tossed the wife's underwear to the side and pulled the dresser drawers from their rails. He ripped clothes off hangers in the many closets, reached up on the top shelves and knocked everything down, checking shoe and hat boxes.

Luchi returned and dropped his discoveries in the middle of the living room: stacks of cash, handfuls of jewelry, an entire brick of cocaine.

"Enjoy it," the husband yelled. "Disfrutalo. Soon you'll be dead y no disfrutarás de *nada*."

Luchi grabbed the husband's pistol, handing his Mac-10 to Adán. Stepping over to the wife, he pointed the pistol at her head.

"Esto es para Griselda," he said.

Luchi pulled the trigger and the back of the wife's head disintegrated. Adán's eyes shot open wide, his gun hand wavering. The wife flew backwards, landing on the carpet next to the other dead body.

The husband screamed.

Luchi walked over to the wife's body and pulled the trigger again, and again and again until the hammer clicked on nothing. The husband screamed louder with each shot, watching his wife's body hop as the bullets tore through her. Tears streamed down the husband's face, his mouth open in a wide grimace. His screams faded to strangled gasps.

The husband looked up at Luchi, spit hanging from his mouth.

"Te mataré," he whispered. "Te encontraré y te mataré."

Luchi raised the empty pistol again.

"Y esto es para mi amigo," he said.

Turning the gun around, Luchi rammed the butt into the husband's nose. The man crumpled, out cold. Tossing the gun on the wife's body, Luchi walked into the kitchen, returning with a trash bag. He dumped the cash, jewelry and cocaine in, nodding from Adán to the husband. Adán hefted the unconscious man over his shoulder. The husband groaned. Luchi grabbed the trash bag, glancing at the two dead bodies on the living room floor. When he looked at Adán again, his pupils were pits of darkness.

Luchi walked over to the man slung over Adán's shoulder like a slab of meat, grabbed the husband's hair and pulled his head up, looking him in the eye. The man's nose was crooked, the space beneath covered in blood, drops of it dripping off his chin to the floor.

"You will hurt," Luchi said. "Bad."

The husband tried to speak but Luchi cocked a fist back and punched him in the mouth. The man went unconscious again.

Luchi took one last look at the bodies in the living room.

The front door creaked as they left, and then there was silence.

To Be Continued...

ACKNOWLEDGMENTS

Special thanks to:

The family and friends (is there a difference?) who've read the many, many drafts over the years. Thanks for your patience and feedback.

Alexa, my muse.

The authors/directors and their works of fiction and non-fiction that helped inspire and inform these events and characters: Edna Buchanan, Max Mermelstein, Trick Daddy, Luther Campbell, Marshall Frank, Marvin Dunn, Nicholas Griffin, Guy Gugliotta, Jeff Leen, David Simon, Tarell McCraney, Billy Corben.

Junot Diaz, Susan Hubbard and Darlin Neal for the much appreciated cover quotes.

J. J. for believing in this project and helping me get it out.

And Miami.

ABOUT THE AUTHOR

    Patrick Anderson Jr. was born in Miami to Jamaican immigrants who relocated to the city in the early eighties. His short stories have appeared in numerous literary journals, magazines and anthologies. Patrick received his B.A. in English from Florida State University and his M.F.A. in Creative writing from University of Central Florida. He is currently a Creative Writing Professor at Miami Dade College where he has taught for over a decade. In his spare time, Patrick records and produces music under the stage name Autonomous Entity.

PatrickAndersonJr.com
Instagram: @PatrickAndersonMusic